When the Sun
Goes Down

Also by Gwynne Forster

Published by Kensington Publishing Corp.

When the Sun Goes Down

Gwynne Forster

Kensington Publishing Corp.
www.kensingtonbooks.com

DAFINA BOOKS are published by

Kensington Publishing Corp.
119 West 40th Street
New York, NY 10018

All Kensington Titles, Imprints, and Distributed Lines are available at special quantity discounts for bulk purchases for sales promotions, premiums, fund-raising, and educational or institutional use. Special book excerpts or customized printings can also be created to fit specific needs. For details, write or phone the office of the Kensington special sales manager: Kensington Publishing Corp., 119 West 40th Street, New York, NY 10018, attn: Special Sales Department, Phone: 1-800-221-2647.

Dafina and the Dafina logo Reg. U.S. Pat. & TM Off.

ISBN-13: 978-0-7582-4700-1
ISBN-10: 0-7582-4700-1
First Kensington Trade Edition: October 2010
First Kensington Mass Market Edition: November 2016

eISBN-13: 978-0-7582-8518-8
eISBN-13: 0-7582-8518-3
First Kensington Electronic Edition: October 2010

10 9 8 7 6 5 4 3 2 1

Printed in the United States of America

Chapter One

The biting cold and harsh January wind stung Gunther Farrell's face and whitened the surface of St. John's Lane, which led to and from St. John's Cemetery just outside of Ellicott City, Maryland. Gunther glanced back over his left shoulder at the sound of rocky soil hitting the wooden box. The wind brought tears to his eyes, but he refused to shed them. His father didn't deserve his tears, and not even the wind could make him do the old man the honor of crying at his demise. Not much of his heart was in that hole, but he knew that his sister, who was younger as well as softer and less judgmental than he, was despondent over their father's death. He slung an arm across her shoulder and tugged her close to him, protecting her as he'd done since they lost their mother when he was fifteen and she was nearing her thirteenth birthday.

"Where are you going, Edgar?" he called to his older brother. "Don't you think you should ride back to the house with Shirley and me?"

Edgar hopped onto the back of a friend's Harley and hooked the helmet under his chin. "Look, I participated in this charade because you and Shirley begged me to be here, but it's enough for me. I'm outta here."

"You could at least go back to the house along with us," Shirley said.

"I'll see you there," Edgar said. "By the way, brother. Did Donald Riggs mention when he's reading the will? You'd think he'd tell me something, since I'm the oldest."

"He hasn't mentioned it to me," Gunther said.

"Me neither," Shirley assured him.

Edgar's friend revved the big Harley, and a minute later, dust obscured the speeding vehicle.

Gunther and Shirley got into the backseat of the rented limousine that would take them to their father's house. Neither of them lived in the family home, so the place would now be home to Edgar alone. After waiting for their older brother for more than an hour, Gunther locked the house and took Shirley with him to his duplex condominium.

"I'm going back to Fort Lauderdale in a couple of days," Shirley told Gunther later as they sat in his living room sipping vodka and tonic. "My cruise leaves for the Mediterranean on Friday."

"I wish you could stay until we settle Father's estate. I'd bet my life it'll be complicated."

"Tell me about it," Shirley said. "I wouldn't be surprised if he left everything he had to somebody's puppy."

Gunther rested his glass on the coffee table, got up, and walked over to the window. The grim weather further darkened his spirit. "Father didn't understand that you and I succeeded beyond what he had a right to expect, considering that we did it on our own with absolutely no help from him," Gunther said. "He never seemed to appreciate that when I was nine years old, I got up at five o'clock every morning in order to deliver papers before going to school and that I worked every afternoon after school. In spite of that, I earned a scholarship to college, worked my way through, and got an MBA."

"It maddened him that you didn't join the fat cats on Wall Street."

"I wanted to develop computer software for games and puzzles and to design games. He said that was nothing and that I should be ashamed. Now I'm doing that. I make a good living, and I can't wait to get to work every morning."

"We're both lucky, Gunther. I wanted to travel, and I have a job as director of public relations for a major cruise line. I could live on a ship if I wanted to. Incidentally, do you think it's odd that Riggs hasn't mentioned the reading of the will?"

"I hadn't thought of it until Edgar mentioned it. Father used to say regularly that when the sun went down on his life, we'd all three come apart like balloons with holes punched in them. So I suspect he's done his best to ensure that his prophecy comes true." He looked at his watch. "I wonder where Edgar went when he left the cemetery."

Shirley sipped the last of her drink. "Who knows? I wish he weren't so angry at everybody and everything."

Gunther got up the next morning, cooked breakfast for Shirley and himself, and sat down to eat. He'd done well for himself. At the age of thirty-four, he owned a company that created and published computer games and puzzles, and he owned an attractive condominium—more like a town house—in a modern building and upscale neighborhood. And moreover, he had substantial savings.

"Edgar's smart," he said to Shirley, "but he wants everything the easy way. One day, that's going to get him into serious trouble."

"I know. And it worries me."

He reached for the phone that hung on the kitchen wall. "I'd better call Riggs. He hasn't said a word to us, and that's not normal. He's been Father's lawyer for at least twenty years, and he's probably executor of the will. He ought to tell us something about this." He dialed the number.

"Hello, Mr. Riggs, this is Gunther Farrell. When are you scheduling a reading of Father's will?"

"How are you, Gunther? My condolences to you and to Edgar and Shirley. There's a problem. I know Leon had a will that was properly executed, because it was witnessed and notarized in my presence, but he did not leave a copy with me. He also didn't tell me where he put it. So we'll have to find it."

"*You can't be serious!* He could have put it under a can in the garage, for heaven's sake."

"Yes. And he was capable of doing precisely that. I had a call from Edgar, and when I told him I don't know where the will is, he said he's going to court and have his father declared intestate."

Gunther flexed the fingers of his left hand in an effort to beat back the rising anger and stress. "Can he do that?"

"I'm way ahead of him. I've obtained an injunction forbidding the disposal of the estate for one year unless the will is located within that time. Leon gave me an affidavit naming me as executor of his estate, but without a will, my hands are tied."

Sensing trouble with Edgar, Gunther asked Riggs, "What can we do in the meantime? I'm not depending on anything from my father and neither is Shirley, but Edgar is always flat broke, so he'll trash the place looking for that will."

"He can do that, because he lives there. You and your sister can do the same, but you can get a restraining order to prevent him from disposing of anything that belonged to your father."

Gunther thanked Riggs, hung up, and related the lawyer's remarks to Shirley.

"Father must be somewhere laughing," Shirley said in a disparaging voice.

"I notice you didn't say he was *looking down*."

"Trust me, I'm not feeling that generous. We've got to get hold of Edgar. Knowing how he loves money and how much he hates working for it, I wouldn't be surprised if he did something illegal, thinking we wouldn't prosecute him."

"Yeah," Gunther said. He didn't trust Edgar. He got up and dialed the phone number at the family home.

"Hello."

"Hello, Edgar. Shirley and I waited for you more than an hour last evening. Sorry we missed you. I see you've spoken with Riggs."

"Yeah, man. That joker's talking nonsense. I'm no fool. I bet he knows exactly where that will is. Damned if he's gonna cheat me out of my inheritance."

"Slow down, Edgar. Donald Riggs is not going to

ruin his life and lose his ability to practice law over
an estate as small as the one Father left us. And
I'm warning you, if you sell one pair of socks from
that house, you'll be breaking the law, and I will
see to it that you suffer the consequences."

"How will I be breaking the law?"

Surely Edgar wasn't going to play games with
him. Edgar knew he wouldn't be fooled by any
phony display of innocence. "Because I will have a
one-year restraining order against you," he told
him. "Every toothpick in that place belongs to the
three of us. Find the will, and we take what Father
left us."

"Suppose there isn't a will anywhere."

"There is, because Riggs said he helped Father
construct it and was present when witnesses signed
it and a notary notarized it."

"Oh, crap. That's all I need! Now I have to wait a
year, a whole bloody year to get myself straight.
Man, I'm in debt over my head. You wouldn't have
a couple of thousand, would you?"

Gunther's hand gripped the receiver. He hadn't
expected it, but he should have known it was coming. "Edgar, I have a firm policy that I apply to
everybody. I do not borrow money, and I do not
lend it. And especially not to anyone who already
owes me. Period."

"Why didn't I know that? And you also never
wear your baseball cap turned backward. Pardon
me for asking."

Gunther looked down at Shirley. "Damned if
Edgar didn't hang up on me."

A quick frown slid over her face, and she patted
his hand, eager for peace as usual. "I know it's hard

to love Edgar sometimes," she said, "but he's our brother."

"Yeah. And if you told him how much like Father he is in some ways, he'd be ready to wipe the floor with you. He's as self-centered as a person can be."

An hour later, the veracity of Gunther's statement was fully demonstrated. Donald Riggs looked Edgar in the eye. "Are you suggesting that I mortgage your father's estate for fifty thousand dollars, give the money to you, and you will relinquish further claim to it? Ten percent for me. Is that what you're asking? How do you know it's worth fifty thousand or that it isn't already mortgaged?"

"Look, man, that house is worth at least two hundred grand, maybe twice that much."

Donald leaned forward and spoke through clenched teeth, using every bit of willpower he could muster to refrain from expelling Edgar bodily from his office. "If you think I'll ruin my life in a shaky deal with you, you're dumber than I thought."

Edgar rose to his full height of five feet ten inches and glowered at Riggs. "Nobody calls me dumb, man. My frigging daddy didn't even do that. I'll see you around."

Donald shook his head, bemused. "At times like this, I'm glad my wife and I don't have any children," he said aloud, and began to map a strategy for finding the will. He couldn't check safe-deposit boxes until he got a copy of the death certificate, and that would take another couple of days. He phoned his wife and told her of his conversation with Edgar.

He could almost hear her yawning. "Honey, I thought you told me Edgar's father didn't think he was worth the energy it took to beget him. Don't you get mixed up with that boy. Betty Lou's gon' drop by around noon, and we'll work on the blankets we're making for the homeless. Let me tell you, Bobbie Dean pitched a hissy fit this morning 'bout something or other. You could hear her all over the neighborhood. I declare, Bobbie Dean's so unladylike."

"I'll try to get home early, and maybe we can go see a movie."

"Honey, you're the sweetest man."

He hung up. Whenever he needed relief from stress, he called his wife. She had a way of belittling the biggest problem and making him believe it wasn't as important as he thought. With the kooks he had to deal with every day, having her was a true blessing. And he was going to need more than one blessing if he was to get the Farrell estate settled. How could one man sire sons as different as Gunther and Edgar? A half-laugh slipped out of him. How could kids remain sane with parents as different as Leon and Catherine Farrell? He let out a long and labored sigh. Finding that will would mean taking his time from other, more urgent cases, but he'd do the best he could.

In the meantime, Gunther arrived at a similar decision, more for Shirley than for himself. "I'm going to take the day off from the office," he told his sister. "If we don't locate that will within a year, the state will take what it wants and stipulate who gets what part of the rest. I have to look for that will."

"Where will you start? Since I'm here, I can help."

"Let's go over to the house and start looking there. By now, Edgar's probably wrecked the place."

They searched for hours until, exhausted, Gunther threw his hands up. "I've lived this long and this well without access to Father's money, and I am not going to exercise myself about that will a minute longer."

"That makes two of us," Shirley said. "Father should have been ashamed of himself for doing such a thing. Let Edgar and the state of Maryland sweat over it."

"Anyway, I want to get out of here," Gunther said. "He's been gone only a week, and already this place has a stale, musky odor."

"Yeah. Sort of like decaying mushrooms. Edgar should open some windows."

Edgar roared up on his Harley as Gunther and Shirley were about to get into Gunther's car. "Any luck?" he asked, his piercing gaze pinned on Gunther.

"Nothing," Gunther replied, "and we've been here for more than four hours. I can't imagine where he put it. I never thought Father was devious, but what else would you call this? He wouldn't spend a penny to execute a will and then destroy it. So he hid it somewhere. Good luck trying to find it."

Edgar stared at Gunther. "You're giving up? You're not going to try again? Man, you can't do that. I need the money. I quit my two-bit job the day the old man died, figuring I'd come into some money. This is terrible. It's the pits."

"For goodness' sake, don't get twisted out of shape," Gunther said. "You don't have to pay rent as long as you stay here, because the estate should pay for the upkeep of the house, and you get a monthly check from Mom's will. So what's the urgency?"

"Look here. Get off your damned high horse. I got debts, and a lot of 'em."

Gunther resisted shrugging his shoulder, because he really did care deeply for his brother, but he knew from experience that if he tried to help Edgar, he'd go right down with him. "I'm sorry to hear that," he said. "Stay in touch."

Three days later, Gunther drove Shirley to the Baltimore / Washington International Thurgood Marshall Airport, where he parked and handed her bags to a porter. "I want you to stop fretting about Edgar and that will. He's the oldest, and he should be leading *us*. If he's broke, it's because he spends his income on weed and gambling."

"You don't mean that."

"Yes, I do, and quitting his job was the most stupid thing he could have done. He's a first-rate guitarist, but how many places are there around here for even the best jazz musician to work?"

"Can't he work in Baltimore?"

"I suppose he can, provided he hasn't bombed out in every place that employs jazz guitarists. Stop worrying. Mom babied him till he became useless, and now you're threatening to take up where she left off. He's thirty-six years old, and if he gets into trouble, he has to be man enough to get out of it." He hugged her and kissed her cheek. "Call me when you get to Fort Lauderdale."

Shirley knew that she made too many excuses for Edgar. She'd done it to protect him from their father's wrath, although she knew he probably deserved whatever Leon Farrell meted out. When their mother died suddenly after falling from a ladder, their father began to ignore them, giving them a home and food and not much else. She and Gunther worked their way through universities with the help of scholarships. Edgar refused to struggle through college, and after he finished high school, he worked for a famed Baltimore musician in exchange for guitar and piano lessons, widening the rift between himself and his father.

She boarded her flight, grabbed one of the flimsy red blankets, wrapped herself in it, and settled in a window seat. As soon as the cabin door closed, she slid down in her seat and went to sleep. Weak coffee, assorted other beverages, and pretzels held no interest for her.

"I hope you're not planning to sleep all the way to Fort Lauderdale," a deep baritone voice said, announcing the presence of a seat mate.

She didn't open her eyes. "If at all possible, I am," she said, and turned so that she faced the window. In her opinion, if a man traveled alone, he forgot the truth and his principles the minute he stepped on a plane. Besides, she had no intention of spending two hours and forty-seven minutes of her life on a "friendship" that had nowhere to go.

She awoke when the plane touched down at Fort Lauderdale–Hollywood International Airport, took out her cell phone, and called Gunther. "Hi. The plane just touched down. Any word from Edgar?"

"None. I will communicate to you whatever happens here as soon as I know it. So don't tie yourself in a knot over this."

"I hear you. I'm sailing day after tomorrow, and with almost thirteen hundred people dropping their problems on me, I won't have time to think about Edgar. I'll be in touch."

She found her town house as she'd left it. "This cathedral ceiling is great when I'm not tired," she said to herself as she climbed the carpeted stairs to her second-floor bedroom. It occurred to her that following a week in wintry weather, the Florida heat immediately depleted her energy. After separating the clothes that would go to the cleaners and those scheduled for the laundry, she changed into a jogging suit and went out to buy milk and a few other essentials.

"Where you headed now?" her next-door neighbor asked as she stepped out of the house. "You sure do lead an exciting life."

"I suppose some people would call it that, but it's so stressful that I sometimes have to remind myself to breathe. Mrs. X can't find her little girl, who walked away while mummy was playing the slot machine. Miss Y ordered breakfast in her room and had to wait a whole twenty minutes for it. Mr. J is furious because he can't bring onto the ship the case of liquor he bought onshore. Some big shot doesn't like his seating arrangements for dinner and wants to sit at the captain's table. But the seats at the captain's table are all taken. I could keep this up for an hour."

"Yeah, but it's still glamorous to me. When are you leaving?"

"Day after tomorrow, but I'll be on ship from tomorrow evening. I'm not really complaining, because I love my work. Just setting the record straight."

She completed her shopping and as she returned home, she heard the ringing telephone, dropped the small bag of groceries on the floor, and raced to the phone. "Hello."

"Hi, sis. This is Edgar."

"I know. What's up?" She had an eerie feeling, because Edgar never phoned her and rarely called her "sis."

"Look, sis. I'm really in an awfully tight spot. I need three grand, and if I don't get it this week, I'll be in serious trouble."

She sat down and took some deep breaths. "I'm not wealthy, Edgar, and my mortgage eats up over a quarter of what I make every month. If I lend you three thousand dollars and if you don't give it back to me by the end of the month, things will be extremely difficult for me."

"I'll give it back to you in two weeks. I swear it. The easiest way will be for you to give me your password."

She jumped up. He had to be kidding. "Edgar, I said I'd lend you the money. I did not say I'd lost my mind. I wouldn't have given *Father* the password to my bank account."

"But I need the money *now*."

"I'll send it to you by wire and for two weeks only. Get busy and find that will."

She'd never dreamed that she would speak that way to her older brother, but she suspected that he wouldn't have sounded so frantic if he didn't have gambling debts. She hated gambling. On every cruise, one or more passengers on the ship came to her begging for transportation home, having gambled away every cent they had. She went out and wired the money, but she had a feeling that she would never see it again.

Two hours before the *Mercury* was due to sail for the Mediterranean, Shirley sat at her desk, frantically urging a messenger to get to the boat with the asthma drugs before the ship left shore. Why would a woman with an asthmatic child leave home without his medicine? It should have been the first thing she packed. She sent an officer to the gangplank to make certain that it wasn't raised before the messenger arrived.

"I sure hope this isn't an omen," she said to herself. "I don't need problems with any more frantic mothers." She dialed Gunther but didn't get an answer. The routine lifeboat drills had begun, and she was about to give up hope that the messenger would arrive in time.

She answered her phone. "Public relations, Ms. Farrell speaking."

"Alphonse here. I have the medicine, and I've just given the captain the all clear."

She let out a long breath of relief. "Thanks. Somebody ought to take that woman in hand. She didn't want to give up her cruise, so she took a chance that the medicine would get here before the boat left. If it hadn't, that child could have died. I'll see how long it is before she comes to ask me if the medicine arrived." She dialed Gunther again but to no effect and made a mental note to call him the following morning.

At the moment, Gunther had to deal with his own minicrisis. He sat on a high stool in Crosby's Bar looking at his girlfriend. She'd had only one sip of that martini, but she was behaving as if she'd drunk two of them.

"You don't have to do what that lawyer says. Where's the evidence that your father made him the executor of his estate? A year from now, he could have spent every penny your father left."

He pushed back his rising anger. "At the age of ten, I went to Donald Riggs to get transportation to school and lunch money when my father conveniently forgot about it. I never knew whether he charged Father for it or took it from his own pocket. I do know that if he wasn't honest to the marrow of his bones, my father—who counted every penny twice—would not have kept him as his lawyer."

"How can we get married if you don't get what's coming to you? I want us to sell that house and build a modern place."

"That house belongs to Edgar and Shirley, as well as to me."

As if aware that she'd made a big error with that comment, she broke her gaze from his, sipped the drink, and looked back at him with slightly lowered lashes. "Honey, you know I'm always thinking about your well-being and what's due you. I don't concern myself with anybody else." She pushed the glass away. "Come on. Let's go home."

He assumed that by "home" she meant her apartment, and he knew what that implied.

"I love my apartment," she said as they entered it, "but I miss the fireplace we had at home. When we build our home, I want fireplaces in the living, family, and dining rooms." He said nothing, because he knew the house in which she said she grew up, and, to his knowledge, it didn't have one fireplace.

"Have a seat in the living room," she said, went to the kitchen and returned with a bottle of pinot grigio, two stem glasses, and a bottle opener. "I'll be back in a minute."

He sat there wondering when he had asked her to marry him and couldn't recall the time. He did know that she had begun mentioning it casually and had gradually spoken of it as if they had a formal agreement. But he hadn't made up his mind, and until he did and until he asked her in plain English and she agreed, he didn't consider himself engaged. Minutes later, she returned wearing a red jersey jumpsuit that showed a good deal of her beautiful breasts, and in spite of himself, his mouth began to water.

"Honey, you didn't open the wine?" she asked in a voice tinged with petulance.

"My mind was on other things."

"You're not serious," she said. "I'll have to do something about that." She handed him the bottle opener. He opened the bottle and poured wine into their glasses, all the while thinking how sweet her nipples tasted. He got only a few sips of wine before, without warning, she took his hand, put it into the bodice of her jumpsuit, and rubbed her nipples with it.

"I've been thinking about this all day," she told him, and rubbed his genitals.

"Oh, hell!" he said, capitulating to his rising passion. He pulled one of her breasts from its confines, bent his head, and sucked it into his mouth as she began to stroke him with increasing speed and pressure.

She tugged at his belt, unzipped him, and took him into her mouth. Then, like a satisfied cat that had her mouse, she looked up at him and grinned. "Want some more?" she asked him.

She knew him too well, but he was damned if he'd give her the satisfaction of behaving as if she could do with him as she pleased. He lifted her as he stood, unzipped the jumpsuit, and watched her slither out of it. Then he put her on the sofa and worked her until she clawed and screamed her release, but he wouldn't give her the satisfaction of knowing he enjoyed it and pulled out, flaccid and proud of it.

"What happened there?" she asked him after she collected her wits.

"Look," he said. "I try to be a gentleman. You wanted it, and I did my best."

She tried to sit up, and he moved, accommodating her. "What do you mean?"

"Just what I said. No more, no less. Sex doesn't solve every problem, Lissa. In fact, if there's a problem, sex can worsen it."

She sat on the floor with her back against the sofa. "I didn't know we had a problem."

He wasn't going to comment on that. Brushing

dirt under the rug had never made sense to him, and he tried not to engage in it. At first, he'd been practically stunned by Lissa's directness, and, later, her wildness in bed had captivated him. But as he got to know her, he realized that, for her, the word *relationship* meant little more than sex and the right to make demands on one's partner. He adjusted his clothing and faced the fact that he was not one bit pleased with himself.

"How about I fix us some ham, eggs, and toast?" she said. "That's about all I have in the house."

"Thanks, but I don't think so. I'd better get on home."

"Why? Don't I always make it nice for you? Besides, you have to make up for that trick you just pulled."

He didn't have to do anything. "Slow down, Lissa. I buried my father three days ago. Remember?"

"Oh, dear. I'm so sorry. That explains it. I don't have my head twisted on right. If you think you have to regroup, honey, that is certainly understandable. Call me when you get home. I need to know you're there safely."

"Thanks," he said, but he didn't promise to call her. Indeed, he was almost certain that he wouldn't. He had to get his life straightened out. He'd been so involved with his software firm and its myriad problems that he hadn't focused on his private life and hadn't realized the inroads that Lissa had made in it. He wasn't a man to allow life to happen to him, and if Lissa was counting on that, she'd better wake up.

* * *

A month passed, and neither he, Edgar, nor Riggs had found the will. Edgar's periodic disappearances perplexed Gunther, but he didn't consider it appropriate to question his older brother about it. When sufficiently annoyed, Edgar neither rationed nor tempered his rage, so, to the extent feasible, Gunther tried to maintain a good relationship with him.

Finally, after several months, he began to wonder if Edgar had discovered the will and was attempting some underhanded measure. He called Edgar. "How's it going, Edgar? Did you get that job back? I'm beginning to wonder if Father's estate will ever be settled."

"I looked for that thing till I started looking in my sleep. I got a gig in Atlantic City, and I've been hanging out there. The pay's better than what you get around here, but there're so many mobsters that by the time you pay everybody off, you're practically broke."

"Sorry about that. I guess that goes along with gambling. Are you playing at the casino hotels?"

"Where else is there to play these days? Man, I'm lucky to get work. Those clubs used to be crowded, but money's scarce everywhere."

Gunther didn't plan to comment on that. Edgar was a skilled guitarist, and if he couldn't find work at reliable jobs, he had to be part of the problem. "How long will you be in town?" he asked, changing the subject.

"Till Thursday. I wanted to give this joint another shot. That will's got to be here somewhere. Father wouldn't have put it where it would be out of his control."

Gunther wouldn't dispute that logic. "Good luck. I'm fed up with it."

"You can afford to be. I can't."

He telephoned Shirley, whom he judged to be somewhere between Sicily and Sardinia, according to her travel schedule. "How's life at sea?" he asked when she answered.

"This has been the best tour yet. Cross my fingers. Not a single tragedy, and we've been out four days."

"You're getting to be a regular vagabond. I want to know something. Edgar's acting strangely. He hasn't asked me for money, hasn't mentioned his debts, and his complaints about the will have recently been low-key. Did you lend him any money?"

"Uh . . . well—"

He interrupted her. "So you did. Don't do that again, Shirley. Did he give it back to you?"

"No. He said he'd return it in two weeks, and it's been three months. I don't expect to see my three grand ever again."

"*Three thousand dollars?* Are you crazy?" He threw up his hands. "Oh, all right, all right. Let that be a lesson well learned. Where Edgar is concerned, sis, you need to stiffen your spine."

"I know, and that's one thing I won't do again. Anyway, as long as he owes me, he won't ask."

"Yeah, but that's expensive insurance. Call me when you get to Nice."

"Will do."

Edgar expelled a long breath and released a string of expletives. He couldn't continue running home every week to look for the will, and Gunther and Shirley didn't much care about it. He was spending more money on transportation than he could afford, and after paying off the goons for letting him do his gig undisturbed, he didn't have enough cash left for the makings of one Mary Jane.

Riding toward the JFK Memorial Highway, he passed a sign that read MONTGOMERY DETECTIVE AGENCY SERVING EASTERN UNITED STATES. In the blink of an eye, he made up his mind and turned back. Following the green and white instructions on a sign, he took the elevator to the fourth floor of the building, walked down the hall to suite 418, and rang the bell. In response, he heard a buzzer, opened the door, and walked into an attractive reception room. A woman of about thirty asked if she could help him.

"I'd like to hire a detective."

She let her gaze travel from the top of his head to his shoes. "Please have a seat. Mr. Montgomery will be with you in a minute."

After a few minutes, a smooth-looking Harvard type opened the door, extended his hand for a handshake, and said, "I'm Carson Montgomery. Please, come into my office."

They sat down, and Montgomery's gaze seemed to pierce him with the precision of a sharp-pointed weapon. "What can I do for you, Mr. . . . ?"

"Farrell. Edgar Farrell." He told the man what his problem was, omitting nothing but the reasons why he needed the money so desperately. "My father was mean-spirited, and he wouldn't care if my siblings and I cut each other up over his money and property. He didn't spend it on us when he was alive, and he's made it as tough as he could for us to get it now. The problem, Mr. Montgomery, is my current lack of big-time funds. If you find that will, you get six percent of my share."

"You drive a mean bargain. Suppose your father was broke?"

"He wasn't, and you can check that with his lawyer, Donald Riggs. Besides, Father owned that huge house and everything in it. He was as frugal as they come."

Montgomery made a pyramid of his ten fingers, leaned back, and closed his eyes. "All right. I'll look into this and call you tomorrow. What is your phone number?"

He gave the detective his cell phone number. "If you want to locate my brother and sister, Riggs can tell you how to reach them. He also has a key to the house. I'm the only person who lives there."

He arrived in Atlantic City more than an hour prior to the time for his first show. He checked into the hotel, and after doing his finger exercises, he phoned Gunther.

"You may get a call from a detective. I'm trying to hire him to find that will. I'm hoping he'll do it for six percent of what I get."

"Where are you?" Edgar told him. "Is the man reliable?"

"If you meet him, you won't ask that question. Ask Riggs what he thinks."

"I definitely will. I talked with Shirley. She was between Sardinia and Sicily en route for Nice."

"She'd better get off that boat, find herself a man, and settle down. Thirty-two is old to start having children."

"Maybe. What kind of example are you setting? Thirty-six is old if you're still single."

"Lay off, man. That applies to people who had empathetic fathers. Gotta go."

"And nobody could accuse us of that. If things turn out all right with Montgomery and he finds the will, I'll share the cost. You pay him three percent of your take and I'll give him three percent of mine. Okay?"

"Right on, brother!"

Edgar looked around his hotel room, disgusted. He could afford that little room, but only the deaf could sleep there. After a shower, he stretched out on the bed for a brief rest, got out his tuning fork, and tuned his guitar. He patted its bridge and stroked its neck.

"As long as you're with me, baby, I'll never starve," he said aloud. Then he remembered how his father hated his guitar and so despised his competence at playing that he wouldn't allow him to play it where he could hear it. But he played and practiced in the basement and in closets and whenever he was alone in the house. The guitar became to him a symbol of defiance. During his father's lifetime, he locked his guitar in the closet in his bedroom, and whenever he couldn't take the instrument with him, he kept it there.

Higher education held no interest for him. As a teenager, he took the money he made on street corners and in clubs and churches and spent it on lessons with accomplished guitarists, both classical and jazz.

He got backstage ten minutes before time for his performance as a side man with the house band.

"You're second guitarist tonight," Mason, the band leader, said. "Jack Vine is sitting in with us."

Edgar stared at the man. "Yeah? Then let him do a solo. I'm a lead guitarist, and I don't do second. I know my shit, man, so knock it off. Vine is a bigger name, but I play circles around that dude, and he knows it. Who's gonna play lead tomorrow night when Vine's in Chicago, or somewhere else?" He took his usual chair and played lead guitar throughout the show. He didn't know and didn't care what Mason said to Vine.

After the show, he put his hand in his pocket and fished out eleven dollars and forty-three cents. Twenty-four hours earlier, he'd had seven hundred dollars. He swore aloud. Something had to give.

Chapter Two

Carson Montgomery had no intention of becoming involved in a fight over a will. Neither he nor his detectives had time for the shenanigans of which siblings were capable. He telephoned Gunther Farrell.

"Good morning, Mr. Farrell, this is Detective Carson Montgomery. Edgar Farrell has asked me to find his father's will, but as you and your sister are also beneficiaries, I'd like to know where you stand in this."

"Thanks for calling. I certainly approve of any legal steps to locate that will, and I'd like to meet you, if you have time. What about fifteen minutes this afternoon?"

"Would you care to meet for a short lunch?" Carson asked.

"I'm on York, not far from Madison."

"I'm on Calvert, about five blocks from you. What do you say we meet at the Frigate? Would twelve-fifteen suit you?"

Gunther looked at his watch. "I can do that. Twelve-fifteen it is. First to get there takes a table."

"Right."

Carson hung up. From that short conversation, he had a sense that Gunther Farrell was an honorable man and that, in some ways, he towered above his brother. He especially appreciated that Gunther wanted to meet him, obviously in order to appraise him as a person. He wanted the same advantage in respect to Gunther.

Minutes before twelve-fifteen, he entered the Frigate, a landmark seafood restaurant, and while he stood at the maître d's desk, Gunther walked up and asked for him. They shook hands, and the maître d' led them to a corner table.

"Thank you for meeting me," Gunther said, and Carson laughed inwardly. The man was set to have the conversation go his way, but he'd see about that.

"It's advantageous for me, too," Carson said. "I like to know who I'm dealing with, and I can't make that assessment over the phone. I confess that your brother didn't make the best impression on me."

"Desperate people rarely represent themselves well," Gunther said, to which Carson raised an eyebrow. "Edgar thinks he lives on his own terms, because he knows that as long as he has that guitar and ten healthy fingers, he can make a living. He's an excellent guitarist, and that's all he seems to care about. He told me how he expects to pay you, and I offered to split that with him. Our father was a rich man who cared little for anything other than his money and property. If you get six percent of a share, you'll get a bundle."

"What about your sister? Where is she, and how will she react to this plan?"

"Our sister is the youngest of the three, and if Edgar and I both agree on a thing, she most often accepts it. She's a public relations officer on a cruise ship that's currently docked in Nice." He seemed to study Carson. Then he said, "This is a clever thing Edgar's done. I hope you'll agree to take the job."

"I'm accustomed to looking for people and for clues to problems. This will be a challenge, but it definitely will not be boring. I'll phone Edgar and write out a contract for him." He looked up at the waiter, whose face bore an expression of exasperation. "I'll have a big bowl of New England clam chowder and a Caesar salad."

"I'll have the same," Gunther said.

"What do you do for a living?" Carson asked Gunther.

"I own a software company that designs, produces, and distributes intelligent computer games and puzzles for all ages."

"How does one get into that?" Carson asked him.

"I've been doing games and puzzles since I was nine or ten. My father hated it, and when I began doing it for a living after having gotten an MBA, my father all but disowned me. He wanted me to join the Wall Street fat cats and get rich. But since I got through college and graduate school with almost no help from him, I figured I could do as I pleased."

"I'm beginning to understand why Edgar thinks you don't care about your father's will."

Gunther lifted his right shoulder in a quick shrug. "Of course I care. But if it's never found, I won't lose a minute of sleep. For Edgar, it's a lifeline."

They finished lunch, walked out together, and shook hands. "I'm glad I met you," Carson said. "I'd certainly like to see who your sister more closely resembles in personality and outlook, you or your brother."

A smile played around Gunther's lips. "Shirley is her own independent self. She loves us, but she does not walk our walk. You may want to interview her, since each of us has a take on Father and the sort of person he was. I hope to hear from you."

"You will indeed." Carson rushed back to his office and jotted down some notes on his conversation with Gunther. He drafted a contract, phoned Edgar, and read it to him.

"Just remember this one thing," Edgar said. "I'm the one you report to. I expect you'll talk with Shirley and Gunther all you need to, but I'm the one you report to."

"I have no problem with that," Carson said, "so long as it's agreed that you're responsible for payment."

He hung up, gave the contract to his secretary for typing, and looked up Leon Farrell on the Internet. He discovered that the man earned a fortune speculating in real estate and was known for his scroogelike reputation. At his funeral, only his children, his lawyer, and the preacher and paid pallbearers were present. Carson phoned Gunther, got his father's address, and contacted the builder of the family home for the house plans. He needed to know every niche in that house and any other of Farrell's properties, such as vacation homes, automobiles, boats, garages, and the like.

Two days later, Edgar signed the contract and gave Carson his first interview. "Man, how long is this going to take?" Edgar asked him. "I need the bread, man."

"If you read the fine print on the second page of that contract, you'll see that I made provisions for harassment. If you do that, I can tear up the contract. And I will do it. I'm not begging for work. You got that?"

"Yeah. I got it, but that will ain't gonna walk up to you and say, 'Hello, Mr. Montgomery. Here I am.'"

"No kidding? And to think I'd planned to get a can of beer, go to your place, sit in front of the TV, and wait for the damned thing to drop in my lap. Look here, Mr. Farrell. You take care of your business and stay out of mine. And if you want to sound clever, try it on somebody else. As far as I'm concerned, that comment was childish. Send my secretary a list of your father's properties. I'm going to examine every one of them."

"Right. I didn't mean to pull your chain, man, but this has been going on too long, and if we don't find it by mid-January, the state takes over, siphons off as much as it wants, and then decides of the little that's left who gets what and what goes where."

"Okay. Just send me that list." He hung up. If he let Edgar Farrell work his nerves, he'd quit the job before he started. He hoped Shirley wasn't frantic about the will. The last thing he needed was a woman plaguing him 24/7.

* * *

Back in his office, Gunther worked on a computer game in which a mouse tried to teach neighboring cats about the unhappy lives of mice that lived in constant dread of their cat neighbors. After watching a group of preschool children terrorize a playmate, he'd designed the game as a teaching vehicle about the effects of cruelty.

"When am I getting a chance to try out that game on my Effie?" Medford, one of his assistants, asked him. "I have a feeling she'll love it."

"Maybe. How old is Effie?"

"She's four, and practically everything she sees excites her. She's pretty good at the computer. She reads, writes, counts, and, man, does she love to sing."

Gunther stopped working as a thought struck him. "Bring her in tomorrow. I'd like to get her reaction to this."

Medford's lower jaw dropped. "You'll pay Effie to have fun with that game?"

"How will I know kids will love it if I don't test it? I'll pay her twelve-fifty an hour."

"Well, I'll be damned. You wouldn't need her for the whole day, would you?" He held up both hands, palms out. "Just kidding. My wife would take my hide off."

"Call for you on line three, Gunther," his other assistant said.

He lifted the receiver and pushed the button. "Farrell speaking."

"Honey, this is Lissa." He rolled his eyes toward the ceiling. As if he didn't know her voice. "Any more news about the will, honey? I mean . . . did they find it yet?"

He was unprepared for the burst of anger that

seemed almost to consume him. "Who do you mean by 'they'?" he asked her. "I haven't been looking for it."

"What? But how can we plan on building a new home and doing all the things we want to do if you don't find the will? I want a big wedding, and—"

It was too much. He interrupted her. "Why do you think we're getting married, Lissa? I have never mentioned marriage to you. We are not engaged because I have never asked you to marry me, and you have no right to assume that we're getting married. If you think I can be railroaded into it, think again." There! He'd told her, and he should have done it the first time she tried that trick.

"But we've been going together over eight months, and I haven't been seeing anyone else. How can you do this?"

"Hold on, Lissa. Did I ever ask you not to see any other man?"

"No, but you took up my time. Every day is important to me. I'm forty-four years old, and—"

He nearly swallowed his tongue. That had definitely been a slip. "Forty-four? But you told me you were thirty." He took a deep breath and exhaled it. "I'm sorry, Lissa, but we'd better call this off right now. I've been concerned that each time we've had even the smallest confrontation, you solved it by seducing me. At first, I liked it. But you made a habit of it, and I began to resent being manipulated. Sex should be an expression either of need or of love. Where I stand, it's not for problem-solving and certainly not for controlling another person. It's been nice knowing you, and I do wish you the best."

Relief flooded his whole being. He hung up and

returned to the game of mice and cats, whistling as he worked, and the pieces began to fall into place.

"I think I've got it," he said to Medford several hours later. "If you don't want to bring Effie here, I could drop by your place with a copy of the game for an hour or so this afternoon."

Medford seemed to ponder the alternatives. "I'd like to have you come home with me, but if Effie sees that game this evening, she'll be uncontrollable for the rest of the night."

The following morning, Medford arrived with his daughter, and she hardly needed Gunther's instructions. He watched, fascinated, as she took to the game as if it were her idea. After testing it and the instructions he had to write for it, he wrote a check for twenty-five dollars and handed it to Effie.

"Give that to your father," he said, and thanked her for the visit. When Effie didn't want to stop playing, he knew he'd hit the jackpot with that game, and he could hardly contain his elation. He'd published only a few games so far, compared to the number of games on the market, and he took pride in their quality and popularity. Some of his competitors had offered to buy him out, and one had attempted to purchase the building in which he had his business. But the building's owner had refused to sell, and he was grateful for that. This time, he was going to publish and distribute *Mice and Cats* himself, and the vultures and thieves wouldn't have a chance at it.

Gunther was still buoyed by his vision of the future when he received a call from Shirley. "I've got two weeks' shore leave," she told him. "Can I hang out with you, or will that louse up things with you and Lissa?"

"Lissa's history. When will you get here?"

"Hallelujah. We dock in Fort Lauderdale tomorrow morning. I'll go home, check things out, and see you day after tomorrow. I hope to sleep indefinitely. How're things? Did Edgar hire a detective yet?"

"Yeah, I met him, and I think he's first class . . . at least as a man. We'll see about his detective skills. He'll want to interview you."

"Fine with me. We can talk about it when I see you. I have this weird feeling that things are going too smoothly. It isn't like Edgar to be so low-key about a thing that's so important to him."

"You're right. That hadn't occurred to me."

"I keep telling you I'm smart. See you in a couple of days. Love you."

"Love you, too. Bye for now."

Gunther hoped that Shirley hadn't had one of her premonitions. She believed so strongly in them that it wouldn't surprise him if she had based her decision to take two weeks' leave on what she called a premonition and which he considered a hunch.

Gunther hadn't guessed correctly, but he wasn't wrong, either. Shirley didn't believe Edgar to be capable of genteel behavior about anything relating to money. To her mind, there'd be a storm between her brothers, and she meant to do what she could to lessen its force. In her Fort Lauderdale apartment, Shirley packed what she'd need for two weeks, phoned for a taxi, and was soon en route to Ellicott City.

Gunther met her at the Baltimore/Washington International Thurgood Marshall Airport.

"Hey. You look great," he said. "I must be in the wrong profession."

"It's breathing that fresh, clean sea air. My lungs appreciate it, and my skin loves it."

"Tell me about it!"

"Did you tell Edgar I was coming? I called him several times, but he didn't answer his phone."

"He might not have paid his phone bill."

"Yeah. I keep forgetting that he doesn't operate like most people. He's not going to like my staying with you, but as much as I love my brother, I can take just so much of him."

"Same here, and it's a pity."

Less than an hour after they walked into Gunther's apartment, the doorbell rang. Shirley opened the door and stared into the face of an angry Edgar.

"Where'd you come from?" he asked her. "And where's Gunther?"

"What's the matter, Edgar?"

"What's the matter? I knew he couldn't be trusted. I'm paying Montgomery, and if Mister Big Shot wants to contribute, he can damned well give the money to me. I'm no fool. If he thinks that gives him the right to give Montgomery instructions and to demand his report, he's lamer than I thought. It was my idea, and I get the guy's report."

"Did this detective tell you that Gunther demanded the report?"

"He didn't have to. I know when I'm being screwed."

"What's the problem, Edgar?"

She wondered how long Gunther had been standing there. Probably long enough to decide how to handle the situation.

Edgar repeated his accusation. "I'm having none of it. This contract has my name on it and mine only as the employer. Got it?"

Gunther slouched against the wall. "I don't know what you're so upset about. If you want me to take back my offer to split the cost with you, fine. It'll be that much more for me."

Edgar seemed to shake with anger. "What is this? Blackmail? You said you'd split it, and I'm holding you to it."

Gunther shrugged first one shoulder and then the other one. "Why doesn't that surprise me? You coming in, or do you plan to continue standing there in the foyer?"

"I'll be watching every move you make, and if you try anything with Montgomery, I'll be on you like scales on a fish, buddy."

Shirley moved forward and rested a hand on Edgar's shoulder. "But, Edgar, can't you see that you're the only one of us who's strung out about this? You want to start a fight with Gunther, and he only tried to be helpful."

"I expected that you'd defend him. But you watch it. Both of you. I hired Montgomery, and from now on, I'm running the show." He left without saying good-bye.

Shirley threw up her hands, exasperated. "The problem is that for Edgar, this is just the beginning of his paranoia about you and that will. Every time he gets in a tizzy because it hasn't been located, he'll find a way to lay at least half of the blame on you. Who is this Montgomery fellow? I'd like to meet him."

"Of course. I'll phone him." Gunther pulled his cell phone out of his pocket and dialed Carson. "This is Gunther Farrell. May I speak with Carson Montgomery?"

"Just a minute, please," the voice said.

"Montgomery speaking. What may I do for you, Mr. Farrell?"

"My sister's in town. If you have time, this would be an opportunity to speak with her."

"Thank you. Do you have a phone number for her?"

"She's staying at my apartment. In fact, she's here, if you'd like to speak with her."

"I would, indeed, if that suits her."

Gunther handed Shirley his cell phone.

"Hello, Mr. Montgomery. I'll be here for about two weeks. When would it be convenient for us to meet?"

"I'm anxious to get as much information as possible about your father and his habits. If I don't find that will day before yesterday, Edgar will have a meltdown. So I'd like us to meet as soon as possible. Tomorrow, if that suits you."

"Fine. We could meet for lunch," she said, "provided that's convenient."

They agreed to meet at the Frigate at twelve-thirty.

She wore a coral-colored, short-sleeved silk business suit and a matching hat of fine Milan straw. *I won't wear white gloves,* she thought, *because that would probably make him think I'm a phony.* But in that blistering sun, she'd wear her hat. Besides, she knew she looked great in it.

She arrived at the Frigate on time and followed the maître d' to Carson's table. He stood as they approached. Why hadn't Gunther warned her? Wasn't it just like a man to overlook things that were important to a woman? He could at least have told her that Carson Montgomery was a humdinger of a man and precisely her type.

Let it go, girl. How would Gunther know who your kind of man is? He probably doesn't think of you in relation to men. She laid back her shoulders, put a smile on her face, and extended her hand.

"I'm glad to meet you, Mr. Montgomery."

He seemed momentarily taken aback, but he let her know that he wasn't easily flustered when he shook her hand as if handling a piece of wood. "Thank you for coming, Ms. Farrell. I'm glad to meet you. I'd been wondering which of your brothers you'd more nearly resemble in manners and behavior."

She bristled, and she knew he noticed it. "I love both of my brothers, Mr. Montgomery."

"Love has nothing to do with it, and I'm sure you're aware of that. I agreed to try and find that will. Edgar signed a contract with me, and for payment, I get six percent of his share. Those were the conditions that he offered, and after speaking with Gunther, I agreed to them. Edgar has an attitude toward Gunther that I find bothersome, but that's between them. Another thing that bothers me is Edgar's insistence that I report what I find only to him, although the will is the property of the three of you.

"Your father's attorney is positive that a will exists and that your father deliberately hid it. That doesn't make sense to me, but I have to accept it. If I'm going to find that will, I'll need the three of you to help me. Where did your father work?"

"He closed his Baltimore office about ten years ago and converted one of the bedrooms in our house into an office. That's a really big house, and I'd bet that when his will is finally located, it will be in that house."

"He could have buried it on the property."

"I doubt that, since he didn't own a shovel. As stingy as he was, he paid a groundskeeper—a gardener or whatever you call them—to care for the property around the house. Father believed in hard work as long as it was confined to work with the brain."

"Not so. He began as a laborer at a milk company."

"I know, but he seemed uncomfortable with even the memory of those days. To my way of thinking, he could have had one of three reasons for doing such a strange thing: He wanted us to be remorseful that we hadn't lived by his rules and complied with his demands; he wanted to shatter our relations with each other, because we cared more for our siblings than for him; or he wanted to force us to spend time, energy, and money to find the will. When I recall how mean and stingy he was—something I wouldn't admit when he was alive—I think all of those apply."

"Why wouldn't you admit it when he was alive?"

"Simple. He was my father, and I was supposed to love him. If I'd acknowledged the facts, loving him would have been too hard."

He noted the waiter's presence. "I'll have New England chowder and a crab sandwich." He looked at Shirley. "And you?"

"I'll have the same."

"Did your brothers find loving him too difficult?"

She leaned back in the chair and studied Carson. He was a shrewd and clever man. Opting for the truth, she leaned forward. "You must have guessed that Gunther is his own man. He sized up his relationship with Father and went his own way. Edgar pretended to care and hung around for what he could get. Father didn't buy it, and Edgar got crumbs."

"That certainly puts things into proper perspective." Their lunch arrived, and he changed his line of questioning. "Mind telling me where you went to school and what you studied?"

"Not at all. I studied psychology and business administration at Morgan State University. I wanted to go to Harvard, and because I had the grades, I was admitted. But I had only an academic fellowship. The cost of living was more than I could afford, so I attended Morgan State and lived at home."

"And you weren't bitter toward your father? He was a millionaire."

"He worked for his and we should work for ours. That was his philosophy."

"Damn. I may never find that will."

"If you don't, I won't cry about it. I've done well for myself with minimal help from my father, and I need him less now than ever."

His facial expression projected admiration, and she could see that she had his respect. "This soup is delicious," she said. "By the way, where did you go to school?" What was good for the goose was good for the gander.

He grinned, as if acknowledging what she'd thought. And did the brother ever have charisma! She tucked in her belly and told herself to focus not on him but on what he said.

"I have a bachelor's degree in criminology and a JD, both from Howard University. I've passed the national bar, and I'm a licensed private detective."

"Have you ever practiced law?"

"I worked as an assistant DA when I first passed the bar, but the idea of getting a conviction without due regard for justice thoroughly disillusioned me. I found that I didn't want to be a trial lawyer, either, and I didn't want to teach. Detective work really suits me. Most of my contracts are with lawyers."

He glanced at his watch. "I could sit here with you indefinitely, but work is calling. When can we meet at your father's house? My plan is to go over that place with each of you separately, and then I'll search it alone."

"Tomorrow morning, if you like. Edgar will be in Atlantic City. Not to worry. Each of us has a key to the house."

He picked up the check, and they left the restaurant. "If you're going back to Gunther's place, I'll drop you off."

As they got into his car, he said, "You were hesitant."

"Yes, I was. I'm a careful person, Mr. Montgomery."

"And well you should be. If you're not driving,

I'd be glad to come by for you tomorrow morning at nine-fifteen."

"In that case, I won't have to inconvenience Gunther. I'll be ready. Thank you."

She couldn't wait to find out what Gunther really thought of Carson Montgomery. She knew what she thought, but with a man like that one, it was probably best not to trust your own judgment. Six feet three inches tall at least, with curly black hair; large, grayish brown eyes with curled lashes; and skin the color of shelled walnuts. If she were stupid, she'd have followed him wherever he was going. But she wasn't stupid, and she had seen many men who were just as good-looking. But there was something about Carson Montgomery that set him apart. She had a hunch that she'd better not bother to find out what that was.

Carson drove off shaking his head and trying to figure out what had happened during that lunch. Years had passed since he reacted to a woman as he did to Shirley Farrell. "Thank God I'm still human and my testosterone is still lively," he said to himself. When he'd finally gotten a divorce settlement after years of pain and angst, he'd been certain that he never wanted to be near another woman. Hell had descended on him in stages: the last two years of living with Darnell, his ex-wife, and the following two years of divorce wrangling. In the end, he'd considered himself fortunate to have retained any semblance of sanity. "The mere thought of it is enough to straighten out my head," he said aloud. "No more of that for me!"

The following morning at nine-fifteen, he rang the doorbell of Gunther's apartment and gaped. Shirley Farrell opened the door. Her hair hung girlishly in a long ponytail, and she wore a red T-shirt, faded blue jeans, and white sneakers. Her face bore not a speck of makeup, but big, round silver hoops swung from her ears.

"For a minute I didn't recognize you," he said, thankful that he'd recovered his breath. "Ready?"

She slung a hobo bag over her shoulder. "Ready as I'll ever be."

They drove in silence to the family home two miles beyond the Ellicott City line. He parked, turned, and looked at her. "I won't succeed unless you and your brothers tell me every relevant thing that you know. This is a big house, and I'm looking for a piece of paper." He considered himself an excellent judge of people, and he observed her closely until she blushed. He could see that he'd embarrassed her.

"I'm sorry, Shirley. I hope you don't mind me using your first name. I have a habit of studying people as carefully as possible. I didn't mean to make you uncomfortable. Shall we go in?"

She guided him room by room through the huge house. Each of the siblings had a room and bath, and the old man had reserved for himself what appeared to be a separate wing in which he could live without encountering any of his offspring.

She answered his many questions, but he didn't find anything that she said more helpful than what he already knew. "How did he spend his time after dinner?" he asked her.

She appeared bemused. "I don't know. I never

saw much of him after dinner. He hated noise, so we never sat together talking, listening to music, or watching television."

"What did you give your father for Christmas . . . after you got a job?"

"I gave him a Montblanc pen, a sweater, an electric shaver, things like that."

It amazed him that she showed so much patience. "I want you to think back and try to remember everything you ever gave him. Not now, but later. What did he especially like?"

"Animals. But he didn't have pets."

He continued the questioning until noon. "I'm starved," he said. "Suppose we get a sandwich or something, come back and search for an hour?"

And so went their pattern for the next three days, but in the end he had nothing to show for it but a pile of notes that he recorded each day after leaving her.

"You mean he still doesn't have a clue?" Gunther asked her after she'd spent three days with Carson.

"If he has, he's keeping it to himself."

"For goodness' sake, don't say that to Edgar. He'll jump all over Montgomery."

"You're kidding. Nobody's going to jump all over that man. Let's eat out. I don't feel like cooking, and you're so tired, you literally flung yourself into that chair. You should have a housekeeper for this big place. Why don't you?"

"I thought several times that I'd do it, but Lissa said there wasn't enough for a housekeeper to do here. So I got a weekly cleaning woman."

"Lissa knew a housekeeper would see straight

through her and her tricks. Get a housekeeper." She
telephoned the secretary of the church to which she
went on occasion. "Ms. Broadus, my brother needs
a housekeeper, experienced and preferably over
forty, not too motherly and not man hunting."

"I think I have just the person for him. She
worked for a family for the past year, but the man
lost his job and can't any longer afford a housekeeper. She's a good Christian woman, so she
won't be drinking and carrying on. You know what
I mean."

She didn't, but could guess. Shirley gave the
woman Gunther's address. "Ask her to come this
afternoon, if possible." She hung up and called to
Gunther, "A woman is coming here this afternoon
to interview for the job as your housekeeper. I got
the contact from the church office."

"Thanks. I'd have procrastinated about that indefinitely. What do I know about hiring a housekeeper?"

"You'll learn this afternoon."

Gunther opened the door to Mirna Jordan,
looked hard at her, and released a breath of relief.
"Come in. I'm Gunther Farrell."

"My name's Mirna Jordan, Mr. Farrell, and I'm
here because I need a job."

A no-nonsense woman. He liked that. "Come in
and have a seat." He liked her face. She had an air
of competence and self-possession. He went into
the kitchen and got two glasses and the pitcher of
sweetened ice tea that Shirley had placed there
earlier, and joined her in the living room.

"It's hot outside," he said, and poured a glass

full and handed it to her. Then he poured a glass for himself and sat opposite her.

"Thank you, sir. After that long walk I had, I was about to burn up."

"A bus stops about two blocks from here."

"I know, but every dollar's important to me these days."

He leaned back, hoping to make her comfortable. "Tell me about yourself."

"I'm a widow, Mr. Farrell, and I have one daughter who's a junior at Spelman College in Atlanta. She lives with my sister and brother-in-law, but I'm paying her bills. I'm forty-eight. I worked on my last job up until last week, when the man lost his job. The company moved to somewhere in the Pacific, and he couldn't move the family there because both his mother and his mother-in-law are very sick. Here's the telephone number if you want a reference. It broke my heart to leave them, but you know life don't promise you a thing."

She shook her head as if perplexed and continued speaking. "No, it sure don't. I'm a good cook, and I can give you meat and potatoes, or I can cook a gourmet meal for twenty-five people. Just let me know what you like and what you don't like, and I'll keep you happy. If you want me to do the shopping, just give me a budget. I know how to run a house."

"I'll check your references and—"

"Excuse me, Mr. Farrell, but I don't mind if you call them while I'm sitting here. I took care of that home and that family as if they were my own. They cried when I left."

He observed her closely for a minute. She needed the job, and she didn't want to give him a chance to hire someone else. He dialed the number. "Hello. May I speak with Mrs. Parsons, please?

"Mrs. Parsons, I'm Gunther Farrell, and I'm interviewing Mrs. Jordan for a job as my housekeeper. She says she kept house for you."

He listened while Mrs. Parsons extolled Mirna Jordan's virtues as a housekeeper and as a woman and decided that he'd be lucky if the woman agreed to work for him. "Thank you, Mrs. Parsons. I appreciate this. Good-bye."

He hung up. "What do you say I show you my apartment? It's much bigger than it looks from here. There're three bedrooms and three baths upstairs, and a living room, dining room, den, kitchen, and lavatory on this floor. A balcony overlooks the garden, which I confess I don't take the best care of."

As they walked through the rooms, she stopped and asked him, "Why did you need such a big apartment?"

"Good question. I figured I should get one in which I could raise a family, when and if I get married."

"I don't imagine you're having any trouble getting married."

"Not really, because I haven't tried. My sister is staying with me for a couple of weeks. She lives in Fort Lauderdale, Florida. Do you smoke?"

"Me? Smoke? No, siree."

"Good. I don't want one puff of smoke in this apartment. I have an older brother, Edgar, who lives in the family home about two miles outside of the city. If you're here alone and he attempts to muscle his way in, don't open the door. He can be devious, unprincipled. No matter how much charm he exudes, do not let him in."

She looked at him as if sizing him up. "Is he jealous of you?"

"That's one way to put it."

"Don't you worry. I get the whole picture, and if you say a person's not to come here, I won't be the one to let 'em in. Not ever!"

He called Shirley. "Come down for a few minutes. I want you to meet Mrs. Jordan."

Shirley ran down the stairs, walked over to Mirna Jordan, and shook her hand. "I'm delighted to meet you, Mrs. Jordan. You won't see much of me, because I live in Florida, but I'm glad you'll be here to take care of my big brother. I hope you'll keep the fat and salt in his food low, because he doesn't concern himself much with his health."

"You needn't worry about that, miss, if I work here. I have to tell you, though, that he and I don't have an agreement yet."

"Heavens," Gunther said. "I forgot about that." He quoted Mirna a salary and added, "You'll have health insurance and, of course, sick and vacation leave."

Mirna stood up and sat back down. "You offering me the job? Lord, I can't believe it. The pay is fine, sir. Well, you will definitely not regret it. I'm gonna keep this place like polished glass. Thank you, sir. When do you want me to start?"

"Tomorrow. You get Sundays and Thursday afternoons off."

"I need to know how much I can spend for food and for dry cleaning each month. I'll do the regular laundry. And let me know what time you eat breakfast and dinner."

They shook hands. After taking her address and social security number, he gave her a key. "See you in the morning. I'll call a taxi for you." He called the taxi, walked out with her, and paid the fare.

"Well, what do you think?" he asked Shirley when he returned.

"I think you've probably hit the jackpot. I got great vibes from her."

"So did I. How old do you think she is?"

Shirley folded her arms and thought for a minute. "About fifty-five or sixty. She looks as if she's had a hard life."

"Maybe. She's a widow, and she said she's forty-eight."

"What? It's been my experience that black women don't age fast, but she just didn't act that young."

He jerked his shoulder in a shrug. "Who knows what she's been through?"

Mirna Jordan relaxed in the taxi and used the cell phone her previous employer gave her to call her friend. "May I please speak with Frieda Davis?"

"Girl, you won't believe this. I got a job. The Lord does provide. And this man gon' pay me a hundred more a month than I was getting at Ms. Parsons's. Plus, girl, there's just him in his big three-bedroom apartment, and the man is sending me home in an air-conditioned taxi."

"I told you not to worry. All worry does for you is make you sick."

"Imagine me with health insurance, sick pay, and vacation time. I'm moving up to your class."

"People ought to pay their housekeepers decent

wages," Frieda said. "And it wouldn't hurt people to pay us LPNs what we're worth, either. I'm happy for you, Mirna. Talk to you later. I have a distressed patient to look after. Bye."

Mirna hung up and called her daughter, using one of her free long-distance calls. And after sharing her good news with the person closest to her, she said a prayer of thanks. Life was good. She'd be all right.

Gunther tripped down the stairs the next morning at a quarter past seven to fix his breakfast, sniffed the odor of food coming from the kitchen, and stopped. He'd forgotten that he'd hired a housekeeper. Thankful that he was fully dressed, he walked into the kitchen.

"Good morning, Mr. Farrell. Breakfast will be ready in a minute. Here. You can have some coffee while I flip these over."

"Good gracious," he said. "You're as busy as a bee. What did you find to cook?"

"You had bread and coffee. I brought eggs, milk, bacon, grits, sausage, and some fresh fruit with me this morning. I know how men keep house. This is ready. You want to eat in the dining room?"

"I'm used to eating in here. Shirley's still asleep, so it's just the two of us this morning. I can set the table. This coffee is really good. What kind is it?"

"It's the coffee you bought. I probably make it stronger than you do."

He set the table for two, and she placed fresh sliced peaches, grits, scrambled eggs, rope sausage, and French toast on the table. "Come on," he said.

"I see I'm going to have to start working out in a gym every day." He cut a piece of French toast.

"I have to say grace before I eat," she said.

He stopped eating. "I was taught to do that, and I see I'm going to have to do better."

He finished eating, stood and looked down at Mirna. "This was a terrific breakfast. I enjoyed every calorie. Here's your budget, and an envelope of petty cash."

"Thanks, Mr. Farrell. I'll keep good records."

"If you do that, we won't have a problem." As he walked out the door of the building in which he lived, he heard the roar of Edgar's big Harley-Davidson. *Now what?*

Chapter Three

Edgar hopped off the motorcycle and headed toward Gunther. "You know I'm supposed to be at my office by now," Gunther said. "What's up?"

"I thought I'd drop by and say hi to Shirley for a few minutes."

"Shirley's asleep. Were you planning to give her the three thousand dollars you took from her?"

"Now look here. I didn't put a gun in her back. She gave it to me willingly."

"She didn't give it to you. She loaned it to you after you handed her a hard-luck story. She's your baby sister, for heaven's sake. You should be taking care of *her*. Don't bother to ask her for any more money, because she isn't going to give it to you."

Edgar didn't want to hear that. Right then, she was his only hope. "Let her speak for herself."

"She promised me she wasn't going to lend you another cent, and you know Shirley keeps her word."

"You've got no business meddling in my business. One of these days, you'll go too far."

Gunther folded his arms across his chest and widened his stance, and Edgar knew that when Gunther did that, a hurricane wouldn't move him. Unfortunately, his younger brother was taller than he by six inches and had the weight that went with a six-foot, three-inch skeleton. He'd have to be crazy to take him on. He wasn't even sure he wanted to. In his honest moments, he'd admit that he had far more natural talent than Gunther, but . . . Oh, what the hell! He swung around, jumped on his Harley, and let his brother taste the fumes that it exhausted.

Gunther stood where Edgar left him, staring at the speeding vehicle until he could no longer see it. He'd give anything if he could connect with Edgar as one brother should with another. He got into his car and drove to his office. He'd learned years earlier that worrying about Edgar and Edgar's attitude toward him was as wasteful as it was painful.

He walked into his office, his adrenaline already pumping from his thoughts of his next game of *Mice and Cats.* If children loved his idea, he'd have to create a new game at least once every three months. He stopped abruptly.

"What the hell!" he exclaimed, staring at Lissa. "What are you doing here?"

"I . . . uh . . . I thought we'd talk. I know you didn't mean what you said the other day."

He threw his briefcase on his desk, walked around to his chair, and sat down. "I meant every word I said, and you're old enough to recognize the truth when you hear it. There isn't going to be anything else between you and me. Not now and not ever. I am not one bit sympathetic with the game you were playing."

"But you enjoyed being with me. You can't deny that."

"I don't want to be coarse, Lissa, so please don't push me to it. I don't entertain women socially in my office, and I don't allow my employees to do it. So, I'd appreciate it if you'll excuse me. Now. And, Lissa, it's over."

He stood, but she waved a hand dismissively. "I know the way out."

What kind of woman would plan a future with a man without his consent, without his ever having told her that he loved her and without having done or said anything to suggest that she loved him? "It's a lesson," he said aloud, "and I will not have to learn it a second time." He got up to lower the air-conditioning and his gaze took in what appeared to be a business card lying on the floor near his desk.

He picked up the card and read EDGAR FARRELL. MASTER OF THE CLASSICAL AND JAZZ GUITAR. He punched the intercom. "Medford, was my brother here this morning?"

"No. The only visitor here today was a woman named Lissa Goins. She said she was your fiancée, so I let her sit in your office."

"I don't have a fiancée, Medford—Miss Goins was attempting to be clever. I do not want her here again. Not ever."

"Man, I'm sorry. She didn't look like she was lying."

"She was lying, and if she comes here again, I will indict her for harassment."

"You couldn't make it clearer than that, Gunther."

He dialed Edgar's cell number.

"Hello. What's up, brother?"

"I'm not sure, Edgar. How do you happen to know Lissa Goins?"

"That's what I call cutting to the chase. She called me, came to the house, told me she was your fiancée and that you found another woman and dropped her like a hot potato. She cried for an hour. I told her no man was worth that much misery and that she ought not to have much trouble finding another dude and getting on with her life. She made a hell of a pass at me, but, man, I won't stoop that low. Sex is too easy to get."

He gave Edgar a summary of his relationship with Lissa, ending with details of their breakup. "Lissa wants a husband, and she wants money. She has no scruples about how she gets either of them. Why did she have your business card?"

"I . . . uh . . . I didn't know she had it."

"If you want a problem, hang out with Lissa," Gunther said. "She'll make certain that you get one."

"Naah, man. I don't want your leavings."

That didn't sound one bit like Edgar. Righteousness was not his forte. It didn't smell right. But for the time being, he'd leave the matter. He'd learned that if he gave Edgar enough rope, he'd become increasingly brazen and soon hang himself.

"Doesn't it bother you?" Shirley asked when he told her about it that night. "I'd be furious."

"You think I'm not mad? I'd like to send my fist through both of them. I don't want that woman to tell people I'm her fiancé, and if I hear that she persists, I'll take out an ad—"

"Don't do that. Indict her and ask heavy damages. That will teach her a lesson. You're not going to continue seeing her, are you?"

"You can't be serious. The other day, I met someone at a trade show who interests me. I'm not sure about her, though, but she's one up on Lissa, because she has a good job and probably isn't looking for someone to support her. I want a woman to marry me because she loves me and needs me."

"As good-looking as you are, there shouldn't be a problem."

"But there is. The only women who think I'd be interested in them are the designer-clothed, picture-perfect narcissistic beauties who bore me to death. Avoiding them is how I got mixed up with Lissa."

"Are you going to let me meet this trade-show gal?"

"That's not a bad idea. She likes baseball. I'll see if I can get three good seats before you leave." He thought for a minute. "Maybe. I don't know. "

"I'm thinking of moving to Frederick if my boss will let me. It will only cost the company my occasional transportation from Frederick to either Orlando or Fort Lauderdale."

Hmm. What was behind that? He knew how she loved living within walking distance from the Atlantic Ocean. It bore watching.

Shirley told herself that she needed to be on hand to mediate misunderstandings between her brothers lest they do irreparable damage to their relationship. But on the following morning when she opened the door to Carson Montgomery, she was not so certain of the rationalization she gave herself for her decision to move back to Frederick. The emotional jarring she got when she looked up at him annoyed her.

"Hi. Why the frown?" he asked her.

"I didn't know I was frowning. Shall we go?"

"Sure. That's why I'm here." So the brother could give as good as he got and wasn't slow about doing it.

"Sorry, but I'm a little discombobulated," she said, and wasn't sure that explanation helped the situation.

He didn't let her off the hook. "About what? It's only nine o'clock."

"Look, Carson. We'd better start over again. Would you like some coffee?"

"Would I like . . . What a switch! Do I dare say no?"

She braced her knuckles against her sides, quickly removed them, and stared at him. "What's going on here?"

"Something that neither of us plans to admit," he said under his breath. Louder, he said, "You going to bring the coffee to me here, or are you going to ask me to come in?"

"That you at the door, Miss Shirley?"

"Yes. It's me."

Carson's eyebrows shot up. "Am I interrupting anything?"

"No. Come in. That's Mrs. Jordan, my brother's housekeeper."

"Thanks for the offer of coffee. All I've had this morning is a cup of Maxwell's best instant."

She closed the door. "Would you mind drinking it in the kitchen? I don't want to get in Mrs. Jordan's way."

"You won't be in my way," Mirna said. "Sit in the dining room, and you'll have coffee in ten minutes."

"Thanks," Shirley said. "Mrs. Jordan, this is Carson Montgomery."

"Glad to meet you, Mrs. Jordan."

"Likewise, I'm sure. I got some waffle batter left from breakfast. Would you like a waffle?"

"If you give me a homemade waffle, I may never leave here."

"Well, get comfortable."

Shirley got a place setting for Carson and a mug for herself.

Ten minutes later, Mirna put a carafe of coffee on the table along with waffles, maple syrup, butter, and half a cantaloupe. "If you'd dropped by earlier, Mr. Montgomery, I'd a given you a real breakfast."

"Thank you. I don't see how it could be more real than this." He sampled the coffee. "This is pure heaven." He ate slowly as if savoring every bite and every minute of the experience. "I'd like to know what set you off this morning, but if you're not comfortable telling me, I'll accept that."

If he had the guts to say what he wanted to, so did she. Instead of answering his question, she said, "You're not wearing a wedding band, and I don't see the print of one on your finger. Does that mean you're not married?"

"That's precisely what it means. I'm divorced, and I don't have any children, though I regret the latter."

"But you don't regret the divorce?"

"No, indeed. I regret the mistake I made in getting married."

Now what could she say to that? "Are you bitter about it?"

"No. If I was, I'd only hurt myself. I'm just very, very cautious. You're not wearing a wedding band, either, nor is there evidence that you've worn one."

"You're right. I'm not, and I haven't. Since college, I haven't stayed in one place long enough to cultivate lasting relationships. Besides, I love what I do, although there's getting to be a conflict between that and the rate at which my biological clock is ticking."

"How old are you?"

"I'll be thirty-two October fourteenth."

"I'm thirty-six, and sometimes I feel as if I've lived a thousand years. In my business, you see so much, move into and out of so many lives, that it's not easy to keep track of your own life."

"But I can tell that you manage it."

"That I do. Otherwise, I'd have a mental problem." He drained his third cup of coffee. "This was an unexpected treat. And to think that you offered it only to make amends for splashing ice water in my face."

"I didn't do that."

"Did so."

"Okay, I did," she said, "but if you hadn't forgiven me, you wouldn't have come in, the prospects of a cup of real coffee notwithstanding."

"Truth can be hard on the ego. I think we'd better get started." He hugged Mirna and thanked her.

"What do we tackle today?" Shirley asked when they reached his car.

"Tell me if you think I'm wrong, but I believe we ought to examine his bedroom and study again. From what I'm learning about him, he put that will out of reach of others, but also where he could watch over it while he lived."

"I can't argue with that," she said, and got into his dark blue BMW and hooked her seat belt. "Father never talked when the simplest of gestures would suffice. *Taciturn* barely describes him. By the time I was in high school, I had decided that he didn't consider us children worth an investment of his precious time."

He didn't comment on that. They reached the family home, and he parked in the garage. "I don't want anybody driving this baby but me," he said, alluding to the high incidence of car theft.

Walking up the stairs ahead of him made her uncomfortable, and she ran up the last few steps. "What's the hurry?" he asked her.

Tired of giving you a free show, she said to herself. To him, she said, "Walking up the stairs is more tiring than running up."

Inside of what had been Leon Farrell's office or den, Carson rolled back the fifteen-by-twenty Tabriz carpet, exposing the bare floor of half the room; he then moved the furniture and rolled back the other half of the carpet.

"Nothing," he said in a voice that suggested exasperation. "Not one thing."

She helped him return the room to its previous condition. "It hadn't occurred to me to do that," she said, relaxing against the corner of her father's rolltop desk.

"You're not a detective. In this particular case, I'm guessing that looking in obvious places will net me nothing. Still, I have to look everywhere. Your father wouldn't have hidden anything under his mattress, but I can't overlook it."

"How do you know he wouldn't?"

"Leon Farrell was not your normal, ordinary man. He was devious, secretive, and self-absorbed. He would never do the expected."

"No," she said, momentarily musing about her past. "I don't suppose he would have."

She watched while Carson examined the draperies, testing to determine whether the will could have been sewn into them. Next, Carson lifted a big desk chair, turned it upside down, and examined the seat. His short-sleeved T-shirt exposed his hard biceps, flexing from the punishment he gave them as he worked.

Shirley couldn't tear her gaze from the action of the muscular body that rippled when he reached, lifted, and pulled at the objects in his way. He dropped to his knees, flipped over on his back, and, by the power of his hips, propelled himself beneath the enormous desk. She swallowed the liquid accumulating in her mouth as his lithe body provoked in her head ideas as to what he could do to her.

With his knees flexed, he swung his hips from side to side until he was clear of the desk and jumped to his feet. "You don't have to stand there," he said. "Sit down. I'm going to open every book on those shelves."

Catatonic-like, she stared at him. How could he . . . She remembered that it was only she who had experienced that rush of desire.

"What is it?" he asked, walking toward her with the rhythmic movements of a dancer. "Is it something about your father?"

She backed away from him, escaping his heat and his powerful aura. But he'd caught her signal, and she knew it. He gazed down at her for a long minute, shook his head slowly from side to side, and, as he walked away from her, muttered, "Damn the luck."

Shirley heard him and understood what he meant, and although she wanted to bait him, she kept her mouth shut. If she had to deal with that man on a woman-to-man basis, she'd feel better equipped wearing her red "Sherman tank" miniskirt with the right amount of cleavage exposed and a pair of five-inch-heel sandals. A little Fendi perfume wouldn't hurt, either. "That guy would be a challenge even if he was madly in love with you," she said to herself, and she didn't need that kind of problem.

She thought she'd been delivered from temptation, but as if he'd had second thoughts, he walked back to her. Her anticipation of something personal was wasted, however, because he assumed one of his no-nonsense stances and looked hard at her. "Tell me, Shirley, did you love your father even a little bit? Gunther didn't, and I doubt Edgar's capable of love. What about you?"

"I am capable of love, if that's what you're asking."

"That isn't what I'm asking and you know it. What did you feel for your father?"

She wanted to tell the truth, but she didn't know what the truth was. Looking into the distance, she heard herself say, "I just realized that I don't remember ever having sat on Father's lap or hugging his neck. Still, I was sorry when he died."

She punished the carpet with the toe of her sneaker-clad left foot. "You won't mind if we drop this conversation, will you? Talking about him this way isn't pleasant. I'm going downstairs. Do you want some coffee?"

"Thanks, but I'd better get on with this."

She didn't want any coffee. She wanted an opportunity to regain her emotional equilibrium, and she stood a greater chance of doing that if she put some distance between her and Carson Montgomery. Earlier, she and Gunther had checked the dining room for the will, but she scoured it again, because she disliked wasting time. After about forty minutes, she heard Carson amble down the stairs.

"I was getting worried," he said. "Are you okay?"

"Yeah. I figured that since I'm down here, I could search the dining room. I didn't find anything, but . . . well, you never can tell."

He shoved his hands into his pockets and let the doorjamb take his weight. "That's right, you can't. But you won't find that will on this floor. If it's in this house, it's in Leon Farrell's bedroom, office/den, or his bathroom, places where no one but he had a right to be."

"I wasn't disagreeing with you; I simply can't stand to do nothing."

She could see that he didn't believe her, and as if he'd read her mind, he pushed himself away from the doorway, smiled, and said, "Come upstairs and help me where it might produce fruitful results." He held out his hand to her, saw that she was not going to take it, half smiled, spun around, and dashed up the stairs, taking two steps at a time.

As she watched him bounding up those stairs, she told herself not to think about the man's strength or his power and what it had potential for. *Suck it up, kiddo,* she told herself, *and keep your head. He's used to women falling all over him.* She waited until he reached the top before she began the climb.

He stood on the landing grinning down at her. "Come on. If you start to fly, I'll bring you back down to earth." Punching him out wouldn't help, but she imagined how good doing so would make her feel.

My Lord. Am I becoming violent? she asked herself, and suddenly laughter poured out of her.

"What's so funny?" he asked.

"Me. I'm a regular riot."

When she reached the top step, he grabbed her left hand and pulled her to the landing. "We have another room to do, and I'm getting hungry. You don't want to be around if I start to starve."

She knew he was making light of a situation that each of them refused to acknowledge, and if she hadn't been so disgusted, she probably would have admired him for it. But he was no better a man than she was a woman. And she meant to make that clear to him before they left the house.

"All right," she said airily, "get out your microscope and let's get to work."

"Right on, lady."

The two of them searched every place and every thing in the bedroom, from the carpet to the drapes, beneath the mattresses, and in every drawer. They took every item from the closets, examined them, and put them back. At twenty minutes past one, Carson stopped and looked at her. "I'm beginning to be starved. Let's get something to eat. As soon as I wash my hands, I'm ready to go."

"I was starved an hour ago," she said, and headed down the stairs. She washed her hands in the guest lavatory, combed her hair, and adjusted her clothing as best she could. The fit of her jeans suggested that she'd lost several pounds since she last put them on.

"So what," she said to herself. "They suit *me*."

She watched Carson trip down the stairs. If she wanted to act the fool, what more pleasing target could she pick?

"Like what you see?" he asked as he reached the floor.

"I'm not sure. I'll think about it and let you know."

He put a finger at her elbow and ushered her out the door. "You'll think about it all right, but that will be the end of it. I've got time for a crab sandwich but not at an upscale restaurant like Frigate. What do you suggest?"

"Franks, if you can stand paper napkins and a glass-top table without a tablecloth."

"I'm hungry enough to eat with no napkin. Let's go."

An hour later, she didn't remember what she

ate. The man bothered her. "You don't have to take me home, Carson. I know you're in a hurry."

"I've got my first time to go to a woman's house for her, spend time with her, and not see her safely home."

He drove to the building in which Gunther lived and walked with her to the door of the apartment. "When are you going back to Fort Lauderdale?"

"Thursday morning. I'm scheduled to join a cruise to Central America, but if you need me, I'll be back here late next week."

"I didn't have the hunt for the will in mind."

"What *did* you have in mind?" she asked him as her nerves began to battle with each other.

"I want to spend a pleasant evening with you when we're not lifting furniture, rolling carpets, and creating a lot of dust."

"I see. Unless my boss thinks otherwise, I'll be back here Thursday afternoon."

"Shirley, I like things cut-and-dried. May I call you here Thursday evening?"

"Yes. I . . . uh . . . I'll look forward to that."

"Thanks for that tiny bit of encouragement. And thanks for your help today. You're a real trouper. Until Thursday next week."

He didn't say good-bye, but merely turned and headed for the elevator.

He'd been so impersonal that she'd be a fool to expect anything other than a pleasant evening—as he put it—as a thank-you for her help the past two days. "No," she said aloud as she locked the door. It was as if he'd decided between giving her a thank-you gift and inviting her to dinner. She shrugged as if it didn't matter. "He's a nice guy, properly brought up, and no guy who looks like that one is without ties."

Carson got back to his office, returned several business calls, and telephoned Gunther. "This is Carson. Shirley and I spent the morning at your father's house. A thorough search of his personal quarters revealed nothing. I need to see his lawyer. Can you confirm for me that Riggs is legally the executor of your father's will?"

"He is the executor. He secured a writ prohibiting any action in respect to Father's estate for one year from the date of Father's death or until the will is located, provided that it is found and produced before the elapse of a year from the time of Father's death."

"Smart man. How much time does that give us?"

"Until the fifth of January."

"I may need to talk with you again around the first of the week. I'll call you."

Minutes after he hung up, his assistant called. "Edgar Farrell on line two, Carson."

"Montgomery speaking. What may I do for you, Mr. Farrell?"

"Somebody was at the house this morning. I put a couple of things in inconspicuous places, and they were moved, not far, but they'd been moved."

He bristled at that. *Don't lose your temper, man.* "Hmm. So now you're the detective. I went through your father's personal quarters this morning and made a thorough search. I don't have to look there again. I put things back as I found them, but I certainly didn't try to fool anybody into thinking I hadn't been there. I was doing my job."

"Yeah. But you haven't found the will yet, and I'm flat broke."

"I'm doing my best, and if you begin to harass me—"

"All right. I get it, but, man, if you were in my situation, you'd feel me better."

"I don't expect to be in your situation, Edgar, because I'm not afraid of work, no matter how hard. I'd better get to work, because I won't find that will while talking with you on the phone."

He hung up and leaned back in his desk chair, musing over the happenings of that morning with Shirley at the Farrell home. The woman was almost as transparent as air, but her innate dignity kept her in line. He hadn't had much experience resisting a woman who attracted him when the attraction was mutual, and he didn't want a relationship with a woman who was, in effect, his client. Yet, he needed an opportunity to clear the air between them, and he hoped a pleasant evening together would be sufficient.

He phoned Donald Riggs. "Mr. Riggs, this is Carson Montgomery. I've searched the house, Farrell's quarters twice, and come up empty-handed. If he had a safe-deposit box, I need access to it."

"You may try Fairmount or Altman Washington. He had accounts in both. I'll give you a notarized permit."

"Thanks, man. I'm anxious to wrap this up."

"I'm sure of that. I'm surprised Edgar hasn't driven you crazy by now."

"My contract with him forbids harassment. I'll be by your office in an hour. Thanks."

Carson found safe-deposit boxes in both banks, but neither contained the will or information as to its whereabouts. He informed Riggs of his findings and, for the first time in his career as a detective, admitted that he faced a blank wall.

Gunther met Shirley at the Baltimore / Washington International Thurgood Marshall Airport, gave her a brotherly kiss on the cheek, and took her bag. "How'd it go in the West Indies?"

"Hot and humid. I don't see why anyone would want to go there on vacation this time of year."

"Simple. It's cheaper."

"Any news from Carson?"

He hadn't known that she called the man by his first name. Interesting. "Why . . . no. When he finds the will, Edgar will no doubt be the first to know. You didn't tell me what you thought of Montgomery."

"When I was with him, his search of Father's quarters was practically microscopic. He is a thorough man."

And you're deliberately misunderstanding me. "I've gathered that much from his questions and the things he's said to me. I mean, as a man, what do you think?"

"Well . . ." She paused as if giving herself time to frame her thoughts. "He's certainly a gentleman, and at the least, he's a no-nonsense man."

"Hmm. You're getting to be a real politician. I suppose dealing with all kinds of people daily would lead to that."

He put her bags in the trunk of his silver-gray Mercedes, got in, locked the car doors, and headed home. He'd like to know if she planned to see Montgomery but decided that it wasn't prudent to ask. If she wanted him to know, she'd tell him.

Mirna opened the door for them and beamed when she saw Shirley. "Mr. G didn't tell me you were coming today," she said, locked her knuckles to her hips, and looked at him with one eye narrowed. "You know if you'd a told me, I'd a had something real good for dinner tonight."

He patted Mirna's shoulder. "Everything you cook is good. If I bring a guest home unexpectedly you'd only have to add a place setting, and we'd have a great meal."

Mirna fixed her gaze on the floor. "Thank you, sir. I try my best to make it like home for you. You love to eat, and I do love to cook. I'm glad you're satisfied. We'll have a nice meal tomorrow evening," Mirna said.

He waited for Shirley to explain her troubled look. "I won't be in tomorrow evening, Mirna, but thanks for the thought."

He followed Shirley upstairs and set her bag in her room. "Who are you seeing tomorrow evening?"

She didn't look at him. "Carson invited me to 'a pleasant evening.' I don't know what it will consist of."

"Is something shaping up between you two?"

"I don't know. He hasn't said or done anything to suggest it."

"I don't believe that. You didn't ask *him* out, did you?"

"Of course not," she said, bristling.

"Then pay attention. If you're attracted to him, it's more than likely mutual."

She walked past him without looking at him. "Thanks for the reassurance. I think I'll rest for a few minutes. I've been up since five this morning."

He remembered that he'd left his briefcase and laptop in the trunk of his car and went down to get them. "You're off this afternoon," he told Mirna. "Shirley or I will cook, or we'll eat out."

"Thank you, sir, but I already cooked your dinner. Just heat up those roasted Cornish hens in the oven. They're stuffed with brown rice. There's a salad in the refrigerator and you can warm up the string beans."

"Wonderful." He put his hand in his pocket, pulled out his billfold, and gave her twenty-five dollars. "Treat yourself and a friend to a movie."

"Oh, dear! Thank you so much. I sure do appreciate this, and I'm gonna spend it on a movie, too." She dashed to the telephone and dialed a number. "Frieda. Girl, Mr. G just gave me money to see a movie with a friend. I'll be off in about an hour. Wanna see *Harry Potter*?"

"Okay. We can make the five-thirty, and I'll have time to go home, fix us a picnic supper, and be at the movie at five-twenty or so. We can have the picnic in Banneker Park. If you go straight from work, you'll find a parking spot not far from the theater. Okay? See you at the movie."

She turned, looked at Gunther, and smiled. "I sure do thank you. My girlfriend is always doing nice things for people, and I feel good that I can take her to a movie. The Lord gon' bless you, Mr. G."

"Thanks, Mirna. I'm already blessed. It took me a while to figure that out, but I know it now."

He hoped he'd helped Mirna raise her status in

her friend's eyes. No one liked to be always on the receiving end of largesse. In a good friendship, giving was reciprocal. Whistling in contentment, he went to the room he used for an office—the smallest of the three bedrooms—took out his computer, and began designing a game in which the children of a community found a way to welcome a foreign-born child who didn't speak English. It wouldn't be an easy task, but if he could pull it off, it would be a big seller.

When the phone rang, he saw Lissa's number in the caller ID and didn't answer. He'd switched his focus to Caroline. As far as he was concerned, Lissa did not exist. A thought struck him. He'd better find out what Carson Montgomery was made of, and he did not intend to wait until the man hurt his sister. He dialed the Ellicott City Police Department.

"Sergeant Fowler, please." He waited a few seconds. "Matt, this is Gunther. Edgar hired Carson Montgomery, a detective, to find our father's will. Do you know anything about this guy?"

"Sure. He's first-rate. Excellent reputation. The department uses him when we're in a pinch. Fine man, too. That must be the smartest thing Edgar's done in years."

"That was my estimation, Matt, but I needed to be sure."

"You mean your old man had a will and put it where no one could find it? That's stupid."

"Mean is more like it. Thanks for your help."

"Any time, friend."

He got busy on his computer game. Thank goodness he didn't have to worry about Shirley and Carson Montgomery. If the man was decent, Shirley could definitely hold her own with him. *Don't be too sure about that. Men are different from women, especially good-looking ones.*

When the phone rang at six-thirty, Shirley raced to answer it. "Hello." She hated that she sounded out of breath.

"May I please speak with Ms. Shirley Farrell?"

"Hi, Carson. This is Shirley."

"I thought so, but I wanted to be certain. How are you, and when did you get there?"

"I'm fine, thank you. My plane got in a few minutes after noon, and Gunther met me and brought me home with him."

"Nice brother. I've looked forward to our date. Will you have dinner with me?"

"Yes. How do you dress for dinner?"

"Depends. For dinner with you, I'll look as sharp as I can. I'd like to call for you at six-thirty tomorrow. Would that suit you?"

"Six-thirty is fine."

"Good. If you've got any questions about the will, ask me now, because that's not on my agenda for tomorrow evening."

"If you had anything to tell, would I have to ask?"

"I'm obligated to deliver the result of my work first to Edgar. But I don't have anything to report other than that your father had accounts at Fairmount and Altman Washington Banks and safe-deposit boxes in both. I checked the boxes. Neither one contained the will."

"Carson, I'm beginning to wonder if my father was loony."

"Your father was as sound as the United States mint. He had a reason for this, and we shall someday know what it was. I'll see you tomorrow at six-thirty. Have a lovely, restful evening."

"Thanks. I wish you the same."

She hung up and flopped down on her bed. If his interest in her exceeded a gracious thank-you for helping him, he had yet to show it. *Keep it cool, girl,* she said to herself, but he planned to look as sharp as he could, so she'd do the same. She opened a shoe box and removed a pair of black patent-leather sandals with three-inch heels. She didn't dare wear the five-inch ones, because she was already five feet, eight inches tall.

"Was that Edgar who called a minute ago?" Gunther asked.

"No, it wasn't." If he wanted her to tell him who called her, he'd have to ask outright.

When six-thirty arrived the following evening, she was dressed in a figure-hugging coral-silk dress, knee-length and sleeveless. Nobody had to tell her that she looked great. Her hair touched her shoulders. Marcasite earrings dangled from her ears, and a diamond sparkled at the edge of her cleavage.

"Good Lord," Gunther said after emitting a sharp whistle. "Whoever the guy is, he's definitely in for trouble. You've come up a few notches since you moved out of Father's house."

"It wasn't difficult. He cramped everybody's style." She had not planned to let Gunther stand between her and that door when the bell rang, but he'd managed it, and she knew he did it intentionally.

"I'll get it," he said, already halfway to the door.

"Hello, Carson. How are you?"

"Fine. How's it going? Is Shirley at home?"

"Yes, I am. And I would have opened the door for you, if my big brother hadn't beat me to it."

He handed her a dozen red roses. "I've met a few brothers in my day. Protectiveness of their sisters seems to be in their DNA. Shall we go?"

"Yes. Thanks for the flowers. I love American Beauty roses. I'll be ready as soon as I put these in the dining room.

"Good night, Gunther," she said, knowing that she had aroused his curiosity with that remark. She couldn't help grinning at the expression of shock on his face.

"I think you upset him," Carson said as they settled into his BMW. "I take it you didn't tell him that you were having dinner with me."

"He wormed it out of me."

"Didn't you want him to know?"

"I didn't mind, but I'm trying to change his perception of me as the family baby."

A deep laugh rumbled out of Carson. "But you are, and both of your brothers will always see you that way. You look beautiful. Stunningly beautiful."

"Thank you. You're practically breathtaking."

She loved his laughter, and he treated her to a good dose of it. "Be careful about saying such things. You wouldn't like me to wreck this car, would you?"

"You said you liked things cut-and-dried, and I hate looking for acceptable synonyms and euphemisms. I belong to the tell-it-like-it-is school."

"That is not true. The second occasion on which we worked at your father's house, you spent the entire time doing precisely the opposite. If you'd said what you were thinking and feeling, we'd be talking about something else right now."

"I didn't get any help from you. Do you think I'm stupid enough to stick my neck out?"

"No. But I thought you were smart enough to see what had to be as clear as spring water."

She turned to face him fully. "Are you saying—"

"Right. The same bug that bit you, bit me."

Chapter Four

As he drove along Old Dominion Pike, he reflected that Shirley hadn't responded to his admission that he was attracted to her. He hadn't imagined that she played her cards so close to the chest, and he still didn't believe it. "You haven't asked me where I'm taking you," he said, deliberately changing the subject.

From his peripheral vision, he saw her draw a fortifying breath. Then she turned so that her back was to the passenger's door. "Carson, I would trust you with the life of my newborn baby, not to speak of my own life. And from the look of you tonight, I think I'd be foolish to question your taste." She then resumed her previous position. "Where did you grow up?"

"I was born in Washington, D.C. I'm thirty-six, divorced, and childless."

"Let me guess. You were born between mid-July and mid-August."

"Yeah. I was. July thirty-first. How'd you figure that out?"

"Because you're the epitome of a Leo. Alpha male from your head to your toes. Where'd you go to school to learn how to be a detective, if you don't mind my asking."

"Hmm. How soon they forget. I don't mind at all. I have a bachelor's in criminology and a JD from Howard. Four years practicing law was as much as I could stomach, and after four years as a police detective, I got a private detective's license. I opened my own agency three years ago, and for the first time, I couldn't wait to get to work. This is also the first time I've taken a job searching for something, and I'm not sure that I should have."

"I'm glad you did."

"So am I, and not for the money, either. Did your studies at Morgan prepare you to be a public relations director?"

"Not really. What I studied in psychology helps, but you actually learn it on the job. What I need for my job is some smarts and a caring heart, because I spend my time helping people and solving their problems."

Now we'll see how much truth there is to her claim that she trusts me, he thought to himself as he parked in front of the Harbor Court Hotel in Baltimore. He got out, walked around to the front passenger's door, opened it, released her seat belt, and held out his hand. She took it and walked with him to the front door of the hotel. He handed his car keys to the valet, accepted the ticket, and walked with her to the elevator. She still held his hand and hadn't said one word. He stepped on the elevator with her and pushed the button to the second floor. He would have liked to see her face when he selected the floor, but he couldn't find the button while watching her.

The elevator door opened, and with his finger at her elbow, they stepped out. "Good evening, madam, sir. Your name please, sir," the maître d' said.

"Montgomery."

"Right this way, sir. Your table is ready." They followed the man to their table. "I hope you enjoy the flowers that Mr. Montgomery ordered for you, madam. If you wish to take them with you, I'll be glad to arrange it." He seated her and left them.

"Carson, this is absolutely splendid, and thank you for these beautiful roses. I didn't know this place existed."

"And you didn't think I was bringing you to a hotel?" he asked her, mildly taken aback. Maybe she really did trust him.

"Not really. You knew I hadn't eaten, and you're too sophisticated to try to make love with a starving woman. Besides, you're not the type to play juvenile tricks."

He stared at her for a full minute. Then he rested his elbow on the table and supported his brow with his thumb and forefinger, dying for the pleasure of letting out a belly laugh. This woman would always keep it up front and center, and he liked that. He knew better than to push it further, because she might issue him a challenge, and he hadn't decided to extend their friendship beyond this one night, though he knew he could learn to care very deeply for her.

After a memorable meal with fine wine, followed by liqueurs and espresso, he asked her, "Do you like to dance?"

"Do I? *Dance* in my middle name."

"Wonderful." He took her hand and walked with her to the elevator. "There's a nice lounge at the Sheraton. The music is reasonably good, provided you like jazz. Do you?"

Happiness suffused her at the thought of dancing with him to live jazz music. She squeezed his fingers. "I love jazz, and it's my favorite dance music."

"Then we'll go. I hope they have one of those New Orleans bands tonight."

"I don't care if the music is canned, so long as it's jazz."

He gazed down at her, not imagining that the prospect of dancing could make a woman shine with such happiness. *I hope I never do anything to dim that light in her.*

Later, he had occasion to wonder at his behavior. Driving home after he left her, he kept thinking that he had wanted to kiss her and that she would have embraced him. Why hadn't he done it? Why hadn't he capped off the most delightful evening he'd spent in years with a warm embrace? "To thine own self be true," he quoted, and directed his mind to the problem of locating the Farrell will.

Flush with delight about her evening with Carson, Shirley walked into Gunther's living room and found him at loggerheads with Edgar. "What is wrong here?" she asked them, rushing to where they stood. "What is this about?"

"Why can't we auction off the whole business, split what we get for it, and let somebody else worry

about finding the damned will?" Edgar said. "You
two don't care, because you're loaded. But I need
the money. What do you want me to do? Go rob a
bank?"

She looked at Gunther, who stood like a statue
with his arms folded, his feet wide apart, and his
only movement the slight quiver of his upper lip.
"Edgar, you know we can't do that. Father didn't
have any debts, because he didn't believe in buying what he couldn't pay cash for. That means his
estate is worth at least a couple of million dollars.
You want to give all that to the highest bidder for
fifty or sixty, even a hundred thousand? Why don't
you get a steady job at a night club or with a sym-
phony orchestra? You could make ten times what
you bring in now."

"I'm a first-class musician, and you're asking me
to put myself down with these chickenshit guys
who don't know a bass clef from a treble clef. You
could lend me some money, but you're so damned
much like Father that you'd rather sit back and
watch me drown."

"Cut the melodrama, Edgar. If I loaned you
money every time you asked for it, I'd soon be as
broke as you," Gunther said. "You could make a
thousand dollars every night, and you've done it,
but you'd rather walk around here with your nose
in the air, superior to everybody you see. Knock it
off, man. I gotta go to work in the morning."

"Tomorrow's Saturday," Edgar said.

"Yeah," Gunther replied, "and I'm working. That's
why I have money."

"He doesn't pay rent or utilities," Shirley said to
Gunther after Edgar left, "and he plays that guitar

most nights. What does he do with the money? You think he's on drugs?"

"I don't think so. I think he gambles, and for high stakes at that. It wouldn't surprise me if he had some gambling debts and that he'll have to pay up soon."

"But, Gunther, that could be dangerous."

"Anybody who tries to make easy money lives to regret it. That's one of Father's sayings that I wish Edgar had listened to. Enough about Edgar. How was your evening?"

"Great until I walked in here and saw the two of you at each other's throats. Carson's a classy guy, Gunther."

"He certainly dressed for you, and you did the same for him. Did he kiss you?"

"Uh . . . no."

"*What?* What kind of guy takes out a woman who looks like you, brings her home, and doesn't kiss her? And why'd you let him get away with it? Did you want him to kiss you?"

"Yeah. I did, but I added the morning we worked at Father's house together plus this evening and considered the man he was on both occasions. It added up to, if I don't ask for what he's not giving, he'll give me what I want."

"Explain that logic to me."

"He knows I'm attracted to him, and he told me that the same bug that bit me bit him. You know I'm patient, Gunther. If he doesn't want me, he'd better stay out of my company."

"Tread carefully, sis. He's sophisticated and worldly."

"I know." She described their evening together. "We danced as if we'd been born doing it."

"And he didn't kiss you. He's a stronger man than I am."

"What will we do about Edgar?"

"If we bail him out this time, next week we'll have to do it again. He owes you three thousand, and he owes me four or five times that much. I stopped being a sucker."

They said good night, and Shirley climbed the stairs thinking of Gunther implying that, given similar circumstances, he wouldn't have willingly left the woman without kissing her. *Not all men are the same,* she told herself. One thing was certain: Before she left for Fort Lauderdale, she'd investigate the Ellicott City housing market. Edgar was desperate enough to attack Gunther, and that would be catastrophic.

She got into bed and turned out the light. Damn. She really had wanted a kiss, but since she wasn't ready for a hot relationship with Carson, she didn't mind that he'd chosen not to do it. Besides, it wouldn't hurt her to learn more about the man. A brother who looked that good could bamboozle a saint with a simple grin. *I'm as much woman as he is man,* she told herself, *and his curly lashes won't make me shrivel.* It occurred to her that she was one up on him, because he had a telltale sex sign that he couldn't hide: When his libido reared up, his brown eyes took on a grayish cast. It didn't make sense to laugh, but she closed her eyes happily and thought about selling her Fort Lauderdale condominium.

A call from Carson the next morning surprised her. "I enjoyed our evening together, Shirley, and I hope you slept well," he said. "I need to talk with you for an hour at least, either at your brother's place or the Farrell house. Can we meet, and where do you suggest?"

Just like that, huh? "If you don't need to go out to Father's house, could you come over here at about ten-thirty?"

"Thank you. I'll be there."

Anger suffused her, and she knew it was unreasonable. She calmed her temper, dressed in white slacks and a pink T-shirt, and went down for breakfast. She greeted Gunther and Mirna, got half a grapefruit, a banana, a piece of cheese, and a cup of coffee, and joined them.

"Carson's coming over at ten-thirty to interview me. He's convinced that the will is in Father's personal quarters. I've told him all I know, so—"

"Maybe he's using it as an excuse to see you," Mirna said. "It's been done before."

"He doesn't need an excuse."

Gunther prepared to leave for work. "See you later. Give Carson my regards."

Carson arrived at the appointed time. "Would you like some coffee?" she asked him after they greeted each other.

"Thanks, but I had some."

She led him to the living room and sat in a chair facing him. "What could you possibly have missed?" she asked him.

He leaned forward. "Did he belong to any clubs? And did he have any hobbies? Did he have a place to work away from home?"

"I don't think he belonged to a club. He would have considered that an unnecessary expense. But he had a very serious hobby, and when we were searching, I didn't see any evidence of it, which is strange."

"What was it?"

"He had a passion for robots and other replicas of people. He made robots and collected many."

"Thanks, Shirley. I have to find them. If they were as dear to him as you say, we may be on the right track at last. I can hardly wait until Monday when Edgar returns to Atlantic City. I'll be in touch."

Carson's search that Monday morning left him perplexed and disheartened. The one robot that he found on the floor beside a chair in the living room and that he'd seen before, a machine-made barking dog, could not have contained the will. Tired and disheartened, he dropped himself into a chair and tried to think. When his cell phone rang, he looked at the caller ID and swore.

"What is it, Edgar?"

"I need some money. Can you advance me a couple thousand against my share of the estate?"

Taken aback by the audacity of the request, he waited a bit before responding. "I've been working on this job for weeks now with no result. If I don't find that will, I've wasted time when I could have been earning a substantial amount. I don't do business this way. The answer is no."

"Who do you think you are? If you don't find it soon, I'll put somebody else on the job."

"Really? Check your contract. I have to get back to work." *One more reason why I don't want to get involved with Shirley Farrell. I want that man as far from me as he can get.*

*   *   *

Gunther got home that evening a little later than usual. He missed his sister's company. Hiring Mirna was the smartest thing he had done recently. The woman kept his home as if it were her own, and her skill as a cook was such that he didn't consider eating out.

"Hi, Mirna. What's that I smell? It's making my mouth water."

"Hope you had a good day, Mr. G. We got somethin' good tonight, so just let me know when you're ready to eat."

"It's always good if you cook it. I'll be away Friday evening, Saturday, and most of Sunday, so you have Friday, Saturday, and Sunday off. I can get my own breakfast Friday morning."

"Thank you, sir. Mr. G, the Lord gon' bless you for being such a good person. I can run down to Virginia and see my mother. She's kind of poorly."

He patted her shoulder. "If I can do anything to help, let me know."

Shortly after noon on Friday, he left his office with Medford and another of his employees and headed to Ocean City. "Nothing like fishing in Assawoman Bay," Medford said.

"It's the best way I know to get rid of your concerns. Totally de-stressing," Gunther said. "What are we going to do with so much fish?"

"Take it home. We can get those refrigerator boxes, put the fish in them along with some ice, and they'll be fine," Medford said. "Fish used to be cheap, but not anymore."

By Sunday afternoon, they had as much fish as they could pack into their refrigerator boxes, but Gunther also had developed difficulty breathing and a high temperature. After he got home, he put the fish into his freezer and went to bed. The following morning, Mirna awakened him.

"Mr. G, it's nine o'clock, and you not up yet. You're hot. I think you have a fever."

He rolled over and tried to focus, felt as if he were on fire, and asked Mirna to bring the thermometer from the cabinet in his bathroom. She put the thermometer under his arm until it beeped, took it out, and looked at it.

"My goodness, Mr. G. I think I ought to call your doctor. It says 103.5 degrees."

"I'll get up in a few minutes."

"I'm gonna call Miss Shirley."

Hours later, Gunther awakened in Johns Hopkins Hospital and was informed that he had pneumonia. "When may I go home?" he wanted to know.

"You've been here a couple of days," the doctor told him. "Pneumonia is nothing to play with, so plan to be here for the remainder of the week and expect a considerable period of recuperation. I suspect you've had this for a while."

"You need someone with nursing experience, Mr. G," Mirna told him when he came home. "You know I'll do my best to look after you, but the doctor said you'd be better off with a nurse or an LPN."

"What's an LPN?"

"A licensed practical nurse, meaning she doesn't have a degree. At least she won't think she's too good for the job."

"I don't know where to start looking for an LPN."

"You can ask the doctor, or I can ask my friend Frieda if she knows anyone. She's an LPN."

"Why can't *she* come? At least we'd have someone you know and trust. Where does she work?"

"Right now she's on a case at Maryland General. I'll call her and see what she says."

"My patient is going home tomorrow," Frieda told Mirna. "Poor man is lucky to be alive, but he gon' be fine now. I took good care of him."

Two days later, Frieda Davis walked into Gunther Farrell's house, a move that would change her life and the life of everyone around her.

The first things he noticed about Frieda Davis were her good looks, her elegant stature, and her air of professionalism. "What strain do you have, Mr. Farrell? Treatment varies according to the type you got."

"Viral."

"Then I guess the doctor told you that patience will be your best medicine. Would you please give me your doctor's name and phone number?" He gave them to her. "We have to work out a routine that you'll be comfortable with."

Gunther didn't like being confined to the house, not to speak of his bed, but Frieda made it as pleasant as possible, making a joke of his usually elevated temperature and of her various daily ministrations.

"What man you know has a gorgeous woman washing his face and making his bed when all he has to do is smile and turn over, huh?"

"The trouble with you is that you're never serious. I want to get out of this bed."

"When I talk with the doctor tomorrow morning, I'll tell him you're beginning to get on your own nerves. Okay?"

He couldn't help laughing. "If you don't let me out of this bed, I'll get on *your* nerves."

"I'll ask the doctor if you can read your e-mail for half an hour tomorrow morning, but if I notice you worrying or looking stressed, we won't do that again. And don't think you can hide it from me. Where's your laptop?"

He told her.

Standing by Gunther's bed, Frieda phoned his doctor. "That's the gist of it, Doctor," she said after relating Gunther's condition and attitude. "What do you think?" She made notes while she listened. "All right. One half hour. Thank you, Doctor."

"The doctor said you could read your e-mail for a half hour, but he wants you to rest. He suggested that if you're bored, you might play some simple computer games."

She left the room and returned with a Bed-Lounge. "Mirna bought this for you yesterday. You can sit up, but we'll use this."

He looked at it. "Let's see how it works. Mirna would make somebody a great mom. I get the benefit of her mothering instinct." He said it jokingly, because he didn't especially like being mothered. He got up, nearly fell due to his weakened condition, and dropped himself on the bed. He managed to sit in the chairlike BedLounge, then leaned back and closed his eyes.

"I guess he likes it," Frieda told Mirna later. "The minute he got into it, he closed his eyes and went fast asleep. I tell you what. You off on Thursday afternoons. I don't need to be off, but I'll get a psychological lift if I can be away for four or five hours on Wednesday afternoons. You wear a mask when you're with him and wash your hands with Purell. Viral pneumonia is dangerous."

"Not to worry," Mirna said. "I'll look after him. He a good man."

"You telling me. Some woman must be crazy letting that man run loose."

"Yeah. If I had ten fewer years on me, I'd go for him in a second."

"Oh, come on," Frieda said. "That man is thirty-four years old, and you kicking fifty."

"Yeah, but he ain't stupid, and a smart fortysomething woman could lead that horse to water and get him to drink."

Laughter poured out of Frieda. "Honey, your screws coming loose. That is funny, but I don't think anybody could make that man dance to their tune. That guy's a born choreographer."

"Thank God, that ain't crossed my mind. I love my job. The pay is good and the work is light. When I look at Gunther Farrell, I don't see *man*. I see boss," Mirna said.

Frieda rolled her big, sparkling eyes. "You and me, too. Good jobs are hard to get, but you can find a dozen penises in every block, and half of them ain't no good."

"You telling me," Mirna said. "And when they good, what they hanging on ain't worth spit. Been there and done that, and I'm a lot happier cooking and cleaning."

"I hope the doctor will let him sit up longer each day," Frieda said. "He needs to be getting some energy. The man can hardly stand up. But I exercise his arms and legs twice every day."

"What kind of medicine is he getting?"

"Some vitamins. There isn't a special medicine; his type of pneumonia doesn't respond to antibiotics. The treatment is bed rest and fluids. But he's improving. It's just slow. His temperature doesn't rise above one hundred now, and that's a blessing. I put cold, damp towels on his face and neck. He don't want me to bathe him, but I put a plastic sheet under him, do most of it, and let him do the rest. We get along fine."

Frieda had been with Gunther three weeks when Edgar paid Gunther a visit. "Who're you?" he asked Frieda.

"I could ask you the same," she shot back. "You resemble Mr. Farrell, but only in looks, 'cause you sure don't have his good manners and upbringing."

"Hmm. So the lady's got a mouth." He started up the stairs.

"I wouldn't go up there if I were you—that is, unless you want to expose yourself to viral pneumonia."

He walked back down the stairs. "You mean he's sick? Little brother is finally flat on his back? Well." He lifted an African soapstone carving from a corner table. "This is mine, so I'm taking it."

Frieda walked past him so that she was between him and the foyer. "Over my dead body, pal. And don't try any rough stuff, because I can throw a man twice your size, which ain't much." She called Mirna. "This man wants to make off with this sculpture, but if he tries to get past me, I'll have him flat on his back."

Mirna walked over to Edgar and put her hands on her hips. "Put that back. Now I know why Mr. G told me not to ever let you in this apartment when

I was here by myself. You a thief, and I'll call the cops and let 'em deposit your behind in the clinker. Shame on you."

"It's mine, but since I can't handle two Amazons, I'll get it from brother dear."

"Could you really have taken him down?" Mirna asked Frieda after Edgar left.

"Don't make jokes. What you think I am? It didn't hurt to have him believe it, though, did it?"

They looked up and saw Gunther on the stairs. "Where did Edgar go, and what did he want?" Mirna recapped the scene for him. "I see. I hate to say it, Frieda, but he isn't a nice person, and he could be dangerous if he was desperate for money. Be careful." They watched while he plodded back up the steps and headed to his room.

Gunther took a seat in the overstuffed chair that Frieda had moved to his room. His luck in getting her to see him through his illness was as remarkable as his success in hiring Mirna for his housekeeper. His cell phone rang, and when he saw Edgar's number in the caller ID screen, he answered.

"Hello, Edgar. What's up?"

"Man, I didn't know you'd been sick. Who was that doll who claims she's strong as an Amazon?"

"You mean Ms. Davis threatened you? That's a good laugh. Did you think she was foolish enough to let you walk off with my Shona sculpture? I've told them about you now, so don't try it again. Any news about the will?"

"Naah. Carson said he searched Father's little cubicle at the library but didn't find anything. The man's looked everywhere. I don't know why Father would do such a mean thing. I'll be over to-morrow morning to see how you are. See you." Before he could respond, he heard the click of the receiver.

After a twenty-minute visit with Gunther the next morning, Edgar sauntered down the stairs and stopped in front of Frieda. "You must be something hot. Your boss is nuts about you."

Frieda narrowed her left eye. She didn't believe ninety-nine percent of what any man said to her. Glen Treadwell gave her a lesson for all time, and he was truly a master. "Stuff it, pal," she said. "Men are born liars."

"You're making a mistake. He spent the entire time telling me about your virtues. I got tired of hearing it. You know men fall for their nurses."

"And I know men are liars, too."

Edgar left and Frieda went up to Gunther's room to exercise his legs. She prided herself in the fact that no patient in her care had developed atrophy or bedsores. She massaged his back, applied lotion all over his body, shaved him—though he swore he could do it—and trimmed his hair.

"You must be the reason why nurses are called angels," he said when she handed him his laptop and told him he could use it for two hours.

"We're as human as other people, Mr. Farrell. Some of us care about our patients and take pride in our work. The doctor said you may come downstairs for your meals, and if you have no temperature today or tomorrow, you may begin taking showers. But if you jump back into the rat race, you may get a setback. So please be careful."

"Thanks, Frieda. Would you believe that in the last three days, working one hour a day, I developed a computer game that's really good? It came together in no time, and it's going to be a big hit. I'm going to market this one to a big company. If it works, I'll be fixed for a long time." He leaned forward as excitement flashed through him. "It's about three devilish little boys and a wonderful nurse who gets them out of scrape after scrape. In a sense, you were my inspiration."

"Well, sir, if I h-helped in any w-way," she sputtered, "I'm gr-grateful."

"You certainly have, and I'm the one who's grateful," Gunther said.

Later that day, Frieda sat in her room thinking first of Edgar's having said Gunther was nuts about her, then musing over Gunther's remarks that she was the inspiration for the game he created. "I don't want to be a fool led by a fool," she said aloud, "but what if Edgar was telling the truth?" In the future, she'd pay careful attention. *Hmm. Did Gunther have a girlfriend?*

"You know, it's strange that no women have called or come to see Mr. Farrell since he's been sick, none but his sister, I mean," Frieda said to Mirna during their afternoon tea and chat time. "That man is definitely not gay."

"Quit fishing, Frieda. If he was gay, he wouldn't tell me," Mirna said. "There was a woman who called here occasionally when I first came. Sometimes he'd take her call, but most of the time he wouldn't. I figured he was breaking up with her. But like I said, I likes my job, so I minds my own business. And people who do that usually don't create problems for theyselves."

Wasn't it strange that Mirna would give her that lecture? Frieda mused as she prepared to give Gunther his four-o'clock regime of medicine and vitamins. She'd been through a lot and suffered a lot to get where she was, and she'd done it without help from anybody. Shortly after turning seventeen, she'd run from her adoptive parents' home to avoid more of her adoptive father's sexual depravity. She'd gotten a bus from the little hamlet of Bixby, North Carolina, to Baltimore, Maryland. Working at night and trying to finish high school in a strange, big city had been difficult, but she'd made it, and she was more proud of that than of getting her LPN.

She hadn't been a saint, and she'd done things that she later regretted. Because she blamed her birth mother for her adoptive father's brutality, she hunted the woman like a posse after cattle thieves until she'd finally identified her; then she found her and did what she could to destroy her birth mother's marriage. In the meantime, she'd seduced Glen Treadwell, the woman's beloved stepson, and done it for meanness. But in the end, she'd paid bitterly, because she fell hard for the man and there was no future in it for either of them.

Frieda reasoned that a good-looking man like Gunther Farrell could have his pick of women. So why weren't there any around him? He wasn't gay, because he'd had an erection the first time she massaged his back. He had tried to hide it, but she saw it. She hadn't paid much attention to it, because it had happened with any number of her male patients. But if he was interested in her, as Edgar said, her life could change for the better.

"I promised the good Lord that if I could get over Glen, I wouldn't do anything else underhanded," she reminded herself aloud when she returned to her room. "So I'm gon' encourage Mr. Farrell if I get the chance, but I'm not gon' try that sexy stuff. It could backfire, and this is a real good job."

While Frieda considered the possibility of making a change in Gunther's life, Carson was beginning to realize that he wanted more from Shirley than he'd let himself believe. He walked out of the researchers' cubicle section in Baltimore's Enoch Pratt Free Library, shaking his head. Leon Farrell had been comparing certain properties of wood and aluminum, obviously in the interest of his work on robots, but nothing personal of the man remained in his little cubicle. What next? He stopped at a nearby coffee shop, ordered a cup of coffee, and tried to think. Not in his personal quarters at home, the man's safe-deposit boxes, his workplace, or the garage. So where else could he look? He didn't remember ever being despondent, not even when his wife had let him down, but he was bordering on it. If something didn't go right soon, he'd start banging his head against a wall.

He took out his cell phone and called Shirley. "Hi. This is Carson. Where are you, and when are you getting back in the States?" He knew he'd sur-

prised her. "Friday morning? What's your address?"
She told him. "Do you mind if I visit you Friday afternoon?"

She said she didn't mind at all. So he hung up
and called his travel agent. He didn't fool himself
with the idea that he wanted to see Shirley for information about the will. He'd called her because
he needed her, and he was not in the habit of lying
to himself. A feeling of contentment pervaded
him. For the coming weekend, at least, he would-
n't have that sense of aloneness, feeling as if he
were a dry leaf at the mercy of the wind, as if nobody cared. It was his fault, he knew, because he
didn't take the time to cement friendships. Work
and his ambitions for his agency came first. But he
paid for it. Oh, how he paid!

In the Fort Lauderdale–Hollywood International Airport, he strode past the luggage carousel
without looking in its direction and headed for the
taxi stand. "Carson!" He heard it a second time, realized that someone could be calling him, and
stopped. A soft hand on his arm got his attention,
and he whirled around.

"Wh— Shirley!" he said, certain that he gaped
at her. "It didn't occur to me that you'd meet me.
What a nice welcome!"

She slipped her hand into his and matched his
stride. "We're going to the garage. It's this way. Did
you have a comfortable flight?"

"I guess so. I slept most of the way. I awoke when
the plane touched the ground."

"Then you didn't eat lunch?"

"No, but if you miss an airline meal, you aren't
out of anything."

He didn't think he'd ever been a passenger in a

car driven by a woman, unless the driver was a cabbie, and it interested him that she sat in the vehicle with the kind of authority that he admired. "I think you like to drive," he said as she sped along South Federal Avenue.

"I like the freedom I feel when I drive in light traffic. That's when I have to be careful not to speed. How long will you stay?" She switched from impersonal to personal so quickly that he was momentarily speechless.

"I'd like to stay until Sunday afternoon, unless you have other plans. I reserved a room at The Ritz-Carlton for two nights. I don't think it's too far from you. Am I right?"

"It isn't too far." She parked in front of what looked like an upscale town house. "Here we are."

"How nice!" He saw the FOR SALE sign. "Are you buying or selling?"

"Selling. If I don't get back to Ellicott City soon, Edgar and Gunther will kill each other."

"Are you serious?"

She nodded as she fished in her handbag for the door keys. "Edgar has always been jealous of Gunther, though I don't know why, and now he's angry because Gunther won't lend him any more money. If we loaned—actually, *gave* is a better word—Edgar money every time he asked for it, Gunther and I would be broke."

"I don't suppose you know what he does with it. He doesn't appear to be on drugs."

"I don't think so, either. I think he gambles. He's always wanted something for nothing, into all kinds of deals."

"He may have gambling debts, and that can be dangerous."

"Yes, I know."

They entered the house, and he liked it. "This place is lovely. It expresses you perfectly, from the high ceilings and huge picture windows to the tasteful furniture and lovely warm colors."

"I'm glad you like it," she said. "I hate to leave it. Why don't I give you something to eat. Then we'll check you into your hotel and go for a swim. Would you like that, or do you have other plans?"

She looked at him so hopefully, seemingly open to his own ideas, and he realized that she wanted to please him, but she wasn't sure of him or of his motive for visiting her.

"I'll take the food. Mind if I remove this jacket? It's linen, but even skin is hot down here."

Her laughter removed the tension. "Of course you can take it off. Want to come with me to the kitchen, or would you rather look around?"

He followed her to the kitchen and admired the granite countertops, stainless-steel refrigerator, stove, dishwasher, freezer, and sink, and the walls of yellow brick. "You've got great taste, Shirley. Say, don't move that to the dining room. Why can't I eat right here?"

She gave him a crabmeat salad, deviled eggs, sliced tomatoes, homemade cheese biscuits, and lemonade. "Aren't you joining me?"

"Maybe I'll eat a biscuit. I love biscuits." She sat at the table across from him.

"I can see why. These biscuits are fabulous. Who made them?"

"Who made what? You mean the biscuits? I did, of course. I wouldn't think of buying a biscuit. Carson, I'm dying to know why you decided to visit me."

He stopped eating, drank some lemonade, and looked hard at her. "Are you sure you want to know?"

"Yes. I have to know, Carson."

"I hit a low point, and I thought hard about myself. It wasn't like me to feel that kind of aloneness. I realized that I needed you and that no one and nothing would lift my spirits except being with you."

"You're serious."

"Yes, I am. I'm not surprised, either, because I've had these deep feelings for you all along, and I knew it. I just hadn't thought I needed to do anything about them. I didn't count on just plain needing you. I hadn't felt anything like that in years."

"You . . . uh . . . you really surprise me. I thought you liked me but that you were probably committed to someone else. Are you?"

"No. I've been divorced for five years, and you're the only woman who's gotten through the shell I erected when I knew my marriage was over."

"You took me out to a wonderful dinner and then danced with me. You dressed to the nines, brought me flowers, had some more on our dinner table for me, and told me good night at the door without even kissing me on the cheek. I wanted a kiss."

She'd thought he'd smile at that, but he looked at her solemnly and said, "I wanted it worse than you could have, but I'd spent the evening thinking things you don't want me to repeat. You really had me besotted. Do you know how you look in that dress? I've never done myself a disservice with a woman, but if I'd gotten you in my arms alone in that dimly lit foyer of Gunther's, I might have. And I knew it."

"Thanks for explaining it. I would have invited you to stay here, but I didn't think our relationship warranted that."

"And you're right. However, while I'm down here, I hope to make progress in that direction." He resumed eating. "This is good stuff."

Chapter Five

Did that mean he was going to take their relationship seriously and try to build it into something meaningful? She knew he wouldn't lie about something that important. Deciding not to comment on it, she said, "Your hotel is right on the beach. I hope you get a room facing the ocean."

She noticed that he either ate or talked and didn't attempt them simultaneously. So she waited for his response. He cleaned his plate, leaned back, and looked at her. "That was wonderful. If you like to swim, I'd be delighted to do that. I don't know when I was last in an ocean."

"Oh, I forgot I made a raspberry strudel. Would you like some? I can warm it in a few seconds."

"I'd love it."

She warmed it and placed a big serving of it in front of him. He tasted it and stared at her. "If you tell me you made this, I may never leave here."

Feigning modesty, she said, "I don't know what to say, then."

"Tell you what," he said when he'd finished the

dessert, "get your bathing suit and come with me while I check in at the hotel. We'll change, swim, dress, see some of the town, and I'll bring you home. I'll make some plans for tomorrow. What do you say?"

"I'd like that. How will you dress after we swim?"

"How will I . . . ? I get it. Jacket and open-collared shirt."

She packed a shower cap, a bikini, and makeup in a small handbag and dressed in a pink on pink flowery voile dress. Claiming that he didn't want her to chauffeur him around, he called for a taxi, and she went with him to The Ritz-Carlton. He waited while she changed into her swimsuit and slipped into one of the white terry-cloth robes that hung in his closet.

"Cheat," he said when she came out of the bathroom with the robe wrapped tightly. "Well, at least you can't swim in it."

She sat down, crossed her legs, and waited for him to change. *If he looks like I think he's going to look,* she thought, remembering how he'd slithered on his hips beneath her father's desk, *I'll be in real trouble.*

He emerged from the bathroom wearing a swimsuit one-quarter the size of a pair of Calvin Klein jockey shorts. She thought she'd prepared herself for it, but she hadn't, because she was sure her lower jaw dropped.

"What's wrong?" he asked with a straight face.

"Nothing," she said, went to the closet, got the other white terry-cloth robe, and threw it at him. "Come on. Let's go."

He hooted for a full two minutes, but he put on

the robe, sat down, slipped on a pair of flip-flops, took her hand, and walked over to the window. "What a view. The Atlantic rolling and tumbling for as far as the eye can see. Imagine seeing the sunset from this balcony."

She thought he'd put his arm around her, but he didn't. "The tide seems to be coming in," she said, mostly to calm her nerves.

"Yeah. Let's get that dip."

Since moving to Fort Lauderdale, she'd become a good swimmer, and she'd discovered that she loved the water. What fun it would be to swim with Carson. They dropped their robes on the two lounge chairs that he rented. She looked up, caught him staring at her, and would have run, but immediately her embarrassment dissolved into pure lust. She swallowed heavily, unable to shift her gaze from his body. Her fingers itched to roam from his broad shoulders to his washboard middle and his tapered waist to his muscular thighs and perfectly shaped legs.

"You . . . you're downright sinful," she said, then whirled around and raced to the water.

He caught her before she reached the edge of the ocean. "And I'd like to experience every centimeter of *you*," he said, letting her know he was aware that she ogled him. "You're all any man could want."

She ran out and dove into the water. Seconds later, he grabbed her, picked her up, and waded to shore. "What? What are you doing, Carson?"

"That water is full of jellyfish, and they have a horrible sting. That's why the swimmers are farther down the beach. Let's go down there."

Shock at the feel of his hands on her bare flesh reverberated throughout her body. *I'd better get a grip on this madness,* she said to herself.

They collected their robes and walked half a mile along the beach. "Don't you post signs about those jellyfish?" he asked a guard.

"We posted them in the hotel. Sorry if you didn't see the sign. It's safe to swim here."

After swimming for half an hour, Carson guided her to shore. "It's getting cooler. Perhaps we ought to go back to the hotel." He held her robe for her but didn't try to touch her body.

If he thinks he's teaching me to trust him, I wish he'd stop. I already trust him.

They dressed in his room, but she decided to take a sponge bath, for she saw no point in testing him by taking a shower. He showered and came out of the bathroom fully dressed. "Let's sit on the balcony for a few minutes," he said. "I want to watch the sunset with you. Would you like a glass of wine, a soft drink, anything?"

So he wasn't interested in plying her with alcohol. "A glass of white wine would be nice." She reached down, tightened the strap on her white three-inch-heeled sandals, then stood and accepted his outstretched hand. Sitting on the balcony, holding her hand, he pressed the button for room service and ordered wine and hors d'oeuvres.

She couldn't help thinking that Carson showed his sophistication in so many ways that she'd be hard put to keep abreast of him socially. Within minutes, a kaleidoscope of colors decorated the sky, and in the midst of it, the sun inched toward its nightly resting place.

She squeezed his fingers. "This is so beautiful,"

she whispered. "I wouldn't have missed it for the world."

When he didn't respond, she wondered if he thought her melodramatic. "Wasn't it wonderful?" she asked him after the sun dropped out of sight.

"I've watched many sunsets, Shirley, but I think this one was different because I watched it with you. It was wonderful."

A waiter brought wine and the snacks. "I forgot that swimming makes me hungry," she said, sipping the wine and eating a shrimp.

"It makes me hungry and sleepy, too," he said. "When we finish this, I suggest we leave. I made dinner reservations for a quarter of eight."

After dinner, he signaled for a taxi, and as the cabbie drove along South Federal Highway, singing the praises of Fort Lauderdale, she didn't listen to him but focused her thoughts on the man beside her. It amazed her that she had no anxiety about what would happen between them when she got home.

At her door, Carson held out his hand for her key; then he opened the door and stepped back until she asked if he'd like to come in. "For a few minutes. Yes." He stopped in the foyer, and she flipped on the light, thinking that he didn't want to walk into a dark place. He shoved his hands into the pockets of his trousers in a way that pushed back his jacket. He tilted his head a little and looked her in the eye.

"From the minute you called my name in the airport until now has been the happiest time I've spent in many years. I feel something for you, and it's no simple thing. It transcends what happens when I look at you in a bathing suit, a dress, or a pair of jeans. It's in here." He pointed to his heart. "Tell me right now whether I'm spitting against the wind. Can you care for me?"

Why didn't he just dump a load of cement on her head? She couldn't even accuse him of attempting to bamboozle her, because he'd put a distance of at least four feet between them. "How do I know?" she said, peeved. "You haven't even bothered to kiss me."

"Why does that matter? You don't need proof of the chemistry between us, but if you want a sample, come closer." As if he knew she was about to accuse him of being a chauvinist, he grinned. "Since we're alone in your house, I don't want to crowd you."

He looks vulnerable, she thought, and pushed back the clever words that came to the tip of her tongue. "You won't crowd me," she said, and opened her arms to him. Maybe she moved. Maybe she didn't. But she was in his arms at last. He stared down at her, and then his lips touched her, and she would willingly have been consumed by the fire in him as she parted her lips and took him into her mouth. She felt his tremors and wondered if he could feel the thumping of her heart and sense the storm that raged inside of her.

He released her and stepped back. "Are you involved with any other man?"

"No. There isn't anyone. What about you?"

"Definitely not, and let me tell you this. My work takes me away from home frequently. If you're the type who can't be alone, I won't take this one minute further."

"Is that what happened in your marriage?"

"Yes. It hurt, and I swore never to care for another woman, but as you know, man proposes and God disposes."

"Are you going to make me pay for what she did?"

"I'm not stupid. Besides, you two have nothing in common. Will you agree not to see other men and to let us find out what we can be to each other?"

"Yes, I'd like that," she said. "You said you didn't have any children."

"That's right. My wife didn't want any, and it proved to be just as well; children need both parents all the time."

"Yes, indeed. I wonder what my life would have been like if my mother had lived. Oh, well, I won't get maudlin."

He stepped closer and took her into his arms again. "From now on, you have me. No matter what happens or where it happens, I'll be there for you. Do you understand that?"

She hugged him as tightly as she could. "Yes, and I'll be there for you, too." He kissed her quickly and left her.

She'd given him more than he'd dared to hope for, and he meant to treat the precious gift with care. Sitting with her on the balcony of his hotel room watching that awesome sunset, he had realized that he didn't want to be without her, that he needed her as he needed fresh air and clean water. But he was no stranger to pain. If it didn't work out, he'd shake the sand from his feet and move on.

He walked four blocks until he reached a convenience store that blazed with neon lighting. He walked in and asked the teenaged clerk to phone for a taxi. After tipping the boy, he was soon on his way to the hotel, where he obtained information about what to do and see in Fort Lauderdale; then he went to his room and made plans for the next day. Sitting on the balcony gazing out at the still, dark night, he asked himself why he'd abandoned his policy of not getting involved with a client. On the flight to Fort Lauderdale, he'd told himself that she wasn't a client, but that was only partially true. He could be headed for trouble.

"But I need her," he said aloud, "and I'm human."

While Shirley waited for Carson the next morning, she telephoned Gunther. "Hi, how are you, and are things with Frieda still going well?"

"I can finally see some improvement in my energy and strength. I asked my doctor if I could let Frieda go, and he said no, so I didn't tell him that I work at night while she's asleep. She lets me work two hours a day, and I've designed a new game since I've been recovering."

"Why do you need her?"

"She gives me exercises and massages, monitors my fluid intake, and has me on a regimen of vitamins and minerals. It's too much for Mirna, though I know she'd try if need be. My doctor said it's either hospitalization, a sanitarium, or a private nurse. The trouble is that Edgar got on Frieda's nerves, and she's got a fast, sharp tongue, so she told him off. Now I noticed that he's snooping around her. I don't like it."

And he had reason not to like it, for Edgar had repeated to Frieda his claim that Gunther was enchanted with her.

"Don't worry too much. Edgar can't resist showing his hand, and he'll do it sooner rather than later."

"I certainly hope you're right. He said he'd been trying for two days to reach Carson but can't get through to him."

"I guess not. Carson is here in Fort Lauderdale."

"He what? What the hell is he doing down there?"

"He called me and asked me if he could visit me, and I said yes."

"Is something serious going on between you and that guy?"

She was standing now, and her breath had begun to come in short pants. "I hope so. All of my adult life, I've been waiting to meet an intelligent, accomplished, courteous gentleman who respects me and himself. Carson fills the bill perfectly."

"Well! I think you just told me to stay out of it. Where is he now?"

"At The Ritz-Carlton. He should be here any minute."

"At his age, he should be married," Gunther said, and she knew he was both fishing for information and warning her.

"So should you," she told him. "The doorbell just rang. Gotta go."

She opened the door and gazed at Carson. Getting used to his stunning looks would take some doing. He seemed unaware of them, and that was a good thing. If he'd been narcissistic, she wouldn't have given him a second glance.

He leaned down, brushed her lips with his, and then ran his finger down the bridge of her nose. "I feel good. What about you? How's my girl?"

His girl, huh? She hugged him, because she couldn't resist it. "Great. You've been listening to James Brown's recording."

"Not me," he said. "His music never got to me. Let's get some breakfast and get started. I've planned the whole day."

She'd known that he'd do that, because she'd noticed that he didn't leave much to chance. "If you can digest cantaloupe, waffles, bacon, and coffee, we can have breakfast here in ten minutes."

"I'd love it. Where do I wash my hands?"

"Right over there." She pointed to the guest lavatory. "Let's see. If I remember right, you take two spoonfuls of sugar. That's too much sugar." She saw his eyebrows shoot up, but he'd have to get used to drinking coffee with less in it. She strolled to the kitchen as if what she'd said wasn't unusual, though she figured he wasn't used to being crossed, lectured to, or confronted in any way.

"Yes, ma'am," she heard him say in a tone of wonder.

They finished breakfast. He insisted on cleaning the kitchen, and later she discovered that he didn't plan on riding around in her car. He seated her in the Buick LeSabre, and she concentrated on dealing with the excitement she felt being with Carson Montgomery on a new and different basis. During the day, he took her to places she hadn't been, such as the African-American Research Library and Cultural Center, where they enjoyed the huge collection of books, documents, and artifacts that reflected experiences of people of African descent.

He took her to the Buehler Planetarium and she hadn't thought she'd enjoy it so much, but after seeing its introduction to space and the horizons, she vowed to get to New York to visit the great Hayden Planetarium. As they emerged into the bright sunlight, she tugged at his arm.

"Being with you is wonderful. You can't imagine how much I enjoyed that."

He gazed at her for a few seconds. "If I've done something that makes you happy, it's more than worth the trip down here." With her hand in his, he went back to the car, and they were soon headed to Seminole Paradise, where they explored the history and culture of the famous Native American tribe.

He took her next to River Walk, the social center of the city. "Weren't you going to tell me that you're hungry?" he asked her. "You must be, because I'm about starved."

She smiled, because peace and contentment pervaded her. "Now that you mention it, my tummy is pinching me."

His laughter was something she could enjoy hearing forever. "You make a guy feel like a giant."

They sat at a table beside the river, and he handed her a bag. She stared at its contents. "When did you buy these? I didn't see them. They're so precious."

"In the crafts shop, while you were examining baskets, I bought those Seminole dolls. I couldn't decide between the boy and the girl, so I got both. I'm glad you like them."

"I love them. Oh, and these beads. Seminole women are famous for their beads. I'm not going to wear these; I could break them. I'm going to display all this in a shadow box where they can't be damaged."

He took her home around three o'clock. "I'll be back for you at four-thirty. A dressy street dress should be suitable for the evening, and if you have a shawl or sweater, you might bring that along."

She raised both arms to him. "Don't I get a kiss?"

"A little one. I can't handle that heavy stuff this time of day."

"Why not?"

"Because it's a signal to me to complete it, and you're not ready for that."

"Are you?"

"Shirley, don't ever ask me a question unless you want the unvarnished truth. Yes, I'm ready for it, and I have been since the second day we searched your father's place together. I've wanted it more and more urgently whenever I've seen you since then and whenever I've thought of you. I'll see you at four-thirty." He pressed his lips to hers and set her away from him. She watched him stride down the walk past the sign that read FOR SALE and watched the car until it was out of sight.

"Well, I guess he twirled my switch."

They spent the evening on the *Jungle Queen,* cruising along the New River and dining on barbecued baby back ribs and shrimp, among other delights. They danced to jazz music of questionable quality, but neither cared. With his arm tight around her, they stood on deck and watched as the boat plied past Millionaire's Row.

"Who needs so much wealth?" she asked, mostly to herself.

"You don't?" he asked, letting her know that he heard her.

"I doubt they're happier than I am. Observing my father taught me that money and things can make you comfortable, but they do not bring happiness. Father never did or said anything that made me think he was happy."

"That's a pity."

When at last he took her home, he stood in her foyer, looking at her as if he hadn't seen her before. "I leave early in the morning, but I'll call your cell phone the minute I get to Baltimore."

"If I don't answer, call my landline. I don't cruise again until Tuesday."

"This weekend has been wonderful, Shirley. Did you agree to be my girl?"

"Actually, I did. I just didn't tell you."

His laughter wrapped around her like a blanket of warmth in the dead of winter. "I care a lot for you. I want you to remember that."

"I will if you remember that you're not seeing any woman but me."

"Don't think for a minute that I'll forget that. Kiss me." He folded her to the warmth of his body and held her there. Then he brushed his lips across hers again and again until she parted them, and he possessed her until she slumped in his arms. He gripped her in a fierce hug, stared down at her for a minute, and left. She turned out the light and made her way up the dark stairs to her bedroom.

"If I had known I'd feel this badly when he left me, I don't think I would have let him come."

* * *

A few minutes before the crew closed the cabin doors for the takeoff of flight 780, Carson phoned his younger, and only, brother. "What's up, Ogden? You called me? Sorry I didn't catch your ring. I must have been on the river. In parts, it looks more like a lake than a river. How are you?"

"Me? I'm fine. What river are you talking about?"

"The New River in Fort Lauderdale. It's something for the eyes."

"Never heard of it. Where in the name of kings *are* you?"

"I said Fort Lauderdale. I'm on the plane headed home, and I'll have to cut this short any minute. What's up?"

"I just got promoted to managing engineer, and in this company, brother, that stands for something."

"Fantastic. Way to go. I'm going to buy a bottle of Dom Pérignon. Only the best for my kid brother. Call you when the plane lands. Bye for now."

He fastened his seat belt, turned toward the window, and went to sleep. He had to testify in court Monday morning, something he hated doing in divorce cases, and he had to find that will. His instincts and his common sense told him that the will was somewhere in Leon Farrell's private quarters, but he'd combed the place with a toothpick. Nothing had exasperated him as much as his search for that will. He told himself to go to sleep. With a lack of sleep, his memory wouldn't be reliable, and he didn't want to ruin his own reputation. Enough people were willing to do that for him.

As soon as the plane taxied to the gate, he dialed Shirley's number. "Hi. We just landed. I slept all the way. I'll be busy for the remainder of the day, but I'll phone you tonight. How are you? By now, you should be missing me."

"Give me a few more minutes."

"What? Am I not worth even a little misery?"

"Good heavens, a real ham. Actually, I started missing you last night before you got back to the hotel."

"That's a lot more like it. If I'm going to be unhappy missing you, by damn, I want company. They're disembarking. Talk later. Kisses."

"Bye for now, and kisses to you."

He got home at a quarter past one, and a check of his answering machine revealed seven calls from Edgar Farrell, the last three of which were abusive and profane. He was getting sick of Edgar, but he felt almost obligated to finish what he'd started. He'd never walked away from a job, leaving it unfinished, but Edgar's behavior threatened to make this a first. He erased the calls and put Edgar out of his mind.

The following Wednesday afternoon, which was her afternoon off, Frieda rushed up the stairs to her apartment at 2911 Franklin Street in Baltimore, threw her bag onto the sofa, kicked off her shoes, and sat down to read the letter. Her fingers shook so badly that she couldn't open the envelope. After struggling with it for a full minute, she went to her tiny kitchen, got a knife, and slit it open.

Seeing her birth mother's return address on the letter had sent her heartbeat into a tailspin, and she could barely keep her balance. She and Coreen Holmes Treadwell were on speaking terms, but that about described their relationship. Not that she blamed Coreen for it as she once did, because she'd hunted the woman, and when she finally confronted her, she showered upon Coreen a barrage of vituperous vengeance. But the meeting, the first time she'd laid eyes on her birth mother, proved just as painful for her. Coreen didn't spare her but poured out the horrifying experience of Frieda's conception—brought on by rape—and the extraordinary misery to which she was subjected while pregnant with Frieda.

After half a year of searching for Coreen and planning ways in which to humiliate her, those moments of confrontation and revenge had left Frieda not triumphant, but empty and sad. Frieda had accepted as balm for her wounds the letter she received from Coreen some three weeks later offering friendship and promising to be there for Frieda if she needed her. She had put the letter in her safe-deposit box along with the government bonds she bought weekly to buy a house. She had written Coreen a letter thanking her for the gesture of friendship, and sent her cards at Christmas, but that was the extent of their exchange.

She opened the letter, began to read, and put it aside. The letter was not from Coreen, but from Eric, Coreen's elder stepson. She went to the kitchen, made a pot of coffee, poured a cup, and went back to the living room. After sipping for a while, she picked up the letter and began to read.

Dear Frieda,
You and I haven't met, but I hope we will very soon. My stepmother, your mother, is very ill and needs a transfusion of bone mar-

row, but we have been unable to find a
match. My stepmother told us to ask you to
help. She said you wrote her and said that if
she ever needed you, you would do whatever
you could. Please say you'll come. I hope this
letter reaches you. I've called you many
times to no avail. If you'll call 555-1676, I'll
come for you and bring you here by car. Sin-
cerely yours, Eric Treadwell

She wondered why Glen hadn't written the letter. After finishing the second cup of coffee, she
telephoned Mirna, related the matter, and added,
"I'm her daughter, so I may be able to help. At
least I should test for it. But who's going to look
after Mr. G? Tell you what. I'll be back there in
about an hour."

"You're not going to try and help your mother?"
Mirna asked, her tone incredulous.

"Mirna, I'm a Christian. I'll do the right thing,
but I'm gon' take care of my patient, too."

She called Eric Treadwell. "Mr. Treadwell, this is
Frieda Davis."

"Thank God. We'd almost given up hope of
finding you."

"I'm a nurse, and I'm on a case. I came home
this afternoon and found your letter. I have to go
back to my job now, but I can take the test tomorrow morning."

"Where will you be tomorrow morning? I'll go
there for you."

She gave him the address. "I'll see you in the
morning, then, Mr. Treadwell. Do you know what
her prognosis is?"

"It's . . . it's all or nothing."

"I'm not surprised. See you in the morning."

She'd planned to do her laundry and then put up her feet while watching *Judge Judy,* but she wouldn't have time for that. She changed clothes, repacked her bag, locked the apartment door, and walked up Franklin to Juno, where she caught the bus. Forty minutes later, she walked into Gunther's apartment.

"I thought you were off this afternoon," he said when she walked into his room, where he sat by the window reading.

She told him enough about her background to enable him to understand why she needed to take the next day off. "As far as I know, I'm her only living blood relative. I can't say no."

She couldn't decipher his facial expression, but it seemed warm and friendly. "You have to go," he said. "I'll miss you, but I'll manage. I'm not so sick that I need a nurse anyway. The doctor's being overly cautious."

So he did care for her. When she got back, she'd definitely do something about that, but now was not the time.

She wrote out instructions for Mirna and told Gunther, "I know Mirna loves to fill you full of soul food, but if you eat that stuff, it will definitely set you back. I'm leaving menus for her, and I want you to see that she follows them."

"Of course I will. Why would I ignore my nurse's advice?"

She smiled inwardly. This would be a bad time to leave him. She should be there working at cementing a relationship with him, but she had a feeling that her birth mother was going to need her. She always tried to keep her promises, even when she didn't want to or when doing so proved inconvenient, like now.

She took the instructions downstairs to Mirna. "Mirna, I know he loves biscuits, pork chops, spareribs, and all the good stuff that you cook so tastefully, but please remember that he can't have it. He has to eat like someone on a diet. I hope my mother will be all right, and I won't need to be gone long. If it ain't one thing, it's another. I was just thinking of taking music lessons. You know, I always wanted to play the piano, and I couldn't afford lessons till now. But I may have to put that on hold, like a lot of other things."

"Everybody has to do that sometime," Mirna said.

"I know, and I'm not complaining. I've got a lot more than a lot of people. It's time he had his massage. See you later."

At ten o'clock the next morning, she answered the door to Eric Treadwell. "Come right in, Mr. Treadwell. I'll be ready in a minute."

As Frieda had expected, Mirna found a reason to appear for an introduction. In her role as housekeeper, Mirna made certain that she knew what went on in that house and that no one tampered with Gunther Farrell's property or violated his rights.

"Mrs. Jordan, this is Eric Treadwell, my birth mother's stepson. He's taking me to the hospital for the test. Mr. Treadwell, Mrs. Jordan is my patient's housekeeper."

"I'm glad to meet you, Mrs. Jordan," Eric said, extending his hand for a handshake. "I hope we won't have to keep Miss Davis too long."

"Likewise, Mr. Treadwell. I'll send up a few

prayers for your mother. That usually takes care of things."

"Thank you, ma'am. I appreciate your concern and your prayers."

"We'd better be going," Frieda said.

It didn't please her that Edgar's motorcycle roared up just as she got into Eric Treadwell's Lexus. Edgar was a devil if she'd ever met one, and he'd be certain to tell Gunther that he saw her going off with a good-looking man.

"Thank you for not changing your mind," Eric said.

"That never crossed my mind. Besides, you said it was all or nothing, depending on whether she got the bone marrow, so what did you expect, Eric? Things will probably never be perfect with your mother and me, but I still have that nice letter she wrote me, telling me she forgave me for trying to ruin her life."

"Did you answer?" he asked, glancing sideways at her.

"Of course I did, and I promised to be there for her if she ever needed me. Strange, but from then on, I had the feeling that I was not alone. I have two wonderful adoptive sisters, but that's not like blood relatives. Like your own mother."

"I guess not. Will it bother you to be around Glen?"

"I don't know. He and I used each other, but fate being what it is, I fell hard for him and he for me, and there was nothing we could do about it. I started it, singling him out because I'd learned that your stepmother had a special love for him. I thought I was seducing him, but I was really no match for his sophistication and experience. I hope he's doing well."

"He is, or so I think. I hope you're both over it."

"We'll see. Nothing would please me more."

"Here we are," Eric said as he parked in the hospital's parking lot.

"Will they let me see her?"

"Of course." He took her arm as they walked toward the front door. "Don't be nervous or anxious, Frieda. What will be, will be."

"Yeah, but I feel like a pan of quivering Jell-O. Is your father here, too? I mean, are things all right between them?"

"Yes, and that was a lesson for all of us. Once her secret was out, she was happier, less secretive, and they've seemed to love each other more than ever. Dad's at work now, but he'll be here later."

"I'm glad. After what she went through . . . It just shows that you shouldn't judge a person unless you have all the facts." She looked up at the darkening sky, and shivers raced through her. "I sure hope this dreary weather isn't a bad omen."

"Be like me," Eric said, opening the door. "I don't believe in omens, so those clouds don't matter to me."

He took her to the diagnostic center and introduced her to the physician in charge. "I'll wait out here for you," he told her. "It will take a while." She looked back at Eric and walked on with the doctor to the examining and testing room. The doctor started to tell her what to expect, but she interrupted him.

"I'm an LPN, Doctor, and I've worked in hospitals and clinics for years. I know what to expect."

She finished the tests, stepped out of the area, and saw Eric sitting where she had left him.

"You must be starved. It's after one o'clock," Frieda said to him.

A half smile played around his lips. "I couldn't eat if my life depended on it."

She realized that he was experiencing all the fear, dread, and concern that she should have been feeling for her mother. Not that she wasn't concerned, but no bond existed between her and Coreen Treadwell, at least not a true mother-daughter bond.

She sat beside Eric and took his hand. "Try to be positive, and when you're near her, think positive thoughts. Attitude has a lot to do with patients surviving."

"Thanks. If you're hungry, I'll get you something to eat downstairs in the cafeteria. We may be here for another three hours."

"You stay here. I'll go. I know the way. I used to work here." She bought sandwiches, coffee for herself, and a container of milk and a Snickers bar for him.

"Nobody feels too bad to eat Snickers," she told him later, and watched while he ate the candy and drank the milk.

"Could I ask you something, Frieda?"

"Go ahead. I don't have to answer."

"Did you feel badly because you were given up for adoption? I mean, did you personally feel unwanted?"

"No. What I felt was hatred for what I went through, but I realize now how wrong I was. Did she treat you and Glen the same? From what I saw at a distance, I thought he was her little pet."

"She loved him more, because he was five when she married Dad. I was seven, and she thought I didn't need her."

"But you did." It wasn't a question.

"Yeah. But I got over that. We were lucky that Dad found a woman who tried to be a good mother to his children."

"You bet you were."

The doctor came out, and both of them jumped to their feet. "You're a perfect match, Ms. Davis. If you haven't taken any painkillers for the last two weeks and there's no alcohol in your blood, we could do this tomorrow morning. I'd rather you didn't eat breakfast. You could stay here tonight, and we could do the transfusion at seven in the morning."

"I think I'd prefer that. Are you using intravenous lines or a needle in the hip bone?"

"Two intravenous lines will give you much less discomfort. Mr. Treadwell, please check her in before dinnertime. I'll make the arrangements."

Frieda phoned Gunther. "I'm a match, sir, so they want me to stay overnight and give the bone marrow tomorrow morning. I gave Mirna instructions as to what she should do."

"Thanks for letting me know. Mirna's managing fine."

What else could she say? She signed off as graciously as she could and then asked Eric if she could say hello to her birth mother.

"Of course. She doesn't yet know that you can donate. She'll be very happy."

"Who's with her? I'm not sure I—"

"Don't worry. My wife, Star, is with her, but Glen may arrive while we're there."

She laid back her shoulders, stiffened her back, and looked at Eric. "Considering what I've been through in my life, I can stand anything."

He put an arm around her shoulder. "Atta girl!"

They took the elevator to the third floor, and after walking down a long, gray, and uninspiring corridor, he knocked on a door that bore the name of Coreen Holmes Treadwell. Holding Frieda's hand as if he were dragging her along, he walked straight to Coreen's bed.

"Mom, you remember Frieda. She took the test, and she's a perfect match."

Coreen's gasp didn't surprise Frieda, but then she opened her arms to Frieda as any mother would. "God bless you, Frieda. I won't try to thank you, because it isn't possible." She tried to hug Frieda, but she only managed a weak gesture and fell back against the pillows. "My, but you're so beautiful. Bates said you look just like me, but I was never beautiful. Oh, I'm so happy that you would do this for me."

"I'm happy that you asked me. Nothing could have kept me away." She felt a hand on her shoulder, looked up, and saw Eric with his arm around a lovely Native American woman.

"Frieda, this is Star, my wife."

She stood and extended her hand to Star. "I'm glad to meet you, Star. You're the first Native American I've met. I'd love to talk with you sometime."

Star hugged Frieda. "I can definitely arrange that."

The door opened, and Bates, Coreen's husband, walked in, followed by his younger son, Glen

Treadwell. *Well*, Frieda thought to herself after they gazed at each other while the room's remaining occupants quietly observed them, *he may still be da bomb, but I don't itch to make him explode.* She smiled and walked over to them. "How are you, Mr. Bates, and you, Glen?" She shook hands with them both and said, "We're in luck. I'm a perfect blood match."

Chapter Six

Frieda wondered why the family didn't leave and give her a chance to talk with Coreen. In her professional experience, that transfusion didn't guarantee long life, and she might not get another chance to talk with her birth mother.

However, Coreen had other thoughts. "If you and Glen need to straighten out anything, Frieda, we'll all excuse you. Everybody here knows what your relationship was."

"Now, honey, this isn't a time for you to worry about that," her husband, Bates, said. "We're just thankful that Frieda wants to do what she can to help. I've been lying awake at night praying that she'd get Eric's messages and that she'd want to help. Whatever's left between her and Glen can wait." He patted Frieda's shoulder. "Frieda, you do what you feel like doing. Nobody here's gonna put you on the spot."

Frieda knew she was the architect of the problem and that she should be the one to erase it. She hoped they reflected that if she hadn't messed things up as she did, they wouldn't have known she existed, and there'd be no one to give Coreen the bone marrow.

Straighten out your mind, girl. She looked at Coreen. "I was hoping for a chance to talk with you."

"That's good," Coreen said. "I wasn't thinking." She closed her eyes, and Frieda could see that the woman was exhausted. She held her head, fluffed the pillows, and adjusted them.

"We'd better put this down a little," Frieda said, lowering the bed to a semilying position. "She's tired." Then Frieda turned toward Glen. "Come on, Glen, let's go down to the cafeteria and get a cup of coffee." If talking to him would make Coreen happy, she was glad to do it.

"Why did you decide to do this?" Glen asked her as they headed for the cafeteria.

"Worrying will make her worse, not better, and I don't want her to be concerned about anything relating to me."

"Gotcha. So there're no hard feelings?"

"No feelings of any kind, Glen. We were both cruel, and we paid for it. I'm over it, and I pray that you are, too. It's a lesson that I will never have to learn again." The minute she said it, her mind flashed to her intention to seduce Gunther Farrell on the basis of Edgar's questionable tale. Shudders shot through her and she stopped walking.

"Glen, this reminds me that God doesn't like ugly. I'm really going to clean up my act."

"So am I, Frieda. That drama with you proved to be too costly, but I still repeated it a few months back. I was lucky to come away from it alive."

"Yeah," she said, "and I was contemplating doing it again as soon as I left here."

"But you won't?"

"No. I need my integrity."

"Come on, let's get that coffee. I think I'm going to enjoy having you for a sister. In spite of what we did, some good came from it."

After speaking with Mirna and Gunther, she checked into the hospital and went to her room. She ate the light supper, watched the evening news on television, and went to sleep, exhausted. At five the next morning, a nurse awakened her, prepped her for the transfusion, and left her. By seven-thirty, she'd done what she went there to do.

"May I go now?" she asked the doctor.

"Not yet. You have to lie down for a few hours, and you must eat, too." They sent her back to her room.

Hours later, free to leave the hospital, Frieda got as far as the front door with Eric at her side and stopped. "You mind waiting a couple of minutes while I tell her good-bye? I want to see if she's got any color since the transplant."

He looked at her, sadly, Frieda thought, and said, "I'll wait, but you shouldn't expect a great change so soon, should you?"

"Sometimes you can. I just have to see for my-self."

"I'll wait, Frieda, but I know you're not saying what you're thinking."

She ran back to the elevator, got off at the third floor, and headed for Coreen's room. But the closer she got, the slower she walked.

"How're you feeling?" she asked her birth mother. She looked closely to judge Coreen's skin and eye color. Relieved at the changes, minor though they were, she smiled her relief. "You look better already."

"I feel a little better, too. Do you think that after this, we can at least call each other once in a while? I'd like that."

"I would, too," Frieda said, "and if you need me, be sure and let me know. I'm an LPN."

"I didn't know that. You've done extremely well, and I'm proud of you."

I'm not going to get weepy here. "Thank you. That means a lot to me. I'll be seeing you. Don't forget now."

"How'd it go?" Eric asked when she returned to him.

"Good. In a way, it's difficult, because she's my mother. I don't acknowledge it to her, and she can't claim it to me. What should I call her?"

"Her name is Coreen. Lots of people call their mother by her first name. I don't think she'd like you to call her Mrs. Treadwell." He grasped her hand. "Come on, sis. Let's go."

"You got a lot to tell me," Mirna said to Frieda when she returned to work the next morning, "and, girl, have I got a mouthful to tell you! Would you believe Mr. G came down here and put Edgar out?"

"How, for goodness' sake? Is Edgar such a weakling that a sick man can shove him around? Mr. Farrell doesn't have the energy for that."

"Oh, yes, he does," Mirna said. "He heard Edgar throwing his weight around down here and came down those stairs almost like a football player. I never saw him so mad. I tried my best to keep Edgar out, but he brushed past me and started acting out. Scared the bejeebers out of me. He won't be back here soon. What happened to you?"

She related to Mirna as much as she wanted her to know. "I'm so excited, because I could see that it did her some good. Already that pale, sickly look was gone. One of her stepsons told me it was all right to call her by her first name. What do you think?"

"Honey, you have to play it by ear. You'll never call her 'Mother,' so call her by her name."

"He practically said the same. I'd better get up those stairs and see about Mr. Farrell."

She knocked on his door and waited for permission to enter. Immediately she realized that she hadn't behaved as if she were his nurse; ordinarily, she knocked and walked in.

"Come in," he said, his voice strong and authoritative.

"I heard about you and Edgar," she said. "Something tells me you no longer need a nurse."

"That's exactly what I was going to tell you. I spoke with the doctor today, and he agreed with me. How did you leave your mother?"

No point in insisting that Coreen was her mother in name only. "Hours after she got the transplant, she was already looking better. She'd lost that awful pallor. But I can see she has a long road to recovery."

Gunther made a pyramid of his fingers, leaned back in his big oversized chair, and closed his eyes. She waited. Finally, he said, "It's true that you're a temp, but I believe in giving a person a fair shake. I'll write you an excellent letter of recommendation and with pleasure, because you're a first-class nurse. And I'll give you your salary for the remainder of the month plus one month's pay."

She let out a gasp. "That's more than fair, sir. I'm not wealthy, and I don't need to be out of work, but it's more than I had any right to expect. If you ever need a nurse, let me know; even if you're flat broke, I'll take care of you. You a first-class person, sir. If it's all right with you, I'll leave in the morning."

His lips curved into a grin. "I hope I'm never flat broke, but I appreciate those sentiments."

Frieda left the next morning and got home around noon. Walking up the steps to her fourth-floor apartment, she stopped suddenly. Gunther wasn't interested in her. Edgar had lied through his teeth, and he'd done it to embarrass Gunther. He hadn't considered that she, who had done nothing to him, could have been mortified and, worse, could have lost her job. "He's an unprincipled person," she said to herself, "and I'm glad to be away from him."

She was about to telephone the hospital and inquire about Coreen when she remembered that, not being a relative, she'd get the standard reply: *She's resting comfortably.* She phoned Eric and asked him.

"Hi. Thanks for calling. She's doing great. The doctor says she can go home in a couple of days."

Frieda thought for a second. She could look after Coreen for a month and still come out ahead. If she let the hospital at which she occasionally worked know that she was available, they'd call her in a minute, and she'd work for half of what Gunther paid her.

"I can look after her for a month. No charge.

After that, she'll need only a housekeeper for a few weeks. I know Star's willing to help. But I'm a nurse."

"You'd . . . you'd do that?"

"Of course. And she won't find a better nurse anywhere."

"I believe you. I'll tell Mom and Dad about your offer. Frieda, you're amazing. I don't know how to thank you."

Gunther walked into his office for the first time in over a month, inhaled deeply, sat down at his desk, and punched the intercom. "Medford, I'm in my office. Come around here, please."

They exchanged fist bumps, and Medford sat in the chair beside Gunther's desk. "You look well, Gunther. I'm glad you're back. We held the fort as well as we could, but you do it best. What's up?"

"I've been working on a dilly of a game, and I know it's one of the best I've ever seen anywhere." He opened his computer, put in the DVD, and sat back to get Medford's take on the antics of the three devilish little five-year-old boys and the reactions of their beautiful and long-suffering nurse.

Three-quarters of the way through the DVD, Medford began knocking his right fist into his left palm and moving his head and torso in a rocking motion. "Man, it's great. It's great. You hit it right on. This is huge!" Medford said at the end of the game. "How do we handle it?"

"I'm giving it to a major distributor, and I want you to design a cover and a video for YouTube and a trailer for the Web site. My father said I could have been wealthy if I'd taken a job on Wall Street, that my decision to start a business of developing computer games was stupid, a lazy man's excuse for work. This would have made him eat those words."

"Right. I'll get to work on the promo stuff right now. You really socked it this time, Gunther."

After Medford went back to his office, Gunther leaned back in his desk chair, musing over what he regarded as a singular achievement. He only had to get it before the public, and he'd soon be a household name. He phoned a top distributor, and one week later, Gunther Farrell Designs, Inc., had a deal certain to make its owner a rich man.

"I'd give anything if the old man could see me now," he said to Mirna as the two of them watched the first trailer on a national TV station. Barely able to contain his excitement, he telephoned Shirley. "Wait till you see this."

"I'll see it day after tomorrow. My real estate agent just sold my condo. You can't imagine how relieved I am. Some of these homes have been listed for months. The moving company is packing my stuff as we speak. How's Frieda doing?"

He rolled his eyes toward the ceiling and blew out a long breath. "I do not need a nurse, Shirley. I let Frieda go a week ago."

"Mmm. Can I stay with you till I find a place? I'd like another condominium, but if I can't find one, I'll settle for a house. I'm sending my things to storage."

"Of course, you may stay with me as long as you want to. You mean you're moving back to Ellicott City?"

"Definitely. My boss doesn't care as long as I'm on that cruise ship when it shoves off. He'll have to pay my airfare to Fort Lauderdale or Orlando, but in the context of the ship's expenses, that's peanuts. I hope I won't be in your way. If you have a girl-friend, you'd better warn her."

"Not to worry. I'd kind of started something, but what with getting sick, I haven't been able to develop it. She's nice. Maybe I'll call her."

"I hope your taste changed since you got rid of Lissa. I did not like that woman."

"I know that, Shirley. Not for one minute did I ever think Lissa would be a permanent fixture in my life. I may do something questionable in a weak moment, but I've never been an idiot."

"No comment. Seen Edgar?"

"Yeah. Pick another topic."

"Whoops! Too bad. See you in a couple of days."

"By the way, has Montgomery been back to Fort Lauderdale?" He wasn't sure about the guy. Who knew why the man decided to court Shirley?

"I've no idea. I've been on the cruise, so if he came here, he didn't come to see me."

Hmmm. He didn't learn anything from that question, and it looked as if she didn't plan to vol-unteer any information about the man. But he'd keep an eye on the guy.

That afternoon, he went to his doctor for a checkup and got a tongue-lashing. "Another week's rest would have done you some good. Be careful that you don't have a relapse."

"I see." He didn't like to hear that, but he'd deal with it. Maybe he should have kept Frieda a week longer.

* * *

However, having released Frieda, Gunther had made possible a phenomenal change in her life. Mirna sat at the ironing board with the hot iron resting facedown on the board while she talked with Frieda on the phone. "You go way from here. Child, you get outta here. You mean you gon' take care of her yourself? Honey, you can't take pay for nursing your own mother, no matter what she done."

"I'm not taking any pay. Eric needed someone to look after her, and I told him I could do it for a month. After this, I'm gon' relieve one of the nurses at the hospital when she goes on maternity leave."

Mirna jumped up, got a wet towel, and put it on the burning ironing board cover. "Now, you just look at that. I was about to burn up the place. Our pastor's always saying there's order in the universe. I guess this is an example of it, 'cause I heard Mr. G say Miss Shirley's moving back for a while. She'll be here today. Three women in this place would be one too many for me. How's your mother doing so far?"

"Her temperature's elevated and her blood pressure is up, but that's not exceptional, since she just came home. She'll be all right."

"I sure hope so. I gotta go. I want to make a lemon cake for supper. Mr. G loves that cake. Be sure and take Thursday afternoon off so we can go to the movies. Bye."

Less than half an hour after she opened the door and welcomed Shirley, Mirna looked through the peephole of Gunther's front door and saw Carson Montgomery. She opened the door. "Well, how d'you do? It's nice to see you again."

"Thank you," Carson said. "I want to see Ms. Farrell." Mirna thought her eyes betrayed her when she looked up and saw Shirley sliding down the banister of the steep stairs. Shirley seemed to take wings as she sped to Carson and into his arms. "Well, I guess that answers the question I was gon' have," Mirna said to herself and headed for the kitchen.

"I looked everywhere for you. Didn't you go to the baggage claim section?" Carson asked Shirley. "Baby, I was afraid you'd missed the plane, so I checked with the airline and learned that you hadn't. You gave me goose bumps."

"I only brought a carry-on. Aren't you going to kiss me? I'll do what I can to get rid of those goose bumps."

"Yeah. I'm sure you'll do your best, but not right here. That'll take more than one kiss." He brushed his lips over hers. "I know you're planning to start looking for an apartment or a house, but I'd appreciate it if you'd go with me to your father's house tomorrow morning. If we don't go tomorrow—"

"I know. Edgar will be home, and I don't think we want to run into him. I think he and Gunther just had a set-to of sorts."

"That's too bad. I'll pick you up tomorrow morning at nine."

"What are you going to do with the nineteen hours between now and then?"

His stern expression slowly dissolved into a grin.

"If you want to share all nineteen of them with me, I'll be as happy as a squirrel in a barrel of acorns."

She pulled his ear. "Oh, you know what I meant."

"If you'll have dinner with me, I'll be here at six in a jacket and tie."

"Why don't you dine with us?"

Shirley's head whipped around. She hadn't heard Gunther come down the stairs, and she said as much. "You forgot that I don't wear shoes in the house," Gunther said. He shook hands with Carson. "I'd be happy to have you join us."

Shirley studied him carefully, and after a glance at Carson, she said, "Thanks, dear brother. We'll take a rain check on that. I haven't seen Carson in ages, and I have so much to tell him." She looked at Carson. "But it's up to you."

Carson eyed Gunther with an expression that said *Help*. "You know I don't have the guts or the faintest desire to turn her down, don't you?" *What man could?* "Thanks for the invitation." He pulled her gently into his arms, pressed his lips to hers, and, as if they were alone, smiled as he looked down at her. "I'm so happy that you're back here to stay. I'll be here at six." He looked at Carson. "See you later, man."

Shirley closed the door behind Carson and turned to her brother. "Gunther, what do you mean by pulling that trick? Hadn't I told you minutes earlier that I hadn't seen Carson in three weeks?"

"You two are pretty close."

"That's right. We are. And we will definitely get closer. If you're planning to supervise my behavior, I can stay at a hotel. Try to remember that I work every day, take care of myself, and vote during local and national elections. I don't break the law, and though my father is dead, I'm old enough, at age thirty-two, to go out with boys without your permission."

He held up both hands, palms out. "Look, sis, we don't know enough about this guy. We've had no results from his searches. Hell, he could already have found the will. Why should you be so trusting?"

"Why? I'll tell you. Because I put on my bikini in his hotel bathroom, and not only did he sit in the suite's living room while I did it, but he also didn't attempt to touch me after I came out. Furthermore, he then changed into that nothing-of-a-swimsuit he wears, and if anybody threatened to get out of line, it was me. So back off. The man's a gentleman."

"Okay, but you're my sister, and it's my duty to look after you."

"I know, honey. But please don't smother me. I like Carson. Your suspicions are unfounded."

She got a book and a handful of peanuts and went out to the park, a small oasis of trees, grass, shrubs, and water fountains in the midst of urban concrete, and sat on a bench beneath a purple ash tree. She stayed on the water so much that the sturdy earth beneath her feet gave her feelings of solidity and security. She opened her book but couldn't concentrate on the story, because the squirrels soon came to investigate her, running across her feet, standing up, and begging for nuts. She put one nut in her right hand and reached down, and the squirrel took it from her. She stayed with the squirrels until they'd taken all of the peanuts, and with the sun still high, she went inside, showered, took a nap, and then began to dress.

"My, don't you look good," Mirna said when Shirley came downstairs. "You work on that, 'cause he a fine man. I'm gon' leave two slices of my lemon cake in a bag on the kitchen counter, and you be sure to give it to him. Little gestures like that endear you to a man. You hear?"

She hugged Mirna. "Thanks. I think he's wonderful, but Gunther's ready to pull the big brother act."

Mirna stuck her fists to her hips. "Now, I think Mr. G's the cat's pajamas, but what he see in a man and what you should be looking for definitely ain't necessarily the same."

"That's part of the problem. I don't know what Gunther sees in Carson. Maybe he refuses to take a close look. Anyhow, it won't cause me a drop of sweat. Growing up without a mother and with a father locked up in himself, I'm lucky to have any values at all."

"I hear you, but don't lean too far in that direction. Some lousy parents have fine children, and some really good parents have very bad luck with their kids. Lots of things other than parents influence children. Parents have to try and control those influences. Did Mr. G give you a key, or does he want you to ring the bell so he'll know what time you come in?"

Shirley couldn't help laughing. "If Gunther knew how well you understand him, he'd be shocked. He likes to think he's complicated. I'm going up there right now and ask him for a key."

"Well, all right, if you insist," he said when she asked him. "This takes some getting used to. It's like you're not my little sister anymore."

She leaned down, braced one hand on the back of his chair, and kissed his forehead. "That's right. I'm not. I'm your younger, thirty-two-year-old sister, and I love you. There's the doorbell. Bye."

"One of these days when you greet me looking like the queen that you are, I'm going to give in to my gut feeling and let out a sharp whistle. You are one gorgeous woman," Carson said. "For two cents, I'd take you to my lair and keep you there."

She looked at him from beneath lowered lashes and added a slow wink. "Couldn't you at least spare a nickel?"

Laughter poured out of him. "Come on, woman. You're temptation enough without adding suggestive remarks."

After dinner at an upscale restaurant in Baltimore, he asked if she'd like to dance. "Of course I would. I love dancing with you."

"A place for good dancing is hard to find in this town. I hope you like Wilson's. The music is . . . well"—with his palm down, he moved his right hand like a rocking boat—"comme ci, comme ça."

"If I'm dancing with you, I won't know the difference."

He stared down at her. "If you mean what I think you mean, I may begin to walk on air."

"I meant what you think I meant, but for goodness' sake, stay down here where I can reach you."

He hugged her, helped her into his car, and headed to the nightclub. They danced until the band stopped and the musicians packed their instruments, and then they left the club with their arms tight around each other.

"Are you still willing to go with me tomorrow morning?" he asked her. "It's after midnight."

"I'll be ready at nine as we planned." He parked in front of the building in which Gunther lived and walked inside, holding her hand.

He opened Gunther's apartment door with her key, returned it to her, and didn't wait for an invitation to go in. He stopped just inside the door and gazed down at her. Wordless. She stared into the dark desire of his mesmerizing eyes, fully aware that she would be a willing victim of the onslaught of passion in which he was about to engulf her.

"I've waited weeks for this," he said, locked her body to his, plunged his tongue into her waiting mouth, and possessed her. "Give it to me. I want your nipple in my mouth. I want to taste your flesh."

With so much cleavage showing, she slipped her right breast out with ease and held it to him. He pulled the nipple into his mouth and sucked it until she could no longer restrain her moans. After adjusting her clothes, he eased her feet to the floor.

"I don't apologize for that, sweetheart. After looking at them all evening, I had to taste them." He cradled her head against his shoulder. "I care a lot for you, Shirley. I'm in pretty deep. If it isn't this way with you and if you think I can't be special to you, please tell me now, and I'll cut my losses."

"I know you were disappointed once, but I'm not planning to do that, Carson. I care a lot for you, too, and I trust you to be fair and honest with me."

"And you can always do that. Kiss me . . . but just a little bit. I'm in enough trouble as it is."

She kissed his cheek. "See you at nine."

"What's the matter, Carson?" Shirley asked him the next morning as he parked in front of her father's house. "You're a blast of north wind compared to the Carson I was with last night."

He turned off the ignition and looked at her. Why hadn't he anticipated her response to the Carson Montgomery who was focused on his work and nothing else? "Sweetheart, I'm sorry. This is the first time I've had a relationship with a client, and I suppose I'm not handling it well. When my mind is on my business, I think of nothing else. Sometimes I don't get hungry or sleepy. I have to find that will, and I'm no closer to it than when I started. Can we agree that when we're dealing with this case, I'm the detective, and when we're not, I'm the man who cares only for you?"

Her eyes widened, and for a few seconds, she gazed steadily at him. "I'm sure this is why you're good at what you do, but don't make a habit of it. Okay, how can I help?"

Inside the house, she followed him up the stairs. "I want you to go into the room that was your bedroom. Take yourself back to the time when you lived here with your father and your brothers, and try to recall what your father did while you were in your room alone or when you played with your brothers. Try to remember what we've missed. I'll be in the basement."

As he passed Leon Farrell's den, he stopped. Why would a man have two wood-paneled walls in his personal office/den when walls in the remainder of the room were painted white? He shrugged. The man probably didn't want to spend any more money on expensive wood paneling. No point in attaching anything to that, considering that the man either hid or destroyed his will. Nothing he did would surprise him. Once in the basement, he began a methodical check of the laundry room and the closet in which the linens were stored. After about an hour, he heard Shirley's footsteps on the stairs.

"You know what? It just occurred to me that I haven't seen any of Father's wooden robots."

He rushed to her. "Wooden robots? I've seen only one plastic robot in this house. Do you think Edgar could have sold them?"

"Maybe, but as I recall, he didn't regard them as valuable. He considered it silly for a man Father's age to collect robots. And when Father began to make wooden ones, Edgar suggested to us that we ought to have him committed. Since only he and Father lived here for the past few years, it's possible that Father hid them from Edgar. He could have put them in storage somewhere."

"I see. Has Edgar mentioned the robots to you since your father passed?"

"Not to me, but he could have spoken to Gunther about them."

"Robots, huh? Can you describe them?"

"He bought plastic and metal ones, but mostly plastic. All were animals—dogs, cats, and bears. I think he must have taken a course in it, because he began to make wooden squirrels and rabbits about two years ago. We joked that he cared more for animals than for humans, but that wasn't really fair."

Carson sat on the edge of a little end table near the steps. "I had that guy all wrong. I'd figured he spent his time reading. So he wasn't an intellectual."

"Not in my estimation," she said. "And it's interesting, because most introverts who prefer their own company tend to be thinkers and intellectuals. Imagine a father of children almost forty years old who lived with him for most of their lives and can't define his personality. Leon Farrell didn't do his job as a parent."

"You'll get no argument from me about that. Why isn't Edgar in Atlantic City on the weekends?"

"He said he works locally on the weekends."

He stared at her. "Does that make sense to you? Are people most likely to go to a resort city on Mondays or on Fridays? Don't believe everything people tell you, not even if the speaker is your older brother."

At dinner that evening, she mentioned to Gunther Carson's skepticism about Edgar's employment arrangements. "Carson thinks it doesn't make sense."

"He's right. It doesn't, and Edgar's probably lying. He might have had a gig there for a short while, but not on a permanent basis. Let's see. Today's Friday. I'll see if he's at that hotel this evening." He took out his BlackBerry, dialed Edgar's cell number, and waited.

"Hello. Farrell speaking."

"How's it going, Edgar? Are you on a gig in Baltimore tonight? I thought I might drop by with a friend."

"Naah, man. I told my boss to shove it. That scum doesn't know good music when he hears it. Like those airheads in Atlantic City. They take a guy who doesn't know a pick from a pitcher and make him lead over a boss guitarist. The hell with all of them. A bunch of assholes."

"Where are you right now?"

"Man, I'm in Vegas. I've been stranded, but this gal I've met is buying me a ticket home. She thinks she's clever, buying me a round trip to be sure I come back. See you in a couple of days."

He related the conversation to Shirley and added, "Looks like he'll always be a deadbeat. I wonder how much he owes that poor woman."

"I hope she can afford it. Carson thinks the absence of those robots may be significant."

"Possibly. It's his job to consider everything. I agree with you. Edgar didn't think enough of them to take them, but Father was a little paranoid when it came to those things, so he probably stored them somewhere. But why would he do that?"

"He had a mean streak, and you know he did. Anyway, Carson wants to talk with you. He's going to find that will or die trying."

"I don't expect you want that," he said dryly.

Since it was Mirna's afternoon off, they cleaned the kitchen together. "I think I'll turn in," he said. "My distributor wants another game. He said the one I gave him is moving. I made it for children, but it seems that everybody's attracted to it. I hope to get this in shape by the middle of next week."

"You're not supposed to work but half a day, so please be sensible about this. And please call Carson in the morning. I may be out for a while. See you at breakfast."

He stopped midway up the stairs. "You may be out? Out where? You were with that guy *last* night."

He could almost see her bristle when she stuck her fists on her hips and glared at him. "What guy are you talking about? One more crack like that one, and I'll move."

"Move where?"

"I'd love to move in with Carson, but he hasn't asked me. There're plenty of hotels here and in Baltimore, so try to keep your bossiness under wraps, please."

"You'd actually move in with Carson?"

"I hadn't considered it until you started getting on my nerves. But the thought of being in a position to have my way with that man is enough to send me over the edge. Good night."

"Are you in love with him?"

"Gunther, please drop it. Carson is important to me, and I don't want to continue discussing him in a flippant manner. We can speak seriously about this another time. Okay?"

"Yeah. As if I didn't have enough headaches."

He heard her cell phone ring, knew it was Carson, and battled with himself as to whether he should confront the man and risk the chance that Shirley would keep her word and move in with him. He didn't want her to do that. A woman was at a disadvantage and with minimum bargaining chips when she removed a guy's chief reason for getting married. Too bad their father hadn't taken the time to give her the facts of life.

*   *   *

Shirley sat on a step midway up the stairs and answered her cell phone. "Hi, how are you?"

"I'm lonely. Want to go for some ice cream? It tastes great this time of night. I know a super place for ice cream. How about it?"

"What are you wearing?"

"Jeans and a collared T-shirt."

"I'll be ready when you get here."

"Gal after my own heart."

She combed out her hair, put on a pair of silver hoop earrings, washed her face, and buffed it with a dry towel. She examined herself in the full-length mirror that hung on the back of the closet door. Black jeans, a red T-shirt, and blue Reeboks. Definitely good enough for ice cream, she assured herself and tripped down the stairs, humming Eric Clapton's "Layla."

"Hi," she said when she looked up and saw Carson at the door. "Mirna left us cake for dessert, but I was saving mine for later. So when you called—"

He interrupted her with a kiss on the mouth. "Why are you nervous? You look great. Let's go."

She was nervous, but she hadn't thought it would show. She hadn't been so casual with Carson, and she didn't know how he'd take it.

"I love your hair down," he said as he drove away from the curb. "And your outfit is raising my blood pressure. Want to go to Three Scoops?"

"I've never been there, Carson, but I'm sure I'll like it."

"Are you always so agreeable? I like that about you, but don't forget that I like to please you. So always let me know exactly what you want and what you like." He stopped for a red light, turned, and looked straight at her. "And that goes for everything, including and especially, when you're in my arms."

She knew what he meant, but she didn't know how to respond. That was as pointed as it could get.

"Do you understand what I mean?" he asked, refusing to let her avoid answering. The light changed to green, and he turned onto Route 144, drove half a mile, and parked in the Three Scoops parking lot.

"You chose an idyllic evening," she said, gazing up at the full, bright aristocratic-looking moon, regal in a field of stars. Down on earth, every leaf seemed content to remain unmoving on its limb, and not the slightest rustle of breeze disturbed the quiet. "I don't even hear an automobile," she said. "This is a little slice of heaven."

"So you'd rather not answer." He flexed his right shoulder in a quick shrug. "The trees and that high wooden panel block out the traffic noise. If you like this, wait until we get inside."

As they passed the lighted counter that displayed the flavors for sale, she chose raspberry margarita. A waitress seated them beside a window that overlooked a waterfall and a brook. Shirley could see their reflections in the water. "This is one seductive environment," she blurted out, "and you don't need any help."

He looked at her for such a long time that she blanched beneath his stare. "Be careful what you say to me, Shirley. I take everything you tell me seriously, even some things said in jest. You just told me that you're attracted to me. I know that, and it's important to me. After all, you've agreed that you're my girl. But that word *seductive* carries a punch."

He was a grown man, and she shouldn't have to mince words with him. "Because I'm your girl, you should expect me to tell you like it is. You're seductive. Period. One of these days, I'll give you some details. And there's no reason why knowing it should blow up your ego."

Both of his eyebrows shot up, and he sat back in the chair and gazed at her, seemingly nonplussed. "Shirley, when you decide to be serious and truthful about what's going on between you and me, please try not to choose a public place in which to do it. If I had you to myself in a private place right now, I would make love to you before I let you out of my sight, and I wouldn't play at it, either."

Her heart began to pound like the hooves of a runaway Thoroughbred horse. "I don't consider anything you say to me as a threat. You . . . You're piling it on. I don't think I'm quite ready, but I'm definitely looking forward to it."

Chapter Seven

Carson hadn't been in the Farrell house twenty minutes that Saturday morning when he heard a key in the front door. He hadn't wanted one of the Farrell siblings with him, because he did his best thinking alone, and something teased the edges of his mind, something he simply could not get a handle on. Whatever it was, it would lead him to that will.

"What the fu . . . ? Who the hell is in here?" a voice yelled, and he knew he'd have to deal with a surprised and irritable Edgar.

He put the desk upright, straightened his clothes, and strolled slowly and with caution down the stairs, every molecule of his body alert and on edge. "What's wrong, Edgar?"

"You? I thought you'd checked this place. No wonder it's taking you—"

"Cool it, man, and act your age. How do you expect me to find that will if I don't look for it?" He'd figured that the best way to handle Edgar was to remind the man of his obvious shortcomings. "I'm successful, among other things, because I'm thorough. Since you're here, do you have any idea why your father's robots are missing?"

"Hell, no, man. He was paranoid about those stupid things. I wouldn't be surprised if he buried them in the cemetery and marked the grave with an expensive headstone. A grown man sitting around playing with toys. He should've been committed, but Gunther and Shirley wouldn't hear of it."

"The man was sane. To have had him committed to a mental facility would have been criminal. Didn't you like your father?"

"He was too harsh. Expected us to be like him. Gunther tried to please Father, but he didn't treat Gunther any better than he treated me. Shakespeare said it all: 'To thine own self be true.' And I been doing my own thing ever since I figured out that nobody could please the old man."

Carson rested his back against the side of a big hutch in the hall between the dining room and the kitchen. "You're just getting in from Atlantic City, I suppose."

"Man, I quit that half-ass job weeks ago. I'm just getting back from Vegas. Now, that's where the action is, and as soon as I can, I'm going back. But, man, that place eats money like a whirlwind sucking up sand. Haven't you come up with any leads yet?"

"Sure, and one by one, they petered out. But after a conversation with Shirley about the type of person your father was, I've begun a different tactic, and it should work. I'd better get busy. See you."

"Man, I'm not staying. I gotta run over to Baltimore and see about making some bread. I need to pick up a couple of gigs. You'll probably be gone when I get back."

"If you're not back in an hour, I certainly will be."

Carson walked back up the stairs, deep in thought. How did a parent avoid creating a person like Edgar? He wasn't born that way, and he had had the same advantages and disadvantages as Gunther and Shirley, but his resemblance to them began and ended with the color of his eyes.

An hour and a half later, speeding down Jones Falls Expressway, Edgar sideswiped a car. He slowed down, but he neither stopped nor looked back, though from his side-view mirror, he should have seen the car spin around 360 degrees and rock precariously before settling on its four wheels. However, in slowing down, he allowed the driver of that car to see enough of him to remember what he wore, though she didn't get his license plate number.

In her usually meticulous way, Frieda Davis jotted down the color and shape of his helmet and drew the shape of the two interlocked red Vs on the back of his white leather jacket. Then she examined her tires, got back into the car, and drove on to Bakerville to continue her care of her birth mother. If she ever saw him again, he'd owe her plenty.

When his cell phone rang persistently, Edgar slowed down and pulled over to the shoulder of the highway. He didn't try to use his cell phone while riding his motorcycle. It would be too dangerous. Besides, he wouldn't be able to hear one word. "Farrell speaking."

"When you coming back, Edgar?"

"Look, babe. I got here this morning, and a lot's facing me before I can leave. Don't be anxious about me going back there. You got my music, babe, and nobody ever played it like you do. You get my meaning?"

"You bet. When you get back, I'll be here just like you left me, honey."

"That's my girl. See you." He put the phone back in his pocket, kicked the starter, and headed to the Eubie Blake National Jazz Institute, the one place where he could always get a gig. While he'd talked with the woman who paid for his trip home, Frieda Davis passed, and as she did so, she made a mental note of his license plate. Edgar parked at the Institute and tried without success to reach Gunther by phone.

But while Edgar seethed in frustration because he couldn't reach his brother, Gunther was learning that *Bravado,* his video game about three mischievous little boys and a nurse, had become the country's best-selling video game.

"We're speaking money here, Gunther," his distributor said, socking his left palm with his right fist. "Yeah, man. Oodles and oodles of green United States money. Man, you're at the summit. I want fifty thousand more copies this week. When the iron is hot, strike it. And you're hot."

Gunther had expected the game to be a hit, but not to the extent that it had. He made an effort to adopt a businesslike demeanor and to resist displaying the excitement that he felt. "I'll order the copies today, and you should have them by Wednesday."

"Uh, by the way, if I were you, I'd open a special account for each product to simplify record keeping. That way, you'll always know exactly what your net gain is from each game."

"Thanks, Ken." He didn't bother to tell the man that he had an MBA from Harvard and knew how to manage a business.

"You keep 'em coming, and I'll put 'em where your customers can get 'em."

Gunther left the man's office shaking his head. Four million copies sold in three short weeks. Even counting what it cost him to produce the video game and get it to stores, he'd made sixteen million dollars net off that one product. Over sixteen times his net worth three months earlier. Frieda Davis had inspired that game, and if he saw her again, he'd make her a present of something valuable. *Leon Farrell, how I wish you were alive to eat the crow I would delight in serving you.*

He reached his car, put his hand in his pocket for his keys, and, along with them, he pulled out a yellow slip of paper that he was about to throw away when he noticed the handwriting on it. A flawless script as might be composed by someone who had studied calligraphy. He stared at it until he remembered the writer and how the slip of paper got into his pocket.

Drops of rain reminded him to unlock the door

and get into the automobile. He put the key in the ignition but didn't turn it. While the rain pelted the car, he made up his mind and dialed the phone number on the yellow slip.

"Hello, Caroline. This is Gunther Farrell. I would have called you weeks ago, but I went on a fishing trip and came down with pneumonia. I'm just back to myself."

"What a surprise this is, Gunther. It's nice to hear from you. I am terribly sorry that you've been ill. How are you now?"

"I'm my old self and very happy about it. Would you have dinner with me one evening? Soon?"

"I'd like that very much. I had about concluded that I wouldn't be hearing from you, and I'm glad you called, because I thought we got on well that one time we were together."

"So did I, and that's why I want to see you again. I have a deadline Wednesday, so I can be free Wednesday evening."

"Oh."

"Wait a minute. We can have dinner again Friday, Saturday, and Sunday evenings, but I want to see you soon, and Wednesday's my earliest free day."

Her laughter floated to him through the wires. "You're smart. I was indeed about to conclude that, to your mind, I was only good for a midweek date. Wednesday it is." She gave him her address.

"Thanks, I'll be there at six-thirty in a jacket and tie."

"Wonderful. That tells me how to dress. I'll look forward to it."

"So will I." Maybe he'd finally begun to get his

life together. He was thirty-four years old and had never had a satisfying relationship with a woman. He'd had plenty of girls, but every one wanted to go to the best restaurant, have the best seat at a football game or tennis match, get the most expensive seat at a concert. He blew out a long breath. He was not a stingy man, but it irked him when a date told him where she wanted to sit at an event. At least Caroline didn't ask where he'd take her to dinner or suggest a restaurant.

If he was lucky, Caroline and he would have common interests, and, most importantly, they would care for each other's well-being. He did not want a woman who had to have the latest fashion, belong to numerous social clubs, and attend every big social function. And he disliked social leeches like Lissa, women whose criteria for a mate consisted solely of his ability to take care of them financially. He wanted a woman who loved him and needed him for things other than financial support. *But I know better than to put too much hope in this. The higher your expectations, the longer you wait for their realization.* Well, he'd waited this long, and though he wanted to settle down and start a family, he'd continue to wait till he was sure he'd found the right woman.

At home that evening, Gunther asked Mirna how she knew Frieda. "Well, Mr. G., I've known Frieda ten years. I worked for a family in Baltimore, and Frieda came to take care of the man's mother. Frieda took care of that old lady like she woulda her own mother. She amazed everybody, even the man what hired her. That old lady loved the ground Frieda walked on. Frieda a real nice person, but if you mistreat her, look out. She don't take no tea for the fever, Mr. G. I know she good-looking, and some men fall for they nurses, but you ain't—"

He interrupted her. "Slow down, Mirna. I asked how you knew her. I didn't ask for a reference, and I am not interested in her as a woman. Got that?"

"Yes, sir. You jes never can tell. Right now, she doing a good deed."

Frieda had given herself a month to care for her birth mother without charge, but after that, she'd have to start earning, because she had to pay the rent on her apartment and save what she could for the house she hoped to buy someday. She had been saving for that house—sometimes as little as fifty cents at a time—since she got her first paycheck, nineteen years earlier. That afternoon, she sat with her mother in a rocking chair on the screened-in back porch of the house Coreen Treadwell shared with her husband.

"Would you like some lemonade?" Frieda asked Coreen. "You'd never drink a drop of anything if I didn't insist. You have to stay hydrated."

"I don't really like water, though I know I should drink it," Coreen told her. "You know," she went on, "I'm kind of glad I got sick. If I hadn't, you and I would never have gotten to know each other. I hope you've forgiven me."

"I'm the one who needed forgiveness," Frieda said. "What happened to me was not your fault. You had already suffered more cruelty than I could have imagined, and I added to the pain. I'm

sorry I did what I did, but I know I'd do it again."
She didn't care to rehash that story and changed
the subject. "A man on a motorcycle sideswiped me
on the highway recently, spun my car all around and
didn't even pause. I got enough information about
him to cause him plenty of trouble, and when I get
ready, I will."

"How much did it cost to fix your car?"

"Oh, don't worry about that. Eric took care of it.
He's a really nice person."

"I see that you like Eric, and I'm glad for that.
Have you forgiven Glen?"

Frieda locked her hands behind her head,
braced her feet on the floor, and moved the rocker
back and forth in a soothing rhythm. "Forgive
Glen for what? He didn't do as much to me as I did
to him. We forgave each other. It's all over."

"I'm so glad. I've worried plenty about that. Maybe
I *will* have some lemonade. I don't know what I
would have done without you, Frieda. You've made
my recovery so pleasant, almost like a nice vacation."

"It is a vacation. You'll be back at work in another month."

"God willing. I sure hope so."

And in another month, she'd be back at the
hospital doing whatever the registered nurses
thought was beneath them. If she ever got a few
pennies ahead, she was going to school and get
her RN. She said as much to Coreen.

"Soon as I can, I'm gon' quit work, go to college, and get my RN. It took me a while to get my
LPN, 'cause I didn't work hard at it, but I'm sure
gon' work hard at that RN."

"I know nursing is hard work, and you have to

be exhausted at the end of the day," Coreen said, "but can't you take a couple of courses in the evenings after work? Then, when you're able to go full-time, it won't take you so long."

"I never thought of that. I can drive to Towson in no time. It's got a great program for nurses. Well, this is my day. Five years from now, you gon' see that RN insignia on my cap, my collar, and everywhere else I can put it."

Coreen's hearty laugh was the response she sought to her comment. She got up, went to the kitchen, got a pitcher of cold lemonade, and gave a glass of it to Coreen. "It sure is good to see you drink that down to the last drop. I won't feel so badly about leaving you at the end of the week."

"We'll be able to manage. All I want is for us to keep in close touch. You call me, even if you don't have anything to say. I want to hear from you."

Frieda took the glass from Coreen, put it on the little table beside the woman's chair, and stared down at her. "Is there gon' be some reason why you can't call me sometime, too?"

Both of them laughed, and Coreen reached out and grasped Frieda's hand. "If we lose touch, it will never be because I didn't try to keep you close to me."

The sound of the front door opening relieved Frieda of the need to respond to Coreen's obvious quest for a closer mother-daughter relationship. Frieda went to see who came in and was glad for the excuse to ignore Coreen's remark. *I'm not ready to cross that bridge,* she said to herself, *and that's a thing I couldn't fake.*

Three days later, at the month's end, Frieda stood at an ironing board, pressing her uniform—

she preferred cotton uniforms to synthetic ones—and talking with Coreen, who sat nearby in a rocker.

"I know I can earn more in private duty, but it means working twelve-hour shifts all the time. In the hospital, I work from seven to three, five days a week. The trouble is with the wages. I won't earn half as much at the hospital as Mr. Farrell paid me. I declare, that is one nice man."

"As who paid you? Who did you say?"

"Mr. Farrell. He's super to work for, and, Lord, that man looks good enough to eat. I'm gon' pack these now, so I'll be ready when Eric comes."

She packed her suitcases, came back downstairs to Coreen, and sat down. She realized that she'd been sitting there five minutes, and Coreen hadn't said a word. *Something's out of gear here,* Frieda thought. *But if I did or said something wrong, she'll have to tell me, 'cause I sure ain't gon' ask her.* Eric arrived, and Frieda would ordinarily have had dinner with them before leaving, but as Coreen remained withdrawn, Frieda told Eric that she had an appointment and would have to skip dinner.

To make sure that a rupture of her relationship with Coreen wouldn't come from any deliberate action on her part, Frieda leaned down and kissed Coreen's cheek. "I'm gonna miss you," she said, and meant it.

She couldn't know that the mention of the name Farrell took Coreen back thirty-seven years to some of the most miserable moments of her life.

Carson sat on a log beside the Patapsco River, picking up pebbles and throwing them as far as he could into the barely moving river. After an hour, he got up, dusted off his trousers, and started back to his car. His gaze took in a huge hollow log that appeared old and nearly white from the ravages of the weather. He went to the log for a closer look and determined that it was no more than a shell. He kicked it and wished he hadn't, for the outside of the log proved as strong as if it were green and freshly felled.

He walked on slowly, trying to summon that idea that teased at the edge of his mind. "This won't do," he said. "I've never had anything beat me like this." He got into his car, started the engine, flipped on the radio, and headed for his office. If he could just get a handle on that something that should be as clear as his hand before him.

"Picking low cotton," Muddy Waters's voice rang out, "sleeping in a hollow log. One more bottle of moonshine, and I—"

A hollow. Some place in that house had a hidden closet, a hidden attic, a gap between the floor and the ceiling. That was it; that was the idea that had been sitting at the edge of his mind for weeks that he hadn't been able to grasp. A devious man like Leon Farrell wouldn't hide anything under a carpet, but he'd make a hole in the floor, cover it up, and camouflage it. Definitely. Carson didn't hear the remainder of Muddy Waters's song. His mind pitched into high gear, and he pulled over, nearly out of his mind with excitement, and dialed Lucas Hamilton's cell phone number. A topflight architect, the man lived in North Carolina, but he knew how to fly.

"Lucas, this is Carson Montgomery. Got a minute?"

"For you? You bet."

He told Lucas briefly of his problem finding the will. "I have a feeling it's between the floor and the ceiling or someplace like that. I don't know why he'd do it, except that he believed at least one of his children was greedy and needy enough to find it no matter where he put it. Can you help me with it? I have the keys and the permission to search the house."

"Sure I can, as long as the house was built after 1940. Earlier than that, I'd have to spend too much time on it. I'd be happier if one of the heirs was there when I entered."

"I can certainly arrange that."

"All right. I'll be at your office tomorrow morning at nine o'clock."

"Great. I have a feeling I'll be able to wind this thing up, and soon. Thanks, buddy."

"Glad to do it."

He telephoned Gunther and told him that he had an architect whom he wanted to look at the house with a view to determining where a person could hide a will. "He wants you there when we enter, no doubt as legal protection. He'll be at my office tomorrow morning at nine."

"I can make that. Let's hope Edgar doesn't show up."

"He may, because he's in town."

"I'll see if I can check his plans," Gunther said. "Edgar can be disruptive."

"Tell me about it. I'll be there at nine tomorrow morning."

So far so good. Now if Providence would only play on Gunther's team, Edgar wouldn't be in Ellicott City before noon. As luck would have it, Edgar met them on his motorcycle several blocks before they reached the Farrell house and evidently didn't recognize Carson's car.

"I hope you're able to help," Gunther said to Lucas Hamilton. "This has been one mind-boggling puzzle." They shook hands. "I won't stay, Carson, because I'd only be in the way. Be seeing you."

"Seems like a nice enough guy," Lucas said after Gunther left, "so what's the problem?"

"He's an all-right guy, from what I've seen of him. It's his brother who's a pain in the ass. He lives here. He was that motorcyclist we met a few blocks before we got here. Trust me, he's shady, at least according to my experience with him."

Lucas examined the floors in Leon Farrell's quarters. "I'm satisfied that these floors have not been tampered with in any way. Now, let's get to the walls." After having examined half of the wall in Leon Farrell's study/den, Lucas called Carson.

"Come here, man. I can see without touching it that this is a false wall." He pointed to the wood paneling on one side of the room. "Whatever you're looking for is probably right here. This entire wall has been paneled in such a way as to camouflage this ruse. Let me see if I can find the key to it."

After searching more than half an hour, Lucas said, "Well, what do you know? It opens electronically. Press the panel in this spot and it slides open."

The wall slid back and Carson let out a loud, sharp whistle. "Man, will you look at that! Nearly a hundred robots."

"Was he a robot freak, or did he make them?" Lucas asked.

"Both, from what I gather." Carson knocked his

right fist into his left palm repeatedly, shaking his head as he did so. "Man, just imagine! I would never have found this. I've searched this room for hours. Well, I'll have to check every one of them and every other inch of this hideaway. Wonder how you close this thing."

Lucas pressed the panel in the spot that opened it, and it closed. "Remember that spot," he said to Carson. "You've got your work cut out. There're numerous places in here to hide a will. Before you find it, you'll probably have solved some other mystery."

They closed the house, and Carson drove with Lucas to the Frigate for lunch. After placing their orders, Lucas leaned back in his chair and a happy grin floated over his face.

"It just occurred to me that you and I have succeeded on every project we've collaborated on. And there have been many. Hats off to us, buddy."

"Hadn't thought of that. How's Willis?"

"Getting rich. His ship's come in. He's a great guy and a true friend."

"That he is," Carson said. "How are Susan and those two great kids of yours? Rudy and Nathan think you walk on water."

"They're all well. Marriage is wonderful, Carson. Find the right woman, and your world will finally sit up straight and spin smoothly. Of course, you have to love each other, and there has to be good chemistry. Then, if the two of you have a lot in common, promote each other and complement each other, and if you're both fully committed to the marriage and to each other, it should be a beautiful ride, man."

"Sounds like the best of all possible worlds," Carson said, aware that his words and tone had the ring of bitterness.

"Come on, Carson. Darnell was concerned with Darnell and no one else. Thank God you didn't have any children. A woman who wants children seems to me a better bet for a wife than one who doesn't."

"She didn't tell me she didn't want any until I suggested we start our family. Next time, I'll get that straight before I buy a ring."

"Good idea. Anybody in the picture?"

Carson reached in his breast pocket for a cigarette and remembered that he gave up smoking years earlier. "Yes, there is, and when I see her tonight, I'm going to ask her that question. I think she's precisely what I need, but we've got some important exploring to do before I take that big step."

"I wish you the very best. You know that."

"Thanks." Carson asked the waiter for the bill, paid it, and looked at his watch. "We'd better head for the airport."

Even with driving at seventy miles an hour in a fifty-mile zone and occasionally beating traffic by driving along the shoulder, Carson got to the Baltimore / Washington International Thurgood Marshall Airport a mere thirty minutes before Lucas's flight.

"Could we possibly have been more circumspect when we were teenagers?" Lucas asked Carson as the car came to a stop.

"I never had my wild days," Carson said. "Maybe it's time. I'll expect your bill in the mail. The estate will pay for it, so be sure and send it. I am in your debt, and I can't possibly thank you enough."

"I was glad to do it. Consulting is a lot easier than drafting." They enjoyed a good laugh at that, knuckle bumped each other, and said good-bye.

On the drive back to Ellicott City, Carson began to plot ways to examine the robots without the interference of any member of the Farrell family. To his mind, it would be unfair to give any of the siblings an upper hand. Edgar would raise hell, and his objection would have merit, but if he found that will, he intended to give it to Donald Riggs, the executor of the estate. Now he had to find out as much as he could about Edgar's schedule, because he definitely was not going to search through those robots with Edgar in the house.

Shirley dressed with special care for her date with Carson that evening. She wanted to appear soft and feminine without looking like a sexpot. Her size 34-D bosom took away some of her options; finding a dress that didn't expose half of it had proved difficult. She'd begun to wonder why dress designers didn't quit flirting with nudity and tell women to go for it all the way. She'd found a sleeveless, V-necked dress with inserts in the skirt that flared below the hips, emphasizing her flat belly and rounded hips. The soft melon color made her cheeks glow. A teardrop diamond, tiny but real, drew attention to her cleavage, and with her hair down to her shoulders and dangling marcasite earrings, she knew she looked great.

"Where are you going dressed up like that?" Gunther asked her when she came down the stairs, her intention being to answer the door before he got to it.

"I'm going out. Why?"

"Who's the lucky guy?"

The flame of irritability slowly furled up in her. He allowed himself the right to make a hideous mistake with that woman Lissa and yet he questioned her association with Carson Montgomery.

She faced him squarely. "I'm going to dinner with Carson Montgomery. We're both over thirty and neither of us is married. Is there some reason why I should ask your permission? We've been on this road before, Gunther."

He spread his hands, palms out. "Look, sis, for all you know, that guy is after your inheritance. All I'm asking you to do is go slowly. We don't know the guy. Edgar picked him up, and you know Edgar's taste in people."

"Listen here, Gunther," she said, her temper rising, "you checked his credentials and his reputation as a detective. What more do you need? Both are an open book. He's an officer of the law and has been for some years. If you're so skeptical about him, I'll stand right here while you grill him, and the first time I see you with a woman, I'll return the favor. I'm also going to find a rental apartment while I look for something to purchase." She could see that she had upset him with that threat, but she meant it.

"All right. All right. No point in getting angry. You know I'm only thinking about your well-being. That's all I've ever done. It won't be easy, but I promise I'll lay off the guy unless I see something I don't like. If I do—"

"Okay, but be careful about what you don't like."

"He's after you," Gunther said, "and I'm a man, so—"

She lowered her left eye in a squint. "I wish I could know what you guys mean when you boast that you're a man. It doesn't explain anything to me. Of course Carson is after me, as you put it. I wonder what his mama would say about the fact that I'm after *him.*" Gunther's eyes widened, and she decided to pile it on. "Oh, yes, and I'll catch him, provided he doesn't catch me first."

"Shirley!"

His intended reprimand was forgotten, for the doorbell rang. She winked at her brother and sped to the door.

"Hi." She gazed up at Carson and imagined that she drooled. "My, but it's nice to see you."

He stepped inside, and with one arm around her waist, kissed her on the mouth. "Hi. If I had two free hands, I'd have done a more thorough job of that." He handed her a bunch of American Beauty roses.

"These are so beautiful. I love flowers. You're a very sweet man. Thanks." She reached up and kissed him on the cheek. Then, having satisfied herself that she'd taught Gunther a lesson, she looked where she knew he still stood, smiled, and said, "Carson, you remember Gunther, my brother."

"Of course I do." He extended his hand to Gunther. "Thanks for helping me out this morning."

"Any luck?" Gunther asked him in a tone and manner that said it was a dutiful question not motivated by curiosity.

"Not yet, but if you can find out when Edgar is out of town, I may luck out. I want to spend an entire day there working without losing my focus."

"He said he was going back to Las Vegas. I'll let you know."

Carson eased an arm around Shirley's waist. "Thanks for your help. Have a good evening."

They hadn't yet reached his car when he said, "Were you and Gunther having some words?"

She nearly tripped up. "Why do you ask? Are you clairvoyant? I was giving him a lecture about staying out of my business."

"He doesn't want you to date? Or he doesn't want you to date *me*? Which is it?"

"Gunther is overprotective of me, and he has been for as long as I can remember. When I was little, I trailed behind him like a lace train behind a bride. After we lost our mother when I was twelve, he was everything to me. He got me a date for my senior prom, helped me choose my dress, and then helped me select a college. Those don't begin to suggest how lost I'd have been if he hadn't looked after me. But I try to tell him that I'm grown now."

He helped her into the car and fastened her seat belt. "What was his complaint tonight, if you don't mind telling me?"

"He thinks I'm moving too fast with you."

"Yeah? If he said that to me, I'd tell him you aren't moving fast enough."

"You wouldn't."

"Trust me. If a man speaks his mind to me, I have no problem dishing it out to him in return. I have to tell you, though, that you're fortunate to have a brother like Gunther. He may be a busybody, but he's a respectable man, and he cares about you. Enough about your brother. You look so beautiful tonight. I'd love to show you off. It makes a guy proud to have a woman like you."

"And I'm proud that you want to be with me. Speaking of looking good, if I knew how to whistle, I'd have done so, loudly and sharply, when I opened the door tonight." She tried to whistle. If truth were known, seeing him in a pair of tight jeans made her want to pant for relief. The man was lethal.

For a few minutes, he drove down Columbia Pike without speaking. He appeared to have come to a decision when, without glancing at her, he said, "I've got an idea. What do you say we have dinner in Columbia and then drop by to see some friends? I hadn't planned that, but they invited me and weren't happy when I declined. I think you would enjoy meeting them."

"I'd love it. I want to meet your friends."

At the elegant restaurant, the sight of a crown roast of pork on a table with eight or ten people made her mouth water, but she ordered shrimp Diablo with saffron rice, because she didn't want to chance soiling her dress with the pork gravy. But she vowed that one day she would drive over to that restaurant alone for lunch and feast on the spaghetti vongole at a time when she wouldn't worry about the slices of garlic that littered the dish of tiny clams, olive oil, and parsleyed noodles.

"Would you like wine?" Carson asked her. "I'd love some, but I don't drink when I'm driving."

"Thank you, but I think I'll skip it." She didn't want to enjoy it when he couldn't.

"Remember me telling you that I love to please you?" he said. "If I drank some wine, would you?"

"Probably, but I'd prefer not to drink right now."

His gaze sharpened, and he seemed to be reading her. It wasn't the first time he'd done it, so he didn't make her uncomfortable. But she decided to beat him to the draw. "You want to ask me something? I'll tell you if I know the answer. This shrimp is delicious."

A smile played on one side of his mouth. "I'm glad you're enjoying that. It's really good. I wish this cook would teach me how to prepare rice. It's wonderful."

"You didn't answer my question."

"No. I didn't. You said you're thirty-two. Does it bother you that you're entering the period when childbearing can be difficult, or does it matter?"

She understood that he hadn't asked the question he wanted to ask, but that her answer would nonetheless tell him what he wanted to know. She didn't believe in pussyfooting around an important issue, so she handed it to him straight.

"If you are asking whether I want any children, the answer is of course I do. I hope I don't give the impression that I don't want any. I have my heart set on a boy, a girl, and a boy in that order, or, if not, I'll be happy with whatever I get." She gave him a level stare. "By the way, was it by choice that you didn't have any children with your ex-wife?"

"Definitely not by my choice. When I suggested we start a family, she said no way."

"Was that the deal breaker for you?"

"That's something you tell a person before you

marry them. Unfortunately, I hadn't thought to ask her. But she knew I loved children, so . . . Well, no point in rehashing that."

"You can't be an only child, Carson. How many siblings do you have?"

"I don't know how you figured that out, but I have a younger brother. He's a managing electronic engineer with Faulks Engineering, Inc. My father's a chemical engineer. Why did you conclude that I'm not an only child?"

"Because you're so generous, and I'm not talking about money. You give yourself, and you don't judge others harshly. That tells me you're not self-centered. Unless parents work overtime to prevent it, an only child is likely to think of me, myself, and I."

He drained his espresso cup. "I'm glad you think I have a congenial personality. Ready when you are."

She stopped at the women's room, brushed her teeth, combed her hair, rubbed a paper towel over her face in a light buffing, and dabbed some Obsession behind her ears. "Who knows where he's taking me? Thank goodness I put on this dress."

"It isn't too far from here," he said. "I almost wish we hadn't decided to go there. This night is something special. Moonlight, a soft breeze, and not a cloud in the sky. It would be wonderful to walk and . . . and just be together."

"October is my favorite time of the year," she said. "Sixty-five degrees and so calm."

Carson grasped her hand and held it as they walked to his car. He started the engine, but then turned it off and looked squarely at her. Was this happening to him, or was he hallucinating? "You really get to me. You know that? Are you happy when we're together?"

She leaned toward him. "Happy hardly describes what I experience when I'm with you. It's . . . As soon as you leave me, I'm lonely for you."

"I care a lot for you, Shirley, and it's deep."

"I . . . It's mutual, Carson."

Chapter Eight

Carson had never liked big parties at which people stood around drinking and making small talk. If he had to socialize with people not of his own choosing, he'd rather do it at a dinner for not more than eight. In that way, he could at least learn something about those guests he hadn't previously met. He drove into a three-car garage attached to a big redbrick house surrounded by beautifully manicured lawn and shrubs and with tall trees near enough to give it summer shade.

He got out, walked around to Shirley, and rubbed her nose with his thumb. "Woman, you exasperate me sometimes. I wanted to open the door for you. I know you are capable of finding your way out of it, but it's my pleasure to open it for you, and you've cheated me out of it."

"How careless and thoughtless of me," she said, slid back into the car, and closed the door. With her hands lying in her lap and her shoulders relaxed against the back of the seat, she looked at him, her face blooming in an innocent smile. He couldn't shake her, as badly as he wanted to do *something* to her. With the long-ago demise of the caveman culture, he couldn't do what he felt like doing, so he opened the door, held out his hand, and assisted her out of the car.

"I owe you one for that, Shirley."

"I imagine you do, and I can't wait to get it. You *will* make it pleasant, won't you?" She dusted the side of his face with the back of her hand. "Don't look so shocked. If I promised you something, you'd be dying to get it, wouldn't you?"

"Quit while you're ahead, Shirley. For two cents, I'd take you somewhere right now, and . . . Look, this is childish. I'm not going to play smartass with something that's important to me, to both of us."

"You're right. I shouldn't have started that, but you were looking so serious that I couldn't help teasing."

"Teasing? You weren't teasing; you were saying some things you wanted to get off your chest. I told you that I take seriously everything you say, including the things you say in jest. How do I introduce you?"

"My name is Shirley Farrell. You know that."

"May I introduce you as my girl?"

"Oh! I see. But we're not intimate."

He grasped her hand and began walking toward the door. "Intimacy is not a criterion." He didn't like that frown on her face.

"It ought to be. But I like the idea, so why not? What's the matter?" she asked when the air seemed to whoosh out of him.

He wondered if he should believe his ears. "You take some getting used to. I haven't met many women who're as candid as you are, and as I recall,

I encountered those in connection with business matters. Do you realize what you said to me?"

She squeezed his fingers and stars twinkled in her eyes. "Sure I do, and I trust you to be sensible with that information."

"You trust me to . . . I try to be sensible all the time, Shirley. But with these challenges you're throwing at me, it isn't easy." He rang the doorbell.

"Carson! My man, this is great. I was beginning to think you wouldn't get here." The man's gaze shifted to Shirley, and both of his eyebrows shot up. "Mmm. I see there've been some changes made."

"Lester Coleman, this is my girl, Shirley Farrell."

"And what a girl! I'm glad to meet you, Shirley. You two come in and meet folks."

"Hello, Lester. It's nice to meet you."

Carson glanced at her from his peripheral vision. Surely she didn't have a reason for that frosty tone of voice. If Lester noticed it, he didn't make it obvious.

"Where's Alma?" Carson asked the man about his wife.

"She's somewhere around. With all these people, I can't keep up with her." Lester introduced them to people who would forever be a blur to Carson, for he didn't attempt to remember their names or their faces. He heard Shirley ask a woman if she knew where the bathroom was.

"There's one down here and another in the basement, but if you're in a hurry, I suggest you go upstairs and turn left." Shirley thanked the woman and turned to Carson.

"Excuse me for a couple of minutes, and please don't move from here, because I'd never find you."

She returned a few minutes later wearing a strange facial expression. "Do you know a woman who's very fair, has reddish hair, light brown eyes, about my height, a heavy bosom, and real full lips?"

"Yeah. That would be Alma, Lester's wife." Someone slapped him on the back, and he whirled around to find a close friend smiling at him.

"You old son-of-a-gun. If I'd known I'd see you, I wouldn't have given my wife such a hard time about coming here. Carson Montgomery, this is my wife, Francine."

Carson accepted the greeting, put an arm around Shirley's waist, and urged her closer to him. "Richard and Francine Spaldwood Peterson, this is my girl, Shirley Farrell. Shirley, Richard has been everything from an ambassador to the secretary-general of an international organization with headquarters in Geneva, Switzerland. Francine and I are in the same profession."

Shirley's eyes lit up with eager sparkles. "You're a detective? How exciting! Are you a cop, too?"

Francine laughed and nodded. "I know. People say I look too tender to be either, but if they mess with me, they have it confirmed that you can't judge a book by its cover."

"Excuse me," Carson said, mainly to Shirley. "I'm going up the stairs. Do I turn left or right?"

"You'd better go down to the basement," Shirley said.

Strange, he thought. But she'd just been up there, so he'd do as she suggested. It pleased him that Shirley remained with his friends, Richard and Francine Peterson. He had worked with Francine on several high-risk jobs during which they became good friends. He'd often wondered if he could work with a partner he didn't like, since his life could depend on that person's loyalty. He had discovered that, as a detective, Francine was as sharp as any man and better than most.

Richard put a hand on Carson's shoulder. "We'd love for you and Shirley to visit us over on the shore. We live in Ocean Pines right on the ocean, not far from Ocean City. It's idyllic. We wouldn't live anyplace else."

"And we have a big house that we built with the intention of having guests," Francine added.

"Thanks for the thought," he said. "We both love the water. Shirley is public relations director for the Paradise Cruise Line, and she's away most weekends, but if she's willing, we'll work something out."

"Please come," Francine said to Shirley. "I promise you'll want to come back." Shirley thanked her, and it pleased Carson that they seemed to like each other. They talked for a while, but the smell of liquor and cigarette smoke got to him. He hated to disturb Shirley, who seemed engrossed in her conversation with Francine, but he longed for fresh air. Finally he caught Shirley's eye and, as if she'd read his thoughts, she said to Francine, "Carson can take just so much of scenes like this, so I suppose we'll be leaving." She smiled at him. "Am I right?"

"As usual, you're on the button."

They told their friends and the host good night, and it surprised Shirley that he didn't appear to be concerned that they were about to leave and hadn't greeted their hostess. A few blocks from Route 29, which would take them to Ellicott City, he turned into the parking lot of a small café and parked.

"Let's go in here. I'd like some coffee."

"Fine. I'd like some, too, and maybe some lemon custard ice cream."

He ordered coffee and the ice cream for both of them, leaned back in the booth, and asked the question that had plagued him all evening. "Why were you so cool to Lester when we arrived?"

"Because I don't like men who flirt with their friend's date."

He stared at her for a second and then laughter rumbled out of him. "Sorry," he said when he'd brought the laughter under control. "I'd forgotten that Lester is a compulsive womanizer. He'll go after any woman who isn't a blood relative. You certainly cooled him off."

She pulled air through her front teeth, surprising him, because he hadn't previously known her to do that. "He should have been upstairs cooling off his wife."

"*What?* What do you . . . That's right. You described her to me. Where did you see her?"

"On top of a man who wasn't Lester. And since her husband didn't seem worried about her absence, I suspect they have an open marriage. I met three couples there who I'd like to see again, but not those two."

"Different strokes for different folks. If what you suspect is true, I'm surprised at Lester. It's been only eight years since he was a certified country bumpkin lured by the sight of every pretty bosom he saw. I'm ready when you are."

He drove through the winding roads and along the beautiful waters in Patapsco Park, lit by a frosty-looking late-autumn moon. "I wonder why I never paid attention to nature," he said as he drove beneath low-hanging evergreen branches through which the moonlight made intricate and beautiful patterns. "When you get right down to it, nature offers the best sedative, the best de-stressing medicine a person needs. And if this environment doesn't seduce a woman, a man had better admit that he doesn't have a damned thing going for him."

"Did you think you had to bring me here in order to seduce me?"

"Why would I do that?" he said, his tone suddenly frosty. "You've already told me you can't wait to get what I owe you."

"Oh, Carson. That sounds terrible. I was being flippant. When it comes to sophistication, you're far ahead of me."

"I know that, and it's one reason why I don't want to engage in one-upmanship with you. It isn't natural, and it can be hurtful."

"But I have a habit of jostling with people I care about."

"And you care about me?"

"Yes, I do."

Straight from the shoulder. He hoped she was as honest a lover as she was in respect to other things. "Don't you care about me?" she asked, her voice a little shaky. His antenna went up. Could it be that her bravado masked insecurity? He hoped not, for it was a part of her that he liked a great deal. Her cell phone rang.

"Go on and answer your cell phone," he said when it continued to ring. A rueful smile slid over his face. "I won't feel neglected."

She fished around in her pocketbook and found the phone. "Edgar! Hi. Where are you?"

"At the Breakers Harbor Hotel. I'm about to go on. When are you going back to Fort Lauderdale? Gunther's getting so highfalutin that I can't talk to . . . What the devil? Hey, I smell smoke. That's an alarm. I gotta get out of here."

"What? Where are you in that hotel?" She heard a dial tone. "Carson. Please. We . . . I have to go to the Breakers Harbor Hotel in the Inner Harbor. Edgar said it's a . . . that he smelled smoke." She repeated what her brother told her. "Suppose he doesn't get out."

"He will get out, sweetheart. Don't worry. Damn these bucket seats. Move closer to me."

She didn't remember biting her nails since she flunked her eighth-grade cooking class. Every nerve in her body seemed torched. Her legs and thighs perspired profusely, and when she tried to answer Carson, her teeth chattered so badly that she couldn't get out a word.

"Lord, p-please d-don't let anything h-happen to Edgar. L-let him g-get out of th-there," she finally stammered. Carson switched from Route 29 that led to Ellicott City, took the transfer to Route 95, and headed for Baltimore.

"Those are ambulance sirens," she said. "What are we going to do?"

"Easy, sweetheart. We don't know that he's in trouble. Let's send out positive vibes and hope for the best." He parked a block from the hotel, because the police wouldn't let him drive into the block. They jumped out of the car, and he grabbed her hand and raced with her to the middle of the block in which the hotel stood. There, two policemen stopped them.

"My brother's in that hotel," she screamed, and

immediately Carson's arm eased around her and brought her closer to him. Still holding Shirley firmly to his body, he handed the policeman his ID card.

"It's a mess up there, sir," the policeman said. "I think you ought to leave the lady here."

"D-did they get everybody out?" she asked the policeman.

"I don't know, ma'am. That's an awfully big building."

She groped for the lamppost and leaned against it, fearing that her liquid limbs would give way. Holding a facial tissue to her nose, she blew as hard as she could in an effort to get rid of the acrid smoke and the odor of assorted burning objects.

"Sit on this, ma'am," a fireman said, and turned a bucket upside down.

She sank to it gladly. "Thank you so much."

Closer to the fire-ravaged hotel, EMS workers wheeled someone up to an ambulance, and she jumped up. But she couldn't determine whether the person was alive. She worried her bottom lip. Why hadn't Carson come back?

A third-floor window belched thick black smoke, and Shirley sprang up and raced toward the hotel and into the steel-like body of Carson Montgomery.

"You can't go there. It's too dangerous," he told her. "You'll be in the way, and you could cost someone's life." He pulled her aside as a man staggered out of the building and collapsed on the sidewalk.

A fireman raced to the fallen man. "How are you? Can you breathe?" When the man gasped for breath, the fireman covered his nose and mouth with an oxygen mask. Shirley clung to Carson, unable to control her trembling. If Edgar had gotten out of the hotel, wouldn't he call? As if he'd read her mind, Carson asked her for Edgar's cell phone number and dialed it.

"Hello."

"Edgar? Where are you, man? Shirley's going crazy thinking that you might have perished in this hotel fire."

"No way. Tell Shirley not to worry. I accidentally found the back way out. Unfortunately, a few people didn't make it."

"Why didn't you call her, man? She's on her way out of her mind. Can I tell her you're all right?" He listened to Edgar's lame explanation, balling his left fist in frustration. He didn't countenance violent behavior, but he'd love to slam that self-centered guy against a brick wall.

"Me? I'm cool," Edgar said. "I'm almost home. I was going to call you in the morning. Is around nine okay?"

"Yeah. Sure." He hung up and stared at Shirley.

"I know what you're thinking, Carson, but it's no surprise to me. I love my brother, but I don't think I know anybody who's as selfish and as self-centered as he is. I don't know why he's like that."

A sharp explosion drew their attention to the building as a third-floor frontispiece fell to the street, barely missing an ambulance. "I need to see if there's anything I can do to help," Carson said. "Can you drive my car to Gunther's place? I'll get it later."

She looked into his determined gaze and saw that the need to help was intrinsic to his being as a man. Yet, knowing that he might risk his life decelerated the pace of her heartbeat and she had to gasp for breath.

He looked her in the eye. "I could save some-one's life."

She stiffened her back and smiled. "Give me the keys. I'll have coffee ready when you get there. Please be careful."

He handed her the car keys, brushed a kiss over her mouth, and raced to the hotel, where people tried to find their way around the chunks of con-crete that nearly blocked the front exit. She stood as he'd left her and watched him bend down and begin to clear the debris from the doorway.

There's a reason why I love that man, she said to herself. *If he can do that, I can certainly do this.*

She got into his car, started to drive off, and stopped. She'd just told herself that she loved Car-son Montgomery, but she had never even imag-ined that she loved a man, *any man.* She moved away from the curb and headed for Ellicott City.

"Where's Carson?" Gunther asked when she walked into his apartment. "Did you two have a spat?"

She walked past Gunther to the living room, sat down, took a deep breath, and let the air swoosh out of her. "It's a long story." After telling him about Edgar and the hotel fire, she asked him, "Did Edgar call you?"

"Not since last week. Thank God he got out of that hotel safely. Where'd you park Carson's BMW?"

"Half a block from the front door."

"I hope he doesn't attempt any heroics at that fire scene. You care a lot for him, don't you?"

She looked at her brother with what she knew was an appeal for understanding and acceptance. "A lot. An awful lot."

Gunther shoved his hands into his trouser pockets, looked into the distance, and said, "I don't doubt that he's a good man and that you'd have a hard time finding a better one, but . . . how does he feel about you?"

"It was mutual from the second we saw each other, and it's developed into something deeper. He shows me that he cares. I know he's his own man, and I accept that."

"You'd better. A man his age rarely, if ever, changes. Incidentally, Frieda called. I think she'd like to come back, but there aren't any sick people here." His white teeth glistened against his smooth brown skin. "And thank God for that. She's really a wonderful nurse."

"So you said. I hope she gets a good job. I've been thinking that we need another nurse on my ship, the *Mercury*, but she's not an RN. Oh, well."

"Can't you find a way around that?"

"That would be up to the supervisor of our clinics, but I'll put it to them. Write me a letter of recommendation, okay? How's her mother? Did she say?"

"Yeah. The doctor thinks her mother may be able to return to work in about a month. Frieda's not without a job; the hospital is anxious to have her back. She said she needs a better-paying job."

"Okay. I'll see what I can do. I promised Carson I'd have coffee ready when he came for his car, so I'd better get in there and see if I can find something to go with that coffee. We finished dinner almost four hours ago."

Gunther walked toward the stairs, stopped, and looked at her. "Suppose it's three o'clock in the morning when he gets here?"

She'd be up if he didn't get there until daybreak, and the flex of her shoulder in a slight shrug confirmed it. "When did you know me to fail to keep my word?"

"Am I invited for coffee?"

She didn't answer, for she knew it was one of his tongue-in-cheek efforts to needle her. When the doorbell rang a little over two hours later, she rushed to it, put the chain in place, and peeped out.

"Carson! What on earth?"

His grin did little to reassure her as she stared at his torn, sooty, and sagging clothing. "You said you'd have coffee ready for me."

She welcomed him with her arms open, pulling him as tightly to her as her strength would allow. "My Lord. You were in that burning building. Come on in and sit down." She pointed to an oversized leather chair.

"Thank you for waiting up for me. There were times when I thought I'd never get here. I'd love to wash my face and hands."

"I always do what I promised," she said, taking his hand and walking with him to the lavatory near the foyer. "Go have a seat while I bring the coffee." She turned on the coffeemaker, warmed some biscuits, and put a glass of water on the tray that she'd prepared earlier.

"This is wonderful," he said when she placed the coffee, warm biscuits, ham, butter, and jam on the coffee table. "I'm fine, just exhausted." He took a big swallow of coffee, put the cup down, and tasted a buttered biscuit. "Hmm. Honey, this hits the spot. I'm hungry, but I think I needed pampering as much as I needed food. I'm exhausted, but I feel great, if that makes any sense. After I helped clear away that rubble, I dragged six people out of that death trap."

She refilled his coffee cup and brought it back to him. "What happened? Don't they have alarms in that hotel? The fire seemed small enough at first to allow people to get out without difficulty."

"Apparently the alarm in some of the guest rooms didn't work. And you can bet some of the guests had been drinking and were in a deep sleep, so the alarm didn't awaken them." He ate another biscuit and ham sandwich. "I know I had a big dinner with you, but right now, I'm starved. That was more manual labor than I'd done in years."

He finished eating, leaned back, and took a long, deep breath.

"Do you want to spend the night here?" she asked him. "We have a guest room."

His gaze, soft and warm, didn't prepare her for his answer. "Thanks. But when I spend the night under the same roof as you, we'll sleep in the same bed." She knew her eyes had widened, but he acted as if they hadn't. "I'd better finish this and go. I've got a busy day starting in six and a half hours."

At the door, he kissed her without passion, but she didn't mind. She'd learned more about him that night than in the previous months she'd known him. He was the man for her. And he'd find that will, too, because he wouldn't let that, or anything like it, conquer him.

* * *

Minutes after Carson reached his office the next morning, his receptionist buzzed him. "Mr. Edgar Farrell here to see you."

Carson stared at Edgar, annoyed at the intrusion and not bothering to hide it. "I thought you asked if you could call me. What can I do for you that requires a visit?"

Edgar took a seat and crossed his knees. "I like to talk business in person. Talking on the phone can land you in trouble."

Immediately alert, Carson sat forward, his eyes narrowed. "What do you have to say to me that could land you in trouble?"

"Look, man. I'm going back to Vegas day after tomorrow morning, because the fire gutted two floors of that hotel. It's closed, and my gig there is up. I'm the one who engaged you for this job, so I'm telling you that if you find that will and it's unfavorable to me, don't tell Gunther and Shirley about it."

As little as he thought of Edgar, he hadn't expected him to sink to that level. He wondered how far the man would go. "How would I get paid?" he asked, appearing to consider the proposition. "If I don't give the will to the lawyer, it won't be probated, and if I do give it to him, he'll share the contents with your siblings."

"I can get somebody else to probate it. I've got contacts."

"Why doesn't that surprise me." Carson stood and leaned over Edgar, almost touching him. "I'm an officer of the law, and even if I weren't, I would not compromise my integrity and ruin my life by

going in cahoots with someone who has no principles. Miss Marks will show you out."

"I'll fire you."

"You can't. Read the contract that you signed.
If you make one more underhanded suggestion to
me, I will terminate the contract and expose you
to boot. Please leave. Now!"

Go easy, his conscience warned. That guy could
someday be your brother-in-law. He grimaced
from the pain of that thought. Another reason why
he should watch his steps very carefully.

The next morning, Shirley dragged herself out
of bed and began sorting out her clothes for the
next cruise. When trips were shorter—as her next
one was—customers seemed to get more involved
with on-board events and were less picayune about
little things. Her cell phone rang and she glanced
at the caller ID before answering. She didn't welcome a call from Edgar, because she was still annoyed with him.

She answered without enthusiasm. "Hello."

"It's me, sis. Edgar. I'm headed back to Vegas tomorrow, and I . . . uh . . . thought I'd let you know."

"Thanks. Have a good time." If she sounded dis-
interested, she couldn't help it.

"A . . . uh . . . brother out there owes me a few
thousand—"

She didn't let him finish. "Yes, and I imagine his
first name is 'slot.' You still owe me three thousand, seven hundred dollars—the seven hundred
you borrowed over a year ago—and I am not lending you any more. Have a safe—"

He hung up. She sat down on the edge of her bed and tried to exhale her anger. When would it end? After wiping away her tears, she said to herself as she got up, "I don't have to go down with a sinking ship, because I can swim."

"I'm having waffles for breakfast," Mirna said when Shirley walked into the kitchen. "Mr. G will be down in a minute. You want some, or you still trying to make your waistline disappear?"

"I want some of those waffles. Yours are the best. I'll set the table."

After breakfast with Gunther and Mirna, she walked up the stairs along with Gunther. "It's been years since you trailed me up the stairs. At home, you did that when you either wanted something special or you wanted to tell me something in confidence. What is it?"

She told him about her call from Edgar. "It was so unpleasant. As soon as he realized that I was not going to give him money, he hung up. No goodbye. Nothing. What's gotten into him?"

Gunther's right arm slid around her shoulder. "I wish I knew. Don't let him upset you, Shirley. Maybe we have to . . . well . . . let him go. I hate to say it, but we can't force Edgar to do what he ought to do and act like a mature man. He had the same opportunities and the same disadvantages that we had. He made his choices, and he's paying for them. I hurt for him, but he won't accept the help he needs. When you're with Carson, pay attention to the little things."

"I do, and especially to the way he behaves when he is not deliberately courting me. In fact, that's what endears him to me. I like the man he is."

* * *

About that time, Carson came to an important decision: He'd give himself one more week in which to find that will. If he failed, he'd cancel the contract and, for the first time, he'd leave a job unresolved. He didn't relish the idea, but he didn't plan to continue looking for a needle in a haystack.

The morning after Edgar left Ellicott City for Las Vegas, Carson arrived at the Farrell home shortly after nine, locked the doors, fastened the chains, and went upstairs to Leon Farrell's den.

He considered not answering his ringing cell phone, but, thinking that his office might want to contact him, he reached into his pocket. A glance told him that Shirley was his caller. He'd prefer not to talk with her right then. She'd ask where he was, and he'd rather she didn't know. He wanted to work without the contribution or the interruption of any Farrell sibling. But on the other hand, he loved hearing her voice. With a word, she could lift his spirits faster than knowing he'd solved whatever problem confronted him.

"Hi, sweetheart."

"Hi, hon. I've just learned that I have to switch travel plans. I have to leave in a couple of hours. I won't be on the *Mercury* this time. I'll be training a new public relations officer for the *Utopia Girl,* our new flagship. The ship sails out of Miami. Here are my phone numbers."

He wrote them down. "What's your route?"

"Colorado, Costa Rica; Puerto Cabezas, Nicaragua; Bahia; Ocho Rios, Jamaica; and back to Miami."

Hmmm. Ocho Rios offered an elegant and attractive setting, and he wasn't a man to lose out on an opportunity. "What if I join you in Ocho Rios and travel back to Miami with you? I'd make my own accommodations."

"I'd love that, but be sure you give me a day's notice."

"As of now, it's a date. I'll give you notice if I can't get accommodations or if some immovable object gets in my way."

"If you have trouble getting accommodations, let me know. I'm fourth-ranking officer on that ship."

"Right on! Are you sure it's all right?"

"Absolutely. I'll be happy if you're with me. Don't you know that?"

"I should, but I take nothing for granted. Besides, it's your work environment, and we'll have to be careful not to compromise your status. I'd hoped we could be together tonight, but man proposes, and God disposes, or so they say. Can you get to the airport all right?"

"Thanks. I've called a car service, and the cruise line foots the bill. I'll miss you."

"Thank God for that. If you wouldn't, I'd be in serious trouble. Take good care of yourself. I'll call you tonight."

He wanted to say more, but they hadn't gotten that far. Still, their conversation left him with a hollow feeling. He put the cell phone back into his pocket and turned his attention to his work. Having talked with Shirley, he didn't have to answer his phone no matter how many times it rang.

As Lucas Hamilton had demonstrated a few days earlier, Carson ran his fingers along the wall until he touched a slightly depressed area; he pressed it and slid the wall panel open. He stared at the objects stored there. In light of the things on view throughout the house, some precious and some of sentimental value, one could only wonder why Leon Farrell had chosen to hide these things behind the wall.

A gilt-framed photo of a beautiful woman, almost the image of Shirley, gazed back at him. He sat on the edge of Farrell's desk almost unable to remove his gaze from it, as her apparent softness and feminine sweetness captivated him the way Shirley had the first time he looked at her.

If this was the woman Leon Farrell loved, married, and lost in a tragic accident, it was no small wonder that after her death he became reclusive and bitter. She was breathtaking.

He thought of dismantling it in case it concealed the will but discarded the idea; such a drastic measure would have to be a last resort. Tampering with that photo seemed an invasion of the man's privacy. He laughed at the thought.

As he stood gazing at the array of different objects, a plan took shape. He separated the plastic and wooden robots, which were mostly replicas of animals, as Edgar had stated in the most disparaging tone.

Behind the robots, he found a worn football on which someone had scrawled "Gunther." He wondered to whom the two harmonicas on the shelf beside the football had belonged, for he'd begun to doubt that Leon Farrell cared much about music. His personal quarters didn't contain a radio, a record or CD player, or even a television. The man seemed to have spent his later years locked up in himself.

The sight of Latin textbooks surprised him. He opened one, saw in it the name Catherine Long, and concluded that Farrell's wife had attended an upscale private high school. More than two dozen vases of porcelain and crystal sat on the bottom shelf, a logical place, apparently, to lessen the chance that they would fall and break. He saw figurines and statues of jade and cloisonné throughout the closet in no specific order, and he wondered at that, for everything else seemed to have been placed with care and thought. In a corner of the shelf next to the top one lay what was clearly a diary, its cover of blue Chinese silk. He left it untouched.

Thinking that he had a good idea of the general contents of the secret closet, he was about to sit down and sketch the plan that had formed in his mind when he glanced toward the ceiling. On a shelf too high for him—a six-foot, three-inch man—to reach, he saw the top layer of what had been a multilayered wedding cake and beside it a photo of Leon Farrell and his bride smiling and obviously very happy. He wondered if the man's children had ever seen it and if they had pictures of their beautiful mother.

He went down to the basement and got a four-step ladder. He had a hunch that he should begin at the top. Oddly, the icing on the cake remained white after almost forty years. He looked under it, searched behind it with a flashlight, and found half a dozen notebooks. A search of each one disclosed only diagrams for what he suspected became the wooden robots that Leon Farrell designed and constructed. To the right on that top shelf, he saw two pieces of fabric, pale blue and about three yards each. He shook them out as carefully as he could, folded them, and returned them to their corner on the top shelf.

"I ought to stop and get something to eat," he said to himself, but he wanted to get as much done as possible that day, so he didn't stop. His cell phone rang, and from a check of the caller ID, he saw that the caller was a lawyer with whom he occasionally worked, so he answered.

"Montgomery."

"Hello, Carson, my man. This is Rodney Falls. I need you in a hurry."

"What's up, Rodney? You caught me at a bad time. I'm trying to finish up a case that's had me dangling since January, and I'm finally zeroing in on it. I need a week. Can't it wait?"

"Well, what choice do I have? I know you can handle this, so I don't want to try anyone else. This guy left his bride-to-be waiting at the altar in front of six hundred and twenty guests. He's filthy rich, and her family's going to eat him alive. He didn't give her a single clue that he wanted out."

"Maybe there was foul play."

"I doubt it. He phoned her twenty minutes before she left home to meet him at the church, and the police don't have reports of any accidents around that time. A generation ago, the two families had a big, public spat, and the families didn't want these two to get married. Did he get revenge for his family, or did her family kidnap him? What do you say?"

"I say I'll be right on it seven days from now."

Returning to his task, he stepped up on the ladder in order better to see the second highest shelf. His gaze caught a large manila envelope tied with cord, and he nearly fell off the ladder when he dived for it. He could hardly believe his eyes when he opened the envelope and saw big bundles of one-hundred-dollar bills. He closed it, retied it, and put it back where he found it. Why, if the man had a bank account and a safe-deposit box, would he store such a large amount of money in his house? Leon Farrell was an enigma.

Examining that shelf more carefully on the theory that Farrell would store the more valuable things together, Carson opened the man's toiletries kit. He didn't expect to find the will in that all-too-obvious place, but he did see Catherine Farrell's engagement and wedding rings, other jewelry of hers, a very old gold watch, and a few other things that Farrell obviously held dear.

An amateur sleuth would have pushed aside the next item Carson found—a *Webster's Dictionary*—but Carson knew at once that it was a place for storage, one that looked like a book but that had a hollow center. He could hardly control his shaking fingers as he grabbed it and made his way to the desk with it. A long, tired sigh escaped him when he examined the contents and found Leon and Catherine's marriage certificate and Catherine's death certificate.

"At least I'm on the right track," he said to himself. Everything that was dear to Leon he had apparently stashed away in that secret hiding place. "You were a cunning old fox, buddy, but I'm just as smart, and unless you gave that will to the undertaker to put in your casket, I'll get it yet."

That was a thought. He took out his cell phone, got the undertaker's number from the operator, and phoned him.

"Never heard of such a thing," the undertaker said when Carson posed the question. "I hadn't had any prior contact with Mr. Farrell."

Carson thanked him, closed the wall, and called it a day. "Yep. That will is somewhere in this place, and pretty soon I'll have it in my hands."

Chapter Nine

While the scent of a roasting chicken wafted through an open kitchen window, Gunther sat on the balcony of his apartment talking with Mirna and wishing there were another female other than his sister with whom he could share certain of his problems. No matter what the situation, it was almost guaranteed that Shirley would stretch logic in order to see and accept his point of view. So he talked with Mirna, his housekeeper, even though she had cynicism down to a fine art.

"You ought to put her to a test," Mirna said. "Leopards don't change they spots."

"Somehow, that doesn't seem fair, Mirna. Still, I don't want to get involved with a woman I don't know well. The problem is that by the time you get to know what kind of person she is, you've already fallen for her, because that always comes first."

The wind picked up, and Mirna tightened her jacket. "I wouldn't a mentioned it, but she called here so fine and ladylike that I got excited thinking you'd found a nice girl. I feel she a good person, 'cause I got the right vibes from her, and my vibes don't usually fool me. Still, you never can tell."

He also got the right vibes from Caroline, but he doubted that he judged his vibes on the same basis as Mirna judged hers. "She's kind and generous," he heard himself say. "She won't pass a homeless person without giving something, and she doesn't rush people. If they're in her way, she waits until they move, or she says 'excuse me.' I like a lot of things about her."

"Why don't you ask her to dinner when Ms. Shirley is here, and maybe Ms. Shirley can invite Mr. Montgomery. They been seeing each other how long now? Four, five, or so months? And she got yet to invite him for a meal here. A woman ought to see a man in her own space. See how he act. 'Course, if he was mine, I'd display him like he was the American flag. That chicken 'bout roasted now. I'll sauté some spinach in five minutes, and dinner be ready."

He sat down to the beautifully set table, grateful that he could enjoy a meal in Mirna's company. He needed a companion, and he was in a financial position at last to afford a family. But he didn't want to rush into anything. Yet he also didn't relish being sixty years old and crawling around his house with babies on his back, trying to be a playful dad.

"This smells so good," he said.

"It gon' taste good, too. I stuffed this chicken with rosemary and thyme, seasoned it and rubbed it good with butter, covered the roasting pan with those little crimini mushrooms and shallots, and seasoned them with butter, salt, and pepper. You can't eat a thing better. Didn't cost much either."

"It's fantastic. So's this jalapeño corn bread. Have some wine."

"Mr. G, you know I don't drink nothing stronger than coffee. Thanks, though. If I drank a glass of that stuff, you or somebody'd have to carry me home."

He couldn't help laughing at the mental picture he got of Mirna inebriated. "In that case, I'll keep it out of your reach. This is a great meal. What would you cook if I invited Caroline to dinner?"

"Nothing I cooked for you so far. I'd pull out the stops, and especially if Mr. Montgomery was here, too. That man loves to eat."

"You like him. Why?"

"Mr. G, I know a man when I see one. It ain't that he so good-looking, though he sure is that. Lots of hot-looking men in this town, and some of 'em ain't worth a rat's tutu. It's 'cause he straight, Mr. G. Whatever a woman needs in a man, she can find right there. Trust me. He's got it, and he solid as the United States mint. You oughta encourage your sister to tie things up with him."

"I'm not sure she needs any encouragement. Mind if I ask what happened to your marriage?"

"No, I don't. If he'd a been a man like you, I'd still be married to him, but he was a lot like Mr. Edgar. Me and gambling is like oil and water. I work for my few pennies, and I ain't putting them on no horses and no numbers. He gambled the roof from over our heads, and I told the judge I deserved better than that. Her Honor agreed. The next man I marry gon' be from Krypton." Her laughter seemed to start in the pit of her belly before it rolled out in pure, ecstatic enjoyment.

"Mr. G, that is really funny, and I mean every word of it."

"I imagine you do. If you try to befriend a gambler, you'll soon be as broke as he. I'm thinking of having a guest for Thanksgiving—that is, unless you want to be with your family." Caroline wouldn't consider that exceptional, he thought, because one would expect them to be together on holidays.

"I don't have no kids, so that's fine with me. You want a turkey or a goose?"

He stared at her. There was more to Mirna than she'd made apparent. "Turkey. We could have a goose for Christmas. What did you do before you started housekeeping?"

"I taught cooking at the Béchamel Institute, but I didn't have no degree in home economics, just a GED and a certificate from a cooking school in Atlanta. So when the new manager took over the institute, he let me go. Restaurant cooking is too hard, and you often have to work a split shift. So I settled for housekeeping."

"That's really too bad." He got up from the table. "Thanks for a great dinner. I'll let you know about Thanksgiving."

He went to his room, looked up the phone number for Shirley on the *Utopia Girl*, and dialed it. "Ms. Farrell's office." He identified himself and asked to speak with Shirley. "I don't know where she is right now, but call this number and you'll get her."

He thanked the woman and dialed the number. "Ms. Farrell speaking. How may I help you?"

"Hi, Shirley. If you've got a minute, I'd like to ask you something."

"Sure. What's up?"

"I'm thinking of asking a friend to Thanksgiving dinner, but I don't want it to seem like too big a deal. If you're not planning something else, how about inviting Carson to have dinner with us—that is, unless he intends to be with his family."

"His brother is his only family, so . . ."

"Tell him to bring his brother and his date. We'll have a big party."

"What's this girl's name?"

"Caroline. She's nice."

"She'd better be, 'cause I see you like her a lot. All right. I'll let you know as soon as I get hold of Carson."

Suddenly, for reasons he didn't examine, laughter poured out of him. He sat on the edge of a chair, nearly missing it altogether, and rocked while he laughed.

"What's funny?" Shirley asked over and over.

When he could control himself, he said, "I asked you. You have to ask Carson. Carson has to ask his brother, and his brother has to ask his girlfriend; then it has to come back up the chain. By the time it gets back to me, it'll be Christmas."

"And that made you hysterical? You've been working too hard."

"Maybe, but my company has sold four million copies of one computer game that I designed and developed, and I've just released another one that's jumping off the shelves."

"Get outta here!"

"No kidding. Frieda was the inspiration for the

first one, and when I get a full accounting, I'm going to give her something. It's about a nurse and three little boys. I made if for kids, but adults seem to love it, too."

"Congratulations. It's too bad that Father isn't here to eat crow."

"Yeah. I think about that often. Wonder what he'd say."

"There's no telling. You know how he loved money," Shirley said. "I'll call you tomorrow about Thanksgiving dinner."

He hung up and sat alone in the dark of his bedroom, trying to decide on his obligations to his siblings. He hadn't adjusted to his sudden wealth; indeed, he hadn't taken it into account. Did he put money in trust for them, especially for Edgar, who would dissipate whatever he got in a matter of days?

"I'll decide after I know what's in that will," he said to himself. "That may change all our lives."

Somewhere between La Barra and Bahia, Shirley locked her office, stopped by the frozen-yogurt machine, got a cone full of it, and headed to her stateroom. She kicked off her shoes, got comfortable, dialed Carson's number, and after they greeted each other, she presented him with Gunther's suggestion for Thanksgiving dinner.

"What do you think?"

"Ogden and I usually get together for Thanksgiving, but this is such a wonderful idea. . . . Look, I'll tell him that if his girl can't come, he should come alone. Be sure and thank Gunther for me. I love the idea. Have you met his girlfriend?"

"No, and I suspect he's killing several birds with one stone."

"I'll call Ogden right now and get back to you."

She thought of Gunther's laughing and worked hard at restraining her own laughter. "Okay, I'll be right here."

"I miss you, sweetheart. I miss you one helluva lot."

"I miss you, too. I can hardly wait till we get to Ocho Rios."

"I'm counting the seconds. We'll talk later."

By noon the next day, Gunther was able to tell Mirna that she would be having six for Thanksgiving dinner, seven with herself. "Pull out the stops," he said. "You've been itching to do it, so here's your chance. You'll need some extra money, so let me know how much. By the way, I hope you weren't out in that storm last night. I'd never heard such a strong wind."

"Me neither. I was home, but it scared me half to death. Over where I live, everything looked the same this morning, but they said on TV that the suburbs got hit pretty hard. I'll make out a menu and see what I need. You can't even guess how much I'm gon' enjoy cooking this Thanksgiving dinner."

Feeling as if life was finally going to be what he'd always hoped for, he sat at the desk in his office, designing a puppy that was obviously a dog but that looked human. "I'll never get away with this," he said, laughing at the idea, when his receptionist buzzed him.

"Gunther, Carson Montgomery is on the phone, and he sounds as if something's amiss." Gunther's antenna shot up. Carson Montgomery was not a man to display emotion. If he did, something had to have gone wrong. Or was it the will?

"Thanks. Put him through. Hi, Carson. What's up, man?"

"I'm at your father's house." Gunther could feel his blood rush. "No, I haven't found the will. That storm last night did some damage to this house. I haven't gone inside, and I don't think I will. That big cottonwood tree near the garage is uprooted. It fell across the chimney, broke off half of the top, cracked panes in two windows, and buckled the garage door. Some other windows may need securing, and I haven't seen how the back of the house looks. We're speaking serious damage, Gunther."

"I'd better contact Riggs about repairs. Thank you for letting me know."

"I'll get over there and assess the damage," Riggs said when apprised of the situation. "It's insured, because Edgar still lives there, but before the insurance company goes there, you'd better stock that refrigerator with . . . you know . . . basic food and some kind of leftovers. That insurance company doesn't insure a house that no one lives in."

"I'll get some stuff out of my kitchen." He called Mirna and told her what he needed.

"I'll fix you a couple of bags full, but I tell you I don't trust no man when it comes to a refrigerator. Put the vegetables—"

He didn't let her get any further. "Mirna, I kept house for years before I met you, and I know how to make a refrigerator look messy."

"Yes, sir, Mr. G. I know you telling the truth 'bout that. It'll be ready when you get here."

It wasn't possible to get the last word with a woman, and especially not that one. "Thanks. I'll be there in half an hour."

Gunther met Donald Riggs at his father's home, and together they made the kitchen look as if it were in daily use. Apart from a pair of detached window screens at the rear of the house, an examination of the property revealed no apparent damage other than that which Carson had reported.

"This is going to be expensive," Riggs said, "but the place is heavily insured, so we ought to be able to get it repaired right away."

"I suggest you get a good contractor."

"Don't worry. I believe in spending money wisely. There's the question of what we'll do if Edgar comes back before we get the place repaired. I may be able to get the insurance company to rent an apartment for him."

Gunther didn't know when he'd experienced such relief. A long sigh slid out of him. "I'm glad to know it. I won't be comfortable having him at my place." He made some notes on what he'd seen there, thanked Riggs, and went back to work.

Looks as if fate is conspiring against me, Carson thought as he stood by the window in his office, looking down at the people rushing along like little ants racing toward sugar. He had promised himself that at the end of a week, he'd have that will or resign from the job. He harbored an intense dislike for Edgar, and he had to get him out of his hair. He also needed to do some serious work on his relationship with Shirley, and he couldn't do that until he either found the will or quit the job. She'd respect him more if he found the will.

I don't dare work in that house until it's been repaired. But I hate the thought of stopping the search right now when I think I'm on to something. Well, I'm not going to waste the time. I have a day and a half before flying to Ocho Rios to meet Shirley. At the thought of what awaited him, sweat poured down his shirt collar and his heartbeat thudded wildly. He admonished himself to get his act together and telephoned Rodney Falls.

"This is Carson. I've got some hours I could use to acquaint myself with your reluctant bridegroom. I'll be over in half an hour."

Later, after getting the gist of the story, he decided to take the case. But he made a note on the contract that his agreement to find the man was contingent upon his conversations with the jilted bride, who was in seclusion and refused to see anyone. Back at his office, he drew a diagram of Leon Farrell's secret cabinet and began to study it. Could it be that the cabinet itself contained a hiding place and that he was wasting time looking into the different items on the shelves? He'd find it if he had to dismantle the entire cabinet.

Thursday finally arrived, and Carson boarded a noon flight to Ocho Rios. After a smooth journey during which he slept, he took a limousine to the *Utopia Girl* and checked into his stateroom. When he had shoved his bag into the room, he rushed toward the window to see what kind of view he would have. But before he reached the window, his gaze took in a huge bouquet of lavender, white, pink, and red orchids, a bottle of Moët & Chandon champagne, and a large basket containing cookies, crackers, cheese, and tropical fruits. He forgot about the view from his window, dropped himself into a big chair, and dialed Shirley's number.

"Ms. Farrell speaking."

"This is Carson. What time do we sail?"

"Carson! Where are you?" The excitement in her voice told him more than any words she could have uttered.

"I'm in my stateroom. Thanks for this wonderful welcome."

"You're already on this ship? Are you serious? I'll be there in fifteen minutes."

"It'll be the longest fifteen minutes I ever spent. Hurry."

After brushing her teeth, combing down her hair, and exchanging her pants for a skirt that flared around her knees, she stepped out of her office, where in anticipation of his arrival she had stashed a change of clothing, and took the elevator to the fourth deck. She reached his stateroom in precisely a quarter of an hour. He flung the door open after her first knock.

"That was sixteen minutes," he said, his face beaming in a wide grin. He picked her up, kicked the door shut, and wrapped her in his arms. "I'm starved for you. Woman, you're even sweeter and more beautiful than I realized." He stepped back, looked at her, and ran his fingers through his hair. "Do I act like a man who's hooked? I must be, because being with you makes me so happy."

* * *

To her, his being there seemed like a mirage. She'd spent the past week thinking of the moment when she'd see him again and be with him in a different, fairy-tale environment, wondering how she'd relate to him and whether her feelings for him would have changed. The only difference was her far greater yearning to be a part of him. When his entire demeanor changed from one of a delighted lover to that of an almost predatory possessor, she knew that what she felt shone in her eyes.

"Aren't you ever going to kiss me?" she asked him.

He stepped closer, bent to her and, with her body pressed tightly to his, he traced the seams of her lips with the tip of his tongue. Like a morning glory receiving the kiss of the sun on an early spring morning, she opened to him and took him in. The symbolism of her rare submissiveness wasn't lost on either of them. She could feel him holding back, and, for once, she did the same.

Still holding her, he asked, "Where is your stateroom?"

"Next door. When you called, I was in my office on the second level."

He cocked an eyebrow. "Is there a connecting door between us?"

"Uh . . . yes, but it's locked right now. Do you like your room?"

"It's elegant. I was about to check the view when I saw your hospitality gifts. You treated me royally."

"Why wouldn't I? You're a king, at least to me."

"Woman, don't say a thing like that to me unless you mean it. And another thing. You're on duty, and I don't want to compromise you in any way. What are your working hours?"

"I'm on leave from ten tomorrow morning until the next trip, when I'll be back on the *Mercury*, my regular ship assignment. But we can have dinner together at seven-thirty—cocktails, too, if you like. I'm not on night duty. Would you like something to eat or drink?"

"I could use something light, some good fish."

She sat down and dialed the restaurant. "This is Ms. Farrell. Would you send broiled swordfish, potato puffs, and asparagus to 4116-A?" She turned to Carson. "What would you like for dessert?" Her eyes widened when he ran his tongue across his thin top lip. If he knew how sensuous he was, would he control the evidence of it? He could light up her libido without trying. "Three big scoops of cherry-vanilla ice cream, a half bottle of pinot grigio marguerita, and no soup or salad, thanks."

She completed the order. "They'll put the wine on your tab. If you need anything else, you have my number."

"I'm glad to know it," he said with a grin spread all over his face.

"I mean my cell phone number, smarty," she said, though she'd lie if she told him or anybody else that she wouldn't dance to his tune.

He shrouded himself in innocence. "Whatever else would I have been talking about?"

"I'll see you later."

"Unless you want the job of assuring your passengers that there really aren't any wild wolves howling on this ship, you certainly will see me later."

Her frown dissolved into a wide grin. "If I thought you were joking, I'd see if you'd really do that. But you look as if you might. I suppose sailing brings out the nuttiness in some people. See you at a quarter of seven. Jacket and tie are de rigueur."

To her delight, she had no serious requests from passengers for service that afternoon. No one seemed to have been left behind in Bahia, no children were lost on the boat, and no one had to fly home in a family emergency. For her, that constituted a banner day. At five o'clock, she hooked the land phone to the operator, closed her office, and went to her stateroom.

Her ship-line phone rang as she walked into her room, and thinking that Carson might be her caller, she ran to answer.

"Ms. Farrell speaking," she said, remembering that she was the ship's PR officer.

"Hi, sis," Gunther said. "I see you're in Jamaica. When are you leaving there?"

"Saturday morning. How're things?"

"Fine with me. We had a terrible storm the other night, and Father's house got some damage. Riggs is taking care of it."

"What? What happened?"

"Actually, it's pretty serious, but the insurance will cover it, so not to worry. I hope Edgar stays in Las Vegas or somewhere until they've completed the repairs, because I don't want to live in the same house with him."

She sat down, contemplating the consequences of that news. "No. I don't, either. There wouldn't be one minute of peace."

"Yeah, and it's a pity. He thinks life's screwing him, and he can't see that he's doing it to himself."

"And to us as well. Where will he stay?"

"Riggs is trying to get the insurance company

to pay for his lodging in a furnished apartment or a bed-and-board accommodation."

"I hope he can manage it."

"Right. I take it you'll be back here sometime Sunday."

"That's my plan. I gotta get ready for dinner. Here, nobody goes late to the captain's table. See you later."

"Right on!"

She dressed in a sleeveless, buttercup-yellow chiffon-silk dress that had tucks from waist to mid-hip, flared to an inch below the knee, and had just the right amount of décolletage. With her hair around her shoulder, gold bangles at her earlobes, and a beguiling perfume at her throat and wrists, she knew she was at her best. If she had doubted the effect, Carson's gasp when he opened the door would have reassured her.

"You're so beautiful," he said, kissing her cheek, "and you . . . you look perfect."

"Thanks. You're not doing badly yourself," she said of his towering good looks and flawless physique in a white shirt, blue and white striped tie, navy jacket, cream-colored slacks, and white shoes.

"Thank you," he said, and it occurred to her, not for the first time, that Carson didn't pay much attention to his looks or that, if he did, he didn't compare his own looks to that of other men. And it was just as well, because he towered over most in ways more than height.

"We're going down?" he asked when she pushed the Down button on the elevator. "I walked around this afternoon, and I thought I saw the restaurant on a higher floor."

"You did, but we're not going there. We eat at the captain's table."

"I'm impressed. Do you always eat with the captain?"

"I'm fourth-ranking officer on this ship. If I were number six, I'd eat somewhere else."

"All right. I stand corrected. You can't blame me for not wanting that guy in my territory."

She raised an eyebrow, but she decided to treat it as an innocent comment and not say anything. She'd promised not to see other men, but if he wanted serious territorial rights, he'd have to give her a reason and he'd have to make it plain and verbal. They entered the captain's dining room, and it pleased her that the captain also had a female guest. *Please God, don't let it be his sister, or any other female relative.*

She walked with Carson to the head of the table. "Captain Meadows, this is Mr. Montgomery."

"Good to meet you," the captain said in his deep, gravelly voice. "Welcome. I hope you're enjoying the cruise."

"I am indeed, sir, and I'm delighted to have this opportunity to meet you."

The captain gestured toward the woman who sat at his right. "This is Ms. Warren. She hopes someday to make an honest man of me, and I'm hoping she doesn't give up, but she's a landlubber, and I can't resist the water. Magda Warren, meet my PR director, Shirley Farrell, and her friend, Mr. Montgomery. We'll be nine tonight. While we're waiting for the others, let's have some drinks." Minutes later, the purser arrived with his wife and small daughter, followed by the ship's doctor and her husband.

Carson seemed to enter freely into the dinner conversation and to show enthusiasm for the ideas bandied around, but Shirley knew that his mind was really on her. With every pause in his speech, he focused on her. It didn't make her nervous; rather, it excited her.

After a memorable meal, they bade their dinner partners good night. "Would you like to see a movie, or dance?" she asked him. "There's a kind of old folks' orchestra playing waltzes, fox-trots, and calypsos on the other end. Or we could sit in one of the lounges and talk."

"Let's find a quiet lounge. I don't care to have to fight with a gang of dudes who want to dance with you."

"Humph. I ought to insist that we dance. It would be fun to see how you'd react with half a dozen women trying to get you to dance. They're out for fun, and they leave the idea of decorum at home. Nowadays, a lot of women feel that they don't have to wait until a man asks them to dance."

"I'm all for that, so long as I'm not the man." He grabbed her arm. "Which way is the lounge?"

She couldn't help laughing. It had never occurred to her that anything would make Carson Montgomery panic. "It isn't funny; women are used to having men act foolish over them," he said, "but *they've* always showed better taste and common sense."

She laughed harder. "I think you mean that as a compliment. Let's sit over here."

They sat beside each other, and he slipped his arm around her shoulder. "I'd like to go into the city tomorrow. Can you go with me?"

"My time is your time." He was being a bit more

casual than she had expected. There didn't seem to be any urgency about what he wanted for them. *Patience, girl! Wait till he shows his hand.*

He squeezed her shoulder. "Thanks. If it's too hot, or you're not enjoying it, we'll come back to the ship. Let's eat breakfast on our deck and leave the ship at about ten?" She nodded. "A few nights ago, Ellicott City had a terrible storm, and your father's house sustained some damage. It's my understanding that the insurance company will pay for the repairs. I thought you should know."

"Thanks for telling me. Gunther called me this afternoon and told me, but he didn't say how bad it was."

Carson told her what he had observed. "I think the worst damage was the uprooting of that cottonwood tree and the breaking off of the chimney top."

She sat up straight, but he pulled her back into the curve of his arm, surprising her. "Just wait until Edgar comes back," she said, as if she hadn't noticed his show of possessiveness. "He'll twist that into something against him. Gunther said that Riggs is asking the insurance company to pay for Edgar's temporary housing, and I hope it will, because when he gets back here from Las Vegas, he probably won't have a penny."

"Oh, he may win something."

"He's the type who would put it right back in the slot machines."

"I never did understand gamblers," Carson said. "The stakes are always against them, and they always think they can beat those odds."

They talked for a while, and she became restless, wondering what he wanted for them. She knew he cared, but she'd begun to suspect that he still hadn't made up his mind about her.

"Shall we explore the place a little?" he asked her. Then he laughed. "I forget that you know this ship inside and out. Come on. You're much too beautiful to be stashed away in a stateroom."

But right then, she wanted to be in a stateroom, and she wanted to be with him. "I think I'd like a glass of tawny port," she said. She didn't need it, but sipping it was a way to prolong the evening.

He stood, took her hand, walked with her to the bar lounge, ordered the wine for the two of them, and had a bottle of it and two glasses sent to her stateroom. "Charge that to 4116-A," he told the bartender. Walking back to their rooms, he dropped her hand and eased his arm around her waist. At her door, she wondered why he stood looking down at her, his gaze unreadable.

"Aren't you coming in?" she asked him.

"Are you sure you want me to?"

"Why are you reticent, Carson? And you are, you know. You want more, a lot more, but you're not asking for it, and I want to know why because this is definitely out of character."

"You don't know how right you are. I've always avoided involvements with clients, because my integrity is a part of my license to do what I do. In a way, I'm working for you, and it doesn't sit well with me. It never has. You're right—I want more, and I need more, but I don't want to appear to use you. You're as important to me as the air I breathe."

"But what about me? Do you care about the way I feel and what I need?"

"You know that isn't a fair question. Imagine a hungry lion let loose among a herd of antelope. That's how badly I want you. But if I can't find that will and your brothers decide that I'm a charlatan who's been using you, will you side with them or with me? I'm doing my best to make sure I don't lose you."

She slid her key into the lock. "Really? I can think of other, more certain ways not to do it. Good night."

She went inside, closed the door, and looked around at the idyllic setting. Carson didn't strike her as the kind of man who'd forgo such an opportunity. Most men would step up to the plate even if they merely liked the girl. She picked up the phone and dialed his room number.

"What is it, Shirley?"

"I'm perplexed. Are you sure you're not married? I'm thinking that I don't know any member of your family or any of your close friends. I don't know much about you." She knew from his long silence that he was battling his temper, but she waited. The ball was in his court.

"Do you have the key that opens the door separating us?"

"I have a key that fits it. Why?"

"Open the door."

Her lower jaw sagged. It was not a request, but a command. A smart retort settled on the edge of her tongue, but she caught herself in time to restrain it. Both his words and his tone of voice said *Don't play with me.* Maybe she'd taken a step too far. After debating with herself for a few seconds, she got up and opened the door.

With his legs wide apart, his hands above his

head, braced against the sides of the door frame, he seemed to her a figure of towering strength. She would have welcomed a smile, but there was none. He merely stood there, filling the space where the door had once been.

She forced her teeth not to chatter the way they did when she was nervous, but it was as if marbles fought for space in her stomach, and perspiration dampened her undergarments. She stared at him, a thing of beauty, powerful and all man. Suddenly, her hand shot out and gripped his belt, in an attempt to pull him to her. He didn't budge, but within a second, she was tight in his arms. He dumped her gently on his bed and sat on the edge of it.

"Let that be the last time you goad me. What is there about me that you don't like?"

"Nothing."

"What do you think I'm hiding from you?"

"Nothing."

"What do you want from me?"

She sat up and looked him in the eye. "Everything."

He sucked in his breath, and his left hand went to his chest as if trying to regulate his heartbeat. His eyes darkened to stormy mists, and his nostrils flared.

"What do you want from *me*?" she asked him.

"Everything. Everything a man can get from a woman," he said, "and I don't want any other man near you." He stood, lifted her from the bed, locked her body to his, and parted her lips with his tongue.

Shock sped through her body as he pressed her to him in a boldness he hadn't previously showed her. But if he thought she would protest, she let him know that he was giving her what she wanted, and she moved into him. He pulled his tongue out of her mouth and gazed down into her face. Unperturbed, she took his hand and rubbed it across the hardened nipple of her left breast. She knew he liked to suckle her, and the lights that flashed in his eyes told her she'd made the right move.

"Yes," he said. "Oh, yes. I've been looking at them all evening, and I want it. Give it to me." She released her right breast and held it to his mouth. He took it, owned it, and owned her. Minutes later he stormed within her, unleashing the power of his masculinity until she screamed her release, and he followed her, triumphant in his ecstasy.

"How do you feel?" he asked her after some minutes.

"I don't know. I've never had an experience like that. It was wonderful, but I don't feel like myself. I—"

He levered himself on his elbows and gazed down into her face. "You are something of a phony. Talking about your needs. You didn't know what you needed, because that's the first time you've had an orgasm."

"How do you know that?"

"Your behavior told me. I'm in this real deep, sweetheart. What about you? Did you mean what you said a few minutes ago?"

"What did I say?"

"I'm serious, Shirley. You told me that you love me."

She couldn't help grinning, because she had what she wanted, and she meant to keep him. "Yeah. I did say that, didn't I? My brothers will tell you that I always keep my word unless it's impossible, and I never lie, even when the truth is painful. Does that answer your question?"

"Not really, but it will do."

"Don't I have a right to know whether you love me?"

He tweaked her nose. "I've loved you for months. Didn't you know it?"

"Know *that*? I knew you cared for me, because you showed me in so many ways." She wrapped her arms around him. "Carson, I'm so happy I want to shout it to the whole world."

Looking down at her, he let his hands stroke her face in gentle caresses. "Right now, I feel as if I've got planet Earth in my own hands. But I know that happiness is a fragile state, Shirley. A lot depends on your ability to trust and respect those you love. Kiss me." She did. He rolled over to his side, pulled the cover over them, and slept.

She lay in his arms, wide awake, trying to deal with what she'd experienced. She'd told him that there were more certain ways of binding her to him, but in truth she hadn't known what she was talking about. Now she knew, and she was much less sure of herself. He'd just taught her that he could control her as easily as she could control him. Perhaps even more easily. And she understood his reluctance to become involved with a person with whom he had a business relationship, albeit a remote one.

He took his time, she conceded to herself, because he knew what intimacy with her could bring, and she'd pushed him, because she hadn't imagined how much it would change her and what it would do to her feelings for him. He had his hand draped loosely across her belly, but suddenly a smile slid over his face. He stroked her breast until her nipple hardened and her libido began to gnaw at her. After about twenty minutes of discomfort, she sat up.

"Wake up, you."

"Hmm?"

"Wake up. I'll bet you're not really asleep. You've got me completely out of sorts." Annoyed because he didn't respond as she would like, she massaged him to an erection and crawled on top of him. He awakened then, flipped her over on her back, and gave her what she needed.

"That's the most wonderful compliment you could have paid me," he said when she had climbed down from an incredible high.

"I wasn't sure you'd appreciate my waking you up."

"Few things can make a man as happy as hard evidence that his woman wants him. Never hesitate, and don't concern yourself about my reaction. I can't imagine not wanting you."

Chapter Ten

Gunther had begun to look forward to Thanksgiving Day as the possible turning point in his life. If he found that Caroline suited his lifestyle, he'd work at strengthening their relationship and teaching her to care for him. He corrected that. He'd court her seriously, and if their attraction for each other intensified, he'd work at making it permanent.

He ran his hand through his hair and lifted his left shoulder in quick, successive shrugs. "I must be getting desperate. No man is more vulnerable to stupidity than a desperate one. I'll just see what happens." He answered the phone on his desk.

"Mr. G, Frieda said she's been trying to get in touch with you. She said it's very important."

"What's her number?" She gave it to him. "Thanks, Mirna. I'll call her."

He dialed the number that Mirna gave him. "Ms. Davis, please."

"Frieda speaking."

"Ms. Davis, this is Gunther Farrell. I understand that you wanted to speak with me. How are you?"

"I'm good, Mr. Farrell. I need you to write me a reference. I been working at the hospital for 'bout eighteen years. They gave me a small raise when I got my LPN four years ago, but I feel they should give me more money, Mr. Farrell. Would you please write me a recommendation and say how much you paid me?"

Was he hearing correctly? "Are you saying they pay you less than that?" he asked her.

"Yes, sir."

He sucked his teeth in disgust. "That's ridiculous. I'll be glad to do it. What's your address?"

She gave him her address but added, "I'd appreciate it if I could drop by and pick it up. I'd like to take it to my supervisor when I get to work."

"Do you mean you've already left your mother? How is she?" He wondered about the relationship, but didn't think he had a right to probe.

"She's up and about. She doesn't need a nurse now, and I'm not one to wear out my welcome, Mr. Farrell."

He'd have to think about that one. "Right. But I'm sure she appreciated the fact that you went to her aid when she needed you."

Was that a sigh? "I think she did. At least things are a lot better between us than they've been. Still, the only things in this life that you can count on are taxes and death, and ain't neither one of them welcome."

"I'd forgotten what a philosopher you can be at times. I'll be home about five-thirty, and your letter will be ready."

"Thank you, sir. You know I appreciate it. See you around six. Bye."

He wrote the letter, all the while thinking that maybe his situation growing up hadn't been so bad. He hadn't had to pay rent, eat, take care of all his other needs, and plan for a future with the amount of money he paid Frieda, which she had considered a windfall. Leon Farrell gave his children at least a comfortable home and plenty of food; although, unfortunately, after his wife died, he gave them very little beyond that. If he'd learned anything from the man who sired him, it was how *not* to be a father.

He walked into his apartment a few minutes before five o'clock, changed his clothes, and went down to the pool on the ground floor of the apartment building. After several laps, he climbed out of the pool, spent ten minutes on the treadmill, swam another lap, and got back to his apartment minutes before Frieda arrived.

"Where's Mr. Farrell?" he heard her ask Mirna. "He paid me forty-three dollars a week more than I get for that backbreaking work at the hospital, and he's giving me a recommendation. I need a raise so I can move from that fourth-floor dump on Franklin Street. Tired as I am when I get home from work, I have to walk up three flights, and that building has high ceilings. But right now, it's all I can afford."

"He a good man," Mirna said. "And whatever he say he gon' do, you can put money on it."

"Don't I know!" Frieda said. "Ain't many like him. And a real gentleman, too."

Gunther took the letter from his pocket and

walked into the dining room where the two women sat talking. "Here you are," he said to Frieda. "I hope it works for you."

She looked at the unopened letter and then gazed at him for a long time until he wondered at her behavior. Finally, she said, "Mr. Farrell, I'll never forget your kindness to me. I wasn't gon' tell you this, but one good deed deserves another. The day I left here driving to Baltimore, your brother passed me on his motorcycle and sideswiped my car, spinning me around in a circle. He could've killed me, and he didn't even slow down."

"What? Are you sure?"

"Sure, I'm sure. I passed him about three miles farther on the highway where he'd stopped to talk on his cell phone. I got his license plate number, looked it up, and saw that Harley belonged to Edgar Farrell. I was without my car for two weeks. But he's your brother, so I won't report him."

"I'm not a bit surprised. You should have reported it. Next time he'll kill someone. Have you had your car repaired?"

"It's been fixed, sir. I don't want you to do a thing about it, but I know you wouldn't want no kin of yours in jail."

He thought about that for a few seconds and surprised himself when he said, "I appreciate your sentiments, but I don't know about that. Maybe getting what he deserves would turn him around."

He surmised that Frieda Davis was not as simple as her apparent warmth and lightheartedness suggested. He knew she took her work seriously and did it with pride, more often exceeding what was required of her. And her ever-ready sense of humor could be as effective as a doctor's prescription. But for all that, she maintained a distance, a right, as it were, to reverse herself and attack if need be.

He walked with her toward the front door. "I get the feeling that you've had a difficult life. My siblings and I have thought that our lives were tough, but I suspect you had it far worse."

She stopped walking and looked up at him. "It's interesting you say that 'cause I try hard not to let it show. I was adopted at birth. My birth mother gave me up without knowing whether I was a girl or a boy. My father—whoever he was—raped her on the way home from school. Coreen—my mother—told me what she suffered during that pregnancy, and I don't know how she stood it. After that was over, she picked herself up, got two university degrees, is head of a big social agency, and has been president of her international professional organization.

"But her life wasn't a bit harder than mine. Starting when I was twelve, my adoptive father raped me whenever he felt like it. I left home in the middle of a winter night wearing my adoptive mother's housecoat and an old blanket and with one hundred and twenty-six dollars that I stole from my adoptive father's pants while he violated me. I blamed my birth mother. I spent nearly two years looking hard for her, tracing leads and trying to make her miserable."

He didn't realize that he'd been holding his breath until he suddenly gasped for air. "I gather you found her."

"Yes. I tried to ruin her happy marriage and her nice family life, but it didn't work. I was glad, too, after she told me what she went through. I caused a lot of pain and trouble for her and her family, and I'm sorry. But we're all on pretty good terms now, and I'm grateful. It's not perfect. I tried to call her Mother, but I couldn't. At least, not yet."

She looked at Gunther and frowned. "Funny thing. I'm the spitting image of her."

He hurt for her. "No matter what's gone down before, Frieda, she probably would have died if you hadn't found her and if you hadn't given her the bone marrow."

"You're right, and I like to think that doing that made up for the trouble I caused. You know, Mr. Farrell, the Lord works in strange ways. Sometimes I just can't figure Him out."

He gave her a light pat on the shoulder. "I don't think we're supposed to. Let me know if you get that raise."

"I sure will. Thank you so much." He opened the door for her. "Hmm," she said, looking up at the sky, "looks like we gon' have some snow for Thanksgiving."

He told her good-bye, went to his bedroom, and dialed Shirley's cell phone number. "This is Gunther. Have you done anything about getting Frieda a job on one of those cruise ships?"

"I gave her application to the head of our clinics and asked her to interview Frieda. As soon as I get to Orlando, I'll push it hard. Not to worry."

"Thanks. She needs a break. By the way, Riggs has been trying to reach Carson. I take it you know where he is."

"I do, indeed," she said, and he heard the preening in her voice suggestive of someone's having won a huge lottery prize.

He told himself not to react. "When is he coming back here? I mean, when will he be home?"

"Sunday afternoon, for certain."

He didn't like that. "I see," he said, and he did. So Carson had scored with his baby sister. He told himself she had a right to live whatever life she chose, but he'd rather not know the details. "I gather you know what you're doing." He didn't believe that, but he accepted that, for Shirley, he probably wouldn't think any man good enough.

She spoke softly, without stridence or a tone that suggested he was interfering where he shouldn't. "I can only judge him by his behavior with me and toward me, Gunther. Right now, he's batting one thousand. He's . . . Gunther, he's wonderful. You'll see."

"It's a cinch I won't see what you see," he said dryly. "I hope it works out the way you want it to, sis. So far, I don't find any fault with him. But I'm waiting for him to deliver. In any case, we'll all be together at Thanksgiving. Give him my regards."

He hung up and let out a sharp whistle. The old man's devious behavior had precipitated changes that Leon Farrell could not have imagined and probably wouldn't have wanted. He disliked government and legal authority and was suspicious of anyone associated with it, including police. Carson Montgomery was a law enforcement officer. Gunther laughed because he needed to release some tension, and laughter was the least painful way of doing it.

Thanksgiving Day arrived with scattered snowflakes falling softly and quietly and darkening clouds that threatened a more wintry day. Shirley set the dining room table, adding tall, yellow candles and a centerpiece of brown, yellow, orange, and red mums and yellow place cards. The fires that Gunther had lighted in the dining and living room fireplaces sparkled and crackled with warmth, and added festiveness to the day.

As she regarded the results of her handiwork, it occurred to Shirley that her mother would be proud of her, for Catherine Farrell had loved and enjoyed beautiful things. With that thought came the realization that, after Catherine's death, their father had rejected the beauty and elegance that their mother had loved and with which she had surrounded them.

Could it have been that Leon Farrell's descent into a mean-spirited, stingy man was his way of dealing with the pain of their mother's loss? If that explained it, perhaps she could forgive him. But she was not convinced.

"If you was smart as I think," Mirna said as she put individual salt and pepper shakers in front of each plate, "this 'ud be the last Thanksgiving you had here in this apartment."

A frown etched deep grooves in Shirley's brow. "What do you mean?"

"I mean this time next year, Mr. Montgomery ought to be at the head of your Thanksgiving Day table in your and his house. That's clear, ain't it?"

Shirley laid her head to the side and looked hard at Mirna. "Why do you say that? You haven't seen that much of him."

Mirna locked her knuckles to her hips and looked toward the ceiling. "Honey, I know a man when I see one, and that man's got everything a

woman could need and plenty of it. Like I said to
Mr. G, he'll make a woman happy, and I ain't only
talking about sex. If he say he gon' do somethin',
honey, I bet my neck it's good as done. He ain't
got no right to be single."

"So far, you're a good judge of people," Shirley
said, patted Mirna's shoulder, and went to her
room. Three days with Carson on the *Utopia Girl*
and exploring Ocho Rios with him had increased
her appetite for the man, and she had made up
her mind that if he remained single, it would not
be her fault.

Caroline arrived first, and after one look at the
woman, Shirley decided that her brother had found
someone wonderful. "I'm so glad to meet you,
Caroline," she said, "and I hope this will be your
happiest Thanksgiving ever."

"Thanks. Me too," Caroline replied. "I've been a
wreck for days thinking about this. I thought,
thank God, I don't have to meet his mother. Then
I shamed myself and remembered that he has a sister. Have you ever been through this?"

Shirley's laugh allowed her to get rid of some
tension and to calm her own nerves. "I'm in the
same boat as you, Caroline. My friend's closest relative, his younger brother, will be joining us today,
and I haven't met him yet. So worry not. I'm in
your corner."

The doorbell rang, and Shirley raced to it, her
heart thundering in her chest. She opened the
door and gazed up at Carson. Speechless. "What
kind of welcome is this?" Carson asked her, stepped
inside, wrapped her close, and kissed her. "Shirley,
this is my brother, Ogden, and Marsha Harris, his
girl."

"Come in, Ogden, Marsha," she said, more nervous than she could ever remember being, for Gunther would have something to say about that French kiss she'd shared with Carson, quick though it was. She completed the introductions with Gunther and Caroline, aware that Carson's arm remained around her.

I'm not going to discourage him in order to please Gunther, she thought to herself as they walked into the living room.

Mirna brought hot hors d'oeuvres, Gunther served drinks, and very soon they chatted among each other like old friends. "Dinner's ready, Mr. G."

They followed Mirna to the dining room, took their assigned seats, and enjoyed a feast of corn chowder, roast turkey, corn bread dressing, cranberry relish, wild rice pilaf, grilled crimini mushrooms, asparagus, mesclun salad, assorted cheeses, bread, and lemon chiffon pie.

"I don't think I ever tasted such delicious turkey," Ogden said. He raised his glass to Mirna. "This was a meal for the gods."

Later, as they sat in the living room having coffee and aperitifs, Marsha sipped her espresso, rested her head on the back of the sofa, and said, "A poem about this entire occasion is tugging at my mind. When it comes to me fully, I'm going to write it down and send it to Mirna."

"That would be wonderful," Gunther said. "She'll probably fly right out of the window. Say, I have a taste for some Duke Ellington. What about it?"

"Right on," someone said.

As the strains of "Sophisticated Lady," one of

Ellington's most famous compositions, filled the room, he sat beside Caroline and eased his arm around her shoulder. Gunther realized that he was proud to be with her in the presence of his sister and of men like himself. She was his type of woman, and he'd see where it went from there. Contented, even a little happy, he squeezed Caroline's shoulder, closed his eyes, and let the music wash over him.

"Mr. G, could you please come here?"

He wondered at the note of what sounded like alarm in Mirna's voice. Someone or something had surely frightened her. He excused himself and rushed toward the sound of her voice just as Edgar brushed past her and stopped within inches of him.

"What a pretty scene we have here," Edgar sneered. "The rich have filled their bellies, and they don't give a filthy damn about anybody else."

"Watch your manners, Edgar. You're in my home."

"You don't say," was Edgar's response. Then his gaze caught Carson, who sat with an arm around Shirley. "What the hell are you doing with your arm around my sister? That's why you can't find that will. Or maybe you found it, and you think that if you're banging her, you don't have to get me my—"

Carson reached Edgar in two long strides. "You take that back. I don't care if you disrespect yourself or me, but you will apologize this second for your insult to Shirley. I'm counting to ten, and if you haven't apologized when I get there, I'm taking you out in that hall and giving you the thrashing of your life."

"You wouldn't dare," Edgar said, seemingly unaware that the others gaped at him in silence.

But Carson knew that all eyes were on him and that Shirley might side with her brother if he gave Edgar the punishment he should have had years earlier.

"You wouldn't touch me in my brother's house," Edgar said, though his voice carried a ring of fear.

Carson took his hands out of his pockets. "I assume you can count to ten. One. Two. Three. Fo—"

"All right, man. I was out of line. I'm sorry, Shirley. I didn't mean it."

"You meant it, all right," Gunther said to Edgar. It pained him to see how Shirley had metamorphosed from a regal queen to a woman who looked as if she'd been shoved out into a wintry blast. His estimation of Carson heightened further when the man went back to Shirley, put both arms around her, and whispered something that evidently invited her to cling to him.

"I'm sorry, sweetheart," Carson said aloud.

Shirley patted his knee. "I don't know him these days. Maybe he was always this way, but I don't think so."

Gunther ushered Edgar out of the living room and spoke to him with impatience. "What do you want? I hope you're satisfied that you ruined my dinner party."

As if the latter were of no import, Edgar focused on his own interests. "The house is boarded up. I got to find a place to stay."

"And you think that after what you just did, embarrassing me in the presence of my guests and insulting our sister, that I should let you stay here?

Don't even dream it. Get hold of Riggs. He'll work something out. I'll see you to the door."

Edgar stared at Gunther with narrowed eyes. "What can Riggs do for me if Carson hasn't found the will?"

Gunther lifted his shoulder in a dismissive shrug. "A violent storm damaged the house, and the insurance company is paying for repairs. Riggs arranged that and got the company to pay for your housing until the house is ready for occupancy."

"Yeah? What about food, man? I'm down to my last fifty-five bucks."

Gunther went to the kitchen. "Mirna, would you please give Edgar a takeout Thanksgiving dinner?"

"Gimmie five minutes," she said without looking at either of them.

She prepared a plate of the dinner and added a container of chowder, a big slice of pie, a can of coffee, bananas, biscuits, butter, jam, sugar, and a package of hot dogs.

She handed Edgar the bag in Gunther's presence, looked him in the eye, and said, "If you'd learn to be nice, you wouldn't have days like this."

"And if you had had the courtesy to at least stop to investigate the damage you did when you spun Frieda Davis's car around on the highway, I'd have more respect for you," Gunther told him.

"Yeah," he said, taking the bag and heading for the door. "Life's a bitch sometimes."

So much for gratitude. Gunther went back into the living room and replaced the Duke Ellington CD with Mozart chamber music. "After that hurricane, I think some peaceful breeze is in order. I apologize for my brother's bad manners."

Caroline seemed troubled, and he didn't like that. She leaned toward him and spoke very softly. "Is he always like that? I mean, is he in a perpetual fight with life?"

At least she didn't move from the circle of his arm. "Edgar is a brilliant but self-centered and self-defeating man who takes what he sees as the shortest way to any and every goal, and en route, he invariably creates a problem for himself." After a few seconds, he drew a labored breath and added, "And for the rest of us."

"Do you love him?"

"He's my brother and, yes, I love him. I just can't tolerate him." He explained to Caroline how Carson became a part of their lives. "Edgar is obsessed with money, and as soon as he gets it, he squanders it."

"That's too bad. I didn't see anything of you in him."

"He's older than I, spoiled and convinced that the world owes him whatever he wants. It's really too bad."

Caroline grasped Gunther's arm in what he regarded as a gesture of support. "I'm sorry for him, Gunther, because he will always be unhappy. I've learned that any time a thing is worth having, it's best to get it fairly and honestly."

"I'm definitely with you there," he said, and to lighten the atmosphere, he added, "I'm being a lousy host." Then he put another log on the fire, stirred it, and went to the bar. "I'm having Rémy Martin VSOP cognac. Who's joining me?"

"After such a meal, a fine cognac would be just the ticket," Ogden said.

Hmm. The man knows his drinks, Gunther thought

in admiration. He looked at Marsha Harris. "What would you like?"

"Thank you," Marsha said. "If you have a coffee liqueur, I'd like that."

He appreciated a woman who had taste. "My pleasure," Gunther said. He wasn't showing off for Caroline's benefit, but it wouldn't hurt her to know that he knew a few things about entertaining.

He handed Marsha the drink, and her eyes sparkled with obvious delight. As he was about to serve the others, the telephone rang, and he held his breath, praying that Riggs had found accommodations for Edgar.

"Carson, would you mind serving the ladies while I answer the phone?" he said, figuring that Shirley would appreciate the gesture to Carson. He took the call in the dining room.

"Gunther Farrell speaking."

"Gunther, this is Donald Riggs. I've put Edgar in Wright's Housekeeping Hotel. I thought that would be perfect for him, since he can do his own cooking and save himself some money seeing that he's perpetually broke. But he threatened first to kill me and then to indict me if I don't put him in a five-star hotel suite. If he calls me about it one more time, I'm going to make it a one-night stand, and he can sleep in the street."

He stifled an honest yawn. "Tell him that, Donald, and you may add that I said he will not stay in my apartment. You won't have any more problems with him. The way to bring Edgar to heel is to call his bluff and hand him an ultimatum."

As had happened many times, his brother had all but ruined the day for him. Edgar's callous, uncaring habit of trampling on what was precious to his brother was something for which he'd resented Edgar all of his life, resented it and suffered. But he had always responded simply by stiffening his back and bearing it. Edgar had better not count on his reacting that way in the future.

He put another log on the fire, stirred the coals again, got his guitar, and plucked a few bars.

Ogden shook his head in disbelief. "Man, you need to tune that baby. How long have you been playing?"

"I play the saxophone well, but my neighbors don't like it. I just started playing the guitar." He passed the instrument to Ogden. "You want a shot at it?"

Ogden ran his fingers over the strings. "This is a nice guitar." He tuned it, fingered a few notes, and moved into a dazzling rendition of "Early One Morning." Soon, their voices filled the room with song. It amused Gunther that the group began with popular songs and soon switched to drinking songs. He thought they'd never stop singing "Waltzing Matilda." *Maybe I'm more sober than the rest,* he thought, thinking that no one seemed concerned about an inability to carry a tune. Ogden, Caroline, and Carson sang reasonably well, but after several rounds of drinks, only the joy of singing with friends seemed to matter.

"It's after seven," Ogden said. "I think we'd better get a move on. I'm working tomorrow morning, and I have to drive Marsha home."

"Y'all want some coffee, Mr. G?" Mirna cleared the coffee table and returned with bowls of ice cream and slices of lemon cake. "Y'all must be hungry by now."

Gunther stared at Mirna. "I thought you'd been home for hours."

"No, sir, Mr. G. I don't see no point in rushing home to be by myself. I'll bring some coffee in a minute."

He relieved her of the tray that contained a stainless-steel coffee carafe, a coffee service, and utensils. "You've done a wonderful job, Mirna. It's been a perfect Thanksgiving."

She shook her head. Sadly, he thought. "Almost, Mr. G. The devil always has to get in the act."

"Yeah," he said, "but he's no more successful than we let him be."

The next morning at breakfast, Shirley barely tasted the food. "Are you worried about Edgar?" Gunther asked her.

"I hate to see him this way, but if I try to help him, I'll go down with him. He—"

"Hold it," Gunther said. "I'll get the door." He went to the front door, slipped on the chain, looked out, and saw a stranger.

"Does Edgar Farrell live here?"

"No, he definitely does not. What do you want with him?"

"But you know where he is," the man said. "That bozo owes me twenty-five grand, and he promised to pay it by the fifteenth, which was last week. If I don't get it by the first of December, he'll never see Christmas."

Icy blood trickled through Gunther's veins, and he had to ignore the perspiration that beaded his forehead and dripped down the sides of his temples and onto his neck. He forced himself to look steadily at the man with an expression of authority and power. "Why does he owe you?"

The man's hard gaze bore into Gunther, suggesting both impatience and ruthlessness. "He don't know a damned thing about blackjack. He also don't know when to quit. If you see him, tell him that if he values his neck, he'd better call this number. I ain't taking no excuse, and tell him Vegas is a small town. If he squeals, I got friends. Good friends. Be sure and tell him that."

Gunther took the slip of paper on which only a telephone number had been written. "I don't promise I'll see him, but if I do, I'll give him this number and your messages."

The man nodded. "You do that."

Shirley met Gunther in the hall as he headed back to the dining room. "I heard that. What are you going to do?"

"First I'm going to get hold of Edgar. Only an idiot would bet with a professional gambler when he doesn't know the game."

"But you know Edgar doesn't have that much money," Shirley said, her voice plaintive and almost pleading. "Are you going to lend it to him?"

"Definitely not. He'd gamble with it and sink deeper into debt. But I don't want that man to kill him."

He dialed Edgar's cell phone but didn't get a response, and fear began to furl up in him until he remembered and dialed Edgar's hotel room.

"Hello."

"Edgar, this is Gunther, and I have a hot, frightening message for you."

"Whatta you talking about?" For once, Edgar's voice lacked its stridency and arrogance.

Gunther explained the reason for his call and added, "That man means business, and this time you'll pay."

"With what?" Edgar yelled, panic-stricken. "I had just enough money to get back here. He can't get blood out of a turnip."

"This is true, but that guy is mad enough and evil enough to get rid of the turnip. Eight days from now, he'll collect, one way or the other. Stay at your hotel, and I'll call you back as soon as I can work something out."

Edgar's heavy release of breath, evident through the wire, suggested that he'd been holding it. "I owe you one, brother. But you be careful. I've been told that guy is always loaded. If he doesn't do the job, his hoods will do it for him."

Gunther shook his fist at the air around him. "Then why the hell did you get involved with him?"

"Look, man. I didn't know who he was till it was too late. And I didn't give him your address. He's got everybody in his pocket."

"If this doesn't teach you a lesson, nothing ever will. Just stay there till I get back to you." He hung up and looked at his sister, the tears cascading down her cheeks. "I had planned to share with you and Edgar some of my take from that runaway electronic game I designed, but I didn't want to give Edgar any money until he got a decent job and settled down. It looks as if he gets it now."

"You're going to give Edgar twenty-five thousand dollars?" she asked, her teary eyes wide and disbelieving.

"Definitely not. I'm going to hand it to that guy in Edgar's presence." He telephoned Edgar. "Be here at noon today, and whatever you do, be here on time."

Next, he phoned the man Edgar owed and asked him to met Edgar at his apartment. He got the cash from the bank and was back home by a quarter of twelve. Edgar waited at the door, because Mirna refused to let him inside the apartment.

Precisely at twelve, the bell rang, and Gunther opened the door. "Come in, please," he said, and the man stepped inside the door, but would go no farther.

"I don't walk into traps," he said.

"This is not a trap, mister," Gunther replied, and beckoned to Edgar. "I'm paying you the twenty-five thousand that my brother owes you in his presence, and I suggest that you don't allow him to get in your debt again. This is it. I'm finished."

"You should have given it to me," Edgar said. "I'd have paid him."

"You're a gambling addict," the man said. "You would have gambled it away. Keep it up, and you won't live long. Incidentally, you ought to thank your brother for saving your life." The man tipped his hat and strolled down the hall to the elevator.

As Gunther's gaze swept over his older brother, he fought back the tears as thoughts of their lives together while their mother lived flashed through his mind. Life had been imperfect then, too, but they were a family. Back then, he would have denied vigorously a suggestion that he abhorred his brother's company.

"As soon as repairs on the house have been

completed, Carson will be able to continue searching for Father's will. When he finds it, I hope you'll do something with your life." He walked with Edgar to the door and extended his hand. "Be seeing you."

Edgar walked to the elevator with plodding steps. That was a close call, closer than he wanted to remember. How had Dutch Holliday found him? He hadn't known that the man he was betting against was one of the roughest hoods in Las Vegas, a man who had pulled time for murder. When he left Las Vegas, he'd thought he was home free, but that bitch must have betrayed him. Not that he blamed her. He wouldn't expect her to stand up to a man like Dutch, and there was no imagining what kind of torture Dutch put her through.

He walked out of the building holding his breath, but when he saw that Dutch hadn't damaged his Harley, he breathed easily. "This can't go on. If I keep this up, I'll be dead before I'm forty."

He jumped onto the big motorcycle, revved the engine, and quickly cut it off. If anybody had told him Gunther would pay his twenty-five-grand gambling debt, he'd have called them a liar. It definitely wasn't just talk that Gunther had saved his life. Dutch meant business. But maybe the most unfortunate part of it was that Gunther had finished with him for all time. He'd said it, and he meant it. Oh, what the hell!

He revved up the engine and headed for Baltimore. What he needed was a week or two of gigs to tide him over till Carson found that will. He appreciated what Gunther did for him, surprised though he still was, but he was on his own now, and he had to make his own bread.

The manager met him when he entered the club. He was willing to beg for work, even on his knees, if necessary. "Man, I've been trying for days to get hold of you," the manager said. "Moody sprained his wrist, and I don't have a decent guitarist. Can you give me a couple of weeks?"

Edgar ran his hands over his tight curls, rubbed the back of his neck, and adopted the facial expression of one sorely put upon. "I'd planned to head north. What's on your mind, man? I mean, what are you offering? I can't support myself on what you pay."

"Okay. I'll up it by one-fifty a week. What do you say?"

Edgar appeared to muse over the offer as if he had better options. Finally, he said, "Look, man, if you can make it two hundred more, I'll cancel my gig. You've been good to me, so . . . well, okay. The regular plus one-fifty. It's a deal, but I'll have to call my gig and cancel. I'll be back here at a quarter of seven ready to work."

Outside the popular club, Edgar wiped the sweat from the side of his face and the back of his neck. And to think that he'd been prepared to work for less than he usually demanded. Maybe his luck had changed. One thing was certain: After losing twenty-five grand in forty minutes, he'd played his last game of blackjack. And as soon as he got his share of that will, he meant to shake Ellicott City's dirt off his shoes and head west for good.

* * *

Shirley met Gunther on the stairs as he headed to his room. "What happened? I didn't want to witness that."

"I gave the man the money and told both of them that I won't do it again. Edgar needs help with that habit. It's dangerous. Unfortunately, it is entirely compatible with certain elements of his personality, and I don't see him quitting without professional help." He lifted his shoulder in a quick shrug. "What to do? I've told him that, but, like most addicts, he thinks he can quit gambling whenever he wants to. I'm going to my office. When are you due back on the *Utopia Girl?*"

"I have to report to the head office in Orlando on Wednesday. I'm sailing on the *Mercury* Thursday afternoon."

"What about Carson? You two have gotten very tight."

"That's true. We have. I'm seeing him tonight."

"I expected as much. Do you think he'd have punched Edgar?"

"I'm sure of it, and Edgar deserved it. I hope you're giving serious thought to a relationship with Caroline. I like her a lot."

"So do I, and I'm planning to work on it. Carson's a good guy." He sped up the stairs, put on his jacket and coat, grabbed his briefcase, and left for his office. Shirley sat on a step midway down the stairs, trying to come to grips with what had happened there that morning. As if she didn't exist, Edgar had neither told her good-bye nor given Gunther a message for her. After nearly half an hour, she got up and went to find Mirna. At least she could be thankful for the fact that Gunther would no longer nag her about Carson.

Shirley didn't like having to go on a two-week cruise at a time when her relationship with Carson had reached the point of decision making. She believed he loved her, but she wanted to hear it from his lips at a time when lovemaking hadn't made him loose tongued. Nobody could rush him, but she thought she'd learned enough about him to guide him to where she wanted him.

"I'm not discounting the fact that he's been this way once, didn't like the outcome, and is unlikely to rush back into marriage. But I am not going to be a convenience for him. Love doesn't cover that." She figured that during the two weeks they'd be apart, Carson would do a lot of thinking and rationalizing. Well, wouldn't she be doing the same?

For their date that evening, Shirley dressed carefully, exposing just enough cleavage to make his mouth water for more. She told herself that the cool, green color of the dress would dilute its brazenness. She lifted her right shoulder in a quick shrug. She was dealing with a man of the world, and she had to use all the ammunition available to her.

Chapter Eleven

Shirley opened the door that evening and walked into Carson Montgomery's arms. "You are one lovely creature," he said. "One of these days, I'm going to take you to my lair and keep you there."

"Can't happen soon enough for me," she replied, her tone as airy as his.

But his expression as he stared down at her was anything but light. "Be careful what you say to me, Shirley. As I've told you before, jokes often cover the truth."

"Really? So when are you sweeping me away to your lair?" she shot back.

He raised an eyebrow. "We could head there right now if I hadn't made other plans. Ogden and Marsha want us to go to her place for supper, after which the four of us would go dancing. Marsha knows a good place. Is that okay with you?"

"Of course," she said, somewhat subdued. "I liked Marsha. Where does she live?"

"East Baltimore, not too far from the university."

She thought for a few minutes. Either Ogden wanted Carson's opinion of Marsha or Carson wanted his brother's opinion of her. "Do you think Marsha is a good match for Ogden?" she asked him, trying to get the answer indirectly.

"She seems to be, but my impressions are not the ones that count."

Hmm. No luck there, but it did mean that Carson was not expressly seeking Ogden's opinion of her. She liked what she'd seen of Carson's brother, but she didn't know his standards for women. She embraced a calm that floated over her when she decided not to second-guess Carson as to why he wanted the four of them to spend the evening together. Four hours later, she reprimanded herself for having thought that Carson had an undisclosed agenda.

They ate a simple, cold supper at Marsha's studio apartment and ended the evening dancing. "Two weeks is a long time," Carson whispered in Shirley's ear as they danced a two-step.

"It'll be just as long for me," she replied, "and I *know* I don't like it."

"If Ogden weren't spending the weekend at my place, I'd ask you to go home with me." He tweaked her nose. "Cover up those tantalizing globes. They're torturing me."

Was he serious? An inch of cleavage was old-fashioned by today's standard. She forced herself not to look at him and didn't respond. At times, she couldn't read his mood, and she'd learned to wait until he showed his hand. Later, that knowledge served her well.

"I'll be on a case until about Tuesday," he told

her as they walked into Gunther's apartment not long after midnight, "but I'll see you before you leave."

When she didn't reply, only gazed at him, he gripped her shoulders, pulled her closer, rimmed her lips with his tongue, and plowed into her. When he released her, she staggered backward, shaken by his possessiveness. And she'd never seen his face bear a more serious expression.

"That's the way it is with me, baby. Think about it."

And she did, long after he said good night.

Her cell phone rang as she got into bed, and although she suspected that Carson was her caller, she had an unexplainable reluctance to answer. "Hello."

"You knew I'd call. I couldn't leave things like that. You're more important to me than I think you realize."

It was what she wanted to hear, but she couldn't absorb it. "Carson, I'm bothered that you thought my dress provocative. If I found a more conservative one, I'd probably have to make it, and I'm not planning to do that. I like that dress."

"So do I, but it was displaying what are for my eyes only."

She bristled and didn't bother to hide it. "If you want the right to make that claim, be prepared to make some changes in your life."

His laugh could have been mistaken for a sneer. "I'm not fool enough to believe you'd let me tell you what to wear no matter what my status was in your life. And you'd be within your right. That is not the issue here."

She did not want to precipitate a cold draft in their relationship, so she said, "You can't blame me for trying to protect my investment, and I have a lot of myself at stake in you. Anyway, you're the one who instigated that exchange."

She imagined that both of his eyebrows shot up before he said, "I think you apologized, and I readily accept."

Her laughter had a ring of happiness. "If you take good care of . . . er . . . things, whether I cover up won't matter."

"If I have your permission, I'll take damned good care of them."

Trust Carson to cut right to the chase, but she refused the bait. "Kiss me good night. I'm sleepy." He made the sound of a kiss, and she turned out the light and began wrestling with the sheets.

Shirley checked in at the cruise line's head office in Orlando three hours early. "I want to see Dr. Larsen," she told the receptionist, and added, "I have an appointment," before the woman could lie and say that Larsen was busy. Shirley had wondered at the receptionist's protective attitude toward Larsen and felt more than a little pity for her. The woman had seen more than fifty years, and meeting Hugh Larsen's office needs appeared to be her whole life.

Larsen stood at his office door with a broad smile on his friendly face, and with his usual fatherly persona, he patted Shirley's shoulder. "Come in, Miss Farrell"—he never said "Ms."—"and have a seat. I suppose you want to see me about Frieda Davis's application."

"Yes. Thank you for considering her."

"Ordinarily I wouldn't, because she isn't an RN,

but her reference is outstanding. So I called a couple of doctors and the head nurse at the hospital at which she works, and I got fantastically good reports. One doctor said she was as good as any RN and that, in addition, she wasn't full of attitude. I want to meet her and talk with her."

"That's wonderful, sir. I can certainly arrange that."

"Good. I'll send her a ticket and put her up overnight. I'm very curious about that woman. Tell her to expect my call."

"Thank you, sir. From what I observed of her when she was taking care of my brother, I'd say she deserves better than she's been getting."

As soon as she boarded the *Mercury* and settled into her stateroom, Shirley called Gunther.

"Hi. I think Frieda has a good chance at a job on one of the ships or in the head office. Tell her that Dr. Larsen, who's head of the health service, is going to call her and ask her to go down to Orlando for an interview at the cruise line's expense. Have you heard from Edgar?"

"Not a word. But he'll show up when he has another problem, or if he's mad about something. When are you sailing?"

"Tomorrow at five."

"Safe trip."

She answered the phone on its first ring, hoping that Carson was her caller, but instead, a clipped voice said, "Ms. Farrell, the captain wants to see you."

She threw up her hands. When was she going to get organized? "Thanks. I'll be right there," she said in her best professional manner. She put on her badge and left for the captain's office.

"Good afternoon, sir," she said. "Ms. Richards said you wanted to see me."

"Yes. Please have a seat. Management has agreed to allow *Around the World Travel* magazine to do a lead story on our cruise line. Because you've done such a fine job as a public relations officer, the interviews will be on our ship and you'll be the central figure in the story. So, during this cruise, a photographer and an interviewer will follow your activities. This is good advertising for the *Mercury*, so I hope you don't mind. They're anxious to get the story in the upcoming issue, so the next two days may be difficult ones for you."

"Thank you for the honor, sir. I'll do my best."

With a reporter and a photographer recording her every move and word, she didn't get a chance to call Carson until her bedtime, and then, he didn't answer his phone. Where could he be at eleven o'clock at night that he couldn't answer his phone?

After chiding herself for that moment of weakness, she told herself that he was asleep. The next morning, she called him as soon as she awoke.

"I thought you'd written me off," he said after they greeted each other.

Hmm. So he was fishing for reassurance of his importance to her. "You didn't think any such thing. I thought you took care of business night before last."

"I did, too," he said, "but the human mind can be fickle."

The human mind, maybe, but not the human body, at least not hers. She told him about the magazine article. "I can't sneeze without wondering how I'll look on camera. I'll be glad when they finish getting the documentation. Do you know how repairs are moving on Father's house?"

"The chimney and windows are done, and they're working on the roof. You can't imagine how relieved I'll be when I finally get that will in my hands. More is riding on that than I thought when I agreed to find it."

"Does that mean I won't see as much of you?" She wanted to bite her tongue for that lapse, but like a plucked flower, it was done, and she had to live with it.

"That question does not merit an answer, Shirley, and you know it. I'm always happy to finish a job, and I'll be especially happy when this one is behind me."

She was not going to make the mistake of asking him why finding that will was more important to him than completing most of his assignments. She trusted him, but she might not want to know his reasons. Maybe she'd better be more cautious. Her deep sigh told a tale, even to her. After the loving he gave her the night before she left Ellicott City, it was too late for caution. Much too late.

Carson sat in Donald Riggs's office, enjoying some of the Belgian chocolates that Riggs always had in his top desk drawer. "When will I be able to get back in the house?" he asked Riggs. "I had to stop just as I thought I was on to something. I had Leon Farrell all wrong at first. Not even his children understood the man. Gradually I realized that he didn't seek understanding and would not have welcomed it. You can't imagine how glad I am that I didn't grow up in that man's house."

"I expect you're right. Leon cared deeply about Catherine, and when she died, he lost interest in people, including his children. It doesn't surprise me that you pegged him wrong; he spent his last ten years locked up in a shell of himself, guarding his property and his money and loving nobody, not even himself. I hope you can find that will, if only to free Gunther and Shirley from Edgar's venom. That man's fixation on his father's will has caused him to deteriorate more with each passing day. Believe me, if I had the keys to heaven, I don't think Leon Farrell would get in."

Riggs's secretary brought in a carafe of coffee, two mugs, cream, and sugar. "I gave up on porcelain cups, man," Riggs said, "so a mug will have to do. Help yourself."

They sipped coffee for a minute quietly, and Carson wondered if he'd have to remind Riggs of his reason for being in the man's office. But Riggs hadn't forgotten. "As soon as the inspector goes over the repairmen's work, you can go in there. But the roofers say they need a couple more days, three if it rains. That means you should be able to get in at the latest by the middle of next week."

"Thanks. I want to finish with Edgar Farrell. I don't like the man, and my tolerance for him is almost nil."

Riggs stretched out his legs, leaned back, and laughed. "Thanks for the company. That makes two of us, but his brother and sister are fine people. This will is creating a chasm between them and Edgar. Neither of them has asked me about that will once. But Edgar's been on me about it since the day after Leon was buried. Edgar's a deadbeat. The other two are used to making their own way, and Leon did not help them as he should have. He didn't always give them money for their school needs, and they came to me."

Carson tried not to appear too eager and had to work at keeping a casual tone in his voice. "How did Edgar turn out so badly?"

"Catherine, his mother, spoiled him rotten. When he was about seventeen, she realized what she'd done, but it was too late to correct him. By the way, did you see that story on Shirley in *Around the World Travel* magazine? I've known Shirley since she was ten or so. She has developed into a lovely woman. Smart, too."

"Yeah. She is that." From the twinkle in Riggs's eyes, Carson knew he'd given himself away. Not that he cared. If he was lucky, a lot more people would know how he felt about Shirley Farrell.

Riggs handed him a copy of the magazine. "You may keep it. My wife and I decided against a winter vacation, so I don't need it."

Back in his own office, Carson read the story of Shirley's work as a public relations specialist for the cruise line and gazed reverently at the pictures of her at work. He didn't think he'd ever been so proud. It called for some serious congratulatory efforts on his part. She hadn't sent him a copy of the magazine, so he had time to make plans.

The evening of the day she returned from the cruise, they held hands in a little ice-cream store not far from Gunther's apartment. Without thinking about it, Carson leaned forward and brushed her lips with a quick kiss. "How would you like to see *The Lion King* or *The Phantom of the Opera*?"

Her eyes sparkled. "You mean they're playing in Baltimore? Great! Let's see *The Lion King*."

"They're playing in New York, and I'll get tickets for Saturday and hotel rooms for Friday and Saturday. How's that? I expect Saturday will be my last free day for a while. Repairs on the house will be finished this week, and come Monday, I'll be back on the job of finding that will."

Shirley showed no hesitation. "I'd love to go, but if I go off with you for the weekend, my brother will ask you about your intentions."

His grin would probably annoy her, but he didn't try to control it, and it bloomed into a laugh. "I'll damned well tell him, too," he managed to say amid the laughter. "Uh . . . you mean Gunther, right?"

It was her turn to laugh. "Who do you think? After your set-to with Edgar Thanksgiving Day, I doubt he'll mention my name to you again." They checked into the Park Lane Hotel at noon that Friday.

It perplexed Gunther that his calls to Frieda went unanswered. He wanted to warn her so that she'd prepare herself to make a good impression on the chief doctor for that cruise line. He went down to the kitchen and asked Mirna for Frieda's cell phone number.

She wrote it on a piece of paper torn from the edge of a brown paper bag and eyed him in her best motherly fashion. "Mr. G, you told me you didn't have no interest in Frieda." She looked toward the ceiling and rolled her eyes. "I tell you . . . Lord, men don't know when they well off."

He couldn't believe what he was hearing. "Mirna, for the last time, I have no interest in Frieda as a woman, and I'm sure that I never will. But if I did, why would you be so set against it? I'm curious. What's wrong with her?"

"She a good person, Mr. G, till you slip up and do something to her that she don't like. Then she the most vindictive person the Lord ever made. Everybody makes mistakes, but if you make one with Frieda, don't expect forgiveness no time soon."

"I thought you said she was a churchgoing Christian. That doesn't sound like it."

"Truth is truth, sir. I guess she must have to pray a lot." She handed him the phone number. "If you need a friend, though, you can count on Frieda."

"I gathered as much. Thanks for the phone number."

He went back to his room thinking of his conversation with Mirna and the one he'd had with Frieda about her life. If she was vindictive, she had probably earned the right; no one deserved the life she'd had, and he imagined that few people would have come through it as she had. In spite of it all, she had maintained her self-respect and integrity. He dialed her cell phone number.

"Hello. This is Frieda."

"Ms. Davis, this is Gunther Farrell. How are you?"

"I'm good, Mr. Farrell. How you doing?"

"My health seems to have been completely restored. I'm calling because Shirley set up an appointment for you with the head of the medical service of the Paradise Cruise Line, the line that she works for, and he wants to interview you. His office is in Orlando, but he'll pay for your transportation there and back and a night's stay at a hotel. His name is Larsen, Dr. Hugh Larsen. Expect a call from him soon." When she didn't respond, he said, "Are you still there?"

"Uh . . . you just knocked the breath out of me."

"I wrote a recommendation for you, and I suppose he checked with your supervisors at the hospital, so let's hope for the best."

"Hope? You kidding? I'm gon' be on my knees praying." After a minute's silence, she said, "But, Mr. Farrell, you know I'm not an RN."

"Of course I know it. Larsen knows it, too. Just put your best foot forward. And let me know what happens."

"I will, sir. I sure will, and I thank you and Miss Shirley from the bottom of my heart."

Less than an hour after he hung up, he received a call from Frieda. "Mr. Farrell, I'm going to Orlando. He called me. He don't usually work on Saturdays, but since I have that day off, he's gon' be at the office—I mean the clinic—just to see me. Mr. Farrell, I think I'm out of my head . . . or something. I'm gon' take Friday afternoon off and fly to Orlando. I can't believe this. Well, I just thought I'd let you know."

"I'll be rooting for you," he said, and he meant it.

He'd met all kinds of people, beginning with the days when, as a nine-year-old, he delivered newspapers to "upstanding" citizens who were slothful about paying him, and he didn't take to people readily. But he had a feeling of compatibility with Frieda that seemed unusual. He shrugged. Why not? She'd been his nurse, and a caring nurse such as Frieda was like a mother. Was it any wonder that he felt so comfortable with her?

He had a feeling of unease about Edgar, but his mind told him that he would see Edgar when Edgar needed him and not before. He got a copy of the *Baltimore Afro-American* and searched the entertainment section until he saw a notice that Edgar was appearing at the Charcoal Club. Satisfied that his brother could at least eat, he put his mind on his own affairs.

His latest electronic game was selling well, but he needed an advertising gimmick that was at least as strong as the ones used to push *Bravado,* his best-selling game, over the top. Medford maintained that they couldn't have equal success with each game, but he planned to shoot for the moon every time. On his way home from work that afternoon, he came within a foot of hitting a man on stilts. He drove another few feet, parked, and walked back to the man.

"Are you all right, buddy? That was a harebrained thing you did. Next time, wait for the light."

"You're right, and I'm glad you weren't text messaging or I'd probably have been killed."

"That's not good enough. What could you have been thinking about?"

"Man, I'm a widower with two children and no job for the past three months. I'm down to my last dollar, and that's all I ever think about."

Gunther thought for a minute. "What kind of work do you do?"

"I'm a typesetter, but I've been picking up odd jobs entertaining kids on these stilts. The problem is that nobody's giving kid parties. Kids love guys on stilts."

Ideas seemed to crisscross in Gunther's mind,

and he eliminated them as fast as they came to him. "I've got it!" he said aloud. "Ever done any camera work, videos, anything like that?"

The man's eagerness was painful to watch. "I've acted. I mean, I was in the theater group the whole four years I was in college."

He gave the man his card. "I'm headed to my office. If you can take off those stilts, you can come along with me."

The man sat on the hood of Gunther's silver Mercedes and took off the stilts. Together, they stored them in the backseat with their ends sticking out of the window.

"Let's hope I don't pass a cop who hasn't issued his quota of tickets today," Gunther said. Medford would probably tell him that he was crazy, but having a man on stilts promote that electronic game was not a bad idea. It would be different, and it would get children's attention.

"Well, what do you think?" he asked Medford after introducing him to Cory Benjamin and explaining his idea.

Medford rubbed the back of his neck. "It's fabulous, Gunther. What I can't figure is how you came up with anything this far-out. The ad will be a huge hit." He looked at Cory. "Let's see what kind of outfit will work best with this game."

Cory looked at Gunther. "Are you going to pay me for this?"

"Sure. A hundred a day for the work and the going rates for as long as we run the ad. I usually pay twice monthly, but you'll get your money at the end of the day, since you said you were broke."

Cory dropped himself into the nearest chair. "Do you mind if I call my aunt? She keeps the kids for me. Even if this job doesn't last but two days, at least we'll be able to eat for a while."

Very little time elapsed before Gunther realized that he'd struck a gold mine in Cory. Working together, offering and rejecting suggestions, Cory and Medford produced a video commercial that Gunther thought equally as interesting as the game he'd created.

"I got an idea, Gunther," Medford said after they sent the video to the distributor's marketing firm. "We've got a good foothold in the industry now, and we could use another hand. Cory is a genius at ideas, he's a good actor, and he knows a few things about the computer. What do you think?"

"I've been thinking the same, and since the two of you got along so well, we ought to keep him if he's willing," Gunther said. "I like his personality. Ask him to come into my office."

"Cory, Medford and I like your work and your attitude. This is a small operation, and we have to get along smoothly. If you'd like to work here full-time, I can offer you fifty thousand a year to start. As we grow, your income will increase. You'll get a bonus at the end of the year, the amount depending on how we've done. What about it?"

"Gunther, you don't know how good it is to feel like a man again. I'll treat your business like it was my own. When do I start?"

Fate had smiled on both Cory and Gunther. He'd never thought he'd be thankful for having almost killed a man. "The day you came here," Gunther said. "I'll draw up a contract to include health insurance for you and your family and paid leave. Welcome aboard."

He answered the phone. "What? You're kidding."

He looked at Cory. "Our marketing people want to enter that video in the annual commercials competition. They're certain that it'll win. Well, I'll be damned." He looked at the glow on Cory's face and noted the strength and solid masculinity that the man now exuded. What a difference it made to a man if he had a sense of self-worth.

What he wouldn't give to see such a transformation in his brother, to see in Edgar the demeanor of a mature, accomplished, and successful man. He fought back the tears. It would never happen, because Edgar could not envisage that in himself. What a wasted life, and what a pity. He filled in a contract form and gave it to his secretary to type up. If he were in Cory's place, he'd want proof that he had a job.

"After you type it, give it to Cory to read and sign," he told his secretary. He went back to his office feeling good, as if spring had bloomed out all around him.

However, Edgar seemed anchored in his same old rut. "You know what you can do, don't you?" Edgar said to the one man who had been eager to hire him days earlier.

"Now, look, Farrell, you can't leave me with no music tonight. Without a guitarist, I don't have a band, and the Charcoal Club has a reputation as a first-class house."

"I don't play with no crappy drummer. Three nights of that two-bit amateur, and I've had it." He turned his back and answered his cell phone. "Farrell speaking. Yeah. What's up, Gunther? Did Carson come up with anything yet?"

"He can't get back on the job until Wednesday. I was wondering if you were still at the Charcoal Club."

"Man, this place sucks. I'm getting ready to head out right now."

"Really? Where are you going? At least that's a job. Where else are you going to find work? Not many people can afford to go to clubs these days, so if a club has enough patrons to hire musicians, I'd stay there if I were you. Unless you plan to panhandle on the street. "

"Yeah. Well, look, man, I gotta go." *Where, indeed! Maybe it wasn't too late.* He went over to the manager. "Like I said when I came here, man. You've been good to me, and one good deed deserves another. Tell that drummer to shape up, will you? All he has to do is maintain the rhythm, and he can do that if he keeps his mind on his work."

"Good. Good. I'll tell him right now," the manager said, looked toward the heavens, whispered something, and went to find the drummer.

That Saturday afternoon, Gunther sat on his balcony listening to a CD of Cream's farewell concert in Albert Hall, London. He'd come of age with Clapton, Baker, and Bruce, and he could still listen to Eric Clapton's guitar for hours and want more. Mirna came out on the balcony and handed him a mug of hot, spiced, hard cider just as Clapton's solo on "Spoonful" began. But he knew she wanted to talk, and he could listen to that music whenever he liked, so he shut it off.

"Thanks," he said, accepting the cider. "This is just the thing for a nippy day like today. Sit down."

She sat with her back to the brick wall. Mirna never seemed comfortable on that balcony. It amused him that she behaved as if it could fall at any time. "I just got a call from Frieda, Mr. G." At that, his antenna went up. "She act like somebody shot her out of a cannon. I didn't understand one word she say. I think maybe she coming down with something. I told her to come by here and let me have a look at her. I hope you don't mind."

The words had hardly left her mouth when the doorbell rang. "That must be her now," Mirna said.

He finished the mug of cider more quickly than he ordinarily would have. To his mind, cider was something you sipped.

"What's come over you?" he heard Mirna ask Frieda, and waited for the answer.

"Girl, you don't know what happened."

"That's right, I don't," Mirna said with a note of exasperation in her voice. "But you'll tell me. I hope you ain't as sick as you sound."

"Sick? I never been so happy in my whole life. Mr. Farrell and Miss Shirley got me a job with that cruise line, and they paying me money. We speaking real money."

Gunther bounded out of his chair and headed toward the sound of their voices.

"Are you saying you got the job?" he asked, looking hard at Frieda.

"Yes, indeed. I tell you I practically flew back here with my own wings. Mr. Farrell, they treated me like I was somebody special. That hotel was da bomb, somebody met me at the airport, and this long black limousine took me back there. It was real special. Dr. Larsen wants me to work in the clinic in Orlando for six months to get used to the way they do things, and then he'll assign me to a ship. He also said that if I take some courses at the University of Central Florida College of Nursing, the cruise line will pay for that. I am sitting on top of the world. I am going right out of my head."

She looked at Gunther. "I'm . . . I'm sorry, but I think I'm going to cry, and I never cry. Never," she said as tears cascaded down her cheeks. "That man said I'm gon' get forty-five thousand dollars a year to start with, plus my expenses, health insurance, paid vacation, Christmas bonus, and an IRA account. I'm finally gon' be able to buy me a little piece of property. I signed the contract. Is that contract legal, Mr. Farrell?"

Her happiness enveloped him. He didn't know when he'd felt so good about a thing that happened to someone other than him. "If both of you signed it," he said, "it will stand in any court."

Frieda pulled out a chair from the dining room table, sat down, lowered her head, and covered her face with her hands. "I just can't believe it, but I sure am grateful." She looked at Gunther. "Y'all never gon' be sorry you got me that job, 'cause I'm gon' do my very best every single day, and that's the truth."

He walked over and patted her lightly on the shoulder. "I know that, Frieda. That's why I recommended you. I'm just as happy about this as you are. Shirley should be back this evening, and I'll let her know you got the job."

He made his way up the stairs. First Cory Benjamin and now Frieda saw their ship come in, and he figured that it was about to happen for Shirley. He thought about Edgar. Nobody could make him believe that their father's spiteful treatment of his will hadn't exacerbated Edgar's failings as a man. Leon Farrell had never given his children what he could and should have, neither materially nor in respect to parental guidance. And, in death, he had simply laughed at them and invited them to tear each other apart. It wouldn't happen. He'd see to that.

Frieda remained where Gunther left her, almost too overwhelmed to collect her thoughts. "You want some tea or some coffee?" Mirna asked Frieda. "When you supposed to go to Orlando? You got to get yourself together, girl."

"I forgot all about putting something in my stomach. I'd love a cup of coffee. I'm gon' clear out of the dump on Franklin Street. The cruise line will send somebody to pack and ship my things. I'm gon' leave that stuff in storage and rent a furnished place till I see how things are going. I gotta call Coreen and tell her I'm gon' be down in Florida. We promised to stay in touch."

"You don't have to justify it to me. Your mother *ought* to know where you are."

"You been a good friend, Mirna, but please don't push me about Coreen. I'm inching along as best I can with her, and if you were in my shoes, you'd understand that."

Mirna held her hands up, palms out. "All right.

That's what I get for not minding my business. Here's some baked ham and some good old butter-milk biscuits. I just made 'em."

Frieda made a sandwich and savored it. "This sure is good. I must have been starving. You just did a good deed." She finished two sandwiches. "I hate to eat and run, but I gotta start packing my personal things. I ain't gon' let those men pack my makeup, toiletries, and underwear. These three biscuits going with me. Thanks. I'll call you tomorrow."

"I'll send up a prayer for you. This is what you been working for, and I know you'll make the best of it."

Frieda walked into her apartment, closed the door, sat down, and dialed Coreen's home phone number. "How are you, Coreen?" There! She'd finally called her by her first name.

"Frieda! It's wonderful to hear from you. I'm up and about and doing just fine. How are things with you?"

"Great. That's why I called you." She told Coreen about her new job and how she got it. She raved on about it, not noticing Coreen's silence. "Am I making tracks or am I?"

"Oh, yes," Coreen said. "You're a wonderful nurse, and you'll do a good job. I'm so happy for you, and I'm really glad you'll have a chance to work toward your RN."

"You know, I was just gon' take some courses. You don't know how glad I am that I called you about this. Lord, this is just too much! Maybe I'll get to see you before I move to Orlando. I'm sure gon' try. Give my best to your husband, Eric, and Glen. I'll send you my new phone numbers soon as I get them. Bye for now."

Frieda hung up, swung around, and hugged herself. She was going to have a job where people respected her, and she was going to college. If Coreen hadn't mentioned working on her RN, she wouldn't have taken full advantage of that opportunity. Something good always came out of the talks with Coreen. She'd have to consider that when she had more time. Right now, she had to get ready for the movers.

She threw up her hands. "I haven't even told my boss at the hospital. I gotta keep those irons in the fire, 'cause I don't know if I'll need to go back there. Never burn all your bridges." After writing a thank-you note to Shirley, she began sorting out her clothes and personal items. "Thank the Lord, I never was one to buy a lot of things I don't need. This is easier than I thought it was gon' be."

Suddenly, she grabbed a chair and sat down.

Something was not right. Coreen didn't seem half as excited about her new job as Gunther had been. As much as they'd discussed Frieda's yearning for better working conditions . . . Perhaps Coreen had been having a bad day and didn't want to spoil Frieda's joy by mentioning it. That had to be the reason. What else could explain it?

"Just my luck," Shirley said to herself when the door opened just as she turned the key in the lock. "Hi, Gunther. Don't tell me Mirna's cooking chicken and dumplings."

"That could be it. Good to see you, Carson. How was Broadway?"

"Great. How's it going? The two shows we saw lived up to their notices. I highly recommend a weekend theater trip, provided you have all of your reservations and tickets before you leave here. I expect the snow's thick up there by now."

"We had some flakes here yesterday. You're welcome to stay for dinner if that suits you. I dare not issue you a genuine invitation, lest Shirley gets her back up."

"If Mirna's cooking chicken and dumplings, Shirley can get her back up all she wants to, but I accept your kind invitation."

Gunther went to the kitchen and came back with a grin spread across his face. He looked at Carson and spoke as if the two of them were alone. "Mirna told me to tell you that nobody makes chicken and dumplings like she does, and that tonight, she's outdone herself. Come on in."

"I've got a lot to tell you," Gunther said to Shirley, but with his tone and demeanor, he included Carson as a rightful recipient of his news. He told them about Frieda, and that she was getting ready to move to Orlando and that he'd hired Cory Benjamin full-time. "Both of these incidents have given me a great feeling. Let's have a drink. Carson, I know you don't drink when you're driving, but how about a glass of wine. It isn't often that my spirit soars like this."

"I'll take a vodka comet with lots of ice," Carson said. "I feel you, man. From what you've said, it seems that both of them not only needed a break but also deserved it. You helped, and you have to feel great. Now, if we could only work a miracle with your brother."

"He phoned me this morning," Shirley said. "He's got a two-week job at the Charcoal Club in Philadelphia beginning tomorrow night. He was on his way to Philly when he called me."

"What happened to his job at the Charcoal Club in Baltimore?" Gunther asked.

"That's an East Coast chain. He said the Philadelphia club is the parent club and that the manager sent for him. He'll be playing solo."

"Let's hope he keeps that job for at least the next two weeks," Carson said. "By that time, I ought to have this cleared up, and it can't happen soon enough for me."

Chapter Twelve

As Carson was about to leave Shirley, she asked him, "Don't you want me to go with you to the house to look for the will? I'm not leaving for Fort Lauderdale until the day after tomorrow."

That was precisely what he had not wanted to hear. "Sweetheart, I've given myself a deadline to find that will, and you would be a distraction that I don't need. I'll call you after I get home."

She seemed somewhat taken aback, but he couldn't help it; he had to maintain his integrity to the extent possible. He rubbed her nose with the tip of his index finger. "This job has taken me three or four times as long as I had anticipated, but I don't quit until I finish. So bear with me, will you?"

She reached up and kissed him on the mouth. "Okay. I won't interfere with your work. See you this evening."

He'd have a talk with her about that. He respected her right to work on a job that took her from her home station for weeks at a time, so she had to grant him the right to do his job as he saw fit. He winked at her, turned, and headed for the elevator.

As was his habit, he called Shirley shortly after he got home. "This past weekend may have signaled a change in my life. It won't be easy in the future; it won't be easy to have days pass without being with you. I still love you."

"And I still love you," she said. "When I'm away from you, I miss you, Carson, but this time, I expect to be miserable."

"We'll work it out, sweetheart. We don't have a choice." And they didn't, he realized after he hung up, because he couldn't do his kind of work solely on cruise ships.

The next morning, he awakened early, feeling refreshed and ready to work. Like an itch in need of scratching, he could hardly wait to get to that house and resume his search. He parked in the garage, entered the house, closed the door behind him, and locked it. Then he secured that and the other two ground-level doors with their chains and headed up the stairs to Leon Farrell's office/den.

With one press of the button, the panel slid open, and his adrenaline began to pump. Carson knew little about fine art beyond what he'd learned browsing in museums in the United States and abroad. He'd had to learn how to spot certain fake sculptures and wooden artifacts. He pulled up a chair, sat on it, and began to examine the Chinese porcelain vases on the bottom shelf. He'd bet that all seven of them were of considerable value and that unless the two blue and white vases were copies, they might date back several centuries. If they were truly valuable, they would be listed in the will. He

handled them carefully. Unfortunately, none of
the seven contained the will.

Neither did a leather box containing Catherine's high school and college memorabilia, as well
as letters from her parents, who hadn't wanted her
to marry the man who had become their son-in-
law. Leon Farrell had worshiped a woman who was
his social better. Had he driven himself to become
his wife's social equal? And had his in-laws cared
that he became very rich? From the letters in his
hand, Carson doubted it.

At about two o'clock, Carson looked at the
many items still to be examined, found a shopping
bag, and put a dozen of the larger plastic robots in
it. He locked the house and took the robots to the
police laboratory in Baltimore.

"I need some lab work, Miles," he said to the
sergeant. "I want to know if these things are hollow, and whether they can be closed to look as if
they've never been tampered with."

"No sweat. We can do that in half an hour.
Somebody hiding stuff in robots?"

Carson didn't move a muscle in his face. Miles
was a good friend, but he didn't want a conversation about those robots. "All things are possible,
man. You know me; I turn every dime sideways."

"Don't I! That's what makes you the best detective anywhere around here."

He followed the sergeant, a man who had been
his squad-car partner when he joined the police
force years earlier. Not only did X-rays fail to show
a will in any of them, but the procedure proved
that if they had been taken apart, it would have
been almost impossible to reassemble them any-

where but in the factory that made them. Disappointed and dispirited, he drove back to the Farrell house, put the robots where he found them, and went home. Nothing, *nada,* zip for a day's work. He considered taking a shower, heating a slice of pizza, drinking a can of beer, and going to bed.

That could have been understandable, when I was eighteen, he said to himself, *but accepting defeat doesn't cut it these days.* As he dialed Shirley's cell phone number, he remembered that he had a date with her. *Wake up, man. You were about to lay an egg of colossal proportions.*

"Hi," he said. "I won't be good company tonight, Shirley, but I want to see you."

"Hi, hon. I gather you didn't have any success today. I know just the tonic for you. Come over here. I'll put on my favorite movie, and we can have pizza, beer, and a lot of laughs. Gunther's out tonight, so I told Mirna not to cook and sent her home early. It's a riotously funny movie. You'll love it."

"Okay, I'll bring ice cream." It did not occur to him to question his elevated mood as he dressed. He bought a quart of black walnut ice cream and a six-pack of pilsner beer and arrived at Gunther's apartment within the hour.

He put as much enthusiasm as he could in his greeting, but he hastened to tell her that the kiss belied his feelings. "What will we be watching?" he asked her.

"*The Russians Are Coming, the Russians Are Coming.* It's a cold-war movie. If you don't laugh, I'll know that you need urgent medical care." She looked at him then, seeming to scrutinize him. "You are down, aren't you? I'm sorry, darling." She opened her arms, and he walked into them, immersing himself in the healing love that she offered.

"You will find it, Carson. If it exists, you will find it. I am as certain of that as I am of my name."

This time, his hug reflected his true feelings for her. "You're what I need, Shirley," he said, took her hand, and walked with her to the kitchen. They heated the pizza, opened the beer, and ate in the kitchen.

Later, when the movie ended, he got up and held out his hand. "I'd better leave now. I have to appear in court at nine tomorrow morning as an expert witness for the state, and that means being in Baltimore by eight-thirty. Walk me to the door, and don't lay it on too thick." The last thing he wanted was the embarrassment of having Gunther Farrell find him in bed with his sister.

"Give me three rings when you get home," she said. "I'll call you tomorrow evening from Fort Lauderdale. Good luck tomorrow morning."

He wrapped her to him, more tightly than was wise, he realized, when he felt the stirring in his loins. Her kiss sent him a message that he didn't need right then. "Get there safely," he whispered, and left while he had the will to do so. As soon as he walked into his apartment, he phoned her and waited until she answered.

"I still love you," he said. "Good night."

"And I still love you."

With his testimony behind him, Carson returned to the work that occupied most of his thoughts. As usual, he parked in the garage, locked and secured all of the ground-floor doors after entering the house, and headed straight for Leon Farrell's secret closet. He told himself to search shelf by shelf, and then search for a hideaway place within that closet. He had already searched the top shelf, so he began with the second.

He nearly fell backward when his hand slid under what seemed to be a plastic envelope beneath a man's woolen scarf. He grabbed the envelope, rushed to Leon's desk, and sat there. Folded inside of an old newspaper, he found a document the heading of which read, "Last Will and Testament." He closed his eyes and took deep breaths for several minutes. At long last!

But almost as soon as he began reading, his spirits sank. He had before him a copy of Catherine Farrell's mother's will. Flipping pages, he saw a bequest, recognized its implications, and sprang from the chair. Shirley's maternal grandmother had left her a hundred thousand dollars, which she was to receive on her eighteenth birthday. If Shirley had been given that money, he doubted that she would have struggled through Morgan State on fellowships and whatever part-time jobs she could get. He noted that the will was probated eleven months after Catherine's death.

"The more I learn about Leon Farrell, the less I like him. Well, I'm not rocking this boat," he said aloud. "Riggs can handle it." A quick perusal of the newspaper revealed a detailed obituary for Shirley's grandmother. He poured coffee from the thermos he'd brought along and drank it as thoughts of possible hiding places for a will occupied his mind. He began searching the next shelf item by item until it occurred to him that before he handled the tissue-fine embroidered linen hand-kerchiefs on that shelf, he'd better put on the latex gloves he'd brought along.

He answered his cell phone after several rings. "Montgomery speaking."

"This is Gunther. You've probably checked this, but I wondered if Father had more than one lawyer or if he'd filed that will anyplace. Just a thought."

"Thanks, Gunther. I can't exclude the possibility that he had more than one lawyer, because he was certainly capable of that, but I can say he didn't file his will in this state."

"Just a thought. Shirley thinks you're being asked to do too much. I want you to know that I don't hold you to that contract."

"Thanks, man, but I'm holding myself to it."

"That doesn't surprise me. See you soon."

I'll finish this next shelf, he said to himself, *and then I'm getting out of here. This place is depressing.*

On the fourth shelf sat nine wooden robots, eight of which were painted different colors. One unpainted robot that was larger than the others stood before him like a challenge. Did he dare dismantle Leon Farrell's masterpieces? He noted that Leon had signed and dated each, until he looked under the belly of the big, unpainted donkey, which had neither a date nor a signature. Carson surmised that Leon hadn't finished that robot. After examining it, he went back to the second shelf and retrieved the sketches of robot construction that Leon had stored there. The diagram of a donkey showed that that robot had been constructed as if it were of two halves. But how were the parts joined?

He spread out a newspaper, put the donkey on it, and began to examine it. Not that he expected it to contain the will; storing it in the robot that stood out from the others in several ways would have been too obvious. But its construction would tell him whether he'd waste time examining the other wooden robots. Carson turned the feet slowly so as not to damage them. He moved the joints and the tail. *This guy turned in a clever job,* he said to himself. *But how the heck did he put these two halves together, since the head seemed to have been carved from a single piece of . . .*

"I've got it!" he yelled aloud. He unscrewed the donkey's head and stared at the inside of the body. He put the robot down and drank the remainder of the coffee from the thermos. Icy, sleetlike darts seemed to attack his arms and legs, and he rubbed his arms as if trying to warm them.

Thinking that he wanted so badly to find that will that he'd lost perspective and was seeing a mirage, he grabbed his leather jacket, went outside, and ran as fast as he could. Oblivious to the dark, overcast sky, the icy wind bruising his face and the sticks, leaves, and other debris swirling around his feet and legs, he ran for three long blocks before turning and running back to the house. Winded, he released a satisfying expletive and told himself, *Go back in there and face it, man. If that's not the will, you'll find it somewhere else.*

After locking and securing the house, he went back to Leon's office and picked up the headless donkey robot, took it to the desk, and sat down. Slowly, with his thumb and forefinger, he eased the sheaves of paper from the belly of the donkey and unfolded The Last Will and Testament of Leon Farrell. His last tear had dropped from his eyes at the grave of his mother seven years earlier.

Shaken, he said a prayer of thanks and wiped his eyes. Then, for fear that the papers in his hands could be one of Leon's tricks, he turned to the last page, saw Donald Riggs's signature as one witness, and laughed aloud.

He'd done it! It had taken him half a year, but he had finally found Leon Farrell's will. *I'd better make a couple of copies of this thing,* he said to himself. *At this point, it's as valuable as my stocks. I wonder what mischief Leon's done with this will.*

He turned to the second page and began reading. Suddenly, the air swooshed out of him. He leaned back in the chair, closed his eyes, and told himself to breathe. After reading all terms of the will, he screwed on the donkey's head and put it back in its place on the fourth shelf. Then he slid the wall panel in place, and with the will secure in a zipped-up pocket inside his leather jacket, he turned out the lights, walked down the stairs, and locked the door behind him. If luck was on his side, he'd been in that dreary place for the last time. The few choice words he spat out didn't begin to express his concern. The Farrell siblings were in for one hair-raising shock.

While Carson fretted over the terms of Leon Farrell's will, Gunther sat with Medford and Cory, checking the distributor's receipts from *Pipper,* the video game that featured Cory on stilts and that had become Gunther's second best-seller. "I want to continue designing handheld electronic games," Gunther said, "because I think that's what I do best, but I can see that *Pipper* is going to be a bigger hit. I'm in something of a dilemma about this."

"I suggest we do both," Medford said. "Let's continue *Bravado* and *Pipper* as series. I think people love series, because we're already getting requests for the next edition of each one. What are you thinking, Gunther?"

"I think it's great, but we need what amounts to a novel or a story for each one. I'm thinking of a long novel presented in installments, sort of like a soap opera. Did you ever do any dancing, Cory? I have in mind a story for Pipper trying out as a dancer."

"I danced plenty in college, even learned to tap, but I don't think I could do that on stilts."

A grin spread over Gunther's face. "You do the choreography and the dancing. We'll photograph it with a green screen behind you, and the computer and I will put the stilts under you."

"I'll make it kid friendly," Cory said, his face the picture of happiness.

The three men talked for several hours, offering ideas, accepting and rejecting them as if they had worked together in harmony all their lives. "I couldn't ask for a better team," Gunther said.

Later, he sat alone in his office with his elbows pressing his knees and his hands together in the shape of a pyramid. Thinking. With his business solidly on track, he could afford to spend more time getting his life in order and, hopefully, getting his brother on the way to becoming a useful citizen. To his mind, changing Edgar required the skill of a good psychotherapist, and getting Edgar to admit he needed one would require a Herculean effort. He'd do what he could.

His thoughts went to Caroline. He cared for her, but with his concerns about the will, his business, and Edgar, he'd been dragging his feet. And he couldn't seem to forget his experience with Lissa. She was nothing like Lissa; indeed, they hardly seemed to be members of the same species, and he had to stop acting as if they had anything in common.

"I'm past the age by which I should have a family," he said to himself. "I haven't behaved fairly with Caroline, and she has a right to know where she stands with me. If she backs off, I'll be in trouble, and she might, because she won't let me string her along." And he didn't want to. He reached for his cell phone. "I'm going for it and I'm going to put my attention on what matters most to me."

He phoned her.

"Hello, Caroline. Could we have dinner this evening and spend tomorrow together?" He got it out in one breath so as not to give her time to question his plan to have dinner with her on Friday evening. Women liked to be busy on Saturdays.

"Sounds like a good plan, but I'm busy this evening. Tomorrow's good. What time?"

Taken aback, he didn't have an immediate response. And it did not escape him that she said not a word but waited for his response. "I suppose I deserve to be disappointed, Caroline, but I'm not going to lie and say I hope your evening is enjoyable. As for tomorrow, I thought we'd put on some really comfortable and warm clothing and go bike riding through a forest trail that I love."

"Where would we go?"

"Out toward Font Hill. I often ride out there alone. It's lovely any time of year, but especially now when it's so quiet and still. I'll pack a lunch, and we can make a fire and rest at a spot I know. If you're not too tired after we get back to Ellicott City, we could have a nice dinner."

"You really meant spending the day together. Well, I'm all for it, and I'm looking forward to it." They talked for about half an hour before saying good-bye. After he hung up, he wondered why he'd thought a woman with Caroline's looks and accomplishments would have nothing to do on a weekend. *Well, I'd better take advantage of what I'm getting.*

He phoned Mirna. "This is Gunther. I'm going bike riding with Caroline tomorrow, and I'd like to treat her to a picnic lunch out on the trail. What can you suggest?"

"You just leave it to me, Mr. G. It's too cold for beer, so I'll put in a bottle of wine and a big thermos of coffee."

"Just the coffee, and remember that I have to pack it in the basket on my bicycle."

"I know that, Mr. G. Just leave it to me. What time you leaving?"

"About eight-thirty in the morning."

"Yeah? It gon' be freezing cold, but I 'spect it'll warm up by noon. I'll have it for you when you ready to go."

He dressed in layers, put socks inside his boots, woolen gloves inside his leather ones, and earmuffs under his woolen cap, and got downstairs at eight that Saturday morning. "I fixed you a real good breakfast, Mr. G," Mirna said, beaming at the table laden with waffles, sausage, scrambled eggs, hash browns, and fresh fruit salad.

She poured their coffee and sat down. "I sure

am glad to see you do something besides work. Miss Caroline's a lovely woman in a lot of ways, and I been wanting to tell you that you should pay some attention to her."

"How do you know I haven't been?" he asked after Mirna said the grace.

"'Cause she don't never call here, and that's 'cause she don't feel comfortable calling you."

"How do you know she doesn't call me on my cell phone?"

"She doesn't. You keep that phone in the inside pocket of your jacket. You come home and pull off the jacket, and half the time you leave it in the foyer closet. If she had a habit of calling you on it, you'd take the phone upstairs with you. Am I right?"

"I'm working on it, Mirna."

"That's all you can do, Mr. G. I fixed you a real nice lunch." She went to the kitchen and returned with a picnic basket. "Everything's in here, and here's a handful of fatwood and a box of matches, if you're planning to stop at a camping site. But you be real careful." He stared at Mirna, thinking that she wasn't old enough to be his mother, and wishing that she were. To hell with it. He took the picnic basket from her, set it on the floor, and hugged her.

"When I hired you, I had no way of knowing the stability and comfort that you would bring to my life. Thanks for this and for thinking of the fatwood and matches."

Caroline opened her door and smiled at him. Dressed in a storm jacket and pants of beige and burnt orange, a matching cap, and heavy boots, she looked like autumn itself. "You always look perfect," he told her, and handed her a pair of fur earmuffs. "These will keep your ears warm." He had an urge to hug her, but he didn't think he'd earned that right.

"I figured that if we ran into a bear, I wouldn't look too strange to him. He should be used to these colors."

He couldn't help laughing at that logic, and when a sense of happiness and well-being enveloped him, he gave in to the urge and hugged her. To his amazement, she returned his embrace. He stared down at her, though he knew that trying to read her would be a useless endeavor. Caroline could camouflage her feelings with the efficiency of an octopus changing its color in order to hide from sharks and stingrays. He stored their bikes on the top of his Mercedes and headed to Font Hill, where he parked and locked the car and its steering wheel.

"I've never been here before," Caroline said, "and I love the outdoors. This is a treat."

He raised the collar of her jacket, doubled her scarf, and tied it around her neck. "Unfortunately, we'll be facing the wind, at least for a while," he said, "and I don't want you to be cold."

"If I get cold in all these clothes, you'll have no choice but to warm me. Where will you build the fire?"

Good thing he didn't respond to the first part of her comment. "There's a camping site about seven miles from here, not far from the river."

"Really? Next time, let's come prepared to fish," she said. "I love to fish."

"If we're going to do it, we'd better beat the first snowfall. When I looked out this morning, I thought we'd have snow." Polite talk as if they were strangers, and whose fault was it? His. They should have become closer by now. They pedaled beyond the gravel to the beginning of the winding road, its breadth sufficient to accommodate standard-sized cars and trucks. He knew the road would eventually narrow and lead them into idyllic scenery.

"These trees are so tall," Caroline said after a long stretch of silence. "They seem to touch the sky."

"The real tall ones are tulip trees. I'm told they're the tallest trees in North America, including California redwoods."

"It's wonderful. Look at the sun filtering through the leaves. I've never been in such a place. Can we come back here sometime?"

"Of course. But if you think this is extraordinary, we have to go to some of the forests in Anne Arundel County over near the Severn River. On a day like this, it's an enchanting place."

"Imagine how wonderful the late summer would have been," she said, "if we'd done things like this. I haven't met many people who love nature as I do."

"I think we might have," he said, "if I hadn't been so focused on my business and my family and, of course, if I hadn't gone fishing in Assawoman Bay and developed pneumonia. Are you tired?"

"Thanks for asking, but I'm not winded yet."

They neared the cove where he knew he'd find a camping spot that offered a wooden table, a couple of benches, and a safe place to build a fire.

"Do you think wild animals come here, Gunther?"

"I'll have a fire in a minute, so you needn't expect any visitors. Out here, a fire is a better weapon against wild animals than a gun is." He built the fire, put a plastic cloth on the table, and spread out the warm slices of quiche, spiced buffalo wings, crab cakes, and buttermilk biscuits. A ziplock plastic bag contained a salad of mixed greens, and in two other containers he found grapes and slices of cheesecake.

"That's enough for four people," she said. "My goodness, you're a thoughtful man."

"Thanks, but Mirna put this together."

"You're still thoughtful," she said, and bit into the quiche. "This is good."

"I'm glad you're enjoying it. Mind if I ask what's between you and the guy you went out with last night? I mean . . . is it . . . uh . . . Are you committed to him?"

"No, I'm not. If that were the case, I wouldn't be out here with you. I date him occasionally."

"I'd like to see you on a regular basis. Does any man have the right to demand anything of you?"

"The answer to that question is a definite no. I'd like us to get to know each other better, and I had thought that by now we'd be on different footing, but you haven't shown much interest."

"I didn't show it, but it's been there since the day we met. I had five weeks in bed with pneumonia. After I was able to get back to work, I had to do a lot of catching up there, and problems with Edgar exploded. I'm not responsible for him, but he's my brother. My business is doing well, my life is getting on track, and I can now put my priorities where they should be."

She covered his hand with her own. "I didn't

mean to ask you for reasons why you let things between us dangle, but thanks for telling me. What are you going to do about your brother? And what can you do since he's older than you are?"

"He's working in Philadelphia right now, but he has some grandiose notions about himself, and as difficult as it is for musicians to find work, he'll quit a job if someone fails to genuflect to him."

"What?"

"You know what I mean. He wants his status as a boss guitarist recognized, and if someone doesn't, he'll ditch the job even if he doesn't have ten dollars in his pocket."

"I gather he hasn't had to sleep on the street in twenty-degree weather."

"You're right. I've bailed him out for the last time, and he knows it." A thought occurred to him that he didn't care for. "Are you judging me by my brother?" He turned and looked straight at her.

"Of course not. From what I've observed, his only likeness to you and Shirley is the color of his eyes." As she spoke, she had been rubbing the back of his hand, unconsciously, he knew, and she did it rhythmically, heating him slowly but surely. It must have shown in his eyes, for suddenly she stopped and looked away as if embarrassed.

"Don't," he said. "It was an honest caress, and I loved it."

"Yes," she said beneath her breath, "it was honest."

Fearing that she would become self-conscious with him, he poured cups of hot coffee and served her a slice of cheesecake. "I assume from this lunch that you like women to have a good deal of flesh on them. This stuff is loaded with calories, delicious though it definitely is."

"If a woman is interesting; has an even temperament; is soft, feminine, and loyal; and everything else is in place, why would I care if she's sporting a few extra pounds? If she complained about it and didn't take steps to change it, I'd get tired of the griping, otherwise . . ." He shrugged. His attraction to women didn't depend on their body type. Indeed, he was damned if he knew what it depended on. On the few occasions when it happened, he'd look at the woman, and something about her would get to him. He spent several hours with Caroline the evening he met her, and though she didn't hit him like an exploding hand grenade when he first saw her, by the time they separated that evening, her hooks were solidly in him. And they sank deeper into him each time he was with her.

"I like a man who prefers substance over tinsel," she said, and held out her cup for more coffee. "I also love to eat."

He wondered if he could risk hugging her. They finished the meal, but she seemed reluctant to leave the fire. "If we weren't on our bikes, it would be fun to sit by this fire with a few bottles of beer," she said, surprising him.

"I didn't know you liked beer."

She turned to face him, and he could see that she wanted him to understand precisely her words and her intent. "Gunther, I am not an elitist. I drink beer with my hot dogs at baseball games. When I'm watching football at home or in a stadium, I drink rum and Coke from a flask or from a glass as the venue warrants, and with my meals, I drink wine."

"If I get tickets to the Ravens, will you go with me? I'll furnish the rum and Coke."

Her face creased into a smile that seemed to make her bloom.

I could get used to this woman, he thought, but what he said was, "You do something to me. Let's go. There's something I want to show you."

They cleaned up, put out the fire, and moved on. About a mile and a half down the trail, he stopped. "We have to be very quiet or we'll disturb them," he told her.

They approached a huge old redwood, its trunk more than three yards in diameter, but it had grown so that about three feet of its lower surface had a deep hollow. A large number of squirrels played in the hollow, scampering up, down, and around the tree. He took a bag of walnuts from the pocket of his jacket and gently emptied them on the ground at the base of the hollow.

Two squirrels came out to examine the nuts. Then they sniffed his shoes, looked up at him, and went back to the nuts. "You've done this before," she said, "and the squirrels remember you."

"I guess they do. This is my fourth time here this autumn. It's about the only recreation I've been able to get."

"And you came each of the other times alone?"

"You're the only person I've ever come here with."

She reached up and kissed his cheek. "Thank you. I'd give anything if I'd brought my camera."

As they headed back home, he realized that he wanted to make love with Caroline. And not be-

cause he'd been celibate for several months, but
because he wanted *her,* needed to be with her and
to share himself with her. It had been a long time
since he'd needed, really needed, a specific woman.
The feeling that he needed Caroline unsettled him.

They pedaled back to Font Hill. He stored their
bikes on top of his car and drove Caroline home.
"It's a quarter past three," he said. "I'd like to
come for you at six-thirty for dinner. I'll be wearing a suit and tie."

"I'll be ready. And, Gunther, thanks for one of
the most delightful days I've had in years. I enjoyed it, and I enjoyed being with you."

When he leaned toward her, she came to meet
him, her mouth soft and warm beneath his, and
the electrifying effect confirmed for him the direction in which he was headed.

When he walked into his apartment half an
hour later, Mirna rushed to him and grabbed his
arm, her face beaming with joy about whatever it
was that she had to report.

"Mr. G, Frieda called and said she sitting in a
chair while the movers wrap and pack her things
and organize them just like she tell them. She say
the cruise company paying for everything and
gon' put her up in a hotel till she find where she
want to stay. She say she has to thank you and Miss
Shirley for changing her life. I'm gon' miss her,
'cause she my best friend, but she has had so much
misery in her life, Mr. G. I think she finally being
blessed."

"I certainly hope so, Mirna. Did Shirley call?"

"No, sir. Didn't she say she'd call tonight? Something tells me you enjoyed that picnic too much."

He couldn't help laughing. "Quit fishing, Mirna.

And thanks for the food. You prepared exactly the right things." He bounded up the stairs, whistling as he went.

Carson left the photocopy store and headed for his bank. He put one copy of Leon Farrell's will in his safe-deposit box and another in his briefcase. The original was in an envelope in the inside pocket of his jacket. "If the original gets lost or stolen, it won't matter too much," he said, got into his car, and headed for Donald Riggs's office.

Why should a will cause so many problems? He suspected that its unavailability had contributed to Edgar's moral, if not mental, deterioration, and it had certainly damaged, perhaps irreparably, the relationships between Edgar and the two younger Farrell siblings. Surely Leon had had the intelligence to foresee that. Yet, the worst might be yet to come, for what he'd seen in that will could cast a permanent cloud over that family, unless Edgar, for one, was more mature than he'd previously given evidence of being.

Carson sat in his car, dreading to get out and go into Donald Riggs's office, but he had no choice. He had promised Edgar that he would report to him before anyone else, but that was before he knew Edgar the man and before he saw the provisions of that will. With the weight of it all bearing down on him, Carson knocked on Riggs's office door.

"Come in, Mr. Montgomery, and have a seat," the secretary said. "Mr. Riggs will be with you shortly."

Minutes later, Donald Riggs opened the door to his private office, looked at Carson, and grinned.

"What a nice surpri— Say, what's the matter? You look as if you're on your way to your best friend's funeral."

Without a word, Carson stood, opened his jacket, and handed the envelope to Riggs.

"Is this . . . I mean . . . Did you actually find it? Come on in here. Something must be wrong. I'd think you'd be shouting for joy."

Carson followed Riggs into his office and sat down. "Yes, I found it, and if I hadn't hired an architect to examine the floor and walls for hiding places, I'd still be looking."

"Where was it?"

Carson told him and added, "He meant to cause friction and maybe a lot of other problems, but I also think it's possible that after he looked it over, he realized that he had exposed himself and hid it in the hope that it would never be found. Did you read it?"

"He never gave me a chance to read the entire document. I merely witnessed when he had it notarized."

"I suggest you take a look at it. I'm supposed to notify Edgar first that I found it, but now that I know him, I realize that he would misuse that information. I'll deal with him when I have to. Another thing, the way that will is written, I may never get paid for six months' work." He lifted his left shoulder in a dismissive shrug. "But what the hell! I've experienced worse."

"I wouldn't worry about that, Carson. If he doesn't pay you, the estate will." Riggs put on his glasses and began reading the bequests. "What the hell's this?" He exploded when reading the first bequeathal. Good Lord!"

Carson stood, preparing to leave. "Like I said, it's a real doozy. I have to tell Edgar that I found it and delivered it to you. He'll raise hell, but I can deal with him. I leave it in your capable hands. When are you going to announce that it's been recovered?"

"I'll set this coming Monday as the date for the reading of the will and send all parties telegrams requesting their presence. You're going to be in trouble with Shirley, but she'll get over it."

"I sure as hell hope so." To himself, he said, *It'll be the perfect time for me to go to Dallas and finish up that job for Rodney Falls.*

Chapter Thirteen

Donald Riggs put the index finger of his left hand at the end of the third mind-blowing sentence, not that he'd lose his place in *that* document. He then stood and shook hands with Carson. "You did your job, man. If I ever need a detective, I'll definitely ring your phone. Am I going to get any more surprises past this third sentence?"

"As sure as my name is Carson Montgomery."

"Where'd you find it?"

"Hidden in a wooden robot, in a closet behind a false wall where Leon kept his treasures, including a wad of money that I didn't count. If I hadn't gotten an architect to examine his den, I would never have found it. There are a lot of valuables in that closet. I don't think he intended the will to be found any time soon, unless he planned to tell one of his children about that panel and died without remembering to do that. Run your hand up and down the wooden panel at the side near the door until you feel the button that opens the closet. See you soon."

Donald sat down, took off his glasses, and rubbed the spot where the frame had pressed his nose. In spite of twenty years of talking with the man on a regular basis, he'd never known Leon Farrell. Half an hour later, having read each line at least three times, he made some notes, got out the telephone directory, and realized that he faced a dilemma. He phoned Carson, and within an hour, he had the information that he needed.

So Carson hadn't reached Edgar when he called him and had decided that he wouldn't inform Shirley. "I wouldn't care to be in his shoes," Donald said to himself.

Two days later, Gunther dialed Shirley's cell phone. "Did you get an invitation from Riggs to come to his office about the matter of the will?"

"Yes, I did. The mail arrived a few minutes ago. It couldn't mean that Carson found the will, could it, because he hasn't mentioned it to me. Our relationship has been a problem for him, probably because I was a recipient of a bequest in the will. He dragged his feet about us for the longest time. Still, he should have told me if he found it."

"Yeah. Then he would have had to tell you about the terms of the will, and that would have been unethical and unfair to Edgar and me."

"The whole thing has been a royal pain. Heard from Edgar?"

"No, but I expect he's already quit his job and is roaring somewhere between Philadelphia and Baltimore."

"Yeah. Poor Donald."

"Who do you think Edgar will take it out on? I

doubt he'll be willing to tie up with Carson," Gunther said, certain that he was in for a set-to with his brother.

"Maybe Carson informed Edgar."

"Sure he did. And the Washington Monument sits in the middle of St. Louis, Missouri. Excuse me a minute. Someone's ringing the doorbell and banging on the door simultaneously. Looks as if Edgar has arrived." Gunther hung up, strolled down the stairs, secured the door chain, opened the door, and looked out.

"Where the hell is that son-of-a-bitch Carson? He was supposed to give that will to me. Where is it? Did he give it to you?"

"Cool off and clean up your mouth. I've never seen the will, and I have no idea where it is, or if he in fact found it. Maybe Carson decided he spent enough time on Father's nonsensical behavior, making a will and then either destroying it or hiding it."

Edgar's entire demeanor seemed to fall like cold molasses dropping out of a jar. "Man, I quit my job and came back here to get my share. This is a bitch."

"You quit your job?" Gunther asked, his face the picture of incredulity. "Did Riggs tell you he had the will?"

"No, but—"

"The problem is that you couldn't wait to quit work. Why do you have all this skill and musical knowledge if you'd rather not use it? Nobody learns to play an instrument as well as you play that guitar without putting in a lot of long and hard hours of study and practice. Why did you do it?"

"Why did I do what, study and practice?" He

shrugged. "I love the sound of a great guitarist at work, and I couldn't stand lousy playing, especially if I was the player. I love to hear myself play. If I miss a note, I can be mad at myself for a week. Nothing pisses me off worse than having to play with guys who don't care how they sound, or if they do care but they don't try to improve. I haven't been in the house for almost two months. I'd better be getting over there. You think Mirna would give me a couple of baking potatoes and a steak or a couple of chops?"

"Sure. Didn't you get paid?"

"Yeah, but nothing's set about the will, and who knows when I'll get another gig?"

"You're never going to learn, brother. I hope for your sake that Carson found that will and delivered it to Riggs. But I'd bet my right arm that if Father left you a hundred grand, you'd be flat broke in three months. Now's the time to decide that you're going to get counseling for that gambling habit. You gamble away money, and you take other serious risks, like quitting your job on the chance that Riggs has the will."

Gunther called to Mirna. "Would you please see what you have in the kitchen that Edgar can take with him to the house—some potatoes, a steak, a couple boxes of frozen vegetables?"

"Sure," she said. "Won't take me but a minute." She walked off after barely sparing Edgar a glance. "Same old, same old," he heard her mutter. But as promised, she was back within a few minutes with a large, heavy bag. "That ought to keep you for a couple of days." She headed back to the kitchen without waiting to hear of Edgar's gratitude.

"What's with her?" Edgar asked Gunther.

Gunther flexed his shoulder in a quick shrug. "Edgar, the Lord promised to pull you up as many times as you fall down, but Mirna's like the rest of us humans. After a while, we don't give a damn."

"Well, thanks, old man. See you Monday at Riggs's office. I gotta look for a gig."

Shirley hung up the phone after her conversation with Gunther and gazed into the distance. Could Carson possibly have found that will, talked with her almost daily, and not said one word to her about it? When he told her that he'd be in Atlanta on a job for about a week, she should have known that he'd either found the will or quit trying. She dialed his number and hung up at the first ring. Damned if she'd ask him about it. He wouldn't be in Ellicott City when she got home Sunday night. Well, she'd find out along with Gunther and Edgar, and it would be a late day in the thirteenth month of the year before she forgave Carson.

She switched her phone to the operator and took the elevator up to the top deck. The feeling of being confined, of needing fresh air and open spaces, closed in on her as if she were claustrophobic. She rushed out of the elevator and sat on a deck chair beside the pool. But immediately a man dressed only in a five-inch bathing suit climbed out of the pool, sauntered over to her, and sat on the edge of her chair. She got up, walked toward the rear of the boat where she knew she'd be alone, and sat at an empty table, watching the vast ocean.

"I can live without him, and I will. Just because he can love me out of my senses doesn't mean I have to let him mistreat me." She blinked rapidly, turned her cell phone on, and went back to her office. He'd been everything to her, but he was just a man.

"You mean Carson still hasn't told you anything about this?" Gunther asked her as the two of them ate breakfast together before going to Riggs's office that Monday morning.

"Not a friggin' word," she said, "and as far as I'm concerned, he's history."

"Don't be foolish. The fact that the two of you are in a relationship is not a reason for him to behave unprofessionally. How could you expect that of him?"

"You don't understand. We're . . . we're really close, or we were. He could have told me and asked for my confidence."

"Oh, yeah! That would have been even worse, because you have a stake in this will. If he'd told Mirna and asked her to keep it to herself, I could accept that, but confiding in you would have been a mean thing to do. My respect for him mounts continually. Let's go, or we'll be late."

"What the . . . what the hell?" Gunther and Shirley heard Edgar exclaim as they followed him into Donald Riggs's office. Gunther's gaze landed on Frieda Davis and a woman who had to be her mother. He didn't speak to Riggs but walked over to Frieda.

"I'm surprised to see you here. How's the job going?" He could see that she was nervous and as mystified as he was. He'd added the question about her new job because he wanted to sound casual.

"Mr. Farrell, this is my mother, Coreen Treadwell. I don't know why I'm here, and from the way Coreen reacted to seeing Edgar when he walked in here, I'm scared I'm gon' hear somethin' I don't want to hear."

He shook Coreen's hand. "How do you do?" he said, and took a seat beside Shirley, who sat near the door. He wouldn't say he was glad to meet Coreen until he found out why she was there.

"Man, do you have the will, or don't you?" Edgar asked, his tone belligerent.

Donald Riggs draped his right ankle over his left knee and made himself comfortable. "Mr. Farrell, Edgar, I mean. If you disrupt me once or behave in the least disorderly fashion, I will have you arrested." He reached over to his desk and pressed the intercom.

"Yes, Mr. Riggs."

"Get a security officer up here and post him at my office door."

Gunther's head snapped up. That meant Riggs was about to read the will and that Edgar wouldn't like what he heard. But what did Frieda and her mother have to do with the will?

"Now, if I may have your attention, please. As executor of Leon Farrell's estate . . ." Gunther jerked around at the gasp he heard. It had come from either Frieda or her mother, and his curiosity about their presence escalated.

"I have the responsibility of disposing of his worldly goods with the aid of his last will and testament, which I have before me." Gunther didn't look at Shirley but reached over and held her hand.

" 'I, Leon Edgar Farrell, declare that this is my will, and I revoke all prior wills and codicils.

" 'I bequeath one hundred thousand dollars to the Severn Sanctum for Injured Pets and one hundred thousand dollars to Coreen Holmes Treadwell.' "

Edgar's oath did not escape anyone present. Neither did Coreen's loud gasp.

" 'I divide the remainder of my property and monies equally among my children, Edgar, Gunther, and Shirley, plus the firstborn child of Coreen Holmes Treadwell, provided that the child passes a DNA test with matches to Gunther or Edgar.' "

Edgar was standing now with his fist balled as if to strike.

" 'And a birth certificate showing that the child was born not more than nine months after Coreen's high school graduation. Edgar is to receive his share, that is his total inheritance, after he has held the same full-time job for one solid year and not before. If he has not accomplished this within fifteen months from the reading of this will, his share is to be divided among my three other children.' "

The door slammed, and Gunther didn't look toward it; he knew that Edgar had left.

"There's more," Riggs said, wiping his brow and continuing to read.

" 'All of the estate's expenses are to be paid before the distribution of inheritances. The child born to Coreen

Holmes is the product of a rape, which I perpetrated upon Coreen, a virgin, at a time and place when she was defenseless and when she trusted me. I've regretted it ever since, and I have prayed that I did not ruin her life and that she has found happiness with her husband and stepsons. Yes, Coreen, I have known your whereabouts for years.

" 'I direct my attorney, Donald Riggs, to effectuate this will to the letter of my stipulations. Leon Edgar Farrell.'

"That's it. As soon as I have all claims against the estate, including the cost of locating the will, I will contact Frieda, who is the eldest, and Edgar, Gunther, and Shirley as to the disposition of the family home. Within a week or two, my accountant will advise me as to your other entitlements. I suggest that the house and its contents should be sold and the proceeds divided equally among you. Any questions?" Hearing none, Riggs stood. "That's all."

Gunther couldn't move. His hand gripped his sister's hand so tightly that she attempted to remove it. Realizing that he'd hurt her, he turned to Shirley and stroked her hand. "I don't know what I was expecting, but this was not it."

"No," Shirley said, "but we'd better go over and talk to Frieda. Do you realize she's our sister?"

"Damn. You're right. Come on." Still holding Shirley's hand, he walked over to Riggs and thanked him.

"I'll have an estimate of the total value of the estate in a few days. My accountant is working on it."

"That's no problem," Gunther said. "I've just learned that I have another sister. Let me go over there and speak with her."

Frieda stood as Gunther and Shirley approached her. "Could you beat this?" she asked them. "I'm in shock, and I know you are, too. I never had any idea who my daddy was, and Coreen refused to tell me. I'm glad she didn't, because I'd a done something terrible."

Gunther opened his arms and brought her to him in a hug. "That's all in the past, sis. I'll take the DNA test as soon as we find a clinic or diagnostic service that does that kind of work. I expect the results will have to go to Riggs." He turned to Coreen. "Can we get Frieda's birth certificate?"

"I know where to get a copy if Frieda doesn't have it."

"I have one, but it doesn't have my father's name on it."

"I don't think that'll be necessary," Shirley said. "All Mr. Riggs needs is your date of birth. How old are you?"

"Thirty-seven."

"That's about right. Edgar's almost thirty-six."

"He's upset," Coreen said. "Is he going to be trouble for Frieda?"

Gunther looked to the ceiling. "He's going to be trouble for all of us, including Donald Riggs."

Coreen regarded him carefully. "You don't seem to resent this. Why?"

"All I ask is the opportunity to make a good life for myself and anybody I'm responsible for. I'm doing that, and I am not depending on what my father accumulated. I would have been happier if he'd spent more time with me and less on his pursuit of wealth."

Coreen looked from Gunther to Shirley. "When I realized that Frieda was working for a man named Farrell, I was terribly uncomfortable, even though she told me what a wonderful person you are and that the two of you got her such a prized job. I didn't expect anything like this when Mr. Riggs called me. At last, Bates and I will have a real nest egg, and we can take a decent vacation. I'd better be going, Frieda."

"I'll take you home, but I have to be back at work Thursday," Frieda said. She looked at Gunther. "Can we get the DNA test while I'm up here in Maryland?"

He turned to Riggs. "Can we?"

"Sure. I'll make the appointment. Somehow I have a feeling that it isn't necessary, but that's what the will requires."

Gunther looked at his watch. "It's twenty minutes past twelve. What do you say we all go to lunch?" He looked at Donald Riggs. "Will you join us?"

"Thanks, but I have a few things to attend to, including making an appointment for that test. I'll call you as soon as it's set. By the way, Gunther and Shirley, I know how unsettling this has been for you, and I'm proud of you both for dealing with it as mature adults."

"We already liked Frieda, so now we'll try to develop closer ties like siblings. I feel sorry for Edgar," Shirley went on, "but he deserves that reprimand. The problem is that Father should have made him shape up when he was a kid."

Riggs nodded, almost as if lost in thought.

"There are many things that Leon should have done but didn't. I'll phone you about the appointment, Gunther."

Outside, Gunther noticed Frieda's protectiveness of Coreen. "You two stay right here, and I'll get my car. It's parked in the next block."

"It's all right," Frieda said. "I drove."

"Leave your car here. I'll bring you back." He looked at Coreen. "I hope this hasn't been too much of a shock for you. We're all in the same boat. You probably made a wise choice to get on with your life. My father was not an easy man to live with, and after our mother died, he became neglectful and uncaring. I hope you at least live in a loving environment."

"I hated him so long for the pain he caused me," she said. "But until today, when I saw Edgar, he'd become a blur that I rarely thought of. I can thank my husband for that. You . . . You're a very kind man. I'm glad Frieda has you in her life."

Gunther drove the short distance to the restaurant, and as they were about to enter, Cory stepped out of the adjoining delicatessen carrying what appeared to be his lunch. "Hey there," he said to Gunther, who detained him with a hand on his arm.

"Hi. Meet my sisters and my older sister's mother." At Cory's quizzical expression, he added, "Not to worry; it's as clear as mud," and they enjoyed a hearty laugh. "My sisters, Frieda Davis and Shirley Farrell," he said. "And this is Coreen Treadwell, Frieda's mother. Ladies, this is Cory Benjamin, one of my associates." He noticed that Cory's gaze lingered on Frieda, and considering her sudden and uncharacteristic shyness in accepting the introduction, he made a mental note to follow up on it. Cory headed for the office.

In the restaurant, they placed their orders, and he marveled that they didn't seem ill at ease. Watching Frieda's protectiveness of Coreen, adjusting her jacket, asking the waiter to exchange her napkin when it slid to the floor, and observing her hawklike, Gunther wondered if Frieda realized that she loved Coreen. He meant to have a conversation about it and tell her it was time she addressed the woman as "Mother."

However, Frieda's thoughts were elsewhere, and her entire nervous system seemed to have unraveled. When Gunther asked her whether anything was wrong, she realized that she couldn't blow him off, and she didn't want to. He was her brother. Unable to control the shaking of her hands, she put them in her lap.

"Calling you Gunther is gon' take some adjusting," she said. "I was just thinking how I'd love to tell Edgar a few things. He told me the biggest lie. Fortunately, I didn't believe him. Knowing what I know now, if I'd followed through on his lie, we wouldn't be sitting here."

Shirley leaned forward. "Go ahead and tell us if you want to. You will learn that integrity is not one of Edgar's character traits."

"He told me more than once that Gunther was attracted to me and that I was a fool if I didn't encourage him. I told him he was lying, that I knew when a man wanted me and that Gunther liked me only as his nurse. I realized that he was trying to foment trouble. I need to ask him how he became so unprincipled and to tell him how close I came to indicting him for that hit-and-run. If I can just tell him those two things, I can start to see him as my brother."

Coreen picked up her glass of water, put it down, and turned to Frieda. "I've learned the hard way that when there are people around you who are in the dark, you have to provide the light. Don't be too hard on him. You never know where your blessing will come from."

Frieda stared at Coreen. Maybe a mother's wise counsel was what she'd missed after she ran away from her adoptive parents' home. Coreen hadn't tried to counsel her, perhaps because they both acknowledged that she didn't have the right, but maybe Coreen hadn't attempted it because she was afraid of losing what she barely had. She patted Coreen's shoulder. "I know you're right, but telling him off would be better than punching him."

Suddenly, she laughed. "When Gunther was sick, Edgar came to the apartment and tried to throw his weight around. I put my hands on my hips, glared at him, and asked him if he wanted me to toss him across the room. He tucked his tail in so fast that I could hardly keep from laughing. I couldn't throw a basketball across Gunther's living room."

"I think we should help Edgar all we can," Coreen said, with the wisdom of an experienced social worker. "Sometimes all a person needs is a chance."

"That's just it," Shirley said. "Edgar gambles away what he makes and what he borrows, and we keep on lending him money. But he knows we won't do that anymore. He's older than Gunther and me, and we are not going to support that awful habit of his any longer."

Frieda nodded. "That's right, because you will wind up right where he is. With absolutely nothing. It's a pity." Suddenly, she changed the subject. "Shirley, I meant to tell you that I'm taking classes at the university, and I can get my RN in two years studying evenings. And the cruise line is paying for it. My ship has really come in."

Gunther looked at Coreen. "You and I have experienced Frieda's wonderful nursing. Want to bet that ten years from now, she'll be head nurse for the Paradise Cruise Line?"

Coreen's face softened into a smile. "I sure wouldn't bet against it. She's a wonderful nurse. I'm so proud of her."

"So am I," Gunther said. They finished lunch, and he took Frieda and Coreen back to Frieda's car. "I want to have a talk with you when you have time," he said to Frieda. "Where are you staying?" She gave him the name of her hotel. "You can stay at my place if you want to. Get there in time for dinner. See you later." He hugged Coreen. "It's been a very good day."

"Are you going to stay at Gunther's house tonight?" Coreen asked Frieda when they were alone.

"I might, since he asked me to. Imagine that. He's my brother and that trifling Edgar was trying to get me to start an affair with him. I've seen the time I'd have made a play for him just because I figured I could. But I thought about my stupidity with Glen, and that was enough to make me use some sense."

"You're over Glen, I hope."

"Yes, but it wasn't easy. I had so much guilt

about it that the feeling for him eventually faded. Glen said the same. We're a lot alike. We attract the opposite sex, and we exploit them. We've both screwed up. I'm through with that nonsense."

"I'm glad to hear it, because that man Cory, who we met before lunch, looks like a decent guy, and he's interested in you."

"He sure threw me for a loop. But that's life. I'll probably never see him again."

"Ask Gunther if he's married. If he isn't, tell Gunther you'd like to see him again, and I'll bet he'll arrange it."

"I didn't think of that. Thanks. Now I know I'm spending the night at Gunther's place."

She arrived at Gunther's apartment at about six o'clock, and Mirna answered the door. "Girl, I heard all about it. You gon' be such a big shot you won't sit up in the movies with me and eat popcorn no more."

"Hi," Frieda said. "That's the first time I ever heard you say anything that even a child could see was stupid. Soon as I get some of that inheritance, you and me gon' spend a week in Italy. I don't want to stay away from work too long, 'cause a lot of people looking for jobs. The good thing is I got some more real nice blood kin; I know who my daddy was, even though he wasn't all that great; and I'm finally gon' get me a little piece of property."

Mirna stared at her and shook her head as if puzzled. "And you telling the truth, too. You ain't never gon' change as long as you live."

Frieda released a throaty laugh. "Good thing you qualified it, 'cause everybody changes soon as they dead. Is Mr. . . . Is Gunther home?"

"He upstairs. Go on up."

"But—"

"You his sister. Miss Shirley would go up without thinking about it."

"But, Mirna, she lives here."

"Girl, don't get on my last nerve."

"Oh, all right." But she couldn't do it, so she went to the bottom of the stairs and called him. "Can I come up, or are you busy?"

"Hi. Come on up. I'm in my office." She walked up, turned left at the top, and went to his office, where he sat at the computer.

He turned off the computer, got a bottle of tawny port out of a cabinet, and poured two drinks. "I was hoping you'd decide to come. I want to talk with you as brother to sister." She wasn't sure she was ready for that. He raised his glass and waited until she did the same. "Welcome to the family. I want you to know that I'm proud to be your brother. After what you've told me about your life, what you've gone through and the battles you fought and won, I truly admire you."

She could hardly believe her ears. "Thank you. I'm not a crybaby, but if I'm not careful, I'm gonna be gushing."

"I think you should reflect on your relations with your mother. I watched you with her today, and I saw that you care deeply for her. Don't you know that?"

"I like her a lot."

"No. You care deeply for her, so stop punishing her and call her 'Mother.'"

She glared at him but was immediately chastened by his stern look. "Is that what I'm doing?

Yes, I feel a lot for her. I think I've been fighting it, but somehow she gets to me. And after hearing what my father wrote in that will, I have to admit I don't know what I would have done if I'd suffered a rape and then gone through the horror she lived for the next nine months. She said her aunt didn't even offer her an aspirin when she was in labor and that she gave birth on a tiny cot that had an inch-thick mattress, the cot she'd slept on during her stay with her aunt. The woman treated her worse than some people treated their slaves."

"Some women put their unwanted babies in the dump," he said. "She didn't do that, and it isn't her fault that your adoptive father proved to be depraved."

"I know, and I shamed myself long ago for blaming her."

"Good. The other thing I want to say is this: If you have any problems with Edgar, let me know. Don't think you can handle it. I know how desperate he can get. Tell me immediately, and I'll take care of it."

"Thanks. You have no idea how much I respect you," she said. "If I ever have any children, which doesn't seem likely, I'm going to teach them to be just like you. I'd better go see if I can help Mirna," she said, suddenly embarrassed.

"Thank you. By the way, Cory Benjamin was taken with you."

She spun around. "*He was?* He sure poleaxed me. Is he married?"

"Hmm. No, he isn't. He's a widower, and he has two little boys, four and six years old."

"Can I meet him?"

"That's what he asked me in respect to you. You

bet you can. He's a fine man. Straight as the crow flies."

"If he goes to church, too, he's for me."

Laughter poured out of Gunther. "If he doesn't, I bet he'll start."

"Where's Shirley? Didn't she come home along with you?"

"I dropped her off at the library. She should be here any minute."

Frieda thought about that for a while. The library had closed at four-thirty, a little over two hours earlier. Was Shirley reacting to the news she got in the lawyer's office? *Lord, please don't let me have to deal with attitude after things went so well this morning,* Frieda said to herself as she started down the stairs. *I declare you just can't depend on nothing.*

"By the way," he called. "Riggs made arrangements for the tests."

She turned and went back to him. "We can get it tomorrow morning. I'll take you."

"Thanks. Coreen said she'd mail my birth certificate to Mr. Riggs."

His look censured her. "*Who* said that?"

"Uh . . . Mom."

"That's better. It won't hurt, and after a while, saying it will feel great."

Frieda tilted her head to the side and looked hard at Gunther. "I always hated people telling me what to do, but the way you put things . . . Well, I don't. I guess the difference is that it's coming from my brother, and I always wanted a brother. Lord, my life is changing so fast it's making me dizzy."

*   *   *

Frieda needn't have worried about Shirley, who had no concern at present other than what to do about Carson. If she walked away from him, she would be miserably unhappy indefinitely. She loved him, and she had believed he loved her. If she confronted him about not having told her he'd found the will, not to speak of the shock she got about Frieda and Coreen, he'd feel as if she had attacked him unfairly, and he'd act accordingly. Shouldn't she expect his unfailing loyalty? Sipping her third cup of Starbucks coffee, she glanced out the window, saw that darkness had set in, put on her coat, and got up to leave. Her cell phone rang.

"Hello."

"This is Edgar. Where did Carson find that will?"

"I have no idea. He has yet to tell me that he found it."

"You want me to believe that? He's your lackey."

"Edgar, if you have nothing else to talk about, please hang up."

"What have you got to be upset about? At least you're getting your share. Father took care of his bastard child and her mother. He had some nerve telling me how to live. Frieda Davis is my sister! Damn! The whole thing makes me sick to my stomach. Do you know where Carson is?"

"He's in Atlanta," she said with a weariness in her voice that reached Edgar though the wires.

"Hey. No point in being depressed. You should be in my shoes. I got debts over my head and no way to pay 'em. I didn't want to put any long-distance calls on my cell, but I gotta talk to Carson."

"I'd better get on home," she said. "It's dark."

"Don't let it drag you. He's not worth it. For all you know, he and Riggs are in cahoots to steal part of Father's property. Something's not right here, and I mean to find out what it is."

"Don't get yourself into a mess over this, Edgar. Carson is honest. I'd swear to it in court."

She heard him pull air through his teeth as if disgusted. "Oh, you'd go to bat for him, even though he didn't tell you he'd found the will? That's the least he should have done, not to mention he should have told me."

One more thing for Edgar to gripe about, she said to herself. To him, she said, "Considering the provisions of the will, it shouldn't surprise you that he decided just to give it to Mr. Riggs."

"You don't say. Well, it wouldn't hurt you to take your own counsel. Be seeing you." He hung up.

When Carson's cell phone rang, he looked at the caller ID, saw that it was Edgar, and swore an epithet. He didn't care to talk with Edgar Farrell, but he certainly wouldn't shrink from it. "Montgomery speaking."

"This is Edgar Farrell. What do you have to say for yourself? You broke our contract, and I've got a mind to sue you."

"Go ahead. After I read that will, I knew that if you got your hands on it, you would destroy it. Further, since you weren't going to fulfill the terms of the will, you wouldn't get your inheritance, and I wouldn't get paid. Right? I decided that giving it to the executor of the estate was the right and legal thing to do. Shirley is probably mad as hell at me right now, but I did what I knew was right and fair."

"Spare me. Where'd you find that will? I scoured that house and every centimeter of Father's room and office. He must have had a secret hiding place."

"I found it in the den. You needn't worry about the payment. Riggs said that the estate will pay for the recovery of the will."

"In the den, eh?" He hung up.

Carson thought for a minute. "I've just made an enormous mistake. Edgar will tear up the room until he finds that panel. Two days later, he'll probably have spent or gambled away the money in that envelope and whatever he gets from hocking those antique vases." As a precaution, he called Riggs.

"Carson here. I wouldn't be surprised if Edgar took an ax and hacked up that room until he finds that false wall. I didn't count the money, but I'd guess he'd find fifty to a hundred thousand dollars in that envelope. There are other valuable things there, including some antique vases and his father's robot collection."

"Thanks for telling me. If he doesn't find it tonight or early tomorrow morning, he'll be out of luck. I'll take my accountant over there and an independent appraiser and have everything catalogued. Spoken with Shirley yet?"

"No, but I hope to within the next hour."

"I wish you luck."

"Thanks. I'm going to need it."

Carson hung up, walked around his hotel room, moving things from one place to another, stared out the window at the cars speeding along the highway, turned on the television, and immediately flipped it off. He decided he'd better eat before calling Shirley, because he might not feel like it after talking with her. He dialed room service and ordered a steak dinner. But as soon as he hung up, he didn't want it. So he called back, canceled it, and ordered a hamburger and a can of beer.

"What the hell!" he said aloud, and dialed Shirley's cell phone number.

"This is Carson. You were going to return my call day before yesterday. What happened?"

"What happened? Is that a serious question?"

"Shirley, if you've got something on your mind, let's have it. Where do we stand?"

"Perhaps I should ask you, Carson. I would have expected you to at least tell me that you had found the will, but no; you let me get a shock. No, several shocks. As close as you and I were"—he flinched at the reference to the past— "couldn't you have warned me that I was about to get the surprise of my life?"

"Had I warned you, I would also have had to warn Edgar and Gunther. I told you I was reluctant to get involved with a client, which you are, because you're behaving that way now. My reputation as an honorable man is just as important to me as what's said of my skills as a detective, and I am not ever going to compromise my integrity and my honor. Edgar offered me a ridiculous deal if I would discard the will in the event that I found it and it was unfavorable to him."

He ignored her gasp and continued to talk. "You've led me to believe that your well-being did not depend on the provision set forth in that will, and you've showed relatively little interest in it. Yet, you're suggesting that because I love you, I should have done the unscrupulous thing of giving you an advantage over your brothers and Miss

Davis. If you're sticking with that position, I've made a gargantuan error."

"What are you saying?"

He heard the catch in her voice and knew her anger was at war with her feelings for him. If she hurt, he couldn't help it; his own pain nearly brought tears to his eyes. "I'm not saying anything. I've said my piece. It's your turn."

"I . . . uh . . . I can't talk about it now. I've got as much on my plate as I can handle, not the least of which is an older sister who I barely know."

He ignored her words and stuck to the subject. "Call me when you can talk about it, but don't take too long. Be seeing you." He hung up. If there was anything he couldn't handle, it was empty words. He called the restaurant, canceled the room service order, put on his jacket and coat, and left the hotel. Maybe if he walked long enough, he'd get hungry.

He wrapped up his case shortly before noon the next morning, but if he'd wanted to rejoice in a job well done, Donald Riggs's telephone call deprived him of the chance.

"What's up, man?" he asked when he saw Riggs's number on his cell phone's caller ID.

"Edgar found that secret panel. Did you say you found the will inside a robot?"

Carson leaned against the hood of his dark blue BMW. He was not going to like what he heard next. "So I did. There were dozens of robots there, all kinds of animals, plastic and wooden. The wooden robots were handmade, and I suspect Leon made them, because I found the sketches."

Riggs's labored sigh reached Carson through the phone. "The place is a mess, and there isn't a robot in sight."

"He told me that those robots were junk. I'm sure he took that money."

"Nope. Poetic justice. He overlooked seventy-seven thousand dollars and took the robots, which he will have to hustle to sell and which aren't likely to net him as much. He also overlooked these beautiful old vases and some fine wood carvings. Well, we'll finish the inventory, and I'll have to figure out whether to indict him, get an estimate and deduct that from his inheritance, or what."

"Look, Donald. It's none of my business. You know he's never going to work at any job for a year. So the robots will be all the inheritance he gets. I wouldn't indict him, though you have to get the agreement of his siblings."

Donald Riggs's calls to Edgar went unanswered until three days later. "Hello, Farrell speaking."

"Edgar, this is Donald Riggs. I don't suppose you're prepared to return those robots that you took from your father's closet? They belonged equally to the four of you."

"Too damned bad. I sold 'em last night to somebody in Baltimore. He came and got them this morning and paid me in cash. Six hours from now, I'll be on a plane to Ghana. I got a buddy over there. This place sucks."

"I guess you'd like to know that I found an envelope containing seventy-seven thousand dollars on the second shelf in that closet. God doesn't love that kind of beha—" Edgar had hung up. Riggs

called Gunther and told him of Edgar's plan to
leave for Ghana.

Gunther telephoned his older brother, thinking
that Riggs couldn't have heard Edgar correctly. His
fingers shook as he dialed the number. "Hello."

"Hi, Edgar. This is Gunther. What's this about—"

Edgar interrupted him. "Hello, brother. I know
Riggs called you. You got your share, you and your
two sisters. I'm never going to get anything else
from that old man, so I'm heading out of here.
Come to Ghana if you want to see me again."

"What's your address there?"

"You don't need it. If I want company, I'll write."

"What about your motorcycle?"

"It's going on the plane with me as freight. See
you." He hung up.

"I sure as hell hope they don't have gambling
joints over there," Gunther said to himself. "This is
going to hurt and hurt badly, but right now, I can't
digest it."

Chapter Fourteen

That morning, Gunther arrived at his office before seven o'clock. He'd skipped breakfast rather than deal with Shirley's lackluster demeanor and her disinterest in anyone and everything around her. He had tried to reason with her and to make her understand that her misery sprang from her own unwillingness to accept the truth and to acknowledge that Carson had behaved fairly and honorably with respect to that will.

"It's time I put a pantry in here," he said to himself after removing two Styrofoam cups of coffee from a brown paper bag. "Furnishing coffee for the people who work for me is the least I can do." He heard steps and walked out to the hallway.

"Why are you here so early?" he asked Cory Benjamin. "It's barely seven o'clock."

"I like working when I'm here alone, when I can't hear a sound. That's when the ideas flow, and I can concentrate. I'm surprised to see you here so early."

He told Cory about the will and the reactions of

his siblings to its provisions. "And can you beat this? I'm thirty-four years old, and I've just learned that I have an older sister who I didn't know about until an hour before I introduced you to her. It blows my mind. Shirley is depressed, but not about our sister. She's concerned about something else. Edgar's way of dealing with this and with that will is about as much as I can take. I could have begun the day as usual with Shirley and played misery loves company, but that's not my style. So I skipped breakfast. Problem with that is I'm beginning to get hungry."

Cory seemed in deep thought. "Miss Davis is your older sister? Do you think you're going to like her?"

Gunther told Cory how he met Frieda. "I liked her a lot, and I admired her attitude toward her work, and her thoroughness, competence, and all-around professionalism. She's a wonderful person. I've written two recommendations for her, not knowing that I was helping my sister. It's strange. I doubt I'll ever see Edgar again, and I feel that I've lost my brother, but I gained a sister. Somehow that blunts the pain of losing Edgar."

Cory ran the fingers of his left hand over his tight curls and gave the floor a gentle kick. "She made a strong impression on me."

"I know. And she told me she'd like to meet you in more favorable circumstances. When she asked me about your status, I told her that you're a widower with two little boys."

Cory's head jerked up. "What did she say to that?"

Gunther could feel his face creasing into a broad grin. "She said something like, 'If he goes to church, he's for me.'"

The sparkle in Cory's eyes betrayed his delight in hearing that she liked him, but his next words were those of a man both modest and cautious. "Do you think she'd mind if you gave me her phone number?"

"I don't think so. She's had a difficult life, betrayed by those she depended on. I doubt she'll trust easily."

"She'll understand decency and sincerity," Cory said, "and I won't ask for more."

"My blessings to you both," Gunther said, making it clear that he would be happy if the two of them developed a meaningful relationship.

Gunther worked well that morning, and he could thank his intense concentration for his need to banish the pain of Edgar's leaving. His design of spacewalkers in the shape of classical nutcrackers hadn't satisfied him, so he'd trashed it and begun working on a family of cartoonlike characters who, with eagle eyes and falconlike wings, descended on Earth whenever they observed from their perches in outer space a need to settle earthly disputes. Riggs's phone call interrupted his progress.

"Hello, Donald. Any news about the tests?" he asked.

"That and other things. When is a good time to get all of you here? We don't need Mrs. Treadwell. I'll send her a cashier's check, but I do need to see you, Frieda, and Shirley. If Edgar comes back here and does as the will stipulates, he'll have to abide by whatever decisions the three of you make."

"Mondays and Tuesdays are usually best for Shirley. She's at my place now, but she's leaving today."

"Unless Frieda can't make it, we'll meet here at my office next Monday. I'll phone her and Shirley now."

"Is that your cell phone ringing, ma'am?" the taxi driver asked Shirley shortly after she got into his cab for the trip to BWI airport. She'd heard the phone, but knowing that it wouldn't be Carson, she hadn't bothered to answer it. She took it from her pocketbook and saw Riggs's number in the caller ID screen.

"Hello, Mr. Riggs."

"How are you, Shirley? Can you be in my office Monday morning at nine o'clock? I want to settle your father's estate."

"But Edgar isn't here."

"I'm aware of that. There are decisions to be made, and according to accepted practice, the majority rule. Edgar isn't here, so he'd be the minority. See you Monday morning."

"All right. Thanks." She hung up thinking that he hadn't given her an alternative. She couldn't blame the man if he'd had enough of dealings concerning that will. What had caused her father to write a will, have it properly executed, and then hide it, knowing that with or without it, his death would adversely affect his children and their relationships with each other?

He was not innocent in this, she thought. *That will aired his dirty linen, and after being honest when writing it, he decided he didn't want us to know what an awful person he'd been in his youth. I deserve whatever he left to me, but considering how he let me struggle unnecessarily to get through school, I do not thank him.*

She settled back in her seat, anticipating the long ride to the airport. How she longed to talk with Carson and to be with him, but she knew that the next move was hers, and she couldn't force herself to make it. She'd been comfortable staying in Gunther's apartment, but her presence there had to inconvenience him, because he hadn't once brought Caroline home with him. After the first of the year, she'd find a house or a condo. Maybe that would make it easier for her and Carson to mend their relationship.

Her mind traveled back over the days since the reading of her father's will. How easily she had accepted Frieda as her sister. Maybe it was because her father wouldn't give a penny to anyone who didn't truly deserve it. Or maybe because Frieda had cared for Gunther so lovingly when she was his nurse. The night after the reading of the will when Frieda stayed with Gunther and her, they'd had a wonderful time exchanging tales of their childhood. And all the while, she'd kept thinking that Edgar would have been a misfit there.

At the airport, she paid the driver and was soon on her way to Fort Lauderdale with the memories of her happiness there with Carson weighing upon her.

She went straight to the ship, checked into her stateroom, and called Frieda. "Nurse Davis speaking. How may I help you?"

"Hi, sis. This is Shirley. I just—"

Frieda interrupted her. "It had better be Shirley. If I get another surprise sister, I may not be able to stand it." Laughter poured out of her. "How are you? And where are you?"

She loved Frieda's deep, throaty laugh. "I'm on

the ship. I just checked in. Did Riggs ask you to be at his office Monday morning?"

"Yeah, but he didn't tell me the outcome of that test Gunther and I took."

"Did you ask him?"

"You bet I did, but he said the three of us would get that information together. My boss said I can have Monday off, but I gotta be at work Tuesday. Do you think Edgar really went to Africa and won't come back here?"

Shirley released a heavy sigh. "Unfortunately, Gunther's right about that. I hate to think of it."

"Me too. He got on my last nerve, but I'd be happier if I thought he was having a good life. I hear tell just about everybody over there in Africa is poor, so what's he gon' do?"

"A lot of Africans are living well, Frieda, but unless Edgar is very fortunate, I doubt he'll be in that class."

"Well, worrying don't do a bit of good. I'm gon' say a few prayers for him and trust the good Lord to do the rest. Stress over something I can't help is definitely not in my DNA."

"Frieda, you're precious. I'm going to try and follow your example. See you Monday."

Monday arrived, and once more, the Farrell siblings sat in Donald Riggs's office awaiting a verdict. "Glad to see everybody's on time," Riggs said. "Never waste another person's time if you can avoid doing so. First, I want to congratulate Frieda on the proof that she is, indeed, Leon Farrell's daughter. The test produced a ninety-nine-point-nine percent match. Of course, no one here doubted it." He pointed to the man sitting beside him. "This is Timothy Hall, my accountant."

Timothy passed out several sheets of computer printouts. "This represents your father's net worth minus the family home and its contents. If you sell the house and its valuables, you'll net about six hundred thousand dollars to be divided among you. Excluding the house and what's in it, each sibling gets one million, three hundred thousand dollars. If Edgar fails to do as the will states, you three will each receive an additional four hundred and thirty-three thousand dollars. The three of you decide what to do with the house and its contents."

"I'm dumbfounded," Frieda said. "I thought I was gonna get four or five thousand dollars, and I could hardly wait for *that*. What I'm gon' do with all that money?"

"When the time comes, you'll retire in comfort," Riggs said.

"Well, I tell you this," she said. "You can bet I won't die poor, not even if I live to be a hundred. The way I heard it, the postman just rings once, no matter what it said in that movie. I'm gon' take good care of this blessing."

"What about the house?" Timothy asked them.

Frieda looked first at Gunther and then at Shirley. "I don't think we should sell that house as long as there's a chance Edgar will come back. That's his home."

"But it and its contents belong to the four of you," Timothy said.

It wasn't his brother, so he could take that position, Frieda thought. Aloud, she said, "Look, I wouldn't like to come back home and find that I didn't have a home, not even if I was a millionaire. Besides, you shouldn't kick a man when he's down."

"I can't insure it if nobody's living there," Riggs said, though he didn't sound very firm about it. "What do you suggest?"

"Frieda has a good point," Shirley said. She looked at Gunther. "Since we don't need the money from that house right now, couldn't we rent it for, say, a year? Fifteen months from now, we'll know one way or the other."

"If Donald approves, then I say we do that," Gunther said, "though I think we ought to store everything that's really valuable."

"We've had everything appraised," the accountant said, "so that should be easy."

Riggs tapped his pen on his desk in a rhythmic fashion. "Darned if you guys aren't the most agreeable siblings I've ever dealt with in money matters. A teacher colleague of my wife's needs a place, and I can vouch for him. He just got a divorce, and he's childless."

Frieda's cell phone rang. "Hello. Frieda speaking."

"Hello, Frieda. This is Cory Benjamin. Gunther introduced us a short while back, and I'd like to see you again. He told me you'd be in town this morning, and I'm hoping we can have lunch someplace before you head back to Orlando."

"Cory . . . oh, dear! This is a big surprise. A real whopper. Yes, I'd like that."

"I'm not too far from that lawyer's office. What time can I pick you up there?"

"I think we're about finished. I'll wait here for you."

"Great. I'm looking forward to seeing you again."

She hung up, looked at Gunther, and said, "I think I'm going to faint. Cory Benjamin is taking me to lunch. Thank you for telling him I'd be here. One of these days, I'm gon' get a chance to do something real nice for you, Gunther. You just wait and see."

"Don't mess up like I did," Shirley said.

"Why can't you fix it?" Frieda asked her. "Does the guy love you?" Shirley nodded. "Then where's the problem? Your pride won't keep you warm at night, but he will. If he hasn't mistreated you, broken the law, cheated, or been too selfish to tolerate, straighten it out."

"He isn't the problem," Gunther said. "She is, and she hasn't got a leg to stand on. She's got a first-class man, and she resents the fact that he wouldn't abandon his integrity and give her an unfair advantage over her siblings."

Frieda looked at Shirley with eyes that reflected the tragedies of her life. "When you've seen as much of life as I have, you'll know that a self-respecting brother who's got what you need and high standards to boot won't come along many times in your life. If you love him, give him the respect he deserves and tell him you're ashamed of yourself. 'Cause you ought to be."

"I've been telling her that. Maybe she'll listen to you. I should be at my office. Frieda, hadn't you better call your mom and tell her about the tests?"

"You right. I was gon' do that, and then Cory called. Well . . . you know how it is."

She went into the little reception room, sat

down, and dialed Coreen Treadwell's number. "Hello. Glen Treadwell speaking."

"Hi, Glen. This is Frieda. Everything all right there?"

"You bet. When are you coming? We'd like you to be here during the holidays."

"I'll get there, Glen, but so many wonderful things are happening to me right now that I don't know my head from my feet."

"That's great, sis. Mom told us what's happening, and I'm happy to hear it. But do your best to remain your natural, honest, and down-to-earth self. That's what makes you so appealing. Don't forget that."

"Thanks, Glen. I appreciate that. Where's Mom?"

"She's . . . Bless you, Frieda. I'll call her. See you soon."

"Frieda? How'd it go, honey? I know what the outcome had to be, and I haven't been a bit concerned."

"Hi, Mom. Everything is great. I got a wad of money, and I have no idea wh—"

"Wait there! What did you call me?"

Frieda had hoped Coreen wouldn't make a big deal out of it. "Mom. Gunther shamed me. He said I was trying to punish you, and I wasn't. It was easier than I thought."

"I'm not concerned with your reasons; I'm grateful that you came to this decision. I . . . I had tried to accept that it would never happen. If you were here, I would hold you and hug you for honoring me this way. How are you getting along with the Farrell children?"

"Wonderful. Gunther and Shirley treat me as if they're happy that I'm their sister. Edgar apparently doesn't plan to abide by the terms for his inheritance, because he left the country in a huff. Gunther said he went to Ghana, so the final settlement is about fifteen months away. I'm gon' send some money to my two adoptive sisters, and I'm gon' take my best friend to Italy next spring. If I can't go, I'll send her. I'm saving the rest, and eventually I'll buy me a little piece of property."

"What about school?"

"I'm doing that university course. In a couple of years, I'll have my RN. I don't know, Mom. I just met this guy, and he's taking me to lunch. He'll be here any minute."

"You mean the man Gunther introduced us to?"

"Yes, ma'am."

"Just be yourself, and he'll adore you. Be sure and come for Christmas."

"I may not be there Christmas Day, but you'll see me just before or just after. Bye for now."

"I'm so glad you called. Good-bye, my daughter."

Frieda hung up, ready to embrace the whole world. "I guess there's a time for all things. She my mom. I told her so, and I feel like I just had a good cathartic, or whatever it is you call those cleaning things. I sure wish Shirley could get herself straightened out. She such a sweet person."

Minutes after Shirley left Riggs's office with Frieda and Gunther, Riggs set in motion the mechanism by which she would get an opportunity to do what Frieda wished for her.

"One more thing," Riggs said to his accountant. "We have to pay Carson for locating the will.

He's due six percent of a sibling share. I'll give him a call."

However, at that moment, Carson was dealing with a matter of life or death—his own. He had located the jilter whom he had chased throughout Atlanta the previous week. Satisfied with a job well done, he drove the rented Lexus into the garage beneath the hotel in which he stayed. As he stepped out of the car, the hairs on his arms burned his skin, and his nerves seemed to rearrange themselves throughout his body. From experiences during his years as a police officer, his antenna shot up, and he swung around just as the man raised his revolver.

Carson ducked behind the side of the car, but not quickly enough. He slid to the concrete, holding the fire-hot wound beneath his shoulder. With difficulty, he pulled the cell phone from his pocket, dialed the police, and reported that he'd been shot. Then he dialed 911 and asked for an ambulance. The police arrived first and took his report, and he awakened in a hospital room.

"You're a lucky man," a doctor assured him. "An inch lower and that bullet would have punctured your lung."

"Yeah? If I was really lucky, the guy would have missed me. How long do I have to stay here?"

"A couple of days. We want the wound to begin healing, and we have to make sure it doesn't become infected. You lost a good deal of blood, too, so I want you to drink a lot of that juice." He pointed to the container of V8 juice on the night table beside Carson's bed.

"You didn't tell me when I can get out of here. Except for this pain, I feel fine."

"Wait until you stand up. If there are no reverses, you can leave day after tomorrow."

"What do you mean by reverses?"

The doctor squinted his left eye, seemed on the verge of saying something, and then changed his mind. "A fever would suggest infection, and dizziness could be due to too much blood loss. Be glad you've got a bed to lie in. Patience can be a virtue."

"That's a parable in which I truly believe," Carson said, miffed at being lectured. "When did I get here?"

"Yesterday afternoon."

"Well, I'll be damned. I missed a whole day of my life." The doctor left, and he dozed off. The ringing sound came from afar, growing louder and louder until he awakened fully, sat up, and got his cell phone.

"Hello. Montgomery speaking."

"Riggs here. I was wondering if you'd drop by this afternoon and collect your pay for finding that will. Settling this estate has become a full-time job."

"I'm still in Atlanta, and in a hospital, at that. A guy I fingered put a plug in my right shoulder, and I'm lucky. I saw him as he raised his revolver and jumped aside, or I'd have gotten it straight on."

"You're telling me you got shot in the chest?"

"Just below my shoulder bone. I hope to be out of here day after tomorrow. This is the last place I want to spend Christmas."

"I should think so. As of now, your pay, at six percent of a share, is seventy-eight thousand dollars plus fifteen hundred for expenses. I'll have a certified check ready for you. If the siblings sell the house, its contents, and the land, we estimate that you'll get about ten thousand more."

"You're joking. That guy was loaded."

"Surprised me, too. Anything I can do for you there?"

"Thanks, buddy, but the only thing I need is freedom from this pain. See you in a few days." Riggs hung up, went into his reception room, and beckoned to Shirley.

"Shirley, I just spoke with Carson. Are you aware that he's in a hospital in Atlanta?"

The shock of his words reverberated throughout her system. "*What!* Who said so?"

"I spoke with him a minute ago."

"Thanks." She hung up and dialed Carson's cell phone number.

"Hello, Shirley. I assume Riggs just called you."

"Yes, he did. Tell me how you are."

"Do you care?"

"I didn't call to be clever, Carson. You know I care. I want to know how you are. What hospital are you in?"

"Don't tell me you want to come down here and look after me."

"Are you asking me to eat humble pie? All right, I'll do that. I've been miserable without you, and I . . . Please forgive me for being selfish. Carson, for goodness' sake, tell me how you are."

"I'm . . . I hurt something awful, but this is nothing compared to the pain I've had since the last time I saw you. I . . . You have to understand that my integrity is important to me and that I'm never going to violate it."

So he wasn't going to make it easy for her. She'd have to put everything on the table, to bare her soul. Well, she'd asked for it. "I love you," she said. "I need you, and I don't want to live without you. Can you forgive me?"

His silence unnerved her, for she knew that whatever he said was likely to be his final answer. "If you tell me that you understand and accept that my ability to make a decent living depends on my reputation for honesty and integrity, and that you agree I did the right thing in giving that information to Riggs, I'll believe you."

She let herself breathe again. "I knew then that you were right and I was wrong, but I was too stubborn to admit it."

"And now you've changed?" he asked in a voice laced with bitterness.

"Oh, yes," she said. "The ache in my heart helped adjust my mind to a capacity for reason. I've never been so miserably unhappy."

"When I get back there, we'll get together."

"Will you let me know when your plane arrives so I can meet you at the airport?"

"I'll let you know."

At least she had a chance with him. She hung up, took the elevator to the building's lobby, stepped out, and stopped. A man with a brilliant smile on his face walked up to Frieda, kissed her cheek, took her hand, and left the building. *Good for you, sis. I'm praying that day after tomorrow will bring me the same and more.*

Gunther started the fire in his living room fireplace and asked himself how anything so beautiful as the flames dancing before him could be so dangerous. Mirna walked in with a pan of cut chestnuts, sat down, and placed the nuts on the ashes at the edge of the fire.

"What we gon' do for Christmas, Mr. G? It's just a week away."

"I know, but I've been too busy to think about it. I'll call Frieda and Shirley and see what they can come up with." He phoned Frieda first. "I'm hoping that you, Shirley, and your dates will have Christmas dinner here," he said after they greeted each other.

"Ain't this something? Last Christmas, I made calls to my two adoptive sisters, but I spent the day alone. This year, you, my mom, and Cory want me for Christmas. I'll try to see Mom just before Christmas, but I hate to give up the chance to bond with Cory and his boys."

"You and Cory can have dinner here and open some gifts on Christmas Eve. And you can be with him and the kids Christmas Day. Okay?" She agreed.

"I'll see if that suits Shirley." He phoned his younger sister. "Carson still has some issues with me, but he said we'd be together. Can we invite Ogden and Marsha, too, or would that be more guests than you want?"

"That's fine. It's a crowd, but you, Frieda, and I can help Mirna. I'll call Ogden and invite him and Marsha."

This sure is something, Frieda thought. *I was about to go to Walmart to get presents for Cory's children when I remembered that I could shop in Bloomingdale's.* She bought things for everyone on her list, including

designer perfume for Coreen and a leather handbag for Mirna, who, she recalled, had never had
one.

"Lord, that's more money than I spent on presents the entire thirty-six and a half years of my
life."

She arrived at the Treadwell home the day before Christmas Eve. "I can't stay too long, Mom. I
promised my girlfriend I'd help her cook Christmas Eve dinner. She's Gunther's housekeeper."

Coreen looked closely at Frieda, seeing more
than her eyes beheld. "You must be the most gen-
uinely nice person I ever met. I'm proud to be
your mother." She took Frieda's hand. "Since you
can't be with us Christmas Eve or Christmas Day,
I'm having a pre-Christmas lunch for the whole
family."

Frieda handed Coreen the package containing
an ounce of Dior perfume and could barely maintain her balance when tears sprang from her
mother's eyes. "This means everything to me,"
Coreen said.

"I know, and to me too," she answered.

Coreen had included her as a member of her
family, and the warmth of all those around her confirmed it. As she sat among them, sharing her first
Christmas with the woman who gave her life, she
couldn't help thinking that she could accept Eric
as a brother and Bates as her stepfather, but she
would never be able to fit Glen in the category of
brother. She could consider him a friend, even a
close one, but after having writhed beneath him in
ecstasy, she could never regard him as her brother,
step or otherwise. What she'd felt for him had
long since dissipated, and how happy she was for

that. A few hours after eating the first food her mother had ever cooked for her, she bade them Merry Christmas and took a train to Baltimore.

Gunther awoke Christmas Eve morning, looked out of his bedroom window, and saw a light dusting of snow on the ground and a haze of whiteness in the atmosphere. After checking the weather forecast, he dressed quickly and raced down the stairs and into the dining room where Mirna and his sisters sat in the kitchen eating breakfast.

"We're in for a heavy snow, so I'm going to get Caroline. Otherwise, I won't see her here this evening. You get half an inch of snow in this place, and everything stands still."

"That's awful," Frieda said. "Cory can't stay away from his kids. It's Christmas."

"It's supposed to snow for Christmas," Mirna said. "He'll be here. Big, strong man gon' let you know he'll go through hell and high water to be with you. Let's finish dressing this tree. It could use a few icicles and a little snow."

Gunther reprimanded Mirna with a stern look. "Did I hear a note of cynicism? She's right to be concerned."

In the act of rising from the table, Mirna glanced at Shirley. "Why you so down? Didn't he say he gon' be here? That's a man who keeps his word."

"I invited him, and he said we'd be together, but he didn't sound as if he was looking forward to it."

Gunther didn't sit down, but poured a cup of coffee, took a sip, and shook his head, as if in sadness, as he looked at his younger sister. "Let this be a lesson, Shirley. Closing the door on a relationship is always far easier and simpler than reopening it, and a lot less painful, too. Use your head. If a man loves you, he needs to know you believe in him. See you later."

The falling snow thickened by the minute, and Shirley's anxiety increased along with it. She went into the living room but left quickly rather than disturb Gunther and Caroline, who huddled before the fire. She started back to the kitchen but went sprawling to the floor as Frieda raced to answer the doorbell.

"Shirley, honey, I'm so sorry. Are you all right?"

"I'm fine." She pulled herself up with Frieda's help.

"Let me answer the door," Frieda said, contrite but obviously anxious to see whether she'd find Cory there.

Shirley dragged herself to the kitchen trying not to hear the happy voices of Frieda and Cory as they greeted each other.

Mirna's arm rested on Shirley's shoulders. "Honey, why don't you get a book or something and pull yourself together? If he coming, he coming. If he don't come and don't call you, you know it's over, and you stick your chin out and say the hell with him. Here. Help me turn this ham. Thank God you don't have to do nothing to a goose after you put it in the oven."

She let out a long breath as if exasperated at Shirley. "And please go get dressed. It's already three o'clock. When he come, you want to greet him looking like you wasn't expecting nobody?" She put an arm around Shirley and hugged her.

"It's gon' be all right. Quit worrying and say a prayer."

But Ogden arrived with Marsha, day slipped into night, and Carson neither arrived nor phoned. At seven o'clock, Mirna complained, "We already half an hour late. My dinner gon' be a mess."

Resigned and more miserable than she'd thought she could be, Shirley accepted that Carson wouldn't be there. "We may as well eat," she said.

Ogden's worried expression infused all of them with intensified anxiety. "He told me yesterday that he'd be here, so I'm sure something has happened."

"He could have changed his mind," Shirley said. She put on a CD of Christmas carols and headed for the dining room. The doorbell rang before she got there, and she whirled around, barely managing to retain her balance as the Persian runner moved with her. She opened the door and gasped as Carson slumped against her.

"Gunther," she yelled. "Come here!" Gunther and Ogden reached them as she and Carson were about to slide to the floor together. Cory joined them, and the three men took Carson up the stairs.

"Put him in a tub of hot water," Mirna called.

Shirley walked from one end of the downstairs hallway to the other and back, tears of anxiety, joy, and hope flowing down her cheeks. "Lord, let him be all right," she prayed until the weight of Ogden's hand on her shoulder caused her to look up at him.

"He doesn't seem to have any frostbite, but he was suffering from hypothermia. Gunther put him in a tub of hot water to thaw out. His car stalled just before three o'clock, and he's been walking since then. He couldn't get transportation."

"I'm going up there," she said to Ogden.

"Go ahead. The two of you probably need a minute together."

"Dinner be on the table in five minutes," Mirna called after Shirley. "You can get lovey-dovey after you eat."

Carson met her at the top of the stairs. "I wanted to call you, but my fingers were so numb I couldn't dial."

"It's all right, love. You're here now, and that's the only thing that counts." The feel of his arms around her was all the Christmas she needed. They strolled down the stairs holding each other's hand.

At the table, festooned with a red linen cloth and napkins, green and red candles, and a centerpiece of red roses nestled in holly, Frieda said, "I know Mirna always says the grace, but tonight, I want to say it:

"Lord, I am so blessed to know and have my brother and my sister, to have my mother, and to have a man who I care for and who cares for me and to be with all these dear friends. Last year, I was alone. Thank you for this and for the food. Please bless my other brother, wherever he is. Thank you."

Nearly two hours later, they finished a meal of oyster stew, roast goose and stuffing, baked ham, cranberry relish, wild rice, turnip greens, candied yams, jalapeño corn muffins, assorted cheeses, lemon meringue pie, and coffee.

"I could hang out here indefinitely," Cory said, got up and kissed Mirna.

"You better kiss me and Shirley, too," Frieda

told him. "I washed the greens and Shirley helped with the ham, plus Shirley and I set the table."

"That's all you want? A kiss on the cheek?" he asked, grinning down at her.

Frieda looked at Gunther. "I thought you told me this man is clever." The comment brought a round of laughter, and Shirley marveled that she could be so happy when only a couple of hours earlier, she had thought she would die of misery.

"We gotta find places for everybody to sleep," Mirna said to Shirley and Frieda. "Can't nobody drive in this weather."

"That's no problem," Frieda said, not bothering to hide her pride. "Cory drove his brother-in-law's truck, and it has a snowplow. I'm going home with him to spend tomorrow with him and the boys, and he said he'll take Ogden and Marsha." Cory confirmed the plan, explaining that the truck seated four—five if three people watched their diet.

"Caroline's staying with me," Gunther said later to Shirley. "Where Carson sleeps is up to the two of you."

The four couples sat in the living room, their only light being the fire's flickering flame and the romantic glow of the lights, bells, and trinkets that bedecked the eight-foot Fraser fir beside the fireplace. Gunther collected the gifts from beneath the tree and passed them out, and Shirley noticed that none of the women opened that special gift from the man who professed to love her.

Long after they had said good night to those who left and to Gunther, Caroline, and Mirna, Shirley sat with Carson in the living room, watching the dying flames and wondering what was next for her. "I want us to be together," Carson said, "but not without a firm commitment from you. Do you trust me always to be there for you, to support you in every way, and always to do right by you?" She took his hands in hers and nodded her agreement. But he needed more. "And if you doubt me, will you tell me what you think and how you feel?"

"I promise." She didn't want talk. She wanted him, but she knew him now, and she hid her impatience.

"I love you. I want to build a home and a family with you. Have you given that any thought?"

"Oh, yes. I want that more than anything. To be with you for the rest of my life is what I want. When I thought I'd have to spend Christmas without you, wondering if you'd had an accident or if you just didn't care, I could hardly bear it."

"At times, I thought I wouldn't make it. I was so cold and so tired. I can't explain how I felt when you opened that door."

Carson stood, took her hand, and climbed the stairs with her.

"This way," she said, pointing to her room.

He stopped. "What about Gunther?"

A grin spread over her face. "The pot can't call the kettle black. He's with Caroline. Didn't you see that tiny package he took off the tree and handed her?"

"Way to go," he said. Dreamy-eyed and happy, he picked her up and carried her to bed. Through her open window, the moon cast a soft light all about them, shrouding them in moonlit beauty. "I love you," he whispered as she swayed to him, besotted by the love that glowed in his eyes.

He claimed her with his hands, his mouth, his tongue, and finally with his body. An hour later, they lay spent and useless, like a pile of discarded old clothing. With reluctance, and much effort, he separated their bodies, got up, and found his jacket. Resting on one knee, he said, "Please give me your left hand." After slipping a diamond on her finger, he asked her, "Will you be my wife and the mother of my children?"

"Oh, yes. It's what I've wanted since that second day we were looking for the will in Father's house." He kissed her, crawled into bed, put his arms around her, and went to sleep.

Epilogue

Fifteen months later, Donald Riggs summoned Gunther Farrell, Frieda Benjamin, and Shirley Farrell-Montgomery to his office. "Glad you're all here. I haven't heard one thing from Edgar. Has he contacted any of you?" Each of them said no. "What have you decided about the house and its contents?"

Gunther rubbed the back of his neck and winced as if in pain. "Shirley and I decided to give the house to Frieda. We hope that can compensate a little bit for what she's been through and certainly would not have experienced if she'd had her father's support. We don't want to live there, and we can't sell it for what it's worth. She has a big family—Cory, his two boys, and his aunt—and that house is perfect for her. If she doesn't mind, we'd like to look in that closet for mementos of our mother."

Frieda's lower jaw sagged. "I don't know what to say. I thank you from the bottom of my heart. Y'all take anything in the house that you want."

"Thanks," Shirley said. "Gunther and I also decided to put aside our portion of Edgar's share in case he ever comes back."

"Me too," Frieda said. "Yes, indeed. Me too."

Riggs exhaled deeply. "You won't see Edgar again, but as long as you keep it, you'll have a nest egg that grows and grows. Think of it as retribution that he's finally paid you."

In this thrilling debut novel from Carrie H. Johnson, one woman with a dangerous job and a volatile past is feeling the heat from all sides . . .

HOT FLASH

On Sale Now

Chapter 1

Our bodies arched, both of us reaching for that place of ultimate release we knew was coming. Yes! We screamed at the same time ... except I kept screaming long after his moment had passed.

You've got to be kidding me, a cramp in my groin? The second time in the three times we had made love. Achieving pretzel positions these days came at a price, but man, how sweet the reward.

"What's the matter, baby? You cramping again?" he asked, looking down at me with genuine concern.

I was pissed, embarrassed, and in pain all at the same time. "Yeah," I answered meekly, grimacing.

"It's okay. It's okay, sugar," he said, sliding off me. He reached out and pulled me into the curvature of his body, leaving the wet spot to its own demise. I settled in. Gently, he massaged my thigh. His hands soothed me. Little by little, the cramp went away. Just as I dozed off, my cell phone rang.

"*Mph, mph, mph,*" I muttered. "Never a moment's peace."

Calvin stirred. "Huh?"

"Nothin', baby, shhhh," I whispered, easing from his grasp and reaching for the phone from the bedside table. As quietly as I could, I answered the phone the same way I always did.

"Muriel Mabley."

"Did I get you at a bad time, partner?" Laughton chuckled. He used the same line whenever he called. He never thought twice about waking me, no matter the hour. I worked to live and lived to work—at least that's been my story for twenty years, the last seventeen as a firearms forensics expert for the Philadelphia Police Department. I had the dubious distinction of being the first woman in the unit and one of two minorities. The other was my partner, Laughton McNair.

At forty-nine, I was beginning to think I was blocking the blessing God intended for me. I felt like I had blown past any hope of a true love in pursuit of a damn suspect.

"You there?" Laughton said, laughing louder.

"Hee hee, hell. I finally find someone and you runnin' my ass ragged, like you don't *even* want it to last. What now?" I said.

"Speak up. I can hardly hear you."

"I said . . ."

"I heard you." More chuckles from Laughton. "You might want to rethink a relationship. Word is we've got another dead wife and again the husband swears he didn't do it. Says she offed herself. That makes three dead wives in three weeks. Hell, must be the season or something in the water."

Not wanting to move much or turn the light on, I let my fingers search blindly through my bag on the nightstand until they landed on paper and a pen. Pulling my hand out of my bag with paper and pen was another story. I knocked over the half-filled champagne glass also on the nightstand. "Damn it!" I was like a freaking circus act, trying to save the paper, keep the bubbly from getting on the bed, stop the glass from breaking, and keep from dropping the phone.

"Sounds like you're fighting a war over there," Laughton said.

"Just give me the address."

"If you can't get away . . ."

"Laughton, just . . ."

"You don't have to yell."

He let a moment of silence pass before he said, "Thirteen ninety-one Berkhoff. I'll meet you there."

"I'm coming," I said and clicked off.

"You okay?" Calvin reached out to recapture me. I let him and fell back into the warmth of his embrace. Then I caught myself, sat up, and clicked the light on—but not without a sigh of protest.

Calvin rose. He rested his head in his palm and flashed that gorgeous smile at me. "Can't blame a guy for trying," he said.

"It's a pity I can't do you any more lovin' right now. I can't sugarcoat it. This is my life," I complained on my way to the bathroom.

"So you keep telling me."

I felt uptight about leaving Calvin in the house alone. My son, Travis, would be home from college in the morning, his first spring break from Lincoln University. He and Calvin had not met. In all the years before this night, I had not brought a man home, except Laughton, and at least a decade had passed since I'd had any form of a romantic rela-

tionship. The memory chip filled with that information had almost disintegrated. Then along came
Calvin.

When I came out, Calvin was up and dressed.
He was five foot ten, two hundred pounds of muscle, the kind of muscle that flexed at his slightest
move. Pure lovely. He pulled me close and pressed
his wet lips to mine. His breath, mixed with a hint
of citrus from his cologne, made every nerve in my
body pulsate.

"Next time we'll do my place. You can sing to
me while I make you dinner," he whispered. "Soft,
slow melodies." He crooned, "You Must Be a Special Lady," as he rocked me back and forth, slow
and steady. His gooey caramel voice touched my
every nerve ending, head to toe. Calvin is a singer
and owns a nightclub, which is how we met. I was
at his club with friends and Calvin and I—or
rather, Calvin and my alter ego, spurred on by my
friends, of course—entertained the crowd with
duets all night.

He held me snugly against his chest and buried
his face in the hollow of my neck while brushing
his fingertips down the length of my body.

"Mmm . . . sounds luscious," was all I could
muster.

The interstate was deserted, unusual no matter
what time, day or night.

In the darkness, I could easily picture Calvin's
face, bright with a satisfied smile. I could still feel
his hot breath on my neck, the soft strumming of
his fingers on my back. I had it bad. Butterflies
reached down to my navel and made me shiver. I

felt like I was nineteen again, first love or some such foolishness.

Flashing lights from an oncoming police car brought my thoughts around to what was ahead, a possible suicide. How anyone could think life was so bad that they would kill themselves never settled with me. Life's stuff enters pit territory sometimes, but then tomorrow comes and anything is possible again. Of course, the idea that the husband could be the killer could take one even deeper into pit territory. The man you once loved, who made you scream during lovemaking, now not only wants you gone, moved out, but dead.

When I rounded the corner to Berkhoff Street, the scene was chaotic, like the trappings of a major crime. I pulled curbside and rolled to a stop behind a news truck. After I turned off Bertha, my 2000 Saab gray convertible, she rattled in protest for a few moments before going quiet. As I got out, local news anchor Sheridan Meriwether hustled from the front of the news truck and shoved a microphone in my face before I could shut the car door.

"Back off, Sheridan. You'll know when we know," I told her.

"True, it's a suicide?" Sheridan persisted.

"If you know that, then why the attack? You know we don't give out information in suicides."

"Confirmation. Especially since two other wives have been killed in the past few weeks."

"Won't be for a while. Not tonight anyway."

"Thanks, Muriel." She nodded toward Bertha. "Time you gave the old gray lady a permanent rest, don't you think?"

"Hey, she's dependable."

She chuckled her way back to the front of the news truck. Sheridan was the only newsperson I would give the time of day. We went back two decades, to rookie days when my mom and dad were killed in a car crash. Sheridan and several other newspeople had accompanied the police to inform me. She returned the next day, too, after the buzz had faded. A drunk driver sped through a red light and rammed my parents' car head-on. That was the story the police told the papers. The driver of the other car cooked to a crisp when his car exploded after hitting my parents' car, then a brick wall. My parents were on their way home from an Earth, Wind & Fire concert at the Tower Theater.

Sheridan produced a series on drunk drivers in Philadelphia, how their indiscretions affected families and children on both sides of the equation, which led to a national broadcast. Philadelphia police cracked down on drunk drivers and legislation passed with compulsory loss of licenses. Several other cities and states followed suit.

I showed my badge to the young cop guarding the front door and entered the small foyer. In front of me was a white-carpeted staircase. To the left was the living room. Laughton, his expression stonier than I expected, stood next to the detective questioning who I supposed was the husband. He sat on the couch, leaned forward with his elbows resting on his thighs, his head hanging down. Two girls clad in *Frozen* pajamas huddled next to him on the couch, one on either side.

The detective glanced at me, then back at the man. "Where were you?"

"I just got here, man," the man said. "Went upstairs and found her on the floor."

"And the kids?"

"My daughter spent the night with me. She had a sleepover at my house. This is Jeanne, lives a few blocks over. She got homesick and wouldn't stop crying, so I was bringing them back here. Marcy and I separated, but we're trying to work things out." He choked up, unable to speak any more.

"At three a.m."

"I told you, the child was having a fit. Wanted her mother."

A tank of a woman charged through the front door, "Oh my God. Baby, are you all right?" She pushed past the police officer there and clomped across the room, sending those close to look for cover. The red-striped flannel robe she wore and pink furry slippers, size thirteen at least, made her look like a giant candy cane with feet.

"Wade, what the hell is happenin' here?" She moved in and lifted the girl from the sofa by her arm. Without giving him a chance to answer, she continued, "C'mon, baby. You're coming with me."

An officer stepped sideways and blocked the way. "Ma'am, you can't take her—"

The woman's head snapped around like the devil possessed her, ready to spit out nasty words followed by green fluids. She never stopped stepping.

I expect she would have trampled the officer, but Laughton interceded. "It's all right, Jackson. Let her go," he said.

Jackson sidestepped out of the woman's way before Laughton's words settled.

Laughton nodded his head in my direction. "Body's upstairs."

The house was spotless. White was *the* color:

white furniture, white walls, white drapes, white wall-to-wall carpet, white picture frames. The only real color came in the mass of throw pillows that adorned the couch and a wash of plants positioned around the room.

I went upstairs and headed to the right of the landing, into a bedroom where an officer I knew, Mark Hutchinson, was photographing the scene. Body funk permeated the air. I wrinkled my nose.

"Hey, M&M," Hutchinson said.

"That's Muriel to you." I hated when my colleagues took the liberty to call me that. Sometimes I wanted to nail Laughton with a front kick to the groin for starting the nickname.

He shook his head. "Ain't me or the victim. She smells like a violet." He tilted his head back, sniffed, and smiled.

Hutchinson waved his hand in another direction. "I'm about done here."

I stopped at the threshold of the bathroom and perused the scene. Marcy Taylor lay on the bathroom floor. A small hole in her temple still oozed blood. Her right arm was extended over her head, and she had a .22 pistol in that hand. Her fingernails and toenails looked freshly painted. When I bent over her body, the sulfur-like smell of hair relaxer backed me up a bit. Her hair was bone-straight. The white silk gown she wore flowed around her body as though staged. Her cocoa brown complexion looked ashen with a pasty, white film.

"Shame," Laughton said to my back. "She was a beautiful woman." I jerked around to see him standing in the doorway.

"Check this out," I said, pointing to the lay of the nightgown over the floor.

"I already did the scene. We'll talk later," he said.

"Damn it, Laughton. Come here and check this out." But when I turned my head, he was gone.

I finished checking out the scene and went outside for some fresh air. Laughton was on the front lawn talking to an officer. He beelined for his car when he saw me.

"What the hell is wrong with you?" I muttered, jogging to catch up with him. Louder. "Laughton, what the hell—"

He dropped anchor. Caught off guard, I plowed into him. He waited until I peeled myself off him and regained my footing, then said, "Nothing. Wade says they separated a few months ago and were trying to get it together, so he came over for some making up. He used his key to enter and found her dead on the bathroom floor."

"No, he said he was bringing the little girl home because she was homesick."

"Yeah, well, then you heard it all."

He about-faced.

I grabbed his arm and attempted to spin him around. "You act like you know this one or something," I practically screeched at him.

"I do."

I cringed and softened my tone five octaves at least when I managed to speak again. "How?"

"I was married to her . . . a long time ago."

He might as well have backhanded me upside the head. "You never—"

"I have an errand to run. I'll see you back at the lab."

I stared after him long after he got in his car and sped off.

The sun was rising by the time the scene was secured: body and evidence bagged, husband and daughter gone back home. It spewed warm tropical hues over the city. By the time I reached the station, the hues had turned cold metallic gray. I pulled into a parking spot and answered the persistent ring of my cell phone. It was Nareece.

"Hey, sis. My babies got you up this early?" I said, feigning a light mood. My babies were Nareece's eight-year-old twin daughters.

Nareece groaned. "No. Everyone's still sleeping."

"You should be, too."

"Couldn't sleep."

"Oh, so you figured you'd wake me up at this ungodly hour in the morning. Sure, why not? We're talkin' sisterly love here, right?" I said. We chuckled. "I've been up since three anyway, working a case." I waited for her to say something, but she stayed silent. "Reece?" More silence. "C'mon, Reecey, we've been through this so many times. Please don't tell me you're trippin' again."

"A bell goes off in my head every time this date rolls around. I believe I'll die with it going off," Nareece confessed.

"Therapy isn't helping?"

"You mean the shrink? She ain't worth the paper she prints her bills on. I get more from talking to you every day. It's all you, Muriel. What would I do without you?"

"I'd say we've helped each other through, Reecey."

Silence filled the space again. Meanwhile, Laughton pulled his Audi Quattro in next to my Bertha and got out. I knocked on the window to get his attention. He glanced in my direction and moved on with his gangster swagger as though he didn't see me.

"I have to go to work, Reece. I just pulled into the parking lot after being at a scene."

"Okay."

"Reece, you've got a great husband, two beautiful daughters, and a gorgeous home, baby. Concentrate on all that and quit lookin' behind you."

Nareece and John had ten years of marriage. John is Vietnamese. The twins were striking, inheritors of almond-shaped eyes, "good" curly black hair, and amber skin. Rose and Helen, named after our mother and grandmother. John balked at their names because they did not reflect his heritage. But he was mush where Nareece was concerned.

"You're right. I'm good except for two days out of the year, today and on Travis's birthday. And you're probably tired of hearing me."

"I'll listen as long as you need me to. It's you and me, Reecey. Always has been, always will be. I'll call you back later today. I promise."

I clicked off and stayed put for a few minutes, bogged down by the realization of Reece's growing obsession with my son, way more than in past years, which conjured up ugly scenes for me. I prayed for a quick passing, though a hint of guilt pierced my gut. Did I pray for her sake, my sake, or Travis's? What scared me anyway?

Connect with Us

Visit us online at
KensingtonBooks.com
to read more from your favorite authors, see books
by series, view reading group guides, and more.

Join us on social media

for sneak peeks, chances to win books and prize packs,
and to share your thoughts with other readers.

facebook.com/kensingtonpublishing
twitter.com/kensingtonbooks

Tell us what you think!

To share your thoughts, submit a review,
or sign up for our eNewsletters, please visit:
KensingtonBooks.com/TellUs.

Grab the Hottest Fiction
from
Dafina Books